MATINICUS

AN ISLAND MYSTERY

DARCY SCOTT

TURTLE
POND
PRESS

Also by Darcy Scott
Hunter Huntress

Cover art by Anna Torborg

Book designed and produced by
Maine Authors Publishing
Rockland, Maine
www.maineauthorspublishing.com

ACKNOWLEDGEMENTS

Matinicus is a real place. I'd give you the Lat/Lon, but so far I've been allowed to sail in those waters and I'd like to keep it that way. Resist the urge to visit. Really.

Quaint this place is not. Rustic doesn't really do it either. Its rather infamous history includes the early arrival of a few scrappy colonist families—ancestors of the same close-knit lobstering clans still duking it out today—who decided to rid the island of the Native Americans so inconveniently in residence by killing and burying them in the vegetable garden.

Today's Matinicans have a well-earned reputation for being suspicious of outsiders, unconcerned with social norms, and intolerant of anything that hints of bureaucracy. So far they've resisted all efforts to establish an on-island police presence—preferring that time-honored mantra, *what happens here, stays here.* They're also openhearted and generous to those who demonstrate a genuine interest in the island and its history. So a big thank you to the great people of Matinicus who allowed me to photograph, record, and otherwise invade their lives—shrugging off my intention to shamelessly appropriate and morph island geography, history, and their "official" 1830 census to suit my questionable literary purposes. I'm indebted to Donna Rogers, whose friendly reception and encouragement granted me the necessary social entrée; to Tom and Eva Clough, keepers of the ghost of the 1799 house that served as inspiration for Hannah's and later Rachel's home; to island historian Suzanne Rankin, who generously allowed me access to her home and the old Young Store records when she was "over in America"; to Sari Bunker, who answered endless questions about Matinicus and turned me on to Elisabeth Ogilvie's *Whistle for a Wind* which provided an excellent window on early out-island life; to Sue Radley of the Vinalhaven Historical Society for hanging around as I pawed through masses of information for the book's historical plotline when she should have been off with her grandson (sorry, Alex!); and to the staff of the Maine Maritime Museum library for their patient education in 19th-century watercraft.

There were several standouts among the countless books I read on Maine shipwrecks, the history of lobstering, island farming, the lives of early nineteenth-century island women, and the island of Matinicus itself. These include an extraordinary botanical catalogue entitled *Flora of Matinicus*

Island, Maine—compiled by Charles A.E. Long in the 1920s and lovingly updated by area botanists many times since; *Matinicus Isle: Its Story and Its People* by Charles Long; and Donna Rogers' *Tales of Matinicus Island.* Virginia Thorndike's *Islander—Real Life on the Maine Islands* also proved an invaluable resource.

As always, love and thanks to my husband, Cleave—first reader extraordinaire—whose eye for continuity is almost scary, and to my other indispensable readers: Adair, Ben, Barb, Roxanne, Chuck, Katherine, and Sarah. Finally, many thanks to Bill Hoadley of the Tuckanuck Lodge—chef, raconteur, and consummate host—who boasts an inexhaustible knowledge of all things Matinicus: the good, the bad, and the really, really juicy.

For Amy and Lacey,
ever dearest;
and for Frank,
who took them to his heart

"Please send by bearer, the following articles...
Four pounds of salt and a small cask of whiskey;
four pounds of lard and a large jug of whiskey; three
stout fishing lines and a quarter hundred weight of biscuit;
the same weight of Cheshire cheese and two large flasks
of whiskey; one paper of limerick hooks and a gallon of
whiskey in any old vessel you don't use; also one pound
of white sugar and a small jug of whiskey.

"P.S. As we shall be gone for several days and as we may
get wet fishing, my doctor, who just stepped in, suggests that
we had better take along a little whiskey. Please send it over
and enter it on your books along with the items above."

—Early provisioning request
Matinicus Island, Maine

God has given me mine eyes
I will see life only once
I mean to make the most of my chance

—Matinicus gravestone

PROLOGUE

"What the hell, Tiff? Ain't like you never done it before."

Just like him to whine like some baby—too lazy to get up and come over, ask her nice. Well, screw him. Tiffany was fifteen now; she didn't need Ivan-fucking-Ames to make up her mind for her.

She stood at the window, the heat like a slap—hip slung against the grimy glass as she gnawed a thumbnail and watched Kathy's dad rocking in his skiff thirty feet below and across the way. A hand on the ladder as he tossed the bag of lobsters up to Gail on the wharf, her stupid green apron with *Kiss the Cook* on the front fluttering in the breeze. Gail was so lame. Like anybody 'round here would pay for lobster salad at some restaurant when they could just make some up from their own catch if they wanted. Yachties, maybe; but there weren't hardly any right now. Wind was wrong.

"What's the matter—you on the rag or somethin'?"

Out in the harbor *Ka-Ching* was in, Cash swinging crateful after crateful over the gunwale—the red staysail with its crossed rifles and that lame Fu Manchu he'd painted on the Jolly Roger holding the boat against the float. Most of the guys sold their catch to Island Lobster right here in the harbor; but he sold over in Rockland twice a week so he could pick up that other crop, the one half of them put in their veins every night. Ivan ever started that shit, they'd be done for good. She'd told him so a hundred times.

Tiffany pried the hair from her sticky neck and fanned herself with it, which didn't do anything but stir up more dust, like there wasn't enough up here already. Sweltering. That's what you called heat like this.

"Take them clothes off, you won't be so hot," Ivan suggested from the mattress.

She shot him a look—glared at that dumb stringy beard, those filthy orange flip-flops, the smelly old futon somebody'd dragged in, and hated him. Not an hour ago she'd liked him good enough to come up here. No use tryin' to figure it.

"Cash'll be bullshit you didn't show this morning," Tiffany said, turning back to the window. "Find himself another kid over to the Sands to go stern with him like he said. Somebody who ain't piss-in-his-pants scared of John and who don't start pukin' soon as the boat clears Indian Ledge."

Ivan glared. "Fuck you. Just 'cause he's screwin' Cheryl don't mean he owns me. Man's gotta do what a man's gotta do. C'mon," he groaned. "What's the big deal?"

And just why they had to do it in the loft above the old store was beyond her anyway. Worse than doing it in his truck, which was just as gross, but at least that had windows you could roll down and a floor you weren't gonna fall through. She hated this place—the nails poking through the roof always catching her hair, the creaky floorboards—the whole history of the island pressing down on her in the smell of oily rags and about a thousand years of fish guts, other things she didn't even want to think about. The heat and the smell about made her want to puke. Plus it was pure dangerous up here; twice she'd stepped through a rotten board, but Ivan had caught her by the arm and dragged her back up. Place should just be torn down. Wasn't a Young left on-island who'd claim it as his own.

Ivan smiled that gooey smile, the one he used when he tried to make up for stuff when all he really wanted was sex. Guys were just pricks. She giggled at the joke.

"What—this is funny now? I'm hurtin' here; look at this huge fuckin' thing." He paused. "Okay, a BJ, then, you gonna be so pissy about it."

She heard it, then, the four o'clock—circling like some monster mosquito heading for the airstrip. Three minutes out, maybe.

"Plane's in," she told him, heading for the ladder. If she didn't get out of here soon, she really would puke. "Gail's gonna skin me I don't get up there. Got some beer comin' in."

"Fuck, Tiffany." Like he couldn't believe she'd do this to him. "I mean it; get back here!"

But she was halfway down the ladder by then, grinning hard as her shoulder punched the door and she burst through to the blazing sun.

ONE

1829

Matinicus, Friday 10 July

    The light fades as I take up my pen, this book my only refuge against loneliness and the troubling omens of a strange new life. These past hours the most unsettling of all since my coming to the island, delivered up as wife to old man Isaac. A time of fire and death, and the arrival of a stranger whose presence in this house leaves me not a little afraid.

    A chill fog having settled with the southwest breeze this noon, it was the smoke and not the sight of the stricken ship that first spoke of danger. My first thought was for the salt hay at the cove grown so close to harvest. Why, I wondered, had not the church bell been rung as is the custom here in case of fire? To be sure, such a thing might finish us all.

    I saw it then, a glow to the west, the light shifting and hovering as if aloft, which as all know means a ship afire. One coming down full upon us.

    Unseen feet pounded past me, setting the sheep to a fearful bleating as men shouted and made for the western cove and the place they call the Rumguzzle, so named for the launching of boats for rescue and salvage, much of it in the way of spirituous liquors. Grabbing my shawl from its hook, I called to Alice to pull the chowder from the fire, to turn the beans in a timely manner, and took myself there as well.

    O, the eerie scene! The boys and few men not gone to the Banks for the summer fishing, Weston Philbrick, Squire Young and old Tyrus Wivell among them, and Tyrus himself half-addled even when not in rum, all of them, young and old, grown silent. Helpless and expectant amid the shale and dogweed of the cove, watching that awful, sulfurous glow until its direction and thus their action might be determined. The children were like puppies among them, happily freed from Weston's schoolroom for the event, making a game of stamping out the cinders raining down upon us all.

That the ship had no steerage was certain; no one experienced as one must be to captain such a vessel would dare travel a fog-choked cut between islands as known for wrecks as is Matinicus. And though we could not as yet make her size, her rigging and sails were clearly ablaze.

Only moments later there came to us such a horrible creaking and grinding as ever I've heard, the ship doomed for certain now, fetched up hard as she was on the rocky ledges ringing this cursed place. And with an unholy holler that chilled my bones, the boys jumped to the rowing boats and made to pull off through the fog: the Crie brothers, Josh Ames, Daniel Norton and the like—the hope of plunder in their black little hearts. Isaac's own Seth among them, though he be but five years.

'Twould serve his father right if he was drowned in this effort. For husband Isaac is at sea, if still living; the ship from which he'll claim a share loaded with as much rum as bait, it is sure. That he too should be lost, I can only hope, for I might then be returned across the bay to Vinalhaven, and happily so. He was a month and a week first widowed and we but a day married when he left for the fishing, with naught but me to care for the unruly brood left him by his dead Patience. She who takes her final rest buried, it is said, with the babe that took her off rather than see itself born.

I was pulled from these thoughts by the sight of Weston on the surf-pounded shore below me. The color full upon his face, sleeves rolled high from his exertion, adding his cries to those of the laughing gulls wheeling unseen above us as he called to the young ones now heading off.

Look to survivors, lads, called he; and leave the salvaging for a time when the fog is not so thick.

Charged as he is with schooling such wild youth as grow here and with so many of their fathers gone now to the fishing, Weston tasks himself with their safety as well. Doubtless he feels there are few enough left as is; no need to lose yet more over such as this.

I had a thought of the chowder then, knowing Alice in her laziness would not think to give a stir to the pot. Mary, though she be but three years, has more wits about her than that one. Supper would surely burn; and there would be nothing but bread and the rest of the milking for the seven of us tonight, and Weston as schoolmaster, boarding with us for the term, certainly deserving of more.

Pulling my shawl about me and turning for home, I was stopped by Weston's sudden shout, a strong foreboding taking me as I drew my head around. Wading urgently through the surf, he struggled toward something so dark and mammoth it seemed the devil himself coming among us. A seaman, I realized, half washing, half crawling from the waves. And as Weston pulled him to shore, old Wivell with his useless, rum-soaked brain latching to the other arm in like errand, I spied another of the kind bobbing face down not ten feet behind. Squire Young, loathe to soak himself on behalf of one so obviously lost, trying for the man instead with a gaffing pole.

I glanced then to my skirts where Mary clung, whimpering and runny-nosed, at my knee. Blonde and as rosy of cheek as an angel, she is not yet infected with the brutal glee such sights bring out in the others. 'Twill not be long before she too sets the cats ablaze for her evening's entertainment, buries brothers too stupid to keep fast to the harbor in a squally sea. And with a prayer that supper not after all be burned, I turned and made for the house, pulling her stumbling and sniveling behind. There was the spinning yet to finish, the mending to tend.

In all, five men, living and dead, came ashore here this day. Four whites, three of them gone to God; and a Black Jack, as they call negro sailors here, barely alive. It was the black Weston pulled from the waters and brought to this very house; the injured white man, with knife wounds, it is said, taken off and put under Lydia Tolman's care.

Thus it is I keep my own knife close, a thing that would surely turn my mother's heart. The negro sleeps before the fire now, an immense creature taking his ease on the rag carpet Weston brought from his own chamber. Warm and safe among us while the fog presses thick without, as if to crush all in this house to very death.

TWO

2005

Hate flying; always have. It's a small plane thing. The one I'm in now, a Cessna 206 piloted by a chatty guy named Doug, is worse than most—its single three-blade prop and lack of landing instruments having much to do with this. Has excellent short field performance, though, which Doug says we'll need. I don't bother asking; I've seen the airstrip out there—a dirt and gravel expanse the width of a driveway, unforgiving rock cliffs dropping into the sea at one end, an enormous barn squatting at the other.

Doug continues his version of the take-off chat, shouting over the noise of the engine. Empty weight of two thousand pounds; freight capacity of sixteen hundred, including three passengers of which I'm the only one on this particular afternoon. Good thing, too, considering all the freight packed around me. Boxes of liquor, bagged grocery orders, cases of Diet Coke and Bud Light, a couple FedEx packages. Topping the pile, where Doug tossed it as he climbed into the cockpit, is a duct-taped paper lunch bag that keeps sliding into my lap. Can't spot my duffle or sleeping bag, but I'm pretty sure I saw someone throw them in right before we took off. I pull the brim of Dad's old Dodger's cap down against Doug's spiel and watch the blue hills of Camden recede over the top of my Ray-Bans, nudging back the stuff slowly shifting into my side. I cheer myself with the thought that the fifteen-minute hop from the airport in Owl's Head to Matinicus beats the wet hour and a half I spent pounding into a nasty head sea on a twenty-eight foot Albin my last time out here, but at least that had radar and a life raft. I think of meeting my end nose-diving into the frigid, cerulean waters of Penobscot Bay, and crane my neck nervously for the scatter of out islands somewhere ahead.

"First time in a week I been able to land out here," Doug yells. "Too muddy with all the rain we've been having. Probably okay now."

Probably.

Then I see it, at least I think it's Matinicus—the deadfall standing guard at the eastern entrance to the bay far worse than last time. Spruce mostly, the spindly trunks tumbled at odd angles like so many matchsticks. Funny how different the place looks from the air. Coming in at sea level, it resembled nothing so much as a hairy pancake as might be observed if your cheek was lying flat against the table, as mine has been on any number of occasions.

We circle lazily and I get a good view of South Sandy Beach where I attempted an ill-advised and spectacularly unsuccessful seduction of Rachel my last time out. The Old Gil, I tell myself as we swing over Wheaton Island and buzz the harbor with its tight cluster of lobster boats and scows, then make a graceful arc around Northeast Point and begin our approach. Below us a line of pickups and ATVs bumps its way along the main road toward the airstrip.

Without warning the plane begins to buck and lurch, buffeted by gusts that come out of nowhere. Doug grips the yoke, cursing; I close my eyes and wait for the inevitable crunch of aluminum against unforgiving rock face. Six months ago it would have been the scariest thing I'd been through. But that was before Annika got me in her sights. For sheer terror nothing beats a grad student-cum-lover who goes whacko on you. You know it's time to throw in the towel when your love life is on a collision course with life expectancy.

Something lands in my lap with a soft thud. The mummified lunch bag.

"Hold onto that!" Doug yells, "or he'll shoot us both."

I stare down at it, so flummoxed by this—could we really be shot for losing some guy's lunch?—I actually miss the miracle of our safe landing. The angry whine of the engine as it kicks up gravel mere yards from the raging surf is my first clue that we've actually touched down. Trees flash by on either side, and as we slow I note a few faces by the ATVs and pickups I'd seen from the air.

"How long you here for?" Doug asks, nodding at those collecting around the door as he slides boxes and bags from the plane.

"Not sure," I tell him, the early August heat boring into me as I step down and hand off the lunch bag. No one gives me a glance; I might as well be invisible. "Couple weeks, anyway," I say, hefting my rucksack.

He tosses the lunch bag to a guy in worn jeans and faded red wife-beater who tucks the thing in his pants then heads off without a word. "You been here before, you said."

"Five years ago."

"Got some real squirrels out here," he says watching the guy's bow-legged retreat into the woods. "And I don't mean the cute, fuzzy type. You'd do best to keep your head down 'til they figure out what you're about." He hands me a card, tells me to call when I'm ready to head back.

I cock my head toward the receding back. Can't help myself.

"So what's in the bag?"

"Payment from his wholesaler over in Rockland. About eighty grand this time—all Matinicus Ones." Shoots me a wink. "That's hundred dollar bills."

Lobstering's been good, it seems.

I join Doug in a contemplative eyeballing of the airstrip. Hardly the length of a football field—Christ.

"It's shorter than usual today," he informs me. "We lose about fifty feet when the tide's this high."

Huh.

A slender girl with auburn hair just brushing her shoulders—twelve, thirteen tops—hefts cases of beer to what I'm pretty sure is a Ford pickup, or used to be. Might have been blue once, maybe green. Hard to tell. No doors or license plate, engine hood secured to the grill with a piece of lob-ster warp. Climbing behind the wheel, she yells to two boys—the oldest can't be ten—carrying off a case of Dewars. I watch in disbelief as they lay it in the back of an old golf cart then bump off down the road, the old Ford peeling out behind.

Surely this can't be legal.

I locate my gear, fork over a Matinicus One for the flight, and giv-ing my cap a tug, strike off toward Rachel's place—maybe a hundred yards down the road. Dropping everything on the back porch—I don't bother knocking; I know she's not here—I head to the harbor to collect the key she promised to leave at the Galley Hatch.

Common sense tells me there's got to be some kind of road or driveway to the place, but the only way I've ever been able to find it is by picking my way along a meandering, trash-strewn path that loosely follows the slow curve of the harbor. I pick it up behind the old Young store, making my way from boardwalk to rocks to planks; over sleeping dogs, across piers and past open shed doors, between long lines of lobster traps and bait barrels, and finally up through a hilly tumble of thorn bushes—old engine parts embedded in the packed earth for purchase—where I reach the open, grassy expanse of yard with its good-sized wharf. There in the opening is the Galley Hatch—a large, weathered gambrel perched on the rocks at the harbor's edge with a view that's nothing short of staggering on even the worst of days.

I take the three steps to a large deck and push through the screen door into a place I remember with an immediate and visceral tug, connected as it is with my frustratingly unfulfilled and therefore compelling infatuation with Rachel. A short lunch counter sprouting twin jars of Slim Jims and beef jerky sits to the right beneath an overhead pole strung with vintage ball caps. The rafters themselves are hung with the same faded buoys and old hub caps I remember from last time, a flag from the Maine Maritime Academy dated 1941. In fact, the only thing that looks to have been added is the illuminated BUD LIGHT sign on the left wall above the regulation-size pool table.

I order a tube steak—mustard, extra relish—from Al, who clearly doesn't remember me. No reason he should, really. People come and go here all the time in summer—boaters, birders, naturalists like myself here to count trees or catalogue the almost staggering variety of plant life.

I devour half the dog as I push out onto the deck and slide onto one of the benches that line the railing. Immediately before me is the harbor, gorgeous as hell in the late afternoon light and full of boats with names like *Hombre, Ka-Ching, Plan Bea*. Not the sweet little vessels you see in magazine spreads about quaint seaside villages but serious, off-shore fishing machines built for long hours in rough, often horrendous weather conditions. These things can cost as much as a house.

Change is depressingly apparent all around me, from the dish antennas sprouting atop most of the ramshackle places ringing the harbor to the guy, farther down the deck, talking on his cell, his other ear plugged with a finger. Sad to think that in the few years I've been gone technology has caught up with this place. Then again, I don't have to live thirty rough ocean miles from the nearest hospital or bank—let alone a real grocery store.

I stuff the rest of the hot dog in my mouth just as the old pickup I saw at the airstrip bounces from between two houses and pulls into the yard. Hopping out, the auburn-tressed teen loses no time in scraping a case of Bud from the truck bed and, using her thigh for leverage, begins humping it our way. The slam of a back door brings Al limping over to grab another. War injury or bad hip; he's of an age where it could be either. Neither speak.

I decide on a couple more tube steaks and a beer to keep them company, and head back inside to wait at the counter. I'm flipping through a dog-eared copy of Uncle Henry's, a local swap magazine, when Al finally appears.

"Another hot dog?" He might be sixty, pleasant looking in faded jeans and blue denim shirt with rolled sleeves, a shock of white hair that matches his close-cropped beard. A little hefty, but jolly enough. An old Philco refrigerator chuckles against the wall behind him.

I nod. "Make it two—mustard, extra relish. You hiding a Heineken back there by any chance?"

He cocks his head toward a cooler, cheek by jowl with a grimy top-loading freezer at the end of the room—the pair of them facing off against a couple minimally stocked grocery shelves.

"Bud and Bud Light. Might be a couple Moosehead left."

He's eyeing my ball cap when I return with a longneck Bud. Maybe I can order a case of Heineken from the pilot? Probably only cost me two or three times what it would on the mainland.

"Noticed your cap," Al says, sliding a plate with the two dogs under my nose. "'55 Dodgers, right? Year they won the Series."

"Yup." The guy's obviously a buff. The ball caps strung along the ceiling tell me this—a '48 Boston Braves, '70 Pittsburgh Pirates, '45 Philadelphia Athletics, and a '28 Yankees from the era of the Bronx Bombers, the Babe and Lou, arguably the best team in history—maybe fifteen in all and each too worn to be one of those newbies available over the Internet. If that's not enough, the grease board on the wall before me features sandwiches named for some of the biggest players of all time—The Rocket, The Hammer, Tom Terrific, Mr. October, The Georgia Peach—along with the promise of a free lunch for anyone able to match all the monikers to their respective players. A serious buff.

"Mind?" he asks nodding toward my cap.

I slide it over, twist the cap off my beer and take a long slug. It's then I catch sight of the baseball on a shelf above the cash register. The shiny brown patina of age, two signatures I immediately recognize.

Al catches me staring. "Gehrig and the Babe. Ball was a power hit to the upper rightfield bleacher, Yankee Stadium, 1928. My grandfather caught it."

"He get the cap then, too?' I ask, cocking my head toward the ceiling.

He nods—impressed, I can tell. As am I. God only knows how I remember this crap.

It appears the sniff and piss game is finally over. "So," he says. "What brings you to the edge of the world?"

There's a kitchen in the back; I can see it through the open door to the left of him. Big cast iron stove, twin basket fryolater beside it, the edge of something that might just be a pizza oven.

I swallow what's left of the first dog. "Rachel Leland said you'd have a key for me," I tell him, wiping a hand on my jeans and extending it. "Gil Hodges." I give it a beat. "No relation. That a pie I see on the stove back there?"

"No shit," he says, giving my hand a pump. "Al Freeman." Which I know. "Hodges was one of the best first basemen in the game—hell, I don't have to tell you. Eight-time All-Star; Boys of Summer, helped put the Yankees down in seven back in '55." Hands on his hips now. "Gil Hodges, and with the cap to boot. I was gonna try and buy it off you, but it would surely be a sin." He glances back toward the stove. "My wife Gail's blueberry pie. Best on the island and on the house for you. Seems only right."

He returns from the kitchen with a huge chunk, pulls a key from a nail on the wall and slaps it down in front of me. "So you're a friend of Rachel's." A different kind of appraisal now—a did-he or didn't-he kind of thing.

"Ben was a student of mine," I say, skirting the implied question. Then, because I'm not sure how much he knows about Rachel's son, "Urban Forestry Program at UMaine."

I knock the second dog off in two bites, the better to get to the pie which wafts of warm berries and cinnamon.

"So you're like a professor of trees or something?"

"Something," I say, wrapping my mouth around a forkful. It's pure ambrosia—the kind of thing you chew slowly, deliberately, swallowing only when you absolutely must lest saliva roll uncontrollably down your chin. This is like trying to talk and have sex at the same time; impossible to concentrate on either. Forced to make a choice—well, there isn't one.

"A shame," Al says. "I liked that kid. Cancer, right?"

"Non-Hodgkins lymphoma." Three years ago this September, to be exact. "How much for the whole thing?" I ask as the door opens and a sunburned guy of about forty comes in, grabs the stool farthest from me. Takes a swig from an open Rolling Rock he's brought in with him—something that bothers Al not a whit.

"What—the pie?" Al laughs, reaching to the top of the fridge and pulling a pack of Marlboros from an open carton and tossing them to the guy. "You're serious." His gaze wanders to the stove, calculating. "Three bucks a slice, six slices, that's eighteen. Give it to you for fifteen since it seems there's a piece missing." A wink as he slides some kind of ledger out from beside the cash register, makes a note, slides it back.

The guy ignores me as he simultaneously lights up and unscrews the glass jar of Slim Jims, drawing one out. He looks like a blown-out Bobby De Niro, but with less hair—snarly weathered face, graying two-day beard, dirty tee shirt with a long smear of something that looks like axle grease across the front. He takes a pull on his beer.

"Clayton," Al says, "this here's Gil Hodges, a friend of Rachel's. Used to teach Ben."

That earns me a hard flick of the eyes. "You missed her. Left a couple days ago. I'll take a bowl of that chili, Al."

"Hell, he knows that," Al says heading to the kitchen. "He's stayin' up at her place." He lays a steaming bowl in front of Clayton, makes another note in the ledger before glancing up at me. "So, just why *are* you here, Gil?"

Why indeed, with the lovely Rachel off-island—wisely opting to avoid another of my attempts at conquest, no doubt. The Old Gil, I remind myself again—gone but not forgotten.

"I'm a botanist," I tell him—a statement that earns me looks of puzzled respect in most circles; here it generally results in hoots of derision. "Dendrology, specifically. Here to catalogue trees." That's what I told myself when I decided on this trip, anyway. Good way to start my sabbatical, I figured—though I expect the answer is a bit more complicated.

A snort from Clayton. "Our tax dollars at work."

"Yup," I agree pleasantly, though this project is actually one of my own invention—my time, my money. Besides, I've no interest in engaging this guy's hostility. I stand, throw back the rest of my beer and pocket the key.

"That it?" Al asks.

I shake my head, making for the shelves. "I'll grab a couple supplies."

The pickings are broad-ranging but slim—everything from tubeless tire repair kits and Wonder Bread to Dramamine, Pampers, and thirty-pound bags of kitty litter—and if there's any kind of order to the stuff, it escapes me. I grab a quart of milk from the cooler, tuck a box of Wheaties under my arm, a loaf of bread. Decide on a cry-o-vac of sliced ham, head of lettuce. Enough. I can always come back and eat chili, devour a nickname or two.

"Weren't no kids, Al, and you know it," Clayton snarls. "Too fuckin' mean to be kids."

Al snorts his disbelief.

I shoot them a look.

"Someone killed Clayton's dog yesterday," Al explains. "Sweet old mutt. Butchered him with a nail gun. Maybe fifty three-inchers. Brutal, nasty mess. Tacked the poor thing to the barn door when he was done."

Jesus. Nothing personal in that.

"Ain't his business," Clayton warns. "And it weren't no kids. It was fuckin' John did it."

Embarrassed silence as I settle with Al and make to leave. Turning at the door, I point with my pie toward the sandwich board. "Roger Clemens, Hank Aaron, Tom Seaver, Reggie Jackson. Only one I don't know for sure is the Georgia Peach."

"Ty Cobb," Al grins. "Friday's pizza night, if you're interested. Got a band coming out, too, long as the weather holds." A wink. "Helluva time."

THREE

I was Ben Leland's academic advisor. He was a terrific kid, bright and open and ambitious. But what I admired most was his passion. Where I fell into my profession more out of laziness than anything else—literally following the scent of a coed I fancied into a botany class one morning the fall of my sophomore year—Ben knew what he wanted from the minute he landed on campus. Urban forestry, described in the literature as the studied use of plantings within the urban landscape to its ecological and human benefit. PR-speak for planting bunches of trees in hopes of improving air quality in metropolitan areas. The very idea intrigued him, God only knows why. Could have had something to do with spending summers on an island almost obscenely rich in plant life, most of it courtesy of an equally wide array of birds flying in on their way up and down the coast. Think of it as a rest stop on the migratory I-95 where they'd chow down, cat nap and, more to the point, shit out countless seeds consumed in varying far-flung locales.

My interest in the place took root, so to speak, when Ben brought me a scientific cataloguing of Matinicus flora done in the early 1900s. At first I thought it was a joke. Over seven hundred distinct species on about the same number of acres. Forty-four kinds of trees alone, including eight different species of willow and five of cherry. Twenty species of fern, fifty-seven different grasses. Berry patches, cranberry bogs, wild orchids. A botanist's dream. Ben's suggestion was that he work on an update of the thing as a kind of independent study over the summer. I thought it a terrific idea; and when he subsequently invited me to the island for a few weeks—a kind of working vacation to check on his progress—I jumped at the chance.

Unfortunately, once on-island I took little notice of anything other than the beautiful Rachel who, I noted with considerable glee, fit my preferred body type: slender and leggy, long dark ropes of auburn hair. I should mention that Rachel isn't just beautiful; she's poised and graceful, and an artist, it happens, of considerable talent. Made sense that Ben would come from such as she. A testament to her distinctive singularity is that she's the only summer person on the island to whom the locals have even remotely warmed. No husband in the picture, either; which I figured left the field wide open for me. Ben tolerated my obvious lust with his usual good humor, though it couldn't help but lessen my value as a field assistant. And if my head hadn't been so far up my ass, I might have realized he saw my company as a chance at the kind of relationship he'd never had with his old man. All this was back when I was still being led around by my prick, mind you. These days I'm lucky if I can find the thing to take a piss.

It was Rachel who told me Ben had found and mapped some twenty-two species of wild orchid. I was half in love with her by this time, and would have happily trekked off behind her through the bracken, nettles, and sumac in search of them, but she had different ideas.

I spent the next week and a half painting her barn.

All of this is running through my mind as Rachel's antique white cape comes into view. I grab my duffel and sleeping bag off the back porch, slip the key in the lock, and step into her 1950s-era kitchen. And here's the thing. Though I've known for days she wasn't going to be here, I'm still disappointed. It's a different kind of place with her gone—with both of them gone—at least I perceive it so. A note on the table greets me on friendlier terms than I no doubt deserve; her home is mine, etc., and informs me she's in the midst of a war with the crows. If I see any I'm instructed to shoot them. The rifle is just inside the barn, loaded and ready to go, along with a full box of shells. And if I see anyone hunting pheasant on her land, which they've been warned not to do, I'm to shoot *them,* as well.

No game warden on Matinicus, no police. No doctors, lawyers or Indian chiefs for that matter—all of which means nothing unless I shoot myself in the foot as I invariably will should I be forced to handle the thing, at which point I'll no doubt die of sepsis before I can find anyone to handle the lawsuit.

Rachel's home, the oldest on the island, is known as the 1799 House— split lathing and horsehair plaster, hand-hewn beams, forged nails—and except for the west-facing back porch and kitchen tacked on the place about a hundred years ago, it retains all of its original flavor. Small rooms, four or five working fireplaces—that kind of thing. I'm an open-concept kind of guy myself, my urban loft being all brick and glass and radiant heating, so I don't really get it. But hey.

I wander from the kitchen into what Rachel calls the keeping room—remembering when, wine glasses in hand, we did her version of the historical tour. Here is the largest room of the house—both the physical and social hub of nineteenth-century domesticity—functioning as kitchen, dining, and work room, as well as the place most guests were entertained. All other first floor rooms open off it—including the only bathroom in the place, which is going to make my occasional nocturnal urges a real pain in the ass. The centerpiece of the room is an enormous brick fireplace with all its original hardware—trammels and pot hooks and the like—an oven built into the side of it above an open ash pit. Back in the day, the door I've just come through opened directly onto what was called a dooryard—the area between house and barn where Rachel tends an impressive flower garden.

By now it's nearly seven, and my low-alcohol light is flickering. I'll reacquaint myself with the rest of the house later, I decide, and instead rummage through my duffel for the fifth of single-malt scotch I wisely thought to bubble-wrap for the trip out here. Grabbing my pie and snagging a glass from the dish drainer, I head to the porch for a sunset that promises magnificence. I drop into an old webbed lounger to enjoy my supper, noting with satisfaction that the mainland—just visible beyond the barn and assorted outbuildings, the hay field where Ben and I pitched our tent five years ago, and a few distant rocky out-islands—has been reduced to nothing more than a long, dark puddle shimmering beneath the molten sun.

It's a little-known fact that pie is best eaten with the fingers. It was Ben who taught me this. I no longer remember just why we opted to sleep out under the stars for the duration of that visit unless it was simply to sleep out under the stars. I do remember staring longingly each night toward the upper reaches of the house, imagining Rachel in something slinky and diaphanous—head thrown lustily back on the pillow surrounded by those long masses of curls. Raputa, Raputa the Buta...flip me down your hair; let me climb up the ladder of your love. Something like that.

I break off a chunk of pie, feel the satisfying burst of berry sweetness and buttery crust. Wash it all down with a slow slug of Laphroaig—those stuffy single malt purists be damned.

Raputa, Raputa. I think I musta got lost.

Ben was taking my second semester Forest Biology course when he was first diagnosed. Non-Hodgkins is a tenacious little fucker, and his was what they call a high-grade lymphoma. A double whammy the kid met head-on with his usual confidence during weeks of brutal radiation and chemo that caused him to miss both his final exam and the make-up I quietly arranged for him. Still, when it came down to it I gave him an A for the course anyway. I mean what the hell. Other than that, I never once reached out. Unbelievable, I know—even to me. Wounded pride, I guess. Three weeks as the fair Rachel's houseguest and not only had I not managed a tumble, the woman seemed utterly immune to my charms. Oh, I came up with all kinds of excuses why I couldn't make the trip to their place in Bennington, and it's true I was still feeling pretty raw from going through the same kind of shit with Dad some years earlier—but when it comes down to it, any unmarried man of forty-two with no children, pets or plants, or anything else that might conceivably depend on him, is pretty much free to go where he wants. Truth is, and I'm not proud of this, I'm not used to failure in the sexual arena. Follow thy prick is a mantra that's served me well over the years, happily rolling as I have from one long-legged, dark-haired grad student to another as we mutually tired of my shallow interest in them.

So, given my atrocious behavior toward Rachel on any number of levels, why did I call her out of the blue a few weeks ago and ask to come back? Good question. I offered some vague plan to finish the cataloging Ben had started that summer. A kind of tribute, I said. Did she believe me? Probably not. Was I hoping for another shot at her? Might have had something to do with it. Thing is, the whole mess with Annika shook me. Badly. Here, now, in the dual glow of a crimson sunset and a couple pours of single malt, I can admit this. Rachel appeared in my mind as a balm to the spirit; maybe I could paint her house this time. But her email of three days ago, informing me she'd be off-island through most of September—something about a series of shows at galleries in Kennebunkport, etc., etc.—but that I should feel free to use her place as my base of operations, cleared up any lingering doubt as to her interest in me.

Probably for the best. Besides, a few weeks of clawing my way through the pruckerbrush might just be the kind of physically exhausting labor I need to set myself right.

The light's fading as I back my way into the kitchen cradling my scotch and empty pie plate—making a mental note to add a couple bottles to the Heineken order I intend to call in to somebody or other in the morning.

Duffel in one hand, bottle by the neck in the other, I pass through the keeping room where, on either side of the fireplace, twin doors open onto identical front parlors—each with its own small fireplace. One of these Rachel uses as a living room, the other a summer studio-cum-gallery. The two come together in a front hall where a narrow split staircase rises steeply to the second floor. It's all I can do to wedge myself, my duffel, and the precious bottle up the torturous thing, and I make a note to look for a piss pot once I figure out where I'm sleeping, lest I kill myself trying to navigate it at three a.m.

I head directly for Rachel's room at the front of the house. Not sure why, exactly, except that the sight of it makes me feel good, connected somehow. Here, simple lace panels hang in the front windows and the walls are covered with a faded blue-flowered paper. Above an intricately carved headboard, the nirvana of my fantasies, she's fashioned the letter *R* from shells and dried sea grass—something at once feminine and girlishly innocent that touches me deeply for some reason. All at once I'm overcome with a fatigue so profound I want nothing more than to crawl between her sheets, lose myself in the smell of her pillow. Sorely tempted as I am, though, it seems a violation that's beyond even me.

As I turn to leave, I'm struck by a painting on the wall by her closet. Not a Rachel Leland, or not her usual style, anyway. Her medium is watercolor, her work all soft washes and light, earthy tones—the suggestion of this, an intimation of that. This thing is clearly an oil, the color almost troweled on. Its focus the nexus of two muddy, grayish-brown walls in what looks to be the corner of a room. A smudge of black mid-wall suggests a window on the left, the edge of what might be a fireplace to the right. A figure, at least I think it's a figure—my impression is of a child but perspective is my only basis for this—is nothing more than a murky, translucent shadow crouching in the corner, face buried in its hands as if crying. The whole thing is a study in darkness, utter despair. Gives me the creeps, frankly, so I continue my tour.

Across the hall, the door to Ben's room is cracked. I nudge it with my foot and catch sight of a bevy of medicine bottles on the night stand, a dusty glass beside them. Appears Rachel hasn't touched this place since his death. He was into lacrosse, I remember now—a kickass center on UMaine's perennially winning team—and his stick still hangs on the wall opposite the door. I bet if I pulled those dresser drawers open I'd find his entire summer wardrobe. No way, I think, closing the door softly behind me. This I cannot do.

There's one more room at the back of the house, and I'm struck by how oddly devoid of personality it seems compared to the rest of the place—not a book, memento, or personal touch of any kind. Single bed on a brown metal frame, night table, dresser—that's it. Oddly, the fireplace in here is bricked up. A dry, musty smell is evidence that the room's rarely used; ergo, perfect for my needs. Place has kind of a freaky feel to it, but I've slept in stranger.

Deep in the night I'm woken when something grazes my cheek. A quick stroke, a feather touch.

"Rachel?" is all I can manage and much of that adheres to the roof of my mouth. I rest my forearm over my eyes, swallow, try again. "Rachel?"

Another touch, or is it a sigh? I reach for her, my hand flopping feebly in mid-air—so absurdly glad she's here, the potential of her presence obscures the utter implausibility of it. I fight the knowledge that the Cessna can't make trips at night, no matter how many Matinicus Ones are on offer. Hell, I don't care how or why she did it; I'll take her any way I can get her.

"Rachel?" I'm slowly coming to now—an amazing feat, considering how much scotch I consumed before falling asleep or, more accurately, passing out.

Something cool along my scalp. A breath by my ear that sounds suspiciously like a child's whimper. Disembodied pain and sadness; an almost desperate longing.

I cock an eye. The tingle along my scalp, I realize, is my hair which has begun to rise—an involuntary response to the small filmy presence beside me. Female for sure, but definitely not Rachel.

I bolt from bed, the bottle of Laphroaig—tightly corked, I can only hope—smacking to the floor and rolling away as I tear from the room in a blind stumble toward the stairs. I fail to remember the physics involved and take most of them on my ass, landing in a sprawl and cracking my head on the newel post. The sharp edge of a table rams my thigh as I streak through the keeping room toward the kitchen door; then, tumbling from the porch, scramble, half-crawling, 'til I'm almost to the barn. Only then do I rise, gaping through the moonlight at the quiet, peaceful-looking house—arms limp at my sides.

What the fuck?

"Rachel?" I croak weakly, stupidly.

Normally, I'm no coward. Any guy who's a tightly muscled six-two and a black belt in Tae Kwon Do doesn't shrink from much; but there's no goddam way I'm going back in there tonight. I stand like this for maybe five minutes, the scientist in me struggling with the obvious incongruities. I can be incredibly stupid when I'm determined to be, and this is apparently one of those times because for all my logic, there's one thing my years of training and skepticism can't chase from my head.

Something very bad happened in that room.

FOUR

1829

Matinicus, Saturday 11 July

 The dead sailors laid in the ground today were three. Not drowned as was first thought, but stabbed, their bodies groomed and prayed over as if they were islanders, then sheltered beneath the stand of rock maples at the farthest end of the burying ground because they were not. The Captain of the vessel, a brig called the Amaranth and Nova Scotia bound, not among them. 'Tis a mystery that must remain so until the wounded seaman at Tolmans' awakes or our own stoically silent Black Jack, whom Weston informs me is called Atticus, deigns to do more than eat on the occasion he opens his mouth.

 It was a sorry gathering to be sure, a scattering of women and children and the few men that could be spared hovering beneath a chill drizzle to see the poor souls off. I would not have gone myself, having no interest in further acquaintance with death, if not for fear of being left alone at the farm with the great brute we are sheltering.

 After the bodies were prayed over, admirably done by Weston since the pastor is at present away, I tarried with Sarah Ames—who is as outraged as myself at Sally Young's brazen flaunting at the weekend's Independence celebrations. So she whispered in unexpected camaraderie, her words warming my heart in the damp chill.

 While none has ever called me handsome, not pink-cheeked or twinkle-eyed as is Sally, nor with the flaming hair of Sarah whose own high color must be put down to her condition, neither am I so hard on the eyes that men must turn away. Yet on this occasion Weston, whose goodness is oft my only balm in this place, had not a word or glance for me. The sight of his dark curls bent cordially toward the heads of Squire Young and daughter Sally, his book of Robert Burns clutched to his breast, distracted me from Sarah's teasing question as to when my own slight figure might show some evidence of married life.

I am but sixteen, I protested, and married not yet these two months.

I did not tell her my first day as a married woman was my only as wife, nor that father's insistence we be joined in such unseemly haste was not explained but for my husband's desire to see me settled before leaving for the summer fishing. This left no time for a proper setting out; indeed, my dowry consisted of little more than a few simple dresses and the open heart I mistakenly carried with me to this place. Still, on first approaching my new home there was promise in the roses abud at the front of the house, the fragrance of lilac pervading the yard. I had barely removed my cap, however, when my husband directed me to the garden to set the squash, while beside me his silent and unhappy girls planted beans that would have been up for quite two weeks if their mother had not been carried off before completing the chore herself. Then, my cheeks ablaze with mortification at having no introductions made me, Isaac himself set off for the plowing of the south field.

Next morn, after a night too humiliating to relate, he bade me wrap some bannock in oilcloth, then set out with his jug to fish the Banks on a vessel well known to him, the cod by then running thick. A month he was to be gone, and that well beyond us now.

Still, I did not much mind Sarah's gentle teasing about such matters until Lydia Tolman, herself immense with babe and a woman I keep little acquaintance of as she makes quite free with her opinions, joined our conversation.

Patience, first wife to your Isaac Burgess, said she as she passed her arm through Sarah's, bore him three children and buried two before the age of twenty.

This I already knew, as Isaac has made it a point.

Dipping her head toward the stone of her husband's grandfather, buried some four years ago after more than a century of life, she reminded us both that he sired twenty-one children by three wives, the last in his eighty-first year. You must hurry, Hannah, says she, if you are to catch up.

Sarah laughed with her at this, the two of them, when together, contrary to me in all things. I could have wept. It is to be the same here as it was at home. Everyone against me, father's unaccountable betrayal the worst of all.

On return to the house I set Alice and Emily, twins as much in lazy habits as in fair and freckled countence, to the milking while I readied refreshment. For Weston brought several of the men back with him, these being Squire Young, Lydia's Mr. Tolman and the bug-eyed Ames who is husband to Sarah.

Together they formed a committee of inquiry against the Black Jack, determined on answers to the mysteries of the Amaranth and its missing Captain, and to the distressing state of the dead. For Weston has managed some basic communication with the black, this Atticus, from whom he discovered the vessel's name and the man's occupation as cook upon it, his having come aboard in the West Indies where he entered this life some twenty-eight years ago.

The men stood awkwardly before the hearth, as men will do of a woman's keeping room, while Weston collected the negro from the smokehouse. It is I who insisted he be put there upon waking, so disturbed were my dreams by his presence before our fire. They spoke not a word to me while awaiting Weston's return, but partook freely of my beere and Indian cake. Indeed, it must seem odd to encounter me thus, offering refreshment in Patience's stead, so recently was she mistress here. There is a sense of her about the place yet; I felt it when I first stepped within, my gaze torn between a hearth broad as three men and the loom where her cloth lay half woven. herbs still drying in the chambers above stairs where even yet the girls cry themselves to sleep for the missing of her. Even I felt a pang for the life of this woman, plucked from her busy day by the wrongness of her unborn babe—leaving all behind in mid-course as if she'd but stepped to the dooryard to stretch her tired back.

The negro looked to flee when brought before the men. Indeed, none could have held him if such was his plan, as he is quite the size of an ox, with a neck easily the width of a dinner plate and a breadth of shoulder that surpasses even the Squire himself. But Weston, with his gentle and reassuring manner, urged him to some beere and a stool at the hearth where the man but turned a miserable countenance to our small fire, as if only there did his salvation lay.

It was the Squire, imposing in flowered waistcoat and strapped trouser, who began the inquiry as I took my place in the corner beside Mary, laying needle to the mending while she combed flax, which at three years she does but poorly and so must be overseen.

Now see here, said he in the prideful tones he uses with all but daughter Sally, whose gentile perfection he is loath to disturb with ugly shows of temper. What caused the fire aboard ship?

Never mind that, said Mr. Tolman—his bald pate agleam with perspiration. Where is your Captain, man? And how is it you alone escaped unharmed? Indeed, I can make not a mark upon you.

The negro continued his grim communion with the fire, making no answer to either query, which piqued Tolman greatly. Likewise Mr. Ames, who bent angrily to him.

We've put questions to ye, man, said he. Be ye deaf?

Enough, Weston chided in gentler tones. Nothing will be had from the man in this fashion. Perhaps he is too distressed by events even yet to impart what he knows.

Mr. Ames, intemperate in all things, pressed nonetheless. May as well speak, man. All will be known once the sailor biding at Tolmans' awakes.

The black became much alarmed at this, eyes going wide and white, upending the stool as he leapt to his feet.

Steady, said Weston, with a hand for his shoulder. This benefits us nothing, gentlemen. More rest is called for, perhaps; some time to recollect the order of events.

It was then that Lavon, gangly and ill-tempered and fresh from the washing of himself in the dooryard, came among us. Glowering at the sight of me as he has from the day his father brought me home as wife, he dropped cagboots dripping with mud by my rhubarb pie warming among the coals. Fourteen years old, and still he acts as does Seth who is but five. A more sullen, bitter boy can not be found among even my surly lot of brothers. He'll hear not a word of counsel nor condolence for the elder brother lost not a month before their mother's own passing. Yet another boy who stupidly drowned himself in the hand-lining of cod outside the harbor; his wherry, found washed ashore at the north beach, reclaimed by Lavon who fishes it now in his stead. This rather than keep to his schooling or lend his hand to the farming, as was his father's instruction upon leaving us all.

The wind goes north tonight, said he by way of greeting, meeting no man's eye as he pushed past making for the upper chamber and earning a sharp gaze from Weston for this rudeness. How the boy knows such things puzzles all. Still, he has a gift for prognostication; this one, should it indeed prove true, boding well for the return of clear weather.

It was Tolman who first spoke on Weston's return from removing the black to the smokehouse.

I like this not at all, said he. The negro is most like to run off before we learn what transpired aboard ship, who murdered the men buried here today.

And where is he to go, sir? asked Weston. The island is but three miles north to south. 'Tis not likely he would slip aboard a schooner unremarked.

We must take care nonetheless, Tolman said. He may be our only path to the truth. The sailor taking his ease with us is not so well as I made him to be in the black's hearing. Indeed, the man is not likely to survive.

Tolman is right, said the Squire, fingering his great moustache as is his wont when agitated. We must press the negro as to what happened, the whereabouts of the Captain. The man may be on the vessel yet—injured and in need of aid.

If so, I'll lay he's quite swelled with seawater, said Mr. Ames. Why else but for the lack of a captain would such a vessel wreck on the ledge with the lights of Matinicus Rock to warn it off?

Did the black own to the number of crew? asked the Squire.

He made it to be twelve, sir, said Weston.

And only five found, nodded Tolman—all but the negro badly cut. Rank as a bait barrel, this entire concern. We must learn the fate of the other seven, and quickly. Only then will we know the cut of man we've brought among us.

Aye, and lay claim to the cargo she carries, agreed Mr. Ames. From the West Indies, did the black not say? Coffee, then; and rum. Molasses and cigars, like as not. We'll gaff on to much of benefit, to be sure.

The Squire grew quite distressed at this. Such depends on where she was bound, Mr. Ames; most likely she discharged cargo on her way north. Some southern port, perhaps.

In which case she carries cotton, said Ames. A boon to our wives and daughters for the fashioning of their dresses, shirt fronts for ourselves.

She'd be Europe-bound in that case, man, or New York—where prices are highest, the Squire told him. And what remains of her cargo is not freely ours for the taking, I'll remind you.

Findings-havings, sir—rule of the islands, as ye well know. And I recollect no complaints from ye when the coal was carried off from one such vessel this past winter—sinking as she was north of the harbor, nor the spool wool and raw linen from another last spring. And Weston's fine schoolhouse is itself built from boardwood liberated not five year back from that wrecked schooner bound from Bath. Though as holder of a third share in a vessel much like the Amaranth, I might can see your reluctance; is not your brig, the Sally Ann, engaged in the same West Indies trade?

The Squire, at his mustache again, nodded his thoughts. Indeed she is, Mr. Ames. Indeed she is.

We'll lose all if we delay—men and cargo alike, said Mr. Tolman. The wind goes north, the lad said. If the vessel has not loosed itself from the ledges by morning, her back will surely be broke from the pounding and thus open to lawful salvage. I say we board her on the morrow.

Salvage on the Sabbath? objected the Squire. The pastor would not have it, surely.

Mr. Ames' eyes looked to quite pop from his head with anger. Then 'tis well the man's not here, barked he.

I trust the Lord will understand, Squire. Always the voice of reason, Weston's attitude became thoughtful, the fore of his arm resting at the mantle below the Queen Anne flintlock that reminds me so much of home. Considering him thus, his bearing far beyond the Squire's in elegance though his clothing is indeed more modest, I determined to fashion a shirt of fine cambric to present him on his birthday but a month from now, the thought pleasing me much.

Consider those souls still onboard, sir, continued he; as well our Christian obligation to provide burial. We might perhaps allow what weather Providence sends to decide us. 'Tis certain we can't proceed with the fog thick as it is.

Aye, said Tolman. If the wind goes north, she'll be clear by morning. I'll speak to the others.

And with this the men took their leave, and about time as there were the dumplings to be made yet for the noon dinner, the stew and what remained of the Saturday baking to be set to the hearth. And thus passed the rest of this troubling day.

I end this now with heavy heart, convinced as I am nothing good shall come of this business of the Amaranth and the hulking black whose shadow, lit by candle, I spy pacing as would a desperate animal in the crack of light beneath the smokehouse door.

FIVE

Rachel doesn't keep a car on the island, so I show up for Friday's four o'clock flight, known affectionately as the Booze Run, pulling a rusting child's wagon unearthed from the barn. Back wheel is slightly bent, lending it a kind of rhythmic grinding screak, but it rolls along easily enough. Besides, it's the only conveyance I could find. My search for the tent Ben and I once shared was less successful. Such things aren't kept in the barn, apparently—which is where I've spent the last two nights tossing and turning in my sleeping bag waiting to be startled awake by the caress of a phantasmal finger—neither are they housed in any of the smaller, unused outbuildings. Clearly, if it still exists, it's somewhere in the house—probably the attic, which is problematic as it would entail another trip to that weird and unhappy second floor.

I trade Doug a couple Matinicus Ones for my case of Heineken and three bottles of Laphroaig; then head back with an eye toward grooming myself for tonight's shindig at the Galley Hatch.

Bumping along, I continue the argument I've been having with myself for the last two days—namely how to explain being loved-up by some witchy ghost girl who can't possibly exist. That she is indeed a girl—or, more precisely, once was—I'm certain, being a connoisseur of the female sensibility, however subtle it might be in its deceased state. Neither do I remember Rachel or Ben ever mentioning such a presence, though there's clearly one in residence.

Back at Rachel's, I unload all twenty-four beers into the fridge. Except for the rather creepy feeling I'm being eyeballed, the house feels normal as any other during the day. Still, I confine my ramblings to the first floor, just in case.

Big joke, right? Me, the no-nonsense scientist, leery of something he knows can't be real. It's a lot like my fear of flying, actually—a visceral, unshakeable remnant of childhood. I remember as a kid hiding in my room on Halloween—no lie—even then preferring things I could touch and measure to the murky netherworld of the unseen.

It's not quite seven when, clothed in chinos and my faded green Frank Zappa tee, and with a couple friends named Heineken along for the ride, I head to Al's for an evening of God-only-knows-what. The sweltering August heat hasn't backed off a bit, the harbor road lined with a dusty riot of wild-flowers—black-eyed Susans, daisies, honeysuckle, wild calla; and I find myself escorted the last hundred yards or so by a pair of obese black labs, whose graying muzzles unfailingly guide me down a series of intersecting driveways I've never before seen. No idea where we're headed, but the grow-ing murmur of voices is encouraging. Coming around a final corner, I find myself surrounded by ten or twelve kids tagging their way through a yard full of pickups and ATVs—the noisy, well-lubricated crowd just beyond jammed cheek by jowl onto the deck of the Galley Hatch.

That illusive second way in. Hot damn.

Inside, the place is all but deserted—a couple guys at the pool table, the band taking a break in the corner—the room fragrant with that greasy cheese and oregano smell you get in really good pizza parlors. I secrete my second Heinie behind the milk in the cooler, take a seat at the counter, and pry the cap off my beer.

"Well, if it ain't Mr. Gil Hodges." Al's in full party mode tonight—jean shorts, loud red and yellow Hawaiian button-down, and a '45 Athletics cap worn bill-back. He follows my hungry gaze to an enormous, nearly empty pizza pan at the end of the counter just as a tow-headed kid of about five runs in from the deck, snags one of the two remaining pieces, and slams his way back through the screen door.

Al grins in approval of this little theft. "All you can eat, six ninety-five. Interested?"

"You bet," I say, reaching for the last slice.

"Not that one," he tells me. "Corner pan's for the kids. Got a pepperoni and a loaded coming out any minute now."

He leans into the counter as a diaper-clad toddler with a cap of black curls and enormous blue eyes barrels from between two of the grocery shelves on a low-riding plastic trike. Half-eaten slice strangled in one hand, with the other he manages a tight, perfectly executed turn just inches from the door and pedals off again.

"Settling in okay?" Al asks.

I nod companionably, feeling it wise to avoid the subject of my spectral roomie. "Thinking about doing some camping out on the point."

"Behind Rachel's? Western Point, you mean."

Makes sense, of course, as I was indeed heading west along a well-beaten path through marshy, grotto-like stands of spruce deadfall and cranberry bog when I stumbled across the place—a long rise to a relatively flat plateau falling away to the spectacular raging surf. Staggering views of Penobscot Bay and the Blue Hills hovering above Camden. Sure beats the hell out of sleeping in the barn, which smells oddly of cow dung despite the absence of any animals save a few mice. Not to mention the unsettling presence of that loaded rifle.

Al's busy with his ledger, so I rise, figuring I'll grab what I need to get me through the next few days before the crowd settles in. Deftly dodging another run of the speed-crazed toddler, I consider a shelf stocked with transmission oil, mayonnaise, disposable diapers, fuses, potato chips, Dawn dishwashing liquid, canned tuna.

I grab a couple cans of this last, some mayo, another loaf of bread—glancing to the long window overlooking the harbor where I fix on what has to be the most stunning sailboat I've ever seen. Forty-five, fifty feet—pristine and gleaming white, like a fine thoroughbred tossed incongruously among the workhorses.

"That's some sailboat," I say, dumping my stuff on the counter.

"Allan Kneeland's new yacht," Al tells me. "Guy made a fortune in manufacturing—polyester hair for Barbie Dolls, believe it or not. Sold out maybe five years back, right after he married Kirtley. They spend summers sailing Downeast, usually stop in about this time."

"Looks deserted," I say, glancing again to the window.

"Kirtley sailed it in about a week ago—day or two before you first came in, matter of fact. Flew over to the mainland this morning. Meeting up with Allan, probably."

"She sails that thing herself? Must be some chick."

"Oh, she's that alright," he chuckles. "You'll see."

Just then the auburn-tressed girl I remember from the airstrip, the one schlepping cases of beer last time I was in, blasts from the kitchen with two enormous pizzas. Close up, what I took for twelve or thirteen might actually stretch another year or two considering the air of bored disdain that precedes her; and it's clear her creamy-complected tan—hard to miss with so little skin actually under wraps—is more than the kiss of the sun. There's an olive component at work here that suggests a Mediterranean contribution to the gene pool. Big green eyes, a spattering of freckles. Her body just beginning to develop, like it hasn't yet caught on to what's occurring up there between her ears. And while I'm no longer in this race, it's clear even to me that she's going to wake up an absolute knockout one of these days if she doesn't bore herself to death first.

Finished with their break, tonight's band—the usual four-piece of lead, rhythm, bass and drums—launches into Neil Young's "Cinnamon Girl," bringing the hordes in from the deck. Jeans and tee shirts, sunburned tans. The loose, unfocused demeanor of serious drinkers who've been at it for hours. Something else, too—an undertone of tension I can't quite suss out. Figure maybe it's me—some tourist crashing their party. Summer complaints, they call us here.

Sliding onto the stool beside me is a boy of perhaps sixteen sporting a stringy starter goatee. He reaches across me for a slice without excusing himself—a variety of male territory-marking used by those light on any real machismo; and having established he can do this without challenge, slaps the pizza on a paper plate and drags it through my pile of supplies. Having made his point—that as a summer visitor I do not exist in his world—he inhales it in two bites, washing the whole molten mess down with a swig from a longneck Bud.

Not to be outdone, I slap two pieces on a plate, drag the thing toward me and am deep into it when the kid pipes up, all innocence.

"How about another piece, Tiff?"

She looks uncertain, a vulnerability I immediately peg as romantic entanglement, then reaches for a paper plate.

"...of ass," he finishes—all but falling off his stool with teenage hilarity.

"Get a life," she snaps, chin nodding toward his Bud. "You pay for that?"

A shrug. "Cash's tab. He said."

She glares, then pulls out the ledger and, flipping the page angrily, makes a note.

The teacher in me stirs, longing to warn him mano-a-mano that this kind of crude treatment of one such as she will not only get him nowhere, it may very well earn him some nasty payback he'll never see coming. But as my own record in this regard is hardly stellar, I instead revert to type.

"Give him another beer on me," I say.

The girl I now know as Tiff plants her hands on those heartbreakingly childlike hips. "You running a tab now, too, I suppose?"

"Already started one." Al points over her shoulder at the ledger. "Here, see? Hodge—that's him. Add his groceries in and bag them for me, will you sweetheart?" He plants a kiss on her head, then says to me, "Our niece,

Tiffany. Lives upstairs with us when she remembers to come home."

The band's on a serious nostalgia bent, snarling its way through Steppenwolf's *The Pusher* as I tuck the bag beneath my feet—pointing to Tiffany with my bottle as she moves away.

"Your girl?" I ask the kid.

"Sometimes." All bravado as he takes another pull on the Bud, his dirty orange flip-flops tapping nervously to the music. "Thanks for the brew," he says, eyes flicking my way for the first time. "Name's Ivan."

"Gil." We do the hooked-thumb and palm dance preferred by the young men of today, then go back to ignoring each other until I've fetched my other Heineken and snagged another slice.

"You a lobsterman?" I ask Ivan, who's turned on his stool to watch the room.

"I stern for Cash—scarred-up dude at the pool table." He points with his beer toward a wiry guy with a Fu Manchu who's long since lost the acne war. A wall of people watch as he chalks his cue, bends for a shot. Even from here I can see the long, white striations of scar tissue along both arms. House fire? Car accident?

I swing back to face a pleasant-faced, slightly jowly woman busy swapping a full cheese pie for the empty pan in the kiddy corner. "My wife," Al tells me nodding toward her. "Gail, this here's Hodge—guy staying out to Rachel's."

Gail's early fifties maybe, and pleasingly round, which I appreciate in a cook. Cropped red hair peppered with gray, a no-nonsense look to her which no doubt makes for interesting dynamics with the petulant Tiffany.

"Killer blueberry pie," I tell her. "Don't suppose you've got another one kicking around back there."

"I bake Wednesdays and Saturdays," she snaps—shooting Al a *who the hell is this guy* look as she drops down to open a couple lower cabinets. "You can special order if you want."

One by one, half gallons of liquor appear on the counter beneath the mirror. Gin, vodka, Mount Gay. A fifth of Jack Daniel's, another of tequila. From the Philco she pulls two liter jugs of coke, ginger ale, soda water and tonic as Tiffany reappears with a square bus bucket of ice cubes. Voila—a bar.

You gotta love this place.

"So you like it—being a sternman?" I ask the kid as yet another obese lab waddles from the kitchen and out from behind the bar, tail waving in an expectant circle. What is it with these things?

"Fuckin' sucks. Dirty, boring, shitty work. Up before dawn, stuffin' bait bags, cleanin' out traps. Always the same thing: old guy drives the boat, young guy does all the work."

I glance again at Cash, the particular old guy under discussion—noting he might be all of thirty-five. Twitchy and amped up. Leatherman on one hip, beeper on the other. A beeper, for God's sake. Maybe fifty people live out here off-season—most within shouting distance of each other. Who the hell needs a beeper?

"Good money in lobstering, I hear."

He shoots me a suspicious look. "What are you, some fuckin' reporter?"

"Me?" I laugh. "God, no."

"'Cause we been getting a lot of 'em out here, you know, with the lobster war and shit. Nosey fuckers."

The room's throbbing with beat now—another Steppenwolf, this one the mega hit "Born to Be Wild." I turn on my stool, trolling the room, wondering vaguely if they do any Zappa when I catch a couple marginally attractive women checking me out from their perch against the long bank of windows, the flashing red of the harbor buoy light pulsing in the glass behind them. Dark, shoulder-length hair on both, same chesty build and skinny legs. Sisters, probably. The one on the left, who I dub Denise, takes a long drag of her cigarette; the other—let's call her Donna—a swig of her Bud Light as they whisper, consider, whisper some more. After a minute, they saunter over and lean casually onto the counter. Denise orders a pony of Jack Daniel's from Al, who's boogying behind the counter; Donna, who's beside me, requests a shot of tequila—her gaze swinging casually in my direction.

"Hi," she says in a voice that's seen the bottom of far too many eighty-proof bottles.

I shoot her a wink. What can I say? Old habits die hard.

"Anyone ever tell you you look like that actor—you know…"

"Jeff Bridges," I finish. I get this all the time, and don't think I haven't used it once or twice to my advantage.

"Yeah, him."

"Nope," I lie, sending her my most winning smile. Can't help myself.

She grins in an unfocused sort of way, proving she's too far gone to get the joke; then glancing down to where the Lab's nudging her leg, pours the dregs of her beer onto my paper plate and puts it on the floor for him. An oft-repeated dance, based on the way he laps it up—leaving little doubt as to how he's acquired the gut he labors to drag around.

Donna turns back to me, gives her shot glass a coy little finger stir. "You here with anybody?"

Women generally like to get a name first, I've found—something to connect with the face in case they forget to ask next morning. The great thing about alcohol, though, is the ease with which it cuts through such overrated niceties as caution and self-respect.

"Nope," I say again.

Last summer I'd have tossed a coin and gone home with one of these two, being maybe six months shy of my own wakeup call; but the possibility does nothing for me tonight—hasn't, in fact, since that last surreal week with Annika.

My glance wanders to where the toddler has finally given it up and slumps open-mouthed over the trike—cheek resting on a pudgy forearm draped limply across the handlebar. This despite a noise level approaching that of a passing train. Amazingly, he's still fisting that mash of pizza, a prize the Lab has discovered and is teasing gently from his fingers. Donna turns, follows my gaze.

"Shit," she says, then shrugs good-naturedly. "Duty calls. Catch you later?"

Only as it turns out, there is no later. Just as Donna is reclaiming her comatose child, a man I vaguely recognize slides to the stool beside me. Though he's just joined our little party, his eyes are the rheumy red of a man who takes his drinking seriously, probably building a steady buzz since morning. I have trouble placing him till someone yells from across the room.

"Clayton, you fuck!"

Of course. The surly, De Niro look-alike I met in here a few days back—the one whose dog was murdered to make some grisly point—only tonight he's traded his grease-smeared tee shirt for a clean, albeit wrinkled, blue denim. His shower-wet hair is slicked back and curling at the neck.

"Tequila," he tells Gail—taking me in from a distance as he wrestles with the jar of Slim Jims. Anywhere else in the country, this place would be shut down for serving a man as clearly shitfaced as this guy is, but if anyone's aware of it, they don't care.

Clayton's shot is dutifully marked in the ledger as he leans across me, swaying slightly on the stool.

"Man's a scientist," he yells over the music toward Ivan, who's bent on ignoring him. "Counts trees." He tries to focus on me, apparently having given up on the Slim Jims.

"How's that comin', by the way?"

I raise my beer in response. Music's too loud to make for decent conversation, anyway, which is fine with me. Besides, there's not much to report, distracted as I've been. First thing tomorrow, I promise myself.

"Clayton Burgess, you cocksucker!"

Clayton ignores the liquor-fueled greeting, trying as he is to light up—hard to do when your Zippo keeps missing the tip of your cigarette. I'm nursing my Heineken, enjoying the comedic aspects of all this, when it dawns on me that the room's gone absolutely still—weird considering the music's still thumping away. In the mirror, the BUD LIGHT sign over by the pool table reads THGIL DUB; beneath it Cash twists the cap off a beer bottle and whips it toward Clayton's head. Misses by a mile. I turn to ask Ivan what's going on but he's faded into the crowd.

"Turn around, you shit-for-brains motherfucker!" Cash's reflection has grabbed a cue and is heading our way.

Clayton seems unconcerned. Amused, in fact—shaking his head as at the antics of children. "Don't hardly think so," he says quietly. A chuckle as he sips.

Cash has the speed of the small and sinewy, but Clayton is faster, as is Al despite his limp—both of them grabbing the cue on its arc toward Clayton's head or, possibly, mine. Last time someone came this close to doing me physical harm, she managed to cut me before I could react—having rather stupidly not expected to encounter an adversary in the guise of lover. This time I duck and slide from the stool with a dexterity more befitting my martial arts training, coming up in open parallel stance, Tae Kwon Do-style.

But it's Al who surprises, pulling an old wooden baseball bat from somewhere beneath the counter and shaking it in Cash's face. "Back off!" he growls. "Now!"

Cash is almost apoplectic with fury—forehead vein pumping, muscle twitching furiously at the corner of his eye as he struggles to keep control of the cue. "You and that fucking uncle of yours can fucking kiss my ass," he spits toward Clayton.

"You don't let that stick go, boy," Al threatens, "this little turf war's gonna be the least of your problems. Whatever this is, it ain't gonna be settled in here."

Some guy with boozy eyes and a butt drooping from the corner of his mouth manages to muckle onto Cash from behind; another pins an arm. It's all they can do to hang on to him as they drag him toward the door.

"Got a lot of fuckin' nerve naming that piece of shit boat after my ma," Cash snarls. "Fuckin' John's the one put you up to it, too, I'll bet. Too stupid to come up with it on your own. You really think I'm gonna put up with that thing sittin' in the harbor every day?"

Clayton's retaken his seat, shoots Al a wink like he's really enjoying this. I haven't met John, of course, but it wouldn't surprise me if this nut Cash was the one behind the gruesome calling card tacked to Clayton's barn door.

"Be a miracle that thing's still floating come morning!" Cash screams, hanging onto the door as the others tug him toward the deck. "I'll sink her where she fuckin' sits!" Fingers peel one by one from the jamb as he disappears. "Cash is king!"—a disembodied cackle receding into the night.

There's nothing like a brawl for emptying a place out, and ten minutes later, with the band tossing back beers and noodling through some riffs, Al and I are alone at the counter.

"All comes down to territory," he explains, pouring a shot of Jack Daniel's for me, another for himself. "You got to be born and raised out here to fish these waters—that's the first thing. Even then, young guys coming up have to get the okay from the others before they start fishing their own boats. Think of it as a kind of private club. If you aren't a member, you don't fish anywhere near here. Period."

I've heard this. Some of the most crustacean-rich waters in the world swirl around Matinicus. I also know that if a man's got a license to fish in Maine, he's got the legal right to drop his traps damn near anywhere he wants—on paper anyway.

"Membership has its privileges," I say, raising my glass.

"Exactly," Al says. We throw our liquor back; fire engulfs my throat, my chest. It's not Laphroaig, but it ain't bad.

"Second thing? If you move away, break faith with the island, you're out of the club—no matter who you are. No appeal. Third thing is, we got a kind of frontier justice out here that guarantees numbers one and two."

Out in the kitchen, the fluorescent overheads are going dark one by one. "Goin' up, Al," Gail calls.

"Be along soon," he tells her and turns back to me. "Now Clayton's a Burgess, see. His family's been fishing Matinicus waters since God was a guppy. Plus, he's a highliner. That means he knows the bottom real good— has a sense where the lobsters are, when they're gonna move and where they'll go when they do. He's the best out here—probably pulls in two, three hundred grand a year."

"Dollars?" I choke.

Al nods. "Problem is, Clayton's uncle, John Burgess—the guy who brought him up in the ranks—retired to the mainland about five years back, bought a fried fish place over to Wiscasset. Technically speaking, he doesn't fish here anymore. Only his traps are still out and his boat's been seen."

He pours two more shots. "Following so far?"

I nod.

"So a couple of the boys get together, take a ride over to the fish place for a talk with John who naturally acts all surprised this should be a problem. Claims since he and Clayton are in business together and since Clayton and the business are still out here, he's got a right to fish, even though he keeps his boat over to Tenants Harbor now.

"So the boys come back and the lot of them thrash the whole thing out, Clayton coming down on his uncle's side. They're family, see, so he doesn't really have a choice. Man has a point, they finally decide. A gray area, for sure, but no one wants another lobster war so they let it go. John can fish.

"Then a week ago, Cash and Ivan are out hauling and spot John's boat. Only John's not onboard. He's hired some guy from the mainland to haul for him. See the problem?"

"Guy's not from Matinicus?"

"Exactly. Now he could just as easily have hired some kid from the island to pull his traps, but this way it feels to the boys like John's thumbing his nose, which he tends to do. Slippery slope kind of thing. No way 'round it, now—island's got to take a stand. So they do the usual—tie half-hitches to his buoy tails so they float at an odd angle. Tells a guy you know what he's doing and you expect him to stop. Problem is, John doesn't stop. Got a different guy from the mainland running the boat now. Bigger, uglier, stronger. Keeps a Remington 870 pump-action shotgun in the wheelhouse."

I state the obvious. "So Clayton's in the middle." Even as I say it, I wonder where the Coast Guard is in all this.

Al nods. "Easier to beat on Clayton than John, seeing as he's here. Safer, too, considering who John is. Plus, you add maybe a little jealousy about how well Clayton does—we got some guys here couldn't catch a lobster if it was crawlin' in a puddle—and so you got Cash, who's a fireballer anyway, comin' at him with a pool cue. A pretty benign weapon around here, actually. Could just as easily been a baseball bat or a knife, maybe. Guns. Cash's big on guns. He's another one you don't want to mess with."

"Every man for himself," I say—thinking Wild West, Earp brothers, shootout at the O.K. Coral. "What was all that about Clayton's boat?"

"Well, and that's a whole 'nother layer to this bullshit. Clayton had a thing with Cash's mama some years back. She was still married then. Didn't last long, but Cash ain't one to forget. Bad blood between 'em since.

"So when Clayton buys himself a new work boat to the tune of three hundred grand," Al says, pouring himself another, "he names her *Bobbi Jean*—that's Cash's mama—sticking it to Cash cause he's been riding him about this fishing business. Just brought her out here today."

I shake my head when he points the bottle in my direction; I have yet to pick my way back to Rachel's, after all.

"Cash ain't all that bad, just so you know—never seen him go after someone like that before, not in here, anyway. Just that everyone's on edge tonight. Uncle Clunk died this morning, see. Heart attack. Sitting in the backyard after breakfast, you believe that? Silvie, that's his sister-in-law—he moved in with her when his brother Jack died a couple years back—she went outside to ask him something and there he was, stone dead in his chair."

"Old?" I ask.

"No, that's the thing got us all scratching our heads. Guess you just never know, right?

"So anyway, back to John—guy who shouldn't be fishing but is. Been terrorizing the island since he was a kid. Tried to mess with Gail when she wasn't but ten—that's the kind of animal we're talkin' about here—but she kneed him in the balls and good. Mandatory subject in school," he winks. "Never said nothin', figurin' he'd do that and worse if she told. Surly, mean motherfucker—even for out here."

The grisly image of the bloodied dog jumps again to mind.

"Funny how things work out, though, 'cause he finally got his. Seven, maybe eight years back he was fishin' alone off Criehaven when his shift lever cable popped off. So he's reaching in to fix it—boat's idling in gear— and his sleeve snags on the spinning coupling. A situation you don't want to be in, believe me. Like that, arm gets wrapped around the shaft, breaks in three places before it gets tore off at the elbow. John managed to get himself over to Rockland before he passed out, though."

Ouch. "Good reason to retire."

"Hell, wasn't the accident; he fished for years after. No, his knees blew out. Seems even scumbags get old."

There seems nowhere to go with this so we change tacks, veering from the island's escalating tensions to a subject closer to Al's heart.

"Billy Martin—now there was a brawler, on the field and off. Didn't have the talent of Whitey Ford or the Mick, but the guy did what it took to win. Hell of a manager, too." A pause. "You have any interest in playing— when you were a kid, I mean? Got the right build for it."

"God, no," I laugh. It was Dad who was obsessed with all this; evidence my name and the hat—one he wore every day during baseball season. He was a numbers nut with an almost obsessive interest in stats. I was immersed in the stuff as a kid—no way I could get away from it. I wonder sometimes if all that exposure led me to my job counting trees, as Clayton put it.

"You collect? You know...cards?"

I shrug. Dad's exhaustive collection is the total sum of my patrimony, which isn't as nutty as it sounds. Most of the cards are in near-perfect condi- tion, including the complete 1952 Topps set—the most popular and valu- able post-World War II—plus all two hundred and six of the Topps '55s, including the fabled Brooklyn Dodgers: my man Gil, Johnny Podres, Pee Wee Reese, Jackie Robinson, Duke Snider, Roy Campanella and the like. Pure gold from an investment standpoint.

"Best card I've got," Al says—glancing around as if for spies, "is a '56 Topps Mantle I found online for twenty-five hundred."

I don't tell him Dad's '52 rookie Mantle card is worth probably ten times that. Not bad for a piece of cardboard originally designed to do nothing more than stiffen a pack of bubblegum.

"I'll pay top dollar, you got any '55 Dodgers," he tells me.

I shake my head. This is intimate stuff—like sex. "Not on a first date, Al."

And with this I rise and, cradling my supplies, take myself off under cover of the moon.

SIX

It was quiet on the wharf mid-afternoon; that's why she liked it. Just the gulls, a couple little kids rowing a skiff too big for them along the store beach. Resettling herself, barefoot and cross-legged atop the four-foot piling, Tiffany stared out across the harbor at the empty float where Ka-Ching would be if it was back, which it wasn't. Only one back in was Mary Kate—Kathy and her dad just finishing up.

Cash and them thought she was clueless, but they were the stupid ones. She knew just what they were up to. Anyone else would have done it at night or in the fog so no one could point a finger, not first thing on a crystal clear morning when you could see halfway to Tenants Harbor. She couldn't decide who was stupidest—Ivan cause he was young and lazy, or Cash 'cause he was high most of the time. Plus, he was a hothead. She knew when he came down on Clayton like that last night he'd end up doing something really dumb, take Ivan right along with him.

And cutting John's traps was the biggest dumb there was, same thing as calling him out. And yeah, she knew all the reasons; she'd heard 'em enough times. *Survival depends on keeping poachers out.* And *life out here is hard enough without people trying to steal your livin' out from under you.* They made rules like you had to own a house with electric service and pay island taxes to run a boat here. And even then you had to get voted in. *Enforcing the bottom is self-preservation*—that was another one, but even with all the stupid rules, more people left every year, moved off so they could have movies and malls and McDonald's. God, she'd kill for some hot, greasy McDonald's fries. Burger King, even. Some of them said the island wouldn't survive no matter what they did. Be nothing left in ten years but the summer people scratching their heads when there was no one around to run the electric company or the post office, get 'em their propane.

She glanced down when she heard the oars sliding home, Kathy climbing the ladder up the side of the wharf ahead of Josh.

"Hey, Tiff."

"Hey, Kath." Kathy was okay—they'd come up through school together, though why anyone would want to go stern for a father or brother was beyond Tiffany. Even though she'd considered going stern for Uncle Clayton—he'd asked her enough times—specially when he started promising to leave her all his money when he died seeing as he didn't have any wife or kids. He was usually drunk when he said it, but still. Anyway, Gail wouldn't let her—too dangerous. Besides, she said, school was too important to miss even a few weeks, which Tiffany would have to do in September to keep up her end of the bargain. So that was that.

And school was another thing. Having one that only went to eighth grade was just dumb. If they really wanted to know why people were moving off, well, that was it. All her life she'd been told they had to pull together, support each other or the island would die. But what do they do? Break up families by sending the kids other places for high school; kill poor old dogs; fight each other over dumb lobsters, like there weren't enough of the things crawling around out there to fill every boat wanted 'em. Plus, a lot of 'em like Cash just spent their money on drugs and got all paranoid—shooting their guns off in the harbor like they were in some old western on T.V.

She gazed after Kathy and Josh 'til their pickup reversed through all the ATVs, up past the old store toward the post office—the sight of the store reminding her of Ivan, the gross way he kept count how many times they did it in there. Halfway up the ladder, he'd remind her—like every time. And thinking about that reminded her of the other thing, but she pushed the thought away. She wasn't going to think about that now; she just wasn't.

She turned back to the harbor, her eyes traveling the horizon out past Indian Ledge—willing the red of *Ka-Ching's* Jolly Roger to come into view, begin its lazy roll toward the breakwater. Saw only *Ocean Pirate* and *Plan Bea* heading in. And Clayton's new boat, *Bobbi Jean*, which Cash would probably scuttle next time he got so high he didn't care if he got shot.

Goddam fucking Ivan; where the hell was he? Not that she was worried; not one little bit. Well, she'd sit right here till he showed up, just so's she could ignore him when he walked past. And anyway, it would serve them both right if they got caught out there. John still had like two hundred traps out—nowhere near as many as the others, but still a lot of gear. She figured it in her head. Hundred dollars a trap times two hundred. That was like a lot of money. There'd be a war for sure now. Somebody would probably die. Maybe a bunch of somebodies.

Plus, it was getting plain weird around here what with Clunk and his stupid heart attack—and wasn't that muckin' things up but good—and everybody at each other's throats like all the time. And Gail so snappy and mean, not like that was anything new. Once, when Tiffany said something about how her mother would be coming for her soon, Gail said if she hadn't been back in all these years, she wasn't going to now, so forget about it. But what did she know? She and Al weren't even her relatives; they weren't anything to her. Calling her their niece was a total joke. Like anyone believed that, other than that stupid scientist guy staying up to Rachel's place. Guy was so lame. Playing up to Ivan last night like he gave a shit. Nobody ever talked to Ivan 'cause he had nothing to say. Tiffany probably wouldn't even go out with him if there was any other boy out here her age. Plus, she hated the way he called his mother by her name. Cheryl this, Cheryl that. Disrespectful, considering there were people around here who didn't even have mothers. Well, she'd be rid of him soon. End of August he'd be over in Vinalhaven, living with his grandparents for the fall term, and she'd be gone to Rockland for school.

She pulled her knees to her chest and stared down, wiggling her toes—but the chipped red polish reminded her of the other thing again. She should just stop thinking about it. She'd wake up tomorrow with her period and that'd be the end of it.

She hooked her hair over an ear and hugged her knees, peering over them at the Kneelands' sailboat—so sparkling white it gleamed. Must have cost like a gazillion dollars. If she had something beautiful like that, she'd just head down the coast till she found her mother, who's probably got some important job in some really cool place like Boston or New York. But it wouldn't matter that it was a city with tons of people in it 'cause they'd recognize each other right away, and her mother would quit her job even though it was really important, because it was more important to be with her daughter. And she'd be really impressed that Tiffany had such a gorgeous boat of her own and could sail it around by herself the way Kirtley Kneeland does, and they'd take off to someplace where it was warm all the time—like the Bahamas, or Florida maybe. Be a family.

And her mother would know what to do about the problem with her period. She'd take care of it all. She would.

Really.

SEVEN

Matinicus, Sunday 12 July

It is said that turning your back on the devil does naught but turn his head toward yours. This must indeed be true, for I fear we've brought a murderer among us and the path we take promises nothing but further evil.

As if in agreement with our plans to lay claim to the secrets of the Amaranth, the Lord's Day dawned clear and warm, the wind having shifted northwest during the night to throw off the fog. And with the tide being high at the noon and thus propitious for the work before us, there was little dissent for the plan. Indeed, I have no trouble with the taking, for why should those things as might ease our lives here go instead to the bottom for lack of a proper owner?

Thus it was that after a service of prayer so brief as might be considered scandalous elsewhere, men and boys broke as one toward the Rumguzzle, so fired were they for what might be found on the vessel. Seth, though only five, is angry with me yet for keeping him back, but someone must be spared to watch over Mary who is still with the clouts upon her, and thus twice the burden of the others. The boy may be young for much, but this at least he might do.

After our return to the farm and the getting of the noon dinner, the children had little interest in their chores, so stirred were they by the sight of the charred hull visible across the fields. The twins, arms entwined, skirts a-twirl in the breeze, ignored all but their own ferocious whispers as they watched for Lavon among the pulling boats abob in the waves. Indeed, it took the switch to stir them to the beating of the rugs, so disregarding were they of me. When I was but *a girl of ten on Vinalhaven, not a year more in age than these two, I had the care of the house much upon me. I will not have more than my share put on me here because they shirk.*

I turned then to a lamb just in from the field with a wound in the neck and needing a dressing of tar; then afterward began a pitching of hay to the manger for the cows, a task Seth was set to but quickly gave up, preferring to chase chickens in the dooryard. I fetched Mary to him with a line about her middle that I might have some use of him yet; and he made much of this new power, pulling her about as he does his pets, heedless as the rest of us to her sobbing.

Such melancholy overcame me then for the missing of my home and family across the bay, even such memories of papa when I was still small and he'd not yet taken against me. Ours was a larger farm than this to be sure, our home with a good many more rooms. My mother had a large and lovely ell to her kitchen, bright and airy, with a cellar dug full beneath the house rather than the smaller one room beneath the buttery as is the custom here. And though we kept much the same number of oxen and cattle, cows and laying hens, we had three colts for our play when there was time for such, and an abundance of sheep, some sixty-odd, where Isaac keeps but four and twenty. And though our soil was stony and thin, we carried twice and more the acreage in salt-hay, and had our orchards, of which Isaac has none.

Indeed, why father sent me away as he did, depriving mother of my industry and I her counsel, I cannot say. I had no knowledge of his long acquaintance with Isaac, a man but a few years his junior, nor had I any of my own. Indeed I had never seen the man before his arrival at our farm, whereupon mama bade me take refreshment to the parlor where I understood papa to be entertaining a guest. My surprise was great, therefore, when I entered to find myself the topic of their conversation.

Aye, said father, eyeing me as if encouraging purchase of a sheep or cow, you'll find she's happy in plain garb and will not pester you for fancy. Carding and spinning and tending the dairy are what she's good for.

The shame of it galls me still.

It was mother who spoke of the matter to me, this after father and Isaac had come to agreement, saying that the union, while unlooked for, offered opportunity quite beyond any I was like to find on Vinalhaven considering recent events. Further, Isaac's farm being without a woman upon it and he without wife for nigh on a month, our marriage might take place as soon as was possible. Thus it was I was sent to housekeeping on my very wedding day, when custom would otherwise grant me the grace of a week or two's time with my own mother to prepare for what awaited me here. Indeed, my new husband took me off with no proper setting out, no string of gold beads or china for my new home as my sisters will certainly have; nothing more given me than my clothing and a few belongings hastily packed among them by my mother's hand, salty-wet from the falling of both our tears.

But I have yet to relay such horrors as were found by the men in the salvaging of the Amaranth. It was while working in the yard that a low murmuring drew me to the smokehouse, the door being slight ajar. One voice I knew well as my own, the other an urgent southern tongue too fast and foreign to my ears to take from it any meaning. Peering within, I spied Weston crouching before the black, his clothing quite wet through, and with a grim countenance upon his face.

The time for prevarication is past, said he. They will come for you sure. You must tell me all and quickly if you care for your life.

My shadow must have fallen across them, for Weston glanced to me. For pity's sake, Hannah, he pleaded, leave off your staring lest the others find us too soon. With that he pulled the door tight, latching it.

And indeed, from across fields awave in the wind marched the men in an agitated and woeful passion, led by the Squire greatly determined in gait. Ames and Tolman I spied as well, Lavon among them but apart, as was old Wivell— all with so darkly glowering a mien I backed myself to the barn as they passed me making for the smokehouse. The girls, playing at their chore in the dooryard, dropped their switches and ran for the house, Mary screaming for fear of it all as Seth dragged her in curiosity toward the men.

Yield yourself up! shouted the Squire, pounding at the door. We know you be within!

The sight of Weston stepping out, tall and cold-eyed, his hand to the negro's shoulder, set them back in surprise.

How is it you stand for this man? demanded the Squire. Did you not see the bodies butchered like so much meat?

Aye, said Ames, and with little left for burying. Stand aside Weston, that the Black Jack speak for hisself.

Be temperate, Mr. Ames, Weston said. Atticus has asked that I relate his tale as his speech is little understood here.

Get on with it then, said the Squire with much impatience, lest we squander yet more time in this business.

And so it was Weston relayed how the Amaranth, encountering strong gales en route from St. Vincent for Nova Scotia, sprung leaks beneath her fore and main chains, putting in for repair at Savannah. There, Atticus was taken aboard as cook, theirs missing and assumed washed overboard in the storm.

A moment, said the Squire. Did the man not tell us he was by way of the West Indies?

Aye, sir. Was but a ruse. He is instead a slave run from master and home in Georgia. The Captain, a man named Lewis and long sympathetic to the *underground, provided him passage north to freedom under guise as a cook and free negro.*

Ames pushed a finger in the black's face. Aye, we saw your captain, man—body flayed like so much bait; his head landlocked in a hogshead of sugar. I'd bet my own you knew of this roguery.

The ship took on others in Savannah, Weston continued—men of violent temperament, it was later revealed—who but a fortnight later and upon losing badly at cards to the Captain and Mate dispatched them in such grisly fashion as we have seen. After which a mutinous brawl ensued, the men breaking for the rum stores and taking against such officers as remained. Apparently, they had not the foresight to spare one who might navigate; thus it was the Amaranth was brought down upon us.

This silenced the assemblage.

Consider yourselves in his place, gentlemen. Once the Captain was no more, friend Atticus was open to discovery and return to the man who claimed to own him. It is hardly surprising he was not immediately forthcoming. Have not all heard what befalls slaves on forced repatriation? There is not one among us who would have done different.

All the more reason to cut the others to bits, snapped Mr. Ames. Thus guaranteeing his escape and the chance to do further mischief.

And the fire, demanded Mr. Tolman—what of that?

He claimed no knowledge of it, sir. He thought it prudent to secret himself when things came to their worst.

Tolman laughed sourly. Convenient, is it not, that all are dead but the sailor under Lydia's care?

As to that, how fares the man? asked the Squire.

Lydia tells me he moans and thrashes about, gripped as he is with fever. Mistress Wivell has stopped, and fears if his wounds don't take him off he's like to be out of his head for yet some time.

The Squire nodded then, his fingers in communion with his mustache before he spoke. We'll make no decision about this now, but hold meeting with the rest tomorrow at the store. Perhaps the sailor will have regained wits enough to put the truth or lie to the Black Jack's story. Until then, Weston, you're charged with seeing to the man, being as you have some knowledge of him. Be sure he doesn't break from the island.

That I will, Weston agreed, with Hannah's help.

With that, all turned as if surprised to find me there, standing yet with my back to the barn. O, the unfairness of my place here, alone and set apart. I am but like the Amaranth—broken and stranded on the ledges, with nothing to succor me but the soft sound of my name falling from Weston's lips.

EIGHT

Matinicus, Monday 13 July

    Leaving the negro's breakfast by the smokehouse door this morn, I turned my gaze west across the fields toward the charred hulk of the Amaranth, only to find the ship and her grisly burden had been sucked from that bony perch somewhere in the night and the ledge upon which she'd fetched up awash with foamy breakers once again. I took it to be a hopeful sign. O, that the day might have continued so.

    Our morning was spent in the tending of the gardens. Mary I put to the picking of peas while I set to hoeing cabbages, Seth and the twins biding at the schoolhouse 'til the noon dinner when Weston dismissed his charges that he might be present for the meeting at Squire Young's store.

    After the meal, I left Alice to the washing up and Emily to the care of the little ones while I tied up my hair, donned my bonnet, and set off toward the harbor to conduct my household business, pulling with me one of the smaller wagons filled with our share of the salvaged coffee for trading at Young's.

    The roads on this island are but two, devised as is a cross, the main a north-south lane of easy passing upon which our farm has the most northerly location. The crossroad to this is marked by Weston's schoolhouse but a half mile to our south, just beyond Tolmans' who are our nearest neighbors, the two properties separated by nothing more than a stretch of field and a thick stand of trees.

    The meeting had not yet begun when I arrived, the men instead conversing in the portion of the storeroom kept for such gatherings, a space open to the

shelved goods and barrels of molasses, sugar, and flour sitting before the counter.
I spied Weston, Squire Young and brother Rufus, Lydia's Tolman, James Burgess
(cousin to husband Isaac and with his same severe, unsmiling mien), Messrs.
Crie and Norton, Wivell with the look of drink already upon him, and Sarah's
Mr. Ames making free with the cigars that were his share from the vessel's hold.
As is island custom, each man taking part in the salvaging comes off with a
share of the goods taken, the Squire receiving two hogsheads of molasses and the
total of the muscavado, Tolman and Lavon (and thus our household) with half
shares of coffee, Wivell the rum for his gin store, and the like. There was much,
it is said, that could not be salvaged even with the drying out, as there are none,
even in such a place as this, willing to eat from that which lay floating with the
murdered men.

To my dismay it was Sally I saw stationed behind the counter, her dress
a high-waisted muslin better suited to one of her father's parties than for such
work as this. Further, her head was bent to that of Lydia Tolman, so close to her
lying-in as to be soon in need of the midwife. At the sight of these two, I would
have turned and left but for the matter of settling the store bill and collecting the
items I had need of. A bit of batting and thread, and some small sugar, dear as
it is, Weston being partial of it for his tea.

I therefore made myself busy at the shelves until such time as Lydia took
her leave which, as it happened, was shortly thereafter. Turning, she spared me
barely a nod when passing, her eyes lit with amusement rather than pleasure at
the sight of me.

"Hannah."

I nodded in like fashion, though I made no greeting. My dislike of the
woman was born only days after my arrival here, though I admit I was quite
pleased when she first knocked upon my door, making me the present of a handsome pound cake. I thought myself to have finally found a friend as I set out
tea and took my seat in the good parlor as hostess to my first guest, until she
deigned to instruct me as to the care of the house and the children brought forth
by my predecessor, much as she might a housemaid and not the new wife of her
nearest neighbor. Indeed, none here have as yet called me Mistress Burgess, as is
my right. They think me ignorant of their whisperings: girl-wife, sloppy in her
housekeeping, unkind to Isaac's children. This last is surely Lydia's doing, for I
received her directives coolly that day, obvious in my distaste at being so rudely
treated.

She best think to her own now, for she takes too much joy in the coming of
this babe when all know to wait until the birthing is done and the child faring
well before bestowing affection. And this, her first, will not survive.

"Good day, Hannah." Sally's smile played false, pleased as she was with
the picture she cut in her frilled cuffs and ribboned hair. Even as she spoke, her

gaze went to Weston who was by all accounts concerned with little but his cigar, thereby earning him comely pouts and a pretty tossing of curls.

I made cordial greeting, informing her of my wish to trade the coffee to clear our debt, this being no small amount what with keeping up the needs of Isaac's family, and him away. Her eyes remained with Weston as I listed my purchases, adding in a pique that came quite suddenly upon me the buttons and three yards of cambric I'll need for the fashioning of his birthday shirt. For smitten as Sally may be, it is at my home and not hers that Weston boards, at my table he takes his food.

Aye, said Mr. Ames, gazing toward the harbor where the schooner I saw on my approach was just then drawing anchor off Indian Ledge. 'Tis best she be off. If she tarries she'll be tide-nipped for sure.

Bound for Havana, the Squire told all, thumb hooked in his waistcoat as he rocked on his heels before the long window. Our load of saltfish putting the cap to a cargo of masts and spars from the Thomaston yards. 'Tis said she can make the run in a fortnight, rigged as she is.

Or three days to the Banks in light winds, said Tolman.

Good speed being more important on the return if the occupation is fishing, suggested Cousin Burgess, his glance darting to me. 'Tis sure Isaac and the others are bearing down on us even now with a full hold. The mackerel run soon, and the ship will need fitting out.

They must surely think me a fool. I have seen enough of such things to know a ship this long past due is not likely to return. Had my wishes the strength of waves, Isaac's vessel would surely be lost.

Did you not hear me, Hannah? asked Sally as she held something toward me. A letter has come for you from Vinalhaven.

It was a moment before I took her meaning, so unexpected was the news. A letter from mama at last, my first since arriving here! The joy I felt was but brief, however, for it was father's cramped hand I saw in the addressing of it, the realization begging the question yet again. Why has not mama written these two months? Surely she knows how I miss her.

I believe I know something of this Captain Lewis of the Amaranth, said the Squire in a puffing of smoke toward the ceiling. Privateered a schooner out of Thomaston during Madison's War, did he not? To come to such an end is a foul thing, foul indeed.

Brings to mind the brig Betsey, don't it? Wivell, a quid of tobacco stowed in his cheeks, gave loose to the spittoon. Out of Wiscasset she was, taken by pirates who dispatched the crew in much the same fashion. Killing them in ways not to be spoke of with ladies present.

His discrete nod toward the counter met with Sally's scowl of irritation, as even this failed to win her a glance from Weston's quarter.

It was then Lavon entered among us, newly come from the unloading of his catch, by the look and smell of him. The dragging of his slimy boots across the fresh laid sawdust of Sally's floor earning him an irate glance from herself. Ignoring all, he approached the counter, whereupon I turned away, tucking the unopened letter in my skirt.

Got a wherry load of cod for the trading, said he.

Sally, still reckoning my account, ignored him.

Rufus there'll be salting her out, he said, nodding toward the men.

Lavon, lad, join us! called the Squire. We've begun about the Amaranth. As you were there at the gruesome findings, you have a right to your say.

Nay, said he. I have bait to dig for the morrow.

There'd be no need of it if you bought from me as do the others, laughed the Squire.

Bad enough the boy gives up a sixteenth share to Rufus for the salting, thought I, when he could do it himself—the salt shed being free to all. It's for certain we could use the money.

Then as he came, so did he leave—with no further word or glance for any as were here. Such are the manners our good Patience taught him.

To the issue at hand, gentlemen, said Weston, who then proceeded with a heartfelt retelling of the negro's story, one I shall not bother to again relate, as I give it small credit.

But the bodies, man! Ames, his blood in a roil, puffed mightily on his cigar. Surely, someone must be made to pay!

Aye, nodded Cousin Burgess. The black claims no knowledge of the fire, but how can this be credited? Indeed, his tale offers explanation for very little considering he was there at the time.

'Tis surely to the man's benefit should none but himself survive, Tolman told all. In which case the sailor under my roof must be protected.

And thus we come to the pinch of the game, said the Squire. Namely, what to do with the Black Jack until such time as Tolman's sailor can put truth or lie to his tale?

Under lock and key for the present, Squire; that's my thinking, said Ames. We have the women to consider.

Surely not, objected Weston. Consider the fellow's sufferings heretofore. There is great injustice in imprisoning a man who's guilt is not proven, and doubly so for such as Atticus whose very life until now has been spent thus. He's shown no inclination to flee; is instead grateful for the saving of his life and the chance to prove his innocence that he might continue his journey to freedom.

Surely you don't propose allowing him to roam free about the island? barked Ames. Why 'twould not be borne. The man is an escaped slave, after all, has slipped off from others with more reason to keep him close than we.

Weston's face grew dark with anger. I remind you, Mr. Ames, that we in Maine do not consider people property; that the importation of slaves as you so term them has been a crime these ten years past—one equal to piracy and carrying the death penalty in the bargain. No, what I propose, sirs, is that he be granted free movement about the Burgess farm until such time as his guilt or innocence is determined. With Hannah's permission, of course.

His glance held such warm entreaty, I could but nod my agreement, the color coming to my cheeks with pleasure, gratified that for the second time in as many days he has linked our names in mutual mission. A pretty pout and the tapping of Sally's foot made me smile the more.

Once his claims are borne out, Weston continued, we are bound by Christian charity to secure him safe passage to Canada if that's his wish. It has not been half a year since another poor soul smuggled to Thomaston and secreted there was betrayed and spirited back to the man who claimed to own him.

Aye, said Wivell. And it ain't but fifteen year past what them Brit press gangs took our men for soldiering, my brother amongst them and never to return. That's as much like slavery as what the black run from, and still it makes my blood boil with the thinking of it. I'm for you then, schoolmaster, long as the negro keeps to the Burgess place.

Agreed, said the Squire. We are all of us reasonable men, after all.

And if the Black Jack proves guilty of the murders and the burning of the Amaranth? pressed Mr. Ames.

If Tolman's sailor names him the attacker, pronounced the Squire, he shall be set adrift in a wherry five leagues east of Matinicus, as is island law. If innocent, we'll grant him protected haven until such time as safe passage is found, that he not be returned to bondage.

And thus was the meeting concluded.

'Tis now quite late; the household finally at rest. I myself shall sleep to the echo of Weston's gentle snores, my dreams filled with that soft look of entreaty, a tenderness lost to me forever should old man Isaac indeed return. Certainly Father's letter offered none, there being nothing within but more of his evil accusations. I save it merely to remind myself how quickly those we love come to betray us, how even monsters such as he might pretend to warm feeling when such is to their purpose. Doubtless the future holds more of the same. I can hardly bear the thinking of it.

NINE

Matinicus, it's been said, is Indian for *land of the rusted automobile*—
the things being plentiful as toadstools out here—but the actual derivation
comes from the Wabanaki word *Menasqueicook*, meaning *grassy isle* or *place
of the wild turkeys*, depending on who you're talking to. The whole place,
seven hundred-plus acres of what was once a dense stand of hardwood, was
systematically deforested by eighteenth century settlers bent on farming the
bejeezuz out of the place, only to have it reclaimed bit by bit by all manner
of vegetation. The result is a mind-boggling plethora of plant life shooting
with lush abandon from what in some of the island's more wooded habitats
consists of little more than a thick bed of moss-covered pine needles. On the
quarter-mile path to the campsite alone, I counted four different species of
fringed orchid and nine varieties of fern, and I wasn't even looking.

I bring all this up because the fecundity of the island aside, never before
in my career have I come across a pile of lobster shells growing spontaneously in the middle of the road as they appear to be doing in front of
Rachel's place.

I'm considering the various possibilities as I venture into the Galley
Hatch—hot, sweaty, bug-bit and famished, for what has become my daily
lunch with Al. This is in flagrant violation of the three-streets-back rule, of
course—a culinary principle I came up with to ensure I eat fresh, cheap and
authentic everywhere I go. Duck a few streets off the main drag almost any
place on the planet and simply follow the locals—never fails.

Exception that proves the rule, right? Because not only is the Hatch right there in your face as you enter the harbor, it's the sole culinary act on the island. What's more, therein can be found some of the best home-cooked I've ever come across.

I snag one of the Heinekens Al's deigned space in his cooler for, and finding myself alone at the counter, pull the morning's notes from my ruck-sack. I've made some decent progress mapping out the island's major habi-tats in the last few days, this in preparation for a thorough and systematic cataloging beginning at the north end and working my way down to South Sandy Beach. The east and west sides are both predominated by dense stands of tall fir and spruce—a lot of this last in deadfall—while the more open interior areas, where most of the homes are located, feature grassy fields and deciduous shrubs like shadbush, elderberry, and alder. What's got me excited, though, was my discovery just this morning of two types of spruce not previously noted here—a soaring *Picea glauca*, a white variety easily identified by its blue-green needles; and *Picea abies* which is the Nor-way species. I noticed another species as well which I believe is *Picea abies* var. *erythrocarpa*, but I'll research it later when I return to the camp.

As usually happens once I've actually begun a project like this, I'm antsy to really sink my teeth in; so I'm already regretting having accepted yesterday's spontaneous offer by Cheryl Ames—a determined flirt trailing the odor of a committed three pack-a-dayer—for a haircut this noon. She caught me wolfing down a quick bowl of Gail's chili, having herself stopped in for some bleach and hose clamps, and before I knew it I'd been teased into a five-dollar trim.

Al and Gail are both back in the kitchen, picking at each other with-out much enthusiasm amid the banging of pots, the slamming of cooler doors. It's early for lunch, but then I've been up since five, woken yet again by a pair of lobsterboats hauling traps a stone's throw from my campsite. Most of them are buddying-up these days, according to Al—this against the possibility of some altercation involving John Burgess or his mob-enforcer stand-in.

Glancing to the mirror, I note a dirt-streaked cheek reflected back at me, a bloody scratch along my chin. I reach for a napkin as Al wanders in with tube steaks and buns for the steamer, an untied chef's apron looped around his neck.

He shoots me a big grin which I return. "How's it hangin', Hodge?"

Always glad to see me, this guy—but then I could well be the only one on the island who even remotely understands his obsession with *the game*. Speaking of which, the sandwich board's sporting a new crop of names today: The Beast, Big Ed, Little Looey, Pudge, Whitey. This last, an odd combination of foodstuffs pale in color—grilled chicken, hard boiled egg, and provolone—is, of course, a trick question. Most people assume it's Whitey Ford, but it's really Richie Ashburn. Dad caught me on that one more than once.

I order the Whitey for no reason other than I can't imagine what the thing tastes like.

Al calls it back to Gail, then leans into the counter—eyes shining with the delight of a true gossipmonger. "You heard about Clayton's car?"

I shake my head, take a pull on my beer—wondering if someone tried to nailgun that to the barn, too.

"Drives an old four-door shitbox to the harbor each day, right? So he gets up this morning, heads out to the drive and finds the damn thing flipped on its roof. Never heard a thing, mind you. How's that for a statement?"

He laughs at my obvious confusion. "Way things work out here, a guy's got a beef with you he don't usually say anything right out—that thing with Cash the other night aside. Up to you to figure out who's pissed and why and take care of it without makin' it look like you did, or even acknowledging there was a problem in the first place."

He's waiting for me to catch on, but the logic eludes me. "What kind of car?" I ask.

He sighs. "It's a good sign, see? They're giving him a chance to square things, get back on the right side of all this before the shit starts raining down. And trust me, it will."

I nod my understanding, but I'm stuck on the image of a car balanced on its roof, the physics involved in getting it there. Silently. How many would it take, I wonder? Four guys? Five?

Al tries again. "When Rachel first bought the old Burgess place, she hired a couple of the Ames boys for the restoration work, right? When the place was done, she wanted some numbers over the door—1799, which was when the place was built. What she got was 1979. They said it must have been the beer they'd been drinkin' all morning, but she knew right away why. Island wasn't too happy 'bout some outsider buyin' up the oldest place on Matinicus—didn't matter no one else wanted the damn thing. Their way of showin' her they weren't impressed, see? She left the numbers just like that, too; like she saw the humor in it. Earned her a kind of grudgin' respect. Problem solved."

Which brings me to that growing pile of lobster shells. I decide to get Al's take.

"Hard to tell," he says. "Could be people aren't too happy with your bein' here. Or your talkin' up Clayton the other night's got somebody thinkin' you've taken John's side in all this now that push is comin' to shove."

The reference, of course, is to the cutting of John-the-Restauranteur's traps, the lack of response from the mainland having everyone on edge. Calm before the storm.

I nod as if filing the information away; then forge ahead with this week's other head-scratcher. "Rachel ever mention an old diary she's got out at her place?"

"Burgess diary—sure," Al says, dragging industrial-sized jars of mustard and relish from the Philco. Gail arrives from the kitchen with my sandwich, my nose detecting horseradish as she slides the odd-looking concoction toward me. "Found it behind one of the parlor walls during the renovation—right, honey? Caused quite the stir. Gail here's a Tolman—related to probably three-quarters of the people on the island. She'll chew your ear off about the place, you let her."

Maybe so, but she's clearly not made her mind up about me, despite my daily visits. Her tone, cool from our first meeting, is decidedly wary now. "Where'd you find that old thing?" she demands. "Rachel keeps it locked away."

It found me, actually. "In the parlor," I say instead. And splayed open on the kind of ornate, Victorian loveseat I've spent my life avoiding. Had it been there fifteen minutes earlier when I passed through the room determined on an illicit and ultimately frustrating snoop through Rachel's art studio? I think not. Still, Matinicans are known to enter each other's homes at all hours and for all manner of reasons whether or not there's anyone around; and who's to say some addled neighbor hadn't stopped in for a quick perusal of an obscure two-hundred-year-old journal, forgetting in her haste to close the gaping corner cupboard from whence it was no doubt plucked? But if that's the case, why this nagging feeling it was left out for me? That and the suspicion that ghostie girl's disembodied little hand is in it somehow?

"Pretty intriguing stuff," I say. "Shipwrecks, murders, escaped slaves." Tugs at me, too, in a voyeuristic kind of way. Reluctant teenage bride, husband as old as, well, me. Enough said.

"Boats used to wreck off these islands all the time, what with all the ledges round here," Al says, back to me as he loads the steamer with dogs. "Most of the salvaging was done right out where you are, come to think of it." A quick glance at Gail. "Hodge here's set up camp on Western Point."

"The old Rumguzzle." She nods, her face deadpan as she scrutinizes me. Warm, this woman is not. "How much have you read?"

"The diary? Just a couple entries so far," I say around my first bite. It's the horseradish sauce that makes the whole thing work, I decide. I swallow, swig, swipe with a napkin. "Let's see...Weston's got Atticus helping out on the farm, though Hannah's not crazy about the idea. Guy's a real workhorse, though—taking on the chores Weston can't and Lavon won't; and the younger kids are clearly fascinated by him, especially the little one—Mary."

There are some great descriptions in there as well, I've noticed, a particularly visual one of the haying process that I like—Atticus and Lavon doing the scything; Hannah and the twins raking and forking it up into the rick, the little kids tramping it down. I can just see it. "Even Hannah admits the harvest would have been lost without him, what with the cutting already started when the weather turned.

"What else. The sailor staying at the Tolman farm is conscious but can't remember anything. Language is a little tough, and I'm confused about a couple things, but I get the gist, I think. What the hell is a *clout*, anyway? Those things Mary wears?"

No response. Selective hearing is a skill honed by the island folk to keep us summer people in our place, and it's one Gail's elevated to an art form. I try another tack.

"I feel for Hannah, you know?" I like her; it's hard not to—little slip of a thing and hard as nails. "In a strange place, no real friends. I mean she's little more than a kid herself, and she's got this farm to run, all these children to look out for. And then she's got this young stud under her roof. You can hardly blame her for hoping her husband never makes it back."

Okay, so the teacher's a bit of a dandy; an early version of the arrogant academic strolling the quad clutching the ubiquitous book of poetry. Thing is, Burns was considered pretty salacious stuff back then. Seems an odd choice for a man entrusted with the education of island youth.

Still nothing, though Gail and Al share a quick, inscrutable look.

"You think Atticus did it?" I press. I'm interested in her take; in truth, I haven't yet decided myself.

Gail turns her back to start another pot of coffee. "Did what?"

Why is this is like pulling teeth? "Killed Captain Lewis and the others on the boat? Started the fire?"

"Best you read it for yourself," she says, avoiding my eyes as she swipes her hands on her apron. "You get to the end, we'll talk about it."

"Can you a least tell me what clouts are?" I call after as she heads toward the kitchen. I turn to Al, but he's busy with his first tube steak order of the day. Lunch, it appears, has begun.

"Clouts?" she laughs, lighting a Salem. "Old word for diapers. You want another Bud?" Cheryl Ames—a.k.a. Ivan's mom—is a cheerful, solid woman of about thirty-five with a wide, pleasant face and a cloud of frizzy brown hair threaded with gray which she wears pinned back at the temples. Her salon consists of a worn, Formica-topped kitchen table dragged onto a deck jutting gloriously out over the rocks in a part of the harbor known as the Sands.

I consider the offer. It would be my third beer today and it's just past noon. Amazingly, I decline, determined on at least a few more hours of field work before I head back to camp.

She takes a pull on her Salem, parks it in a plastic ashtray beside a comb, two pairs of barbering scissors, a worn blue-flowered hand towel; then runs both hands through my hair, working a little scalp massage into it. Gauging the work ahead, I figure. Feels fucking great.

"Thick," she says approvingly, her voice exactly what you'd expect from a woman who keeps a cigarette burning incense-like beside her at all times. "Just a trim, you said? Buzz cut would be cooler in this weather."

No doubt, but I've never cared for my hair short. The shaggy, roguish look of the rebel professor is more me. "Ummm," is all I can manage.

"I'll take that as a no," she laughs—the sound a drowsy echo of the warm sun on my face, the gentle lick of water against rocks directly beneath us.

She's working my neck now and I go with it, amazed I could have forgotten the way a woman's touch completely unhinges me. It's not for nothing they have the power to give birth; their obvious link to the life force gets me juiced every time.

"You're staying at Rachel's, someone said. You taught Ben."

I nod. Shoulders, I silently plead. Just dig right in.

"Nice kid. Wish mine had that kind of spunk." A sigh as she gives my shoulders a quick teasing squeeze then inhales another lungful, exhaling over my head toward a line of old bait bags reincarnated as bird feeders. "Okay, then."

I hear the snap of the towel, feel material being tucked into the collar of my shirt. Damn.

"I appreciate you taking the time," I mumble.

"Look around you, honey," she chuckles. "All I got is time. Don't mean the same thing out here, case you hadn't noticed. Instead of days, think wind and weather; for hours, think tide. Like that."

She slides the comb through my hair, makes a couple efficient snips before pausing to smoke. "Problem with my boy is no ambition. Kids out here got it made if they want a life lobstering. It's just handed to them, you know? Good money in it these days. And the ones from the old families like ours—Ames, Tolman, Philbrick, Burgess—we got the harbor land, too."

Smoke curls from her fingers as she points a slow arc along the waterfront on either side of her small cape. "Thirteen acres held in common from way back, each of the original families splitting up and deeding shares to their kids, on and on down through the generations. Can't be sold, just handed down. Gives you the right to build something here, if you can find the room. Mostly it's the guys' shops, where they work on their gear and such, but a few got homes here like me.

"Anyway," she says, snipping at my hair again, "Ivan got a student lobstering license from the state a couple years back, but gave it up. Too much work keepin' all the records they gotta have, he said. Less hassle to go stern for somebody else. Pay's decent for out here, and you can work your way up in the ranks without having to maintain your own boat. Problem is, he's lazy. Half the time he wakes up in the morning and don't go—it's too cold, he's hung over, whatever—leavin' Cash high and dry and swearin' something awful down there on the dock. Some mornings he charges right up here and drags Ivan outta bed. I mean, guy's gotta make a living, right?

"Thing is," she says, tapping the comb lightly, "if Cash was harder on the kid to start with, he wouldn't pull this shit. Got a soft spot for him, bein' he's my boy and all. But the man ain't no saint—anyone knows that, I do—and one of these days Ivan's gonna wake up with no job. Lose his girl too, he's not careful."

Tiffany, I realize—the Mediterranean beauty with the attitude. "Al's niece," I say. Or is it Gail's?

"Oh, hell, she ain't their niece any more than I am. Mother's Deb Burgess, for God sake; father's a guy went stern for Josh Philbrick one summer, then ran out. Good riddance, too. Can't even remember his name. We get all kinds wash up here, bottom-of-the-barrel types the guys pick up in some bar over to Rockland. Some of them don't last a week; those that stay like as not can't go back 'cause there's a bench warrant out for 'em or some such thing."

More combing, more snipping, more feeling up my head. Any more relaxed and I'd be dead.

"I need another beer," she announces, heading toward the kitchen. "Sure you don't want nothin'?"

"Some water would be nice."

A snort of derision. "So anyway," she says, slamming the fridge door and heading back to me, "Deb was an island girl—which means her people never lived anywhere else but here since anyone can remember—but then she has this kid by some coked-up guy from away, so that makes Tiffany's position here kinda iffy despite the fact she's a Burgess. One of us but not of us, you know?"

"Even though she was born here." The tap water is cool and clear, the pink plastic tumbler and matching plastic ice cubes kind of kitschy. I like this woman. I do.

"Right. She's considered a *local* cause she's always lived here, but not an *island girl*, 'cause one of her parents was from away. The cat might have kittens in the oven, but that don't make 'em biscuits—know what I mean?"

"I do."

"Anyway, Deb didn't take much to mothering; just up and left when Tiffany was five or six. Gail was Deb's best friend back then, so she took the girl in. Not that she's really the nurturing type. Don't think I ever seen her as much as give that girl a hug. But who else was gonna take her, you know? No other family out here to speak of. Clayton or John, maybe, since they're uncles—John was still livin' out here, then—but they're both bachelors live like animals. And givin' John a little girl to raise? Might as well just shoot her and be done with it.

"Thing is, nobody but Tiffany much cares where Deb is anymore, since any Matinicus left in her's long since worn off. Feeling is she broke faith with the island. It's been like eight, nine years since anyone's heard from her, but Tiffany's sure she's coming back to get her. Absolutely convinced, poor kid."

We let that recede.

"You're a scientist, they say. Got a thing for Rachel, too."

That stops me.

A pause as she blows on my neck, sending messages to parts of my body I've all but forgotten existed. "Okay, then; you're done."

No, but I could be if she tried a little harder.

"And what about you—bet you've got men all over the island," I tease—covering my startled reaction with the sort of come-ons I used to rattle off in my sleep.

"Oh, Cash and me been together for years." She gives the flowered hand towel a shake. "He's got a temper, sure—but that don't bother me. I mean he never hit me or nothin'. Problem is sex." She glances my way, eyes a-twinkle. "Know what he likes to do?"

I open my mouth; shut it again.

"Get naked and drive his Yamaha Grizzly up and down in the woods while I throw mud at him. Kinky, you know?" A shake of the head. "Ain't like I got a lot to choose from out here. 'Til now, that is." She ruffles my hair playfully and throws herself down on the chair beside me. Takes a swig of her Bud.

God, don't I love a flirt. Two thoughts occur, besides an obvious and overwhelming desire to avoid any wooded areas scarred with ATV trails lest I come across these two in mid-pseudo-sexual exploit. My first is that this woman is a wealth of information with none of Gail's reluctance to share; and second, that the battle-weary vulture of my libido is circling shamelessly again, drawn as it's always been by even the subtlest whiff of female interest.

"Cash live here with you?" I ask glancing around. This is the old me, checking the vicinity for other males before making a move, no matter how ill-advised. The new me mentally reins the beast in and kicks it in the nuts, as more than one woman has threatened to do.

If you think I'm beating myself up pretty hard over my checkered sexual past—trust me, it's a beating I deserve. Thing is, I thought I had all this figured out, had come out the other side a little battered maybe, but with a modicum of self-respect. What's worse, while I'd convinced myself I was here to work, I'm clearly on the trail again. Changing women used to be as easy for me as changing drinks; in this case switching from the promise of a cool Pinot, i.e., Rachel, to the rough feel of, say, tequila—vis-à-vis a tumble with the very obviously available Cheryl.

Amazing what you can see when you pull your head out of your ass.

"Cash—live *here*?" Cheryl cackles. "Hell, no. Gets too wild when he's mad. Broke up my place once. Drunk and feelin' mean, his usual state. And I can't have that—not with Ivan here. No, he's got that old RV out there on the harbor road."

I pass the thing daily. Looks like a slightly larger version of my uncle's 1964 Coachmen Cadet, this one set on blocks and tricked out as a house trailer—plywood shack tacked on its side along with a small half-finished deck. The logistics of getting such a thing out here have my mind reeling.

"Wait till he finds out Ivan's gonna be over on Vinalhaven rest of the week," Cheryl grins. "Orientation thing at the high school. Which means Cash won't have no sternman. I know Ivan ain't told him yet, 'cause he ain't had a meltdown."

"I'd stern with him for a day if it'll help him out." I say this without thinking, remembering too late Ivan's description of the job—something about Up Before Dawn and Dirty, Shitty Work. Still I plow on. "I was thinking of paying someone to take me around the island for some photos of the tree lines, anyway." Which is true. "Think he'd do it?"

"For money?" she laughs. "Hardly." She purses her lips, considers. "Tell you what, though. Bet he'd trade you for sterning. Hell, I'll make sure he does." She laughs, again, shakes her head. "Hope you know what you're in for."

Which gives me pause. But really, how bad can it be?

TEN

Just two mornings later, I gather my things in the inky darkness of three a.m.—rucksack with camera, lunch, and water bottle; and the rolled-up rubber overalls someone helpfully dropped onto my sleeping bag just inside Ben's 1960's era tent. Jesus, the smell. It's not for nothing they call them foulies.

Pure luck finding the tent the way I did. Good thing, too, as the weather's due to turn sometime in the next couple days. After searching the barn and other outbuildings any number of times, I remembered Rachel's mentioning a cellar; figured it was worth a shot. Finding the place in that crazy warren of rooms was another story. I finally stumbled on it while searching for a steamer pot in her pantry—a weirdly sunken, dirt-floored room maybe ten degrees cooler than the rest of the house, where women of yore kept their dairy cans and churned butter and such. I almost missed the small door in the opposite wall. Can't be, I thought. But lo and behold. In addition to the tent poles, canvas, and other attendant paraphernalia, I unearthed a trove of other camping equipment from that small, dank space—an old Coleman lantern, beer cooler, and pretty serviceable stove. Hits from the sixties and seventies, all of them. A bit worn and battered, but then who's not these days?

I slip my cap on, sling the rucksack and overalls over my shoulder, and head toward whatever the day will bring. Rounding the front of the house, I ignore the growing mound of lobster shells—how much of this stuff can these people eat, after all?—and strike off down the road wondering how many pamphlets on paralytic shellfish poisoning I should order.

If Matinicus can be said to have a commuter hour, this is indeed it. Pickups and ATVs streak through the darkness as I make my way toward the harbor. Eventually, a mud-encrusted pickup slows alongside and a big bear of a guy with a full red beard and the liquid brown eyes of a spaniel offers me a ride. Introduces himself as Josh Philbrick. Turns out Uncle Clunk, the man whose heart gave out last week, was a distant cousin—a transplant from over in America, which is what the locals call the mainland. Been out here five years, maybe. It was Josh who ferried the body back to Rockland aboard the Mary Kate.

"Guy was only forty-three," he says pulling onto the wharf. "Weird, don't you think? Didn't smoke, didn't drink—unusual for out here." He shrugs. "Go figure, right?"

As Josh is himself heading out for the day, he willingly rows me over to Ka-Ching—where the diesel engine is already chugging away, the red steadying sail with its Jolly Roger raised and flapping in the breeze. I toss my pack into the boat and climb aboard, Josh waving off my thanks as he pulls away.

Cash ignores my outstretched hand—turning instead to the wheelhouse to crank up the radar and flip on some kind of circulating pump that begins sending water churning through the metal tank behind me. All this without saying a word. Tense as a coiled spring, this guy. God only knows what Cheryl had to promise to get me this far. Extra innings in the mud games would be my guess.

I take this time to slip into my own gear and check out my surroundings, keeping my breathing shallow in an attempt to avoid the rancid smell wafting from the barrel beside me. The harbor is ringed with a scattering of onshore lights, but the real activity is out here on the water, the guys shouting insults as they slide gear around, one by one dropping mooring lines and heading out. I'm rather philosophically pondering the nexus of these two worlds when Cash whips round, firing off a string of instructions.

I'm to remain in one place, he snarls—keep myself braced between the bait barrel and lobster tank. He doesn't have time to stop and fish me out of the water because I'm too stupid to keep from falling overboard. As to my duties, I'm to keep the bait bags coming. Fill them with herring, then run a skewer through the bag and through two pogies using their eyes.

Nice touch.

He tosses me a pair of filthy gloves and an equally nasty glare as he guns the engine, warning me the loaded skewers better be full and ready when he's set to drop the bags into the traps. "And I ain't gonna stop special for no pictures. You'll take em when you got the chance. Understood?"

I tell him I think I can manage.

We say nothing more for maybe twenty minutes. This might have something to do with the rock music he's blasting as we leave the harbor, the combined sounds of the engine and pump, or just his surly mood.

It's cold, the night sky just beginning to brighten as we clear Indian Ledge and thread our way between a line of red and green buoys in the kind of choppy swell I remember from my first trip out here. I managed not to be sick then and I'll be damned if I'm going to lose it now. Still, it's a trick to keep my balance; and as we make our way from one string of traps to another out in open water, the chop grows into the kind of long ocean swell that makes bracing myself between the barrel and tank the only way to remain vertical.

The dawn is spectacular—fingers of coral crawling a blush-pink horizon—and despite the swell, as *Ka-Ching* slows for another string I manage to extricate my camera and get off a few shots of both this and a copse of maples bordering the white sands of Markey Beach. Then the boat lurches, the electric winch brings up the first trap, and we're off and running again. Traps slapped onto the skids, tops flipped open, catch sorted, traps rebaited and returned to the water amid the melee of gulls that trails us.

By mid-morning I've got the job pretty much down, so Cash starts me clearing traps—throwing back the juveniles and egg-bearing females, and banding the keepers. By now I'm so busy I've got no time for the photography I came out here for. Still, I'm into it—the boat, the fish, the salt air. Even the swells are manageable 'til I've been smelling rotten herring for four or five hours. By eleven, we've pulled maybe a hundred traps and I'm alternately queasy and famished. As if reading me, Cash pulls into the lee of a cove at the island's southern tip and idles back 'til we're barely drifting.

"Short break," he barks, walking to the stern and back in a long overhead stretch—those welts of scar tissue tensing along his arms as he hops up to sit on the gunwale.

I pull a PB&J from my sack, a bottle of water. Cash lights a joint.

A few minutes of this and he grows positively chatty. Boat talk, of course. Thirty-six feet, six-hundred-ten horsepower—twice as fast as anything else in the harbor, he tells me, which makes for quick trips to and from Rockland.

Drug runs would be my guess.

"So," he says, deadpan. "You doin' Rachel or what?"

Engines and women—the basic building blocks of all male conversation.

I'm saved from having to respond when the VHF cackles to life. "*Ka-Ching, Ka-Ching.* You out there, Cash?"

I'd know that smokers' rasp anywhere.

He reaches to the instrument panel and snaps up the mike. "Yeah."

"How's Hodge doin'?" Cheryl asks. "You ain't pushed him over or nothin'?"

"Still thinkin' bout it. Ain't tossed his cookies yet, anyways," he adds grudgingly.

They've been chatting maybe a minute when Cash suddenly whips out the binos, peering toward the hot shimmer of another boat about five hundred yards to our west. Suddenly he stiffens. "Motherfucker!"

With that the engine leaps to life and all six-hundred-ten horses are instantly on a plane, the misty spray soaking what's left of my PB&J as I'm knocked backwards on my ass. Meanwhile Cash is screaming into the mike at Cheryl. "I got *Jaws* poaching off Cato Cove. Get the others out here now!" He throws the mike at the panel where it bounces off, swinging wildly by its cord.

"Get the shotgun!" he barks as we bear down on the guy. "Racked up there under the panel. Shot's in the chamber."

I stumble forward, barely managing to stay on my feet as I find and then release the thing—almost dropping it in the process, it's that heavy. Everything I know about these things can be summed up in two words— long and dangerous—and I immediately extend it toward Cash.

"Hold it like you're gonna shoot the guy," he demands. "Up on your shoulder. Try not to look like a fucking pansy, all right?" Shakes his head. "Today of all days I gotta get stuck with you."

He throttles back, and some complicated interaction between this and the mysterious alchemy of current and tide brings us within about thirty feet of *Jaws*—a boat whose name crawls from the mouth of a cartoonish shark painted on its wide stern. Cash cuts the engine and we begin to drift down on her.

Our poacher's broad as a refrigerator, his back to us as he picks calmly through a trap I now recognize as one of Cash's, based on the color of the attached buoy. He knows we're here, of course—I can see it in the set of his shoulders—but he waits for maybe a count of five before turning. He's got the barrel-chested body of a bouncer, the optimistic sneer of a brawler who's never met a fight he didn't like. Buzz cut, tats on every exposed piece of flesh from the neck down.

They eye each other for maybe ten seconds while I keep the rifle shouldered, feeling utterly ridiculous.

"Lost?" Cash finally asks.

"All John's traps seem to got themselves mislaid." The accent is Boston—not a good sign. "He says to tell you we're gonna be sharin' your catch 'til they get found. Otherwise, some boats might get themselves sunk, a couple throats cut. Maybe more than a couple. One by one. In the night, like."

"Poachers get themselves shot out here—he told you that, too, right?" Cash's voice is deadly calm, but the little muscle at the corner of his eye is twitching as madly as the night he charged Clayton with the pool cue. "You best close up that trap and put her back. Now, boy." Over his shoulder he mutters, "You ready?"

Ready for what? He can't seriously think I'm going to shoot this guy.

"Might be smart you listen to me, get out of here while you still can," Cash tells him quietly. This as a low rumble of engines bursts round the island's southern tip and a small army of lobster boats roars toward us. To me he says, "Put one across the bow."

Huh?

"Pull the fucking trigger, you idiot. Do it now."

Amazingly, I do—this as the other boats begin settling around us. I'm smart enough to aim skyward however, loathe as I am to add *accessory to murder* to my curriculum vitae. And I get the shot off okay; it's the recoil that knocks me to the deck.

And with that I finally hurl.

Cash swears, grabs the shotgun and chambers a shot.

I imagine a long stretch in the state prison in Thomaston, my teaching career going up in flames. All for shooting a fucking poacher.

Shooting. Of course. Sliding over to my pack, I dig through it for the camera. Standing brings the urge to hurl again, but I fight it—snapping off countless photos of *Jaws*, the ape driving it, and most damningly, his hands still buried in Cash's trap. I keep shooting 'til the chip's full, and still I click away.

In the end, cooler heads prevail; and after sending John's lackey off minus Cash's lobsters and with the warning that should *Jaws* be seen in Matinicus waters again she'll be summarily scuttled, the fleet steams at a leisurely, we-be-bad pace back to the harbor for an impromptu assessment meeting. A short day for these guys, which is frankly fine with me. The adrenaline's long since fled my system, leaving me weak and emotionally wrung out, not to mention hungry again. Besides, there'll be no more photos 'til I find a way to download my camera chip.

We're rounding the corner into the harbor when Cash fires up a second joint—this one pulled from a hollowed space behind what I've all along assumed was the cover of yet another piece of pricey navigational equipment.

Ah, island ingenuity.

He takes a few hits, extends it my way. "That voodoo-hoodoo shit you pulled at the Hatch last week?" he leers, holding in the smoke. "Pretty fuckin' cool."

I shrug modestly and take the joint. It's been years, yet with a level of paranoia that would make any druggie proud, I glance round the empty ocean for a cop before taking a toke and passing it back.

We back and forth it a couple more times 'til something else grabs his attention.

"Well, HELL-o," he says slowing as we approach the sleek white sailboat I first noticed last week at Al's. Fiberglass, teak deck, lots of gleaming stainless—the name *Bounder* scripted in gold leaf on the stern.

Cash grabs the VHF. "Yo," he says to whoever might be listening. "Kneelands are back, boys. And the missus is out here doin' her thing."

I glance over, do a double take. There, sprawled in the cockpit, lays a stunner of a brunette sunbathing in the raw, or so it first appears—her bikini some flesh-colored number offering barely legal coverage. An intriguing trompe-l'œil designed to titillate, and successfully so. Nothing else on her but a gorgeous tan and a pair of designer sunglasses. Hot damn.

"Been on that thing," Cash tells me. I'm assuming he means the boat. "Tricked out awesome below. Laptop computer, flat-screen TV, surround sound. They bought some weed off me last summer and we smoked a bone."

We circle shamelessly, taking in the view from any number of angles. Must say it's nice to finally put a body to the name Kirtley Kneeland. Eventually, reluctantly, we head back to Cash's float to off-load the catch—all the while keeping a weather eye for any movement in *Bounder's* cockpit. Unfortunately, our view is somewhat compromised by the five or six other boats circling now—though not even this level of scrutiny flusters the lovely Mrs. Kneeland. Nor should it. Not an ounce of fat on her.

I'm further surprised when, after rowing us back in, Cash hands me a bag containing five good-sized lobsters. "You earned 'em," he says with a gruff nod. Keeping hold of the bag 'til my eyes meet his, he adds, "And I want them photos soon as you get 'em."

I promise to send the chip out with Doug on tomorrow morning's flight; then, thoroughly whupped and with a wicked case of the munchies, I trudge toward home.

ELEVEN

The cicadas are revving up hard as I reach to the cooler, brilliantly positioned beside the webbed lounger to avoid the physical stress of anything like standing. I work the cap off a Heineken, take a long pull, and return my attention to the notes I'm pretending to make on a new class I'll teach in the spring. I call it *Edible Forest Gardens* after a book I once read. A pretentious name for a low-level college course, to be sure; and really, the whole thing is feeling pretty irrelevant right now—lulled as I am by the sound of the waves, the warmth of the afternoon sun, and all this goddam natural beauty.

Peering toward the three lobsters I managed to jam into the steamer pulled from Rachel's pantry, I determine that they're doing quite nicely and take another pull on my beer. When I again glance up, the magnificent Tiffany is standing quiet and still at the edge of my campsite—skimpy top, ragged pink short-shorts, canvas sneakers at the end of those slender bronzed legs. How come they didn't make 'em like this when I was a kid?

"Hey," I say, slapping at another mosquito as she pulls what looks suspiciously like my Dodgers cap from her back pocket.

"Cash found this on *Ka-Ching.*"

"Thanks." I'm a little bothered that its absence escaped my notice; then again, I haven't left camp all day—gripped as I've been by an all but crippling lethargy since yesterday's adventure on the high seas. "Tell him the photos will be back Monday." Another Matinicus One bites the dust.

She begins a rambling inspection of my camp, eyeing the contents of my tent with cool interest as she tosses the cap within. Turning those gorgeous green eyes on me, she chin-nods toward my beer. "Can I have one of those?"

No doubt I've got some sort of moral responsibility here, but I'm not up to it today. Besides, I reason, if kids on Matinicus are driving at ten, they're surely drinking by twelve. Flipping the cooler open, I pull out a Heinie and pry off the cap. Hand it over.

"So, how did yesterday's meeting go?" I ask, slapping at my thigh again. I'd planned to get over to Al's for some bug dope today, but nixed the idea in favor of a noon nap. "About the poaching, I mean."

"You don't know nothin' about this place, do you?" she snickers, removing the lantern I've set on a low tree stump and replacing it with her lovely derriere before taking a long, far too experienced pull on her beer. "Most of the time these guys can't stand each other; getting 'em together's like throwing a bunch of cats in a bag. Even something like this, they still can't agree. Half of 'em want to bring in their traps in case John starts cutting 'em away—which he would do, believe me. Other half want to post a guard in the harbor each night case he tries to scatter the fleet. They brought Uncle Clayton in, too, made him *volunteer* to bring in all his traps 'til everything's settled, seeing as he and John are still kind of partners. So he can't fish at all. That'll piss John off big time."

"What does Cash say?"

"Cash just wants to go shoot him about fifty times." She shakes her head. "Guy's so lame." Another sip. Above us, an osprey circles a lazy figure eight.

"He do well out there on the water?" I ask.

She shoots me a look. "You mean money? They never talk about that; it's like a law. All they'll say is they're working three times as hard, fishing twice the number of traps and putting less money in their pockets than ten years ago, but I know for a fact some of 'em just put it up their noses. It's, like so gross."

Smart, this one. I've seen all the recent demographics on island communities, and they're pretty depressing. Matinicus more than most. Traditional ways are on their way out; the easy life easing its way in. Traps are wire mesh instead of wood, the pots Styrofoam, boats fiberglass. Upside is there's less maintenance, things last longer. Downside is all the traditional crafts are being forgotten, the guys have more time on their hands. A recipe for trouble. Still, if this place has a chance, it'll be kids like Tiffany who'll keep it alive.

"You really count trees for a living?" she asks.

"Well, I do some teaching, too."

She shakes her head. "Why? What's so special about trees?"

I'm surprised by the question; it's something almost no one ever bothers to ask. My opinion of her continues to edge north. "Well, a lot of things really, but I guess if I have to choose I'd say it has something to do with the way they stand a kind of silent testament to all that goes on. I mean, imagine all the stuff that's happened here on Matinicus in the last couple hundred years. A lot of the big trees here saw it all. They just keep going—through good times and bad."

She grins over at me, all loose and friendly now. "Like the energizer bunny, right?"

I smile back. "This isn't your first beer today, is it?"

"C'mon, Hodge," she whines as I rise to check the lobsters. "So, if I was a tree, what kind would I be?"

I don't even have to think about it. "A sequoia," I say, dumping the water. "Determined and strong." In First Nation spirituality, sequoias are emblems of tenacity and perseverance, the stubborn will to survive at all odds. I'm not sure how I know this about Tiffany, but I do.

She covers her surprise with another sip, turns to the water so I can't see the flush of pleasure this simple compliment has given her. A small enough gift, I figure, considering all she's lost.

"You got kids?" she asks.

I laugh. "None that I know of, no." I cock my head toward the lobsters. "You want one of these?"

She shakes her head. "People say you got a thing for Rachel."

What, her too? What is it with these people and my sex life, or lack thereof?

"And that you were Ben's teacher. He was cool; I liked him. Most everyone did, but they'll never admit it. They're all so lame." She stares off over the water a minute, picking at a blade of grass. "Ben and Rachel were like really tight. It was nice."

The wistfulness in her voice unleashes a surge of empathy that so completely undoes me I find myself incapable of a single flip comment. This girl's no different from Hannah, I realize—much the same age, same emotional isolation. Both Burgesses, too—one by marriage, the other by birth—not that it's done either of them any good here. I make a mental note to ask Gail if the two are related by more than just their names; if Hannah and Isaac had progeny from whom Tiffany descends.

She stands, throws back the rest of her beer. "I got to get back. Pizza tonight." She extends the empty bottle almost shyly. "You coming? We got the band again."

Oh, goody—more Neil Young. Dare I hope for another brawl?

I shrug, slap at another mosquito.

And with that my decision is made. Not so strange, really—I've made far more important ones based on the scratching of some itch.

The band's good and warmed up, grinding out a decent rendition of "Truckin'" by the time I make it in. Gail's pizza is pepperoni at this particular point in the evening, and despite my lobster feed, I snag a slice on my way to the shelves where I unearth a few jugs of bug dope and some triple A's for my book light. I've got no intention of making another drunken night of it—I'm still a little buzzed from this afternoon, after all—but as both Al and Gail are busy with the bar and Tiffany's just plain ignoring me again, I cave and return to the cooler for one of my hidden Heinekens before grabbing another slice. Just one and I'm out of here.

The room is absolutely packed—an amorphous mass of bodies, cigarettes and beer bottles in hand, swaying and bumping to the beat. Since the only guy I know at the crammed counter is Clayton, ignored by everyone as he sits at the far end morosely knocking back shots of tequila, I park myself against the butt end of one of the grocery shelves and survey the scene. Blotto, every one of them.

"When you gettin' them pictures back, Hodge?"

I turn, surprised, extend my hand as I recognize the thick red beard, the carbed-up build. The guy who fishes the *Mary Kate*. Jay, John—something like that. Josh, that's it.

"Josh," I nod. "Thanks again for yesterday."

He gives my hand a quick pump. "That was fast thinkin', what you did out there."

Which part, I wonder—the part where I shot a hole in the sky or the part where I tossed my cookies in the cockpit? Then I remember. *Mary Kate* was part of the posse steaming out to yesterday's little dust-up.

"Morning flight on Monday for the photos, Josh," I say. "Double prints." I nod meaningfully.

The band breaks at this point, and we're joined by a couple others who launch into a play-by-play of yesterday's face-off with *Jaws*—their names less memorable than those of their boats. *Hombre* buys me a shot of Jack Daniel's which he tells me comes courtesy of Cash, over in America tonight on some mysterious errand or other.

I down yet another slice and accept the gift of a second shot—this one from *Plan Bea*. I'm tempted to ask my new buds about the results of yesterday's meeting—a subject Tiffany quite conveniently slid over—but one look at Clayton's brooding presence stops me. Might be better not to know. Healthier.

Plan Bea points his long-necked Bud toward the deck. "Been soakin' up the rays all afternoon—showin' off the wares, so to speak."

I glance over to where the dark-haired beauty I last saw sprawled delightfully in her cockpit stands nursing a beer in the waning light, her audience a few bleary-eyed sternmen from the boarding house over at the Sands. It's my first real look at her—in actual clothing, anyway—and she doesn't disappoint. She's so distinctive, in fact, I'm amazed I missed her on my way in.

Tall for a woman—five-eight or nine, maybe—she's in cropped jean shorts that show off the lithe legs of an athlete, and is gloriously braless beneath a gauzy white number accentuating her tan along with other delightful things. The Old Gil is on full alert, and I can hardly blame him. The new Gil tries for aloof, casually craning his neck for a better look.

Out of nowhere comes a low rumble from Clayton's corner. "Oh, you're in it now, boy," he mutters to no one in particular. "Ain't no doubt about that."

I'm suddenly uneasy—caught as I am with my mind in another man's cookie jar. Or might this be some cryptic reference to yesterday's fun with guns?

"Weird nobody's seen the old man," Josh says. "Figured he'd be flyin' back out with her."

Plan Bea considers. "Might be he's sick," he suggests, shooting me a wink lest I think yesterday's little hurling incident will be forgotten anytime soon.

Al leans into the counter, nods toward the deck. "You met Kirtley yet?" he asks.

I admit I haven't had the pleasure.

"Way Allan tells it, she was born in Gibraltar, and by the time she was six she'd lived in thirteen countries and could swear in four languages. Laughs like hell when he says it, too."

My kind of girl, I think.

"Husband's okay," *Plan Bea* says. "Always buys the drinks their first night in."

Which reminds me it's my turn to ante up, and I do. Nothing for myself this time, though. Believe it or not, I have been known to exercise restraint on occasion.

"So where is he?" This from *Hombre*, a question he utters as we all stare toward the deck.

The band starts up again, the crowd shuffling in to "Margaritaville." I've managed a stool by now and am helping to finish off the pizza when a glance toward the mirror finds the fair Kirtley approaching—her long, fluid strides those of a runway model or an animal casually out stalking the sub-Saharan plain.

Close up, she's even more amazing. Thirty-five, maybe—dewy, brown eyes and dark, silky hair in a casual chin-length bob my mother would have called a pageboy. And barefoot. If she exuded any more sexuality we'd have to send the kiddies home. Al hasn't exactly said so, but I get the feeling the husband is considerably older. A trophy wife, then.

A somewhat confident man myself, I'm accustomed to boldly and successfully approaching such stunners, but maddeningly and for the second time today, all my playful lines elude me.

Clayton is perking up fast, though.

"Hey, there, Kirtley," Al says when she's ordered a tequila. "Welcome back. Allan with you tonight?" Gail's giving her the cold shoulder normally reserved for me, so he pours the shot himself.

She throws the liquor back in lieu of a response, then slaps the glass on the counter for another. Husband problems, I think; and as she turns her cool gaze my way, there's an immediate connection—a quick flash of something familiar I can't quite put my finger on—that fixes me down to my toes. If someone put a gun to my head just now I swear I couldn't tell you what Rachel Leland looked like.

Clayton seems quite suddenly sober, or sober enough that his antennae pick up my antennae, and we turn to consider each other. Pistols at ten feet or shall we just drink each other to death?

Kirtley slides onto the vacant stool between us and, incredibly, fixes on Clayton, relegating me to the role of voyeur—something I immediately sense she likes. It's a part I've played a good many times before and often enjoy, it having to do with my own twin foibles of danger and risk. But this feels, I don't know, like I'm being finessed. Still, I tend to be a good sport when it comes to such things, and so I nosh on yet another slice and nod in time to a weak version of Bob Seger's "Against the Wind"—all the while absorbed in the rich, deep cadence of Kirtley's voice.

A few shots later, they're thick as thieves. Another and they're dancing. And boy, can she. Clayton does his best to stumble along, hands trying for purchase all along that lovely bod, but she proves pretty deft at sliding out from under his grasp.

I'm turned on my stool watching the show, elbows parked on the counter behind me, when Al leans in close.

"Told you she was something, didn't I?"

"You did," I agree. He offers another shot on the house but I decline, opting instead for a final beer from the cooler to even out the night.

When I return to my stool, Kirtley's doing a solo atop the pool table to Van Morrison's "Moondance." Abandoned to some steamy internal rhythm—eyes closed, face flushed, hands slowly gyrating above her head. Quite a show, as the hoots of approval attest.

"If there's a God, she'll take her shirt off," *Hombre* mutters.

"I'd like to know where the hell her husband is," Gail says from behind me.

"Probably had some fight," Al tells her. "She's just blowin' off steam, is all."

"Uh-huh."

Maybe it's me, but the whole thing is starting to feel a little hinky. Could be I'm just too old and jaded to enjoy such displays anymore. My watch says nine-ten, but it feels like half past too late, which oddly depresses me. What I really want, I decide, is more of the innocent company of Hannah and her reluctant brood.

With that I grab my goodies and take my leave—surprised to see Kirtley's eyes on me all the way to the door.

Yessiree. Hinky as shit.

TWELVE

Matinicus, Friday 24 July

Dare I write the words? Weston has called me My Dear! 'Tis true. Moreover, I'm to accompany him to a gathering at the home of Squire Young tomorrow evening. I shall not sleep this night for happiness, though I hardly care, for does not this invitation betoken a warmth of feeling for me?

It was after the taking of our supper that such wonders occurred, though our discourse did not begin well, the both of us being unusually out of temper. Weston, thoughtful before the hearth and with the sound of the black laying shingles to the barn outside, began making argument for allowing the man to sit with us of an evening that he might learn the history of the island on which he now finds himself.

I was aghast, of course, and couldn't imagine why the man should care. Still, I kept my temper, wishing to encourage the easiness that has grown up between Weston and myself these months.

Is this indeed wise? I asked. He is not yet free of suspicion, after all.

Suspicion is a heavy armor, quoted he from Mr. Burns, and with its weight impedes more than it protects.

It is for the children I worry, and not myself, I said. Once the door to such freedom is opened, 'tis too easily flung wide. I will not have such as he wandering about the house at will.

He would hardly think to make so free, Weston countered. Has he not proven himself honorable these past weeks? It's plain he wishes only to make *himself useful until such time as his future here is determined. Your concern for the children is likewise unfounded, surely. Have not many remarked on the gentleness with which he treated little Mary's wrenched arm not two days past, carrying her across the island to Mistress Wivell for care?*

And thus breaking faith with us by leaving the farm, I reminded him. Was he not directed to stay within its bounds until such time as his guilt or innocence was proven?

His concern for the girl being the cause and a laudable one indeed, Weston pressed. Matinicus has long-welcomed men of such a hard-working and God-fearing nature, and I dare say Atticus has proven himself both.

Surely, Weston, you're not suggesting the man settle here. Certainly there's no future for him on the island with no others of his kind.

Should he choose to stay among us after his account of the Amaranth is borne out, as it most certainly shall be once the sailor under Lydia's care regains memory, I should expect he would be welcome indeed, industrious as he has proven himself to be. I can't speak for the man, himself, of course. He may well wish to continue his journey to Canada, though it's my understanding he has no people there. He might choose instead to make his way to Portland where a thriving populace of free negroes lives in harmony amongst the larger citizenry.

Weston sighed then, pinching his forehead as if a headache was taking hold.

The point, my dear Hannah, said he, is that in an island community of but two hundred souls, all can be made useful.

My Dear.

Floating on his words, I began to find less trouble in the proposal. For the negro's presence before the fire would require Weston's own. Indeed, my insistence that the man's lodgings be moved to the smokehouse has brought me only grief, as it is there Weston now tarries long past dark, returning distant and thoughtful rather than sitting with me before the fire as has long been our habit. Thus it was I allowed that the black might join us this very night, insisting he first bathe in the tub kept behind the barn for the gutting of the piglets, the smell of him being considerable.

It happened that Weston chose for his first discourse the general history of the island, one I know as well as my own, as it is to Vinalhaven that Matinicus is annexed. Used first by the French traders and Penobscot tribes for fowling and seal hunting, men of our kind then arrived to settle and farm, clearing the land of its trees and setting rout to the heathens. Weston's telling of it distressed me, I must say, as he inclines to favor the Indians' cause against Mr. Ebenezer Hall, founder of this island, whom the savages slaughtered, carrying off his wife and children to unthinkable fates. Which I have on other occasions pointed out to him.

That perhaps had to do with the two of their tribe the man shot and buried in his garden, was Weston's reply, so I have kept my peace on the subject since. He's well known for his liberality on such issues, I am told, having a gentle and forgiving nature; still, 'twill not be long before he finds I'm right about the black, as bloodthirsty as any Indian he shall surely prove to be.

No doubt Weston took the negro's silence as interest, for the man remained mute and watchful throughout, with not as much as a glance to he who hoped to better his understanding. Weston proceeded then with the history of fishing as was developed here a full century ago, telling of the forbearers of some even now in residence: Ames, Young, Tolman, Burgess, and the like, and how their mutual reliance, while of benefit to all, detracted nothing from the natural independence common to island folk.

Support of the one for the other is the ticket, said he; should strife and discord make their way among us, a community such as ours could not hope to survive.

The twins, in from the evening milking, passed among us with the cans for the buttery just then. Mary, snot-nosed and ill-kempt, trailed behind her sisters with a shy smile for the black, which he returned in kind as the girls dragged their jugs within. I charged them with her care, and though they acknowledged me not, our angry words of this afternoon not yet forgotten, it seems, they took her hands between them and made for the upper chambers.

At length the negro raised himself, and with a nod addressed Weston in an accent thick with his southern birth.

I be sayin' gudnight, then, suh.

And with not so much as a glance to she who cooks his meals and suffers his habitation here, he took his leave.

The girls appear upset this evening, remarked Weston.

As ever, I said, all anger and tears as I fashion a quilt for Lydia Tolman's babe from their mother's dresses.

His startled look stopped my fingers in their work.

Surely the woman has no further use for them, Weston, and the fabric does quite nicely. Is it not fitting to use what remains from one life to benefit the start of another?

But is this not precipitous? asked he. Might not the girls be afforded some time to grieve before such things as these are undertaken?

They have been at their grieving long enough. Life affords little time to pine for what cannot be changed, and I'll not waste such goods as these to ease a stubborn child's tears.

His disbelieving laugh stung me. Is your lot so very hard, then, Hannah? asked he. Yours is a handsome home, your husband a good man and strong. It won't be long before you have children of your own, I'll warrant, which can't help but ease your way with the others. You beside Isaac as his helpmeet, serving

God and the future of this island. T'will be a good life, indeed.

Not if Isaac has part in it, thought I hotly.

Remember if you will, he said, it is for you and this young family that he fishes the Banks with its countless dangers; spends lonely months with only the rude company of his shipmates. Indeed, here before the fire with you these evenings, speaking calmly of the day's events, even I begin to feel the pull of family life.

For all his knowledge, Weston understands little of a woman's heart. For how else could he read in my words some longing for a husband I can barely stand? Is it nothing to him that should Isaac reclaim his rightful place in this house, these restful evenings he so values shall be at an end?

He was thoughtful for some moments, then, arm draped at the mantle as he studied the dying embers of the fire.

I wish to speak further of Alice and Emily if I might, said he. I've been meaning to do so for some time. They run a bit wild, it has been pointed out.

The tattle of malicious neighbors, said I. A touch of the switch is what brings them 'round; they have need for more of it is all.

Their concentration as scholars is not as I might have it either, he continued. This is owing to nothing more than their so recently having lost their mother, I'm sure. Still, perhaps some diversion is called for, the enjoyment of such refined entertainments as might begin to ready them for young womanhood.

There was some point he wished to make, I realized. Men will oft circle a thing to death before making to the heart of it.

And you keep too much to yourself as well, Hannah, if I might be so bold. You should have friends among the other women; it would ease the time until Isaac's return. I can't help notice they flit about each others' homes in flurries of domestic industry, sharing all manner of goods and labor between them. As it happens, the Squire and Miss Young are planning an entertainment tomorrow evening, it being Saturday and the weather promising fair; and as I'm to attend, I can think of nothing more pleasing than to have yourself and the two fine Miss Burgesses accompany me.

It cost me dear to hide my surprise at news of such a festive gathering. I'd not have him know how little my friendship is looked for here that I'd not myself been invited. Indeed, my humiliation at being passed over in such a way was dispersed only by the glow of Weston's words.

Atticus might be useful to us in this regard as well, he continued. Allowing him the care of Mary and Seth in our absence, I mean. Surely you've noticed how they follow him about; 'tis clear they hold him in much regard.

The thought of arriving at Squire Young's home on Weston's arm made my heart quicken, the look on Sally's face alone worth the venture. The negro making free in my home was a less agreeable proposition to be sure, yet I determined to allow it this once.

Perhaps Weston shall call me My Dear again.

Matinicus, Saturday 25 July

How I despise the name Sally Young! It is but testament to Weston's goodness that he keeps patience with such simpering and unlooked-for attentions from one such as she. My hand shakes with rage even yet at the thought.

It was well beyond the noon hour when I first allowed to Alice and Emily that should they finish their chores and find for themselves something passing to wear, they might accompany Weston and myself to the Squire's this evening. Indeed, I was busy with my own attire, having nothing suitable but the white muslin in which I took my vows, finding among Patience's garments a fine petticoat and cotton stocking, and a bit of handsome blue trim from an old gown which did nicely upon my own. To this I added her best shawl of summer weight and a bonnet likewise affixed with a bit of the trim, and thought the effect quite pleasing.

Weston, taking a cheroot upon the stoop, bowed deep when we joined him.

I apologize for the lack of suitable conveyance for three such worthy ladies, said he.

Indeed, I am glad of the walk, said I, venturing to take his arm. The girls giggled much at this play of manners and skipped off ahead, their arms as always entwined.

We walked a bit in silence, accompanied by the singing of the birds, the glory of the summer wildflowers swaying in the fields around us. There was an air of elegance about Weston this night that had little to do with the grandness of his silk cravat. O, that he were my own young husband, the pair of us taking the air concerned with little but the future before us.

Sighing, he ventured something of Mr. Burns:

The snowdrop and primrose our woodlands adorn,

and violets bathe in the wet of the morn.

Is not it glorious, Hannah? he cried. Look around us, my dear. The sky so blue, the flowers in such a riot of color. 'Tis a paradise, truly.

A paradise indeed when I am on your arm, I ventured boldly, my own spirits being quite high.

He smiled, then, patted my hand as if in agreement. I had hoped for more in this vein, yet when he again spoke, it was in regard to our host.

Have you visited the Squire at his home as yet? asked he.

I allowed I had not.

You'll find it a fine one indeed, quite suited to a man of his station. He entertains with much the free hand, as well. I've enjoyed the finest of liquors and West Indian delicacies at his table.

You are often there? I asked, a shadow creeping over me at the discovery of such intimacy.

O, we are great friends. the Squire and I, Weston assured me, looking quite pleased with the fact. His is a sad tale, you know, his wife being taken off in the birthing of their son, the boy himself completing his own short course only hours later. The Squire might have chosen the comfort of a second wife, of course; most do, as you yourself know; but instead dedicated himself to the upbringing of our Miss Young. Selfless and valiant efforts, to be sure; still, Sally has suffered for the want of a mother these many years.

I had not a single word to advance on the subject, finding no sympathy for a woman kept in the most fashionable of clothes and relieved of much of her housework by maidservants.

The sound of Wivell's fiddle greeted us long before the grand home o'erlooking Indian Ledge was in view. As we stepped within, laughter and excited bursts of conversation quite filling the large front room, I spied the girls being greatly fussed over. Alice, in familiar embrace of Sarah Ames' considerable girth, made me a haughty look bespeaking the lack of affection between us. It is a foolish child, indeed, who risks angering me thus.

I held fast to Weston's arm as we joined those waiting to greet the Youngs, Sally's smile paling for the smallest moment when she found me at his side.

How pleased I am to see you, she told him while making pretty with her curtsy, and how kind of you to bring poor Hannah and the girls. This as her eyes traveled the length of me, boots to bonnet, eyes widening for a moment as she took note of the shawl once belonging to Patience—her own dress being of the new gingham so much in favor at present, her feet clothed in the soft calfskin boots I have seen at four and fifty in her father's store. How frivolous she is. Fashion being so capricious and she so flighty, she'll no doubt spend much time in the altering and remaking of such trifles as these.

Weston lad! The Squire was in red-faced good cheer, the look of rum already about him. Hannah, he said kindly, welcome to our home. It is beyond time, and I fear it is I who hold the blame.

Having performed this duty, he clapped a hand to Weston's shoulder and made for the gathering of men in the parlor beyond. With this Weston turned, unwinding my arm from his.

I claim too much of your time as it is, Hannah, said he in gentle tones. I shall leave you in the good hands of Miss Young that you might find refreshment. Then, more softly and to me alone he said, remember you are here to encourage friendship with such as she.

Sally, it was plain, possessed even less interest in such friendship than did I; still there was nothing for it but to follow her toward the chattering assemblage of women beyond. Indeed, I have never seen such an elegantly appointed room. At its center was a fine table whereon all manner of food was laid: a large stew with dumplings, pies of blueberry and rhubarb, sweet cakes and custards, and the soft gingerbread of which Weston is so fond. A large chest set against the wall served for refreshments of cider, tea, and wine. Yet when I turned to compliment Sally on such a fine setting-out, she had quite vanished. It was instead Sarah I found by my side, fit to burst with news of some kind.

Have you heard? whispered she. Lydia's lying-in is begun. Is it not exciting? Ah, here is Mistress Wivell to report the news of it.

And eating quite freely of the table, thought I, if the crumbs on her bosom are to be believed.

They live first-rate here, do they not? Mistress Wivell commented on our approach. And with a maid for the serving in the bargain.

Has Lydia's confinement indeed begun, Mistress? Asked Sarah. Shall I go to her now?

Not yet child, chewed she, for the woman makes the unfortunate habit of mixing food with word and sharing both quite freely. Progress is only now just begun, though the babe will surely come tonight. I knew it upon waking; I quite feel it in my bones when one of my ladies is at her time. Crushed and boiled the betony just this morning, I did. Gave it her not an hour past to ease the pains plaguing her now in earnest. But even I must take time for refreshment.

With this she placed a hand upon Sarah's own swollen belly. Two weeks, said she. No more, 'tis certain.

The woman's eyes then flicked to my own. Pray tell, Hannah Burgess, how is little Mary's arm? A sweet child, she is; much like her mother in countenance, I think.

She improves daily, I said. I applied a simple of burdock leaves wilted in alcohol for the soreness of her wrenched arm, and she complains of it not at all. Had the negro brought her to me at the first, it would have saved you the bother of her care.

Wivell himself, his coat quite the worse for snuff, was upon us then, his fiddle tucked beneath an arm as he pushed past for some gingerbread.

Squire cuts quite the forest of belly timber, eh, wife? said he. Ain't never seen so much food laid out in one place.

I meant to inquire how such a wrenching occurred, Mistress Wivell pressed, ignoring her husband's remark. It was exceedingly bad for one so young, and the child would say nothing to dispel the mystery of its origin.

Seth plays roughly with the child, I told her, feeling a flush of anger at such importuning. He has felt the switch for it, you can be sure.

A bad wrenching indeed, said she. Quite as if her arm were twisted slowly and with much purpose.

Now, now, laughed Sarah. The day is too fine for such as this. Perhaps, Mistress, you might instead offer your view on the taking of Fowler's solution for one so close to her lying-in as myself? My face has suffered for its lack these many months. Indeed I look to be quite five-and-twenty!

'Twould not be wise, said she, filling a goblet with wine. Young children, being sensitive to arsenic's properties, are easily carried off; a babe in the belly might likewise be lost.

With this she drained her wine, and filled the goblet yet again. For stamina, she explained, as I must return forthwith to Tolmans'.

Wivell took up his fiddle again just then, and as the sound was exceedingly loud, I excused myself to go in search of Weston. The chambers being overly crowded and there being quite the press at the parlor door, I did not at the first see him. I wish even now I had not, for there in my place at Weston's side, and quite affixed to his arm, stood Sally, rapture in her upturned face. The sight stopped me cold.

To the negro Atticus! shouted the Squire, the men raising their glasses as one. I wish only that I'd had the foresight to employ the man myself!

Indeed, said Weston. His skill as a cooper must be seen. Barrels, buckets, casks, kegs; there is nothing he cannot fashion.

I have seen him at the plow in Isaac's field as well, said Mr. Ames with a puff to his pipe. The man does the work of three, though he was no doubt trained to such exertions in his former home.

Yes, yes, thought I. Be done with it, will you. For the press of so many bodies had left me with a headache, one all the worse for the look of adoration in Sally's face. I quite itched with anger at it. I wished only that Weston might soon extricate himself from such unlooked-for attentions and see me home.

His is a sad story indeed, Weston continued. It was while enslaved that he acquired such skills and was thus spared the work of a field hand; while his wife Dorcas, being what he himself terms a house nigger, served as nursemaid to the master's children, itself a position of trust. All was as well as such an arrangement might permit until the morning Atticus came upon such a scene as would...well, gentlemen I'll not mince words. At the sight of his bloodied wife being forced into unholy congress at the hands of an overseer, Atticus struck the man dead with a single blow.

At this, Sally's hand flew to her throat and Weston looked down upon her with a fondness I felt tighten my chest.

My apologies, said he with a pat for her hand, but such brutalities must be as brutally told. The outraged master, he continued, choosing between murder of friend Atticus and the sale of him off the plantation, chose the latter. Financial considerations, you understand. Atticus would have himself preferred death since his wife and sons were forced to remain behind without protection or hope of reunion. Such a separation has the finality of death, the visiting of slaves between plantations being forbidden.

There was much grumbling at this, the Squire pouring yet another round of spirits into the breach.

An existence of utter despair, as you might imagine, said Weston. Think Squire, if you will, of never seeing your Sally's lovely face again; or you, Mr. Ames, your wife and the babe just now being born. The punishment given Atticus for nothing more than the defense of his wife's honor was bitter indeed, but as his new master sent him to the fields, he managed several escapes into the swamps of the area, only to be tracked down and punished in ways I cannot in mixed company relate. Still he persevered, eventually reaching the port of Savannah and the good Captain Lewis, who aided him on his journey north to freedom. His only wish now being to work for the funds necessary to purchase the freedom of his wife and children, assuming they're still alive, a fact he knows not.

There followed a general murmuring of good feeling toward the negro, a man I have come to hate almost as I do Sally Young, whose face was now quite flushed with excitement.

And when I apologized to the man for the crude habitation in which he currently finds himself, continued Weston, the smokehouse upon the Burgess farm being not ten feet by eight, he assured me it was finer and of greater proportion than the lodging permitted the total of his family before they were so cruelly parted: a flea-infested hut with only a dirt floor on which to lay, gentlemen. Miserable habitation indeed.

Mark me, gentlemen, nodded Ames. This slavery business will come to no good.

Weston, I fear you've quite forgotten your promise to escort me through the gardens, said Sally with a pretty pout. It appears Papa and his political pourings-forth have captured you for the duration.

Does no good to fight the lass when she's set her course, laughed the Squire. I fear we'll have to yield you up that you might accompany her.

Why my dear, laughed Weston, 'twas but my sole reason for coming tonight. My Dear.

This was not to be borne. For 'tis I who takes the daily care of him, I who packs his dinner pail with dainties when he stays noons to the schoolhouse. I who truly love him. There, I have said it at the last and will feel no shame in it.

Hannah Burgess loves Weston Philbrick.

I turned then and took my leave with word to no one, my rage such that had I passed some poor soul on the road, my very look would have struck him dead.

It is only now I hear Weston and the girls returning, their laughing voices raised in song.

Such merriment galls me the more. I shall keep to my chamber, then, let them fare as they will. For I am not to be trifled with.

Not I.

THIRTEEN

Tree Genus & Species

Taxus (Yew): 1 species found: canadensis
Pinus (Pine): 4 found: strobus, rigida, banksiana, resinosa
Picea (Spruce): 5 found: canadensis, rubra, mariana*
Acer (Maple): 4 found: pennsylvanicum, spicatum, saccharum, rubrum

*P. glauca and P. abies var. erythrocarpa, undocumented in previous
studies, are common at Matinicus as well.

I pause again, this time to contemplate death. Death at sea, specifically.

Before I began teaching, I put in some time with the U.S. Forest Service out in Washington State. It was there I met Jim Eberle—a fellow biologist and, like me, single malt scotch aficionado. Poured me my first shot of Laphroaig, as a matter of fact. More to the point, he was a balls-to-the-wall sailor. Absolutely obsessed, spent every weekend on the water—Puget Sound, San Juan Islands, the annual Baja Ha-Ha Rally from San Diego to Cabo San Lucas—you name it, he was there. Three weeks before he was due to sail across the Pacific with his father, the old man died—heart attack at forty-eight, no less. Jim nixed the trip but took a couple weeks on the water to do his grieving and scatter the ashes. Thing is, he never made it back. Just sailed off and was never heard from again. No distress call, no wreckage—nothing. Coast Guard figured his boat was hit by either a whale or a container ship and went down quickly. Fucking useless way to go.

The image of Jim simply disappearing into the sea has been stuck in my head since my conversation with Al this noon. Seems Kirtley Kneeland's husband was himself lost during some offshore passage about three months back—something she didn't discover 'til she came up on deck for the four a.m. watch change and found the cockpit deserted. Stormy night, rough seas, no way to know where or even when he went overboard. In other words, not a chance in hell of finding the guy.

Al wasn't told any of this directly, mind you. The information was instead relayed to Clayton of all people, during his steamy little tête-à-tête with Kirtley a couple nights ago. Island drums did the rest.

Gone in a heartbeat, just like Jim. Hell of a note.

I decide on an impromptu toast before I do another goddam thing. It's nigh on beer o'clock, so I grab a Heinie from the cooler and raise it toward the western sky. Suddenly, and for no reason I can figure, I think of Hannah's husband Isaac, likely also lost to the insatiable appetite of the sea. This kind of loss is such a palpable part of life here you can all but taste it.

"To boats and the men who sail them," I say, taking my first pull. I've massacred the quote, I'm sure, but it's the thought that counts.

Wandering to my work table, I riffle through the photos of the maples shot from *Ka-Ching* the other day, stir them with my finger. Focus is the problem, has been all afternoon. Imagine being Allan Kneeland, tossed unceremoniously into the sea, numbed by the sight of your boat sailing off without you. You've gotta know it's over, right? Whole thing has me feeling about as pensive and philosophical as I ever get. If the meek shall inherit the earth, Jim liked to say, the brave will get the oceans. Literally so, it appears. What brave thing was I doing three months back, I wonder, besides slinking around campus trying to avoid Annika?

But it's more than my own lack of adventure that's got me churned up; it's the afternoon's other unforgettable image—the one I stumbled on while clawing my way out of the bramble of a huge cranberry bog onto the sandy white stretch of Markey Beach. There, not fifteen feet from me, the two of us separated by nothing more than the gossamer curtain of a dispirited volleyball net, I perceived the sumptuous person of Mrs. K. catching rays in a state of complete undress.

It was a glorious sight, believe me, and I wasn't above enjoying the view. I look at it this way: a woman who indulges in this kind of thing wants to be admired, and personally I'm happy to oblige. I was maybe thirty seconds into my ocular homage when, no doubt honing in on my interested gaze, she sat up and glanced over at me—turning straight on that I might more fully appreciate the high-rent acreage.

There's nothing particularly original about a horny widow looking for a little action or sympathy, or even both, and I haven't been out of the game so long I don't know a come-hither look when I see one; still, I knew right away I was going to pass. Can't explain it, really, except that I've never been a fan of sex in the sand—too much grit in all the wrong places. And while I'd no doubt delight in a romp with one as delectable as she, public humping simply isn't my style. Despite the current moral drift, sex for me remains an intimate celebration of physical pleasure best carried out in silkened, pillowed privacy. And then there was that eye-opening conversation with Al over lunch, which had a decidedly jarring effect on my encountering her thus. Nobody here seems at all surprised to learn of yet another yachtie dumb enough to fall overboard at night—happens more often than you'd think, according to Al—but I can't shake the image of the poor schmuck treading water, praying hypothermia got him before the sharks did, while she so gloriously before me slept below.

Neither of us said a word.

Tacit offers like this have a shelf life of maybe ten seconds, I've found, and it seemed only fair to allow her the dignity of withdrawing the invitation before I turned away. Which she did by casually resuming her sunbathing, and I by slipping silently back into the brambles from whence I'd come.

Do I regret it now? Depends on which part of me you ask.

A familiar rumbling from the stomach sends me hunting for my stash of camp food. Along with the processing of my camera chip, the latest Matinicus One to fly from my wallet bought me my first real grocery order from the mainland. A small one admittedly, but a first step in cutting the Galley Hatch umbilical. Doug actually laughed handing the box off to me, shaking his head as he turned away.

I open it, peer in. Canned ravioli, baked beans, Spaghettios, Spam. Triscuits for fiber. A box of Wheaties—breakfast of champions.

Below me, bobbing silently in the wash of water against rock, are a couple of gulls and terns, some double-breasted cormorants. Sea birds have longer memories than a lot of people I know, and ever since my lobster feed the other day, these particular specimens fly in for a look-see every time I even appear to be thinking about food.

I work a can of beans with the opener, grab another beer, and stretch out on the lounger.

What I need now is a newspaper, a novel—something to distract me. I'm too sloppy an eater to even consider Hannah's diary. Besides, Weston's pedantic little act is starting to piss me off. All that cutesy poetry; strolling the country roads, tra-la-la.

I register the sound of someone coming along the path as I fork up another mouthful. Christ, if I'm going to start entertaining, I'll need more chairs. I make a mental note to order up another lounger or two from Doug as I glance back.

It's ironic that I don't believe in fate, because there's certainly some element of it in the approach of the lovely widow Kneeland—clothed this time, thank God. Jeans, sandals, and a man's white tee gathered and knotted at the waist the way the college girls do—the better to show off her smooth and, from what I determined earlier, seamless tan.

How do these people keep finding me? Has some schnockered island minion tacked a sign up to one of the withering Spruces on the road? This way to the tree-nut with a sneaker for Rachel Leland.

Kirtley stops at the edge of the camp, taking it all in—me, my tattered lounger, the can of beans. The smile she shoots me is crooked, playful.

"Knock, knock."

"Please," I manage around a mouthful. No doubt some sympathetic comment about her husband's death is called for here, but it strikes me I've twice seen her naked, or close to it, and we've yet to be properly introduced. I rise and move toward her, hand extended. Some perverse reaction to that intense, brown-eyed gaze keeps me from doffing my Dodgers cap, however.

"Gil Hodges," I say.

"Kirtley Kneeland."

Confident grip without stripping me of my masculinity. I like that.

We stand awkwardly for a moment 'til my manners kick in. "Beer?" I ask, parking the beans on a tree stump.

"Unless you've got something more interesting."

All right, then; single malt it is. I hold up a finger while moving to the tent, pull out the last of the three bottles procured via Doug. The one I brought with me makes four, of course, and I've been here not quite two weeks. I try not to do the math.

"Amazing," Kirtley says. "My husband's drink of choice."

I make the usual condolence noises; apologize for having nothing else on offer.

"No, it's perfect," she laughs. It's a great laugh, too, wouldn't you know—deep and musical; the ideal match for a voice suggesting private school, horse farms, summers in the Med. "We'll toast to Allan, then, shall we?"

I gesture for her to take the lounger as I locate two somewhat clean glasses, pour a couple fingers in each.

Her shirt's got some kind of boating logo printed on the breast and she catches me staring. "You know," she says as I hand her the glass, "You look like that actor..."

I shoot her my goofiest Jeff Bridges. "Uncanny, isn't it?" Why is it women are the only ones who notice the similarity; men don't know who this guy is? I reach for something from my repertoire of urbane comebacks designed to catapult me toward sexual conquest, but I'll be damned if I can come up with a single one. No idea why, but Kirtley's starting to have the same brain-numbing effect on me she did the other night. My decision at the beach is beginning to feel a bit precipitous.

"Clayton tells me you're a tree doctor."

She would bring him up. Rumor has it they've spent much of the last few days together, but I console myself with the fact it was me she flashed on the beach a couple hours ago.

"Botanist, actually," I tell her. "I'm here cataloging trees."

"Allan was a chemical engineer way back when. Polyesters." Leaning back on her elbows, she stares off toward a Western sky only now starting to show a bit of color—the avian audience below us bobbing patiently. "It's quite beautiful here," she says. "Very dramatic."

"Beauty and drama—that's me."

She's wearing an anklet, I notice—gold chain with a tiny charm I can't quite make out. The wedding band is gone though, if she ever wore one at all, ring finger perfectly tanned.

"Front's coming in, you know—three-day storm, they say. What will you do then?"

"Hunker down in manly camper fashion," I say, chin-nodding toward the tent. "Stomp around the fire and pound my chest, roar toward the heavens—that kind of thing."

Another crooked grin. "I like you," she announces. "You're fun."

"My claim to fame."

The old me stirs, rolls over, cocks an eye. Together we watch her body language.

She stretches, considers me with those chocolate orbs—her gaze a little edgy, hinting of pleasures both delicious and dark. Definitely my kind of woman. She shakes her head when I extend the bottle, dismissing such distractions. It's then I remember we're supposed to be toasting her husband, old what's-his-name. Do I mention this? Hell, no.

Then there's the other one. Where is Clayton in all this, I wonder? And where is he, like, right now?

"You sail?" Kirtley asks.

"No," I admit, perusing the tree line for that glowering De Niro-like visage. Meanwhile, the old me has entered intense negotiations with my libido—their whisperings so fast and furious I can barely hear myself think.

"You can come with me sometime," she suggests.

I'll bet I could. "Beautiful boat," I offer, trying to distract the libidinous hordes. "Where does the name *Bounder* come from?" I'm thinking something nautical. Over the bounding main—like that.

"Allan's first wife called him that. He liked to chase the girls. Bought his first boat after the divorce and named her *Bounder*. Technically, this one's *Bounder II*."

I consider this. Starter boat, starter wife—both traded in for newer, sleeker models. Way of the world, it seems. And the reason I'll probably never marry.

"Were you one of the girls he chased?" I ask.

She beams at me—a grin that could light the heavens. "And I made sure he caught me." She shifts, crossing and double-crossing those amazing legs—a contortion I haven't seen since grade school, and it mesmerized me then, too. Her feet even do a funky little wrap of their own.

"I have prehensile toes," she explains, amusement in her eyes. "I can do anything with them—and I mean anything."

Oh, man. I'm supposed to flirt back now, but things are shifting pretty fast here and I admit to a little confusion. Maybe it's me, but isn't all this laying around naked and dancing atop pool tables—not to mention the blatant sexual come-ons—somewhat tasteless under the circumstances?

The old me screams that it's been three months; what's a chick supposed to do?

Could be the husband was a flaming asshole, I admit. Pompous and possessive, lousy in the sack. Yeah, that must be it. Gone and gladly forgotten.

What to do?

The amusement's still there in her eyes; if anything, Kirtley seems to be enjoying the turmoil she's obviously set in motion. "They warned me you were the serious kind," she chuckles.

"Half the lies they tell about me aren't true," I hedge.

"What?" she laughs.

"Just something Yogi Berra once said."

Then it hits me, and I know what all my waffling's about. What I felt at Al's that night—that vague sense of familiarity, expectation, the almost electrical thing that continues to draw me to Kirtley Kneeland—is nothing more than the familiar whiff of risk, of life on the edge.

Annika.

Christ.

The similarities are simply too compelling. Annika Gunderssen was my grad student in dendroclimatology—a tree science sub-specialty focusing on ring analysis and climatic change—and the most spectacularly kinky sex partner I've ever had. Oddly enough, she wasn't even my physical type—spiked blonde hair, ice-blue eyes set deep in a sculpted Nordic face, the muscular body of a lifelong skier. All this in lieu of the auburn-tressed, mother-earth sort I usually gravitate toward.

Like Kirtley, she made the first moves and was aggressive about it. Tremendous passion between us, but you could hardly call us friends. In bed we were rough to the point of punishing—her endurance like nothing I've ever seen. She'd try anything and enjoyed all of it. Nothing was taboo or too weird for her, and if she exhibited an almost breathtaking callousness at times—an emotional shallowness that rivaled, well, mine—it hardly mattered. We were there to fuck, and fuck we did.

Problem was, our magic in the bedroom morphed into an explosive cycle of ardor and combat outside it—exhilarating, terrifying. And addictive. Annika messed with my head constantly—liked to draw me in, knock me off balance, watch me unravel. A month into it she began reading my mail, searching my place for evidence of other women. Ludicrous, really. I was barely holding my own as it was.

And it only got worse. Shifting realities, erratic behavior, physical fights. One night she dragged me to a campus party where, true to form, she inexplicably flipped out. Minutes later, the two of us were going at it, rolling around the terrace slugging and biting each other until she whacked me so hard with a beer bottle I passed out. When I came to, what was left of my self-respect was bent over me shaking its head. Whispering I was soon to lose my job and what remained of my reputation if I didn't cut this shit out. It was a tough moment, and when this remnant of my civility finally pulled me to my feet, I knew it was over.

I'd broken with Annika a couple times before, but she'd always managed to draw me back. This time would be different. She was clearly unstable now, or maybe always had been, and I'd just overlooked the fact in my rush to get her horizontal.

Took her a while to really get it, but then she did a typical one-eighty. Suddenly she didn't love me anymore; she hated me. Well, this I could understand. Hell, it was part of the normal progression I went through each time I'd shed one of these chicks. Not pretty, but there it is.

Then things really got weird.

She stalked me for a while, even managed to draw me into a quickie once or twice.

Incredible, I know. Then the threats started. She had explicit photos of us she'd send to the Dean, she said—she didn't, of course. Claimed she was pregnant—also false, thank God. This kind of thing dragged on for a while, but it was basically over and we both knew it.

The whole thing shocked me deeply. Scared me. *I* scared me. There was absolutely nothing sane about any of it. And ever since—well.

I wisely applied for a fall Sabbatical, something the college was only too happy to grant. No doubt they were as relieved as I was—hoping, I'm sure, that I'd use the time to get myself under control. That or opt for a career change. Me? I just wanted to get out of town, give bizzaro-chick time to fixate on someone else.

Fortunately or unfortunately, making this little connection breaks the intoxicating spell of the here and now. Kirtley will have to make do with Clayton; letting the old me out of the box isn't even an option.

She seems to sense my hesitation. "Why don't you come out to the boat later?" she suggests, unwrapping herself from the lounger. "We'll drink some of Allan's scotch. I can probably come up with something a little more appetizing than baked beans for dinner."

"Alas," I say—pointing to the pile of notes fluttering beneath the rock-cum-paperweight on my work table. "Work calls."

"That's twice today you've declined my offer," she teases. "Is it Allan? Because I'm pretty sure he won't mind."

Ouch. I give her my best shy Bridges, a couple hackneyed responses running through my mind. *It's not you; it's me. I'm not ready to get involved.* Both are true, inadequate, and would, in fact, be insulting to a woman of Kirtley's charms. Not to mention my own.

"Couple things," I call as she heads out. "Someone's been releasing rabid raccoons up at Markey Beach—part of some war of intimidation they've got going just now. You might want to be careful; they can get pretty aggressive. Raccoons, I mean."

She continues up the path with a dismissive little wave.

Oh, and you might want to steer clear of any muddy ATV trails, I think.

Or not.

FOURTEEN

It's Sunday noon and I'm once more headed to Al's, hands shoved deep in the pockets of my rain gear, cap pulled low against the thick mist of a precipitating fog—the leading edge of the front Kirtley promised two days ago. Right on time, too. Perhaps all this moisture will finally wash the smoke of her presence from my camp. I can only hope.

I'm making my way along the harbor road when Paul, a.k.a. *Plan Bea*, pulls up in his truck and offers me a lift.

"Headin' down to the harbor?" he asks as I climb aboard, burning his image into my brain for future reference—fifty, maybe, with a scruffy old gomer hat and pitcher ears. One of the innumerable, obese Labs they grow around here immediately pops up from the floor behind us—tail thumping wildly as he slimes my neck.

"The Hatch," I correct, gently urging the beast back.

"Ain't nobody there but Gail, 'cause she got pies in the oven. Special order or somethin'. Everyone else is down watchin the fight."

Parsing this proves impossible, distracted as I am by the word pie. Breakfast was a bust, the Wheaties having grown soggy from the damp. The thought of Gail in thrall to her ovens sets my mouth watering.

I nod, pretending knowledge of whatever fight he's talking about as I continue my own battle with the wet nose and the dank, swampy smell of rain-soaked dog.

He drops me at the turn-off and I pick my way along muddy drives toward the promise of lunch, ducking beneath clotheslines straining under the weight of undershirts and bleached-out jeans drying in the drizzle. The smell of chili hits me as I step inside, slapping the rain from my cap and shrugging my rain gear onto a counter stool. Even from here I can hear the jeering down on the wharf, the cheers of encouragement. State law bans lobstering on Sundays 'til after Labor Day—some attempt to forestall overfishing, I'm told—so there's an enthusiastic audience for this kind of nonsense.

I'm well beyond the age where I have any interest in watching a couple guys beating each other senseless, but I'm curious enough to move to the window where an aproned Gail bears silent witness, arms crossed over her chest.

The wharf is maybe a hundred yards in front and to the left of the Galley Hatch, which makes for perfect viewing—like the skybox at a ballgame, only closer—ideal for watching Cash and Clayton trading tired punches out there in the wet. They've been at it a while, too, from the look of them.

"This about John?" I ask, ruffling the moisture from my hair.

Gail shrugs. "What else?" Impassive, like she's seen it all. "Clayton drew harbor watch tonight, wants someone to trade with him—probably so he can go off with that Kneeland woman. Down to him and Cash now. Loser takes the watch."

Rumor has it John's planning to loose the boats from their moorings under cover of darkness and set them adrift outside the harbor—known in local parlance as scattering the fleet—so a kind of security detail's been set up. Each night one of the guys—Cash, Josh, Clayton, two or three others—stands watch, ready to raise the alarm should John or any of his lackeys have the balls to actually show up.

"Not that it takes much to set those two off," Gail says. "Been bad blood between 'em forever."

Cash's mom, I think, noting the *Bobbi Jean* rocking contentedly not fifty yards from all the action.

Clayton lands a solid right to howls of derision, sending Cash sprawling into a truck with a smashed windshield—par for the course here, except that the two of them look to be stumbling around on freshly broken shards.

"What's with all the glass?"

"Cash put an axe through Clayton's windshield this morning. Clayton returned the favor maybe an hour ago."

"Al's down there," I comment, watching him cheer as Cash head-butts Clayton.

"Somebody's got to keep 'em from killin' each other."

My eyes wander to where *Bounder* swings gently on her mooring, an enormous white awning shielding the cockpit from the rain. I feel as if I've just left there. Dreams are like that—last night's vividly steamy number stirring the old obsession with Annika. She might even have been there, come to think of it. All that baggage leaving me with an emotional hangover tinged with the kind of longing I've learned only means trouble. Last thing I need is some pissing contest with Clayton over sexual turf. Not to mention the waking of my own monsters.

Someone's rummaging back in the shelves, and I turn to see *Mary Kate* snag a can of hydraulic fluid, heft a gallon jug of Dawn before heading toward us.

We nod.

"Hodge."

"Josh."

He heaves a sigh, glancing wearily toward the two men locked in mutual embrace, lurching their way dangerously toward the edge of the wharf. Dance of the troglodytes.

"You gonna call Cheryl?" he asks.

"Not unless they start in with the oars again," Gail says.

He nods, purses his lips. "They're like to fall in."

"Tide's high enough; won't kill 'em." And with that, they turn for the counter, where Gail notes his supplies in the ledger, drops them in a recycled grocery sack. Neither of them so much as flinch at the splash and subsequent roar of approval.

It's decidedly cool for mid-August, or Fogust as they call it here, so I pass up the sandwich board and go for the chili. Gail, chatty as a coed now it's just us two, ladles with a free hand. She seems to have warmed to me overnight—no idea why—and not only is her reticence gone, I can't seem to shut her up. It's from her I learn that though the weather has grounded Doug and his Cessna for God only knows how long, I can in fact order up provisions to be delivered by the state ferry which just happens to be making its bi-monthly run out here tomorrow—this if I call the order in before three today. Laphroaig, I think gleefully. Heineken. I decide I love her.

The chili is outstanding—that and her baked beans rank high in the weekly top-five power rotation—and we continue to talk as I tuck into it. Turns out she isn't just the island historian, she's town clerk, treasurer, school board member, and one of two EMTs out here. She went to Bangor to train for this last, she tells me, but had prior experience of a sort. I ask about this.

"Cutting up bodies," she says refilling my bowl. "Seven years. Chop, chop."

I eye her, reassessing. "You're kidding."

"Wish I was. Studied as a forensic nurse when I was a kid. You know—autopsies. All 'cause I had a crush on that guy Quincy on TV. Real thing's nothing like television, though—I can tell you that. Last one I did was probably twenty years ago—four-year-old boy. Child abuse. You can imagine."

I can't, actually—nor do I want to.

"Halfway through it, I just freaked. Quivering, twitching mass on the floor. Suddenly none of it made sense anymore. This world." A shake of the head. "So I came back to the island. Might be a little rough out here, but it's a small place and I can get my mind around it."

I'm placing my booze order—Gail having dutifully noted the five-dollar phone charge in the ledger—half-wondering if I can stretch our new-found camaraderie to the acquisition of one of the pies I see cooling back there in the kitchen, when Al comes through the door leading a rain-soaked throng. Six middle-aged teenagers, laughing and pumped, in enthusiastic, post-game fever. I recognize *Hombre*, *Plan Bea*, a couple other guys whose names escape.

Al takes the corner of the counter with a pronounced limp; physical exertion does that to him, I've noticed. Out comes the Jack Daniel's, the shot glasses.

"Man, that was a good one." This from *Hombre*. "Ain't had a fight like that out here since John left the island."

"Hodge?" Al grins as I retake my seat. "You in?"

I've made some progress with the boys, I reason; can't stop now. I thank him, order a piece of blueberry pie as two bowls of chili have left me in need of something sweet.

Al pours. "First time I ever seen Cash best Clayton. Man must be distracted or somethin'."

"Woman'll do it every time." *Plan Bea* shoots back his drink. "Leastways he's washin' regular now."

"Hell, I'd shave my legs, she wanted me to," *Hombre* jokes.

Howls of laughter at this.

I grimace at the idea of Clayton as stud, the two of them rolling around in bed. An image that could fuse the retina.

"Fucking ironic about the old man, though. I mean here's this guy—world-class sailor, right? Some wave hits the cockpit and that's it?"

"Hey, you know what they say. Most of these guys get found with their flies down if they get found at all. Trip while they're takin' a whiz or somethin'."

"Or gettin' a blow job."

"Man, I'd give my right nut…"

More laughter, another round.

"Imagine comin' on deck and he's just gone? Christ, what d'ya do then?"

"Trim up them sails and just keep going, would be my guess."

Al's still pouring. "Middle of the night, screaming wind, twenty-foot seas—what else are you gonna do? She called the Coasties on the sideband, according to Clayton; filed some kind of report when she made land."

"Next Sunday's the twenty-first," Gail announces, glowering from the kitchen doorway. Makes no sense to me, but everyone else flinches. "Cleanup day at the schoolhouse. Expect you'll all be there. Barbecue after."

There's some minor grumbling, the nodding of a couple heads.

"Room needs painting this year, too, remember." She narrows her eyes at *Plan Bea*. "Paul, you and Bea offered to come up with paint. Two gallons should do it."

More grumbling as the men toss back what's left of their drinks and slink toward the door. Party over.

Al gimps his way over, dropping onto the stool beside me. "How's things at the dugout?" His new name for my camp.

"Wet," I tell him, waving off his attempt to refill my glass. To be honest, I'm more than relieved at the change in weather. The huge areas of deadfall I've come across in the last few weeks are a tremendous fire hazard. If the sun blinks too hard, this whole place will be one big fireball before anyone knows it.

Back in the kitchen, Gail's still going off about the schoolhouse—the same one-roomer in use since Hannah's day, it seems—and how no one's yet offered housing for the new teacher. A total of five students this year. Five.

"Clayton's supposed to be headin' all this up," she calls. "Woman's gonna be here in two weeks. Can't put her up in the parsonage, either, what with all those leaks; and I don't see nobody jumpin' on that job neither."

"Man's been busy," Al yells over his shoulder. Then sotto voce and with a wink for me, "Potential RBI situation, if ever I saw one."

"Well, I don't like it," Gail grouses, returning from the kitchen with the cherry pie she's decided to grant me—real fruit, too, none of that canned crap we've all gotten so used to. Triple-bagged in plastic against the damp, bless her. "Way she flaunts herself. It's trampy."

Out comes the ledger. Another eighteen dollars added to a bill that's multiplying faster than the national debt.

Al grins at me through a bourbon haze, cocks his head toward her. "Gail doesn't like Kirtley—rivals for my affection that they are."

"What I don't like," she corrects, "is Tiffany chewing on that woman's ear way she does. The two of them out there on the deck like that the other night; made my stomach turn. Girl's gotta stop thinkin' every female sails in here means Deb's right behind.

"And that's not all, Al. I caught the woman stealin' the other morning.

Thinks I'm not gonna notice she's walkin' out with a couple rolls of Bounty under her arm?"

Al shrugs. "So she's a klepto; so are half the people on the island, case you haven't noticed." Then, more softly, almost pleadingly, "She ain't that bad, honey."

"And you know this how? You point your dick in her direction and listen to it hum? What is it with you men?"

Yeah, what is it with us men?

Kirtley and her goddam prehensile toes—that's what.

FIFTEEN

I'm fully awake despite the hour—bad news has that affect on me.

"Who found him?" I yawn, scrubbing my face with my hands. Last time I saw Clayton, he and Cash were slugging it out on the dock over who'd walk the harbor last night. Looks like Clayton got the short straw in more ways than one. I glance at my watch.

Six-thirty-two. Christ.

"Paul."

Plan Bea, I think. Guy with swamp dog.

Yesterday's mist is today's soupy fog, and Cheryl grips the wheel against the dual threats of unseen potholes and near-zero visibility—swiping at tears as we bounce down the harbor road toward Cash's shop. "Found him sprawled on the rocks when he rowed out about three, like maybe he tripped in the fog. Called Gail right off, but Clayton was already gone." Her hand shakes as she fumbles for a Salem, snaps her lighter at its tip.

No need to roll down a window, seeing as Cheryl's pickup has no passenger-side door—a wildly disorienting feature made worse for the nebulous wall of gray whizzing by. No seat belts either, of course, so I grip the outside of the roof to keep from being catapulted into the road. The surreal feeling of all this is heightened by the fact I've no idea why I've been summoned for whatever it is we're doing at this ungodly hour.

To distract myself, I consider what little I know of Clayton—marathon drinker, wannabe womanizer, bachelor scion of an island lobstering family burdened with unfortunate relatives. No better and no worse than the rest of these guys, I figure. Strangely enough, I'll miss him—even though he sticks out chiefly in my mind for his chummy association with Kirtley, whose shimmering sexual presence continues to slink through my dreams—the old me hot on her tail, and pleased as shit at the demise of his only rival.

I'm rescued from these highly inappropriate thoughts when Cheryl swings a wild right onto the narrow incline leading to the Sands—blowing past her own home toward the gun and drug-infested corner of the harbor where the rowdiest of the sternmen board. From the water, it looks like nothing more than a tight-packed tumble of ramshackle buildings and piers jutting precariously out over the rocks; but from this perspective there's a kind of symmetry in the tight grouping of small buildings connected via narrow, serpentine boardwalks. The land held in common, I remember Cheryl telling me. An enforced kind of solidarity, you might say.

We park at the end of a long line of pickups and ATVs, make our way down the packed dirt path and across a short wooden walkway to where an open door enters into Cash's shop—one room, maybe ten-by-fifteen. Tiffany and her attitude are here, as is Ivan—forearm looped possessively around her neck as he smokes. Alarming, considering all the volatiles in the air. Sure enough, behind these two I catch sight of a long work table scattered with tools, a partly dismantled motor, jugs of hydraulic fluid and a good-sized dish of resin, as if Cash was busy laying up fiberglass when he got the word. The smell is overpowering, though no one else seems to notice.

I stand by the door, just in case, breathing through my mouth as I take in the faces around me. Altogether there are maybe ten of us, all badly shaken. Most are holding something—cup of coffee, can of beer—as if gripping a bit of normalcy against the reality of Clayton's demise. I greet Al and Josh, nod to Cash and *Hombre*; do the thumb-shake thing with Ivan.

"Hell, I don't know," Cash growls in response to some question I missed. "Some fuckin' Homeland Security bullshit."

My gaze follows theirs to the window and the relative visibility of the harbor where, despite the early hour, two enormous orange and black Coast Guard Zodiacs bob gently against the wharf. Twenty feet each, I'd say—twin screws, loaded up with radar towers, whip antennas, the whole bit. Four orange-jacketed Coasties strapped with sidearms stand on the dock chatting with Gail and Paul; at their feet is a long shrouded lump that can only be Clayton. I glance away, focus back in on the conversation.

"This fuckin' sucks," Ivan says, concentrating on a smoke ring. "What do we need them assholes for? Never showed up for Uncle Clunk."

"Violent death," Al says. "Lots of blood, no clear cause. So they got to do an autopsy. Clunk was a just a heart attack. Gail signed off, he got buried. Simple as that."

"Cause of death was he got his head smashed in," Ivan shoots back. "Don't take a genius to figure that one out."

"Saw him last night around dusk," *Hombre* says. "Drinkin' with Kirtley at the Hatch."

Al nods. "Tequila—both of them. Three shots each. Clayton hung out 'til she left for the boat, then he made for the harbor. I told all this to the Coasties this morning after they interviewed Kirtley. She was pretty shook up; thinks she should have heard something."

We watch as three of the guys strain to load Clayton's body into one of the Zodiacs. They strap him in, cover him with an orange tarp, then bungee that down as the last of them hands Gail a clipboard. She signs a couple times and hands it back.

"They said Clayton's head was all stove in, like he landed on a pick axe or somethin'," Ivan tells the room. "Just bled out on the rocks."

"All right, all right," Tiffany whines, shrugging him off. "Can you stop?"

I smile—can't help it. It's this place where her hard edge meets her vulnerability that gets me every time. Looks a little wan today, though. Clayton was some kind of uncle, I remember now; hell, he was probably related to everyone in the room except me—this place being the genealogical nightmare it is.

Josh shakes his head. "Don't see him fallin' like they're sayin', though. Guy's been crawlin' around the harbor since he was in three-cornered pants. Knows every rock and tidal pool out there."

"Foggy night?" *Hombre* suggests. "Tequila shooters? Shit. Man was a boozer; we all know that."

"And who here ain't?" This from Cheryl, arms crossed as she stands with her back against the open door, eyes on the street. "Except for Clunk. Weird, don't you think—the two of them dyin' back-to-back like that?"

Cash ignores them, eyes Josh. "What're you sayin'?"

"I think somethin' happened out there."

There's a stirring at this, a nervous shifting along the wall. Half the island cheered on yesterday's knock-down, drag-out, after all—the other half filled in on it all by nightfall. The implication hangs over us like so much bad air.

Josh's gaze stays cool, impassive, even as color pools in Cash's cheeks— his eye starting its little dance again.

"You accusin' me of somethin?" he growls.

A sigh as Josh glances to the window where a series of throaty revs announces the Zodiacs' imminent departure. "Nope. You wanted him dead, you'd have done it ten years ago." He shakes his head. "Can't see him fallin'; that's all I'm sayin'."

Cash considers, watching the boats make their way slowly through the mooring field—disappearing briefly behind a deserted-looking *Bounder* before going wide-open off Indian Ledge.

"You're thinkin' it was John," Cash finally says. "Don't gotta remind you, the man's Clayton's uncle."

"Didn't stop him from killin' the man's dog, though, did it? Coulda been a warnin'."

"Don't know it was John killed the dog," Al reminds them.

I'm dying to jump in here, point out a couple other obvious possibilities like a stroke or the pinpoint of an aneurysm lying in wait since birth—maybe even a heart attack like Clunk—but I tend to agree with Josh. Besides, I know better than to open my yap. Whatever reason these folks have for amusing themselves with my presence, any unsolicited opinion about their goings-on is not part of the deal. Besides, Clayton's death is only the tip of the conversational iceberg here. Far weightier matters lay beneath the surface—issues like trust, loyalty, mutual reliance—the island's fragile sense of community hanging in the balance.

"John had to know Clayton pulled his traps rather than keep fishin'," suggests *Hombre*, trying the theory on. "Might've figured he'd come over to our side in all this."

"Could be he sent a couple goons out here to scatter the fleet and they run into Clayton," Josh nods. "Things got outta hand."

Good point; my single enduring impression of John's steroid-fueled flunky was one of barely controlled violence. Hired muscle who'd kill without giving it a thought.

Tiffany rolls her eyes. "Maybe he just *fell?* He gets wasted like every night; can't find his way home half the time."

Cash ignores her. "What I'm thinkin'," he says, "'til we figure out what's goin' on, we have guys at different spots on the island let us know anything looks funny. Al, you got the harbor since you're there anyway. Josh'll cover the south end, I got the north side. Hodge is out at Western Point—good place to spot someone comin' down on us from the mainland."

I nod my assent, relieved to be given something to do in all this, though I've frankly no idea just what I'll be on the lookout for. I can hardly tell one lobster boat from another, even in broad daylight.

"And if it wasn't John?" someone asks.

Cash stares out the window, lips pursed. "Then he's gonna think I done it. Fuck." The possibility apparently just now occurring to him.

Tiffany's clearly had it with this bunch. "Well if it *wasn't* an accident, which none of you think it was, John musta done it. I mean who else could it be? And he ain't gonna think you done it if he did it himself, now is he?"

Cash, I should mention, is deceptively small—steely in that wiry way you want to look out for; and if yesterday's little show is any indication, he could snap our girl like a twig, something he'd clearly like to do right about now. He sends a warning glare in her direction—one she returns watt for watt.

Attagirl.

"Ain't no sense going on about all this now," Josh says. "Leastways 'til we know what's what. Just like Clayton to leave a mess like this, though, ain't it?"

"Guy was a dub, for sure." But there's affection in the comment and a soft chuckling makes its way through the room.

Hombre laughs, tilts his head toward the water. "Member the time that boat outta Camden anchored right out here, made a show of cookin' up lobsters they bragged about poachin'? Clayton tossed that bucket of engine oil down the companionway? Thought I'd shit my pants."

"Never came back though, did they? Bet they never got the smell out, neither."

And so it begins. One memory teases another. Someone pulls out a bottle—there'll be no fishing today, not after what's happened. A second one appears, and like that our little pseudo-inquest morphs into a wake. Never have I felt more the odd man out, so I slip through the door and head for the dugout—moving quickly against the ominous sensation nipping at my heels.

I've got a really bad feeling about this.

SIXTEEN

"My mother has a boat like this," Tiffany said, accepting a can of Diet Coke and relaxing against the soft, white cockpit cushions. She felt a little guilty about the lie since Kirtley was being so nice, inviting her out to *Bounder* and all. And anyway, it wasn't really a lie if she didn't know for sure it wasn't true. Her mother probably had lots of really great stuff. "She's going to teach me to sail. I'm just waiting for her to get back; then we'll leave together, go live some place really cool."

She sipped at the soda, looked around as she took another bite of her pretzel. It was so shiny clean, so…organized—what with all the lines tied up neat, the fancy little covers on the instruments. Made *Ka-Ching* look like a dump truck, which it was. Didn't surprise her at all that Kirtley could sail this whole thing by herself, she was that smart. And classy, like maybe she was really a princess, only her kingdom had been stolen away by some bad knights and she was out sailing around 'til things got straightened out.

Tiffany watched Kirtley settle across from her, take a sip of wine. Plus, her clothes looked so great all the time, which was just about impossible since she lived on a boat and all. Like today she had on this light shimmery thing that slid off one shoulder, and a pair of jeans that Tiffany would swear had been pressed. Maybe there was a washer down there and an ironing board. She craned her neck, ogling the companionway. She'd heard some of these big yachts had washers and driers, dishwashers even. Yup, she could definitely live like this.

"Your aunt's the one who examined Clayton this morning, wasn't she?"

Kirtley asked.

Tiffany didn't bother correcting the aunt thing this time. No way she wanted Kirtley to know she didn't belong to anyone out here at all, so she just nodded.

"She's the EMT—well, one of them," she offered. "We have two. Nobody's died here in a long time, though—well, other than Clunk with his heart attack. Nothing bloody, I mean. They're all pretty upset."

"Any theories about what happened?"

"Some of them think it was an accident," Tiffany told her. "And some of them think it was John—his uncle who lives on the mainland? There's like this war going on between him and everybody on the island. I don't think he did it, though." She'd finished her pretzel but wasn't sure if it was okay to reach for another, so she nibbled at her cuticle instead.

"And why's that?" Kirtley laughed—that cute little ankle bracelet she always wore bouncing as she wiggled her foot. Tiffany'd bet anything it was real gold.

She shrugged. "Family's too important out here, even family you hate. I think he just slipped, myself, but nobody ever listens to me." She nipped angrily at the cuticle; and when it started to bleed, stuck the hand behind her back. Last thing she wanted was to look like some stupid kid couldn't keep her hands out of her mouth.

"Well I think you're right, if that matters."

God, she was so nice. Maybe if Gail talked to her like this they'd get along better. Probably the reason Gail didn't like Kirtley was because she took the time to be friends with someone younger instead of being so busy all the time and only saying things like *don't even let me catch you on that woman's boat*. Well screw her. Plus, nobody could see her out here anyway, what with the fog rolling back in so thick.

"So how long has Gil been on the island?" Kirtley said then, trying to sound like she wasn't interested, even though Tiffany could tell she was— just like Kathy Philbrick when she asked about Ivan's cousin Harley who'd been out at Christmas. Next thing you knew, they were caught screwing in the church basement. Harley got sent home real quick.

"Couple weeks, maybe," Tiffany said, disappointed the subject had changed to guys so fast, even though she thought Hodge was okay. At least he talked about interesting stuff. The rest of them, all they ever thought about was sex and money and drugs. "He's staying at Rachel Leland's place while she's away. She's like this really famous artist. Why, you like him or something?"

Then Tiffany remembered about Kirtley's husband who just fell off the boat one night while she was sleeping. Not all that long ago, either, so she was probably still feeling pretty crummy about it.

"I'm sorry your husband died and all," Tiffany said, because being nice to people like Kirtley and Uncle Clayton was important—people with money who could help with all kinds of things if they liked you.

Kirtley sighed and took another sip, then looked at Tiffany like she was trying to decide something. "Okay," she said. "Woman to woman? Allan's not really dead."

Tiffany blinked. "But you told Clayton he was."

Kirtley shrugged and even that looked elegant. Tiffany decided to practice the way she lifted just one shoulder like she was almost too bored to even do that.

"Wishful thinking, probably. He's in New York winding up some consulting work. He'll be back next month sometime; then we'll take the boat to Boston."

"Oh."

"Let's keep it a secret, though, just between us? They're kind of fun, secrets—don't you think?"

Cool—telling secrets just like girlfriends. And Tiffany would keep the secret, too—forever if she wanted.

Kirtley re-crossed her legs and sipped at her wine. "Your family's been on the island a long time, I understand."

Tiffany rolled her eyes. "Like forever—on my mom's side, anyways. Nobody ever talks about my Dad." She racked her brain for something that might impress Kirtley, some secret she could trade back, prove she was somebody worth being around.

"My like great-great-great grandfather? He was some sailor who got shipwrecked here when his boat caught fire. Everybody else died." She paused for effect, like she'd seen on TV. "He was a black guy. They don't think I know, but I do." Atticus something-or-other. Ivan had thrown it in her face one time when he was really pissed, the prick.

Kirtley smiled. "So that's where that gorgeous complexion comes from. I thought you might have some Greek in you—Italian, maybe."

Tiffany blushed, which she never ever did. Nobody ever complimented her on anything—except Ivan, who only said nice things when he wanted to get laid.

Then she wondered if it might be okay to tell Kirtley the other thing—the one that kept making her sick in the morning. She'd know that Tiffany was really a woman then, even though she still looked like some kid. Suddenly the words were right there in her mouth and she knew she was going to say them no matter what.

"I think I'm pregnant," she blurted, the sound of the words making them suddenly real. "Well, I guess I pretty much know I am."

She knew right away she'd made a mistake—a really bad one, because Kirtley went all quiet; even the pretty ankle bracelet stopped moving. Stupid, Tiffany thought, staring down at the Coke can. Stupid, stupid, stupid. No way Kirtley would want to be friends anymore now she knew Tiffany couldn't manage something as simple as not getting pregnant.

"How far along?" Kirtley finally asked, real soft like. Not mad at all.

"I just missed my second period," Tiffany said, not daring to look up.

"So a couple months. Does the father know?"

"Ivan? God, no! He'd totally freak." She risked a glance. "What should I do?"

Kirtley sat back, shook her head. "Get an abortion. Right away."

It wasn't like this hadn't occurred to Tiffany before; problem was it made her think of her mother. What if she'd had Tiffany sucked out and thrown away back when she got pregnant, the way Kathy did after Harley got chased off? No one was supposed to know about it, which meant they all did. Thing is, if she had this baby and kept it, Cheryl and them would want her to marry Ivan, and she definitely didn't want to marry that jerk. Not to mention it would ruin all her plans.

She could adopt it out, she knew, but that still meant getting fat with it and everybody knowing.

Then Kirtley leaned forward and put a hand on Tiffany's arm, which was a real girlfriend thing to do, like sharing secrets. "You're too young to be tied to a mistake for the rest of your life," she said, looking at Tiffany so hard it was scary. When she turned her eyes on you like that, it was like you couldn't look anywhere else.

"The reason I said Allan's dead? He's incredibly...possessive. Beyond possessive. And insanely jealous. I could tell you things..." Kirtley shook her head and looked so sad—just like the way Tiffany felt a lot of the time. "But I won't; it wouldn't be fair. I guess I just want to feel single and free again for a little while; does that make any sense?" She squeezed Tiffany's hand, then, and Tiffany squeezed back. "That's what I mean about not tying yourself to a mistake. You have this baby and Ivan will think he owns you, like Allan does me."

Mr. Kneeland must be like a total asshole, Tiffany thought, pushing someone as beautiful and smart as Kirtley around. And anyway, she was right. Ivan already acted like he owned her and he didn't even know about the baby. Well, she'd be out of here soon; just let him try and stop her.

And then it hit her, like maybe Kirtley's coming here was a sign, the kind she sometimes got when she was on the right track with something.

"Maybe I could just go with you when you leave," she said, but it came out all wrong, like she was begging, which she wasn't. Begging was for losers afraid to take things into their own hands.

"And miss your mother when she comes back for you?" Kirtley grinned, like she knew Tiffany wasn't so dumb she hadn't already figured out her mother wasn't really coming back. Not making fun, though, more like playing along. Almost like she was reading her mind. Real mothers could do that, Tiffany'd heard—not pretend ones like Gail, who didn't know half the shit she pulled.

"You have any kids?" she asked, watching Kirtley closely for signs.

"No," Kirtley laughed, almost choking on her wine. "No kids." She smiled really sweet then. "But if I had a daughter I'd want her to be just like you. Someone pretty and friendly who loves to talk about the people here."

Tiffany smiled back. Her mother would talk to her just like this when they were finally back together; she just knew it.

"Now," Kirtley said, settling back. "Tell me more about Gil."

SEVENTEEN

Matinicans call it shut-down rain—downpours that go on for days at a time—and after thirty-six hours of it, the dugout is a real mess.

I'm in survival mode as I lug a couple blue tarps from the barn, thinking to cover as much as I can, but one of them is immediately sucked up by the wind—twenty-five knots would be my guess. Last I saw the thing, it was soaring toward the mainland like some tipsy manta ray taken to the sky—Rachel's webbed lounger chasing after, skipping maybe a dozen yards across the water before sinking in fifty feet of frigid deep.

Shit.

My raingear is completely inadequate in this kind of deluge, the true meaning of the term "soaked to the skin" obvious to me now. It's at times like these that my obstinate side asserts itself and it does so now, however briefly. I manage to secure a corner of the second tarp to a tree and drape it over the tent, but the ground's grown so soggy the pole I'm affixing it to can't find any purchase, and the whole mess is threatened with imminent lift-off.

Hell with it, I think, and instead turn my energies to stowing as much as I can inside the tent until the return of Mr. Sun. The barn leaks like a sieve, so I'm forced to suck it up and head toward the house. Warm and dry trumps any reluctance to encounter restless little spooks—I'm that wet right now.

Chilled to the bone by the time I push into the kitchen—soggy sleeping bag tucked beneath one arm, plastic-wrapped box of essentials cradled in the other—I shed my dripping clothes right there on the floor. All of them.

Ah, that's better.

An hour later, after cramming all six-two of me into Rachel's claw-foot tub for a steamy soak, a place replete with all manner of delightful fantasies involving my lusty triumvirate: Rachel, Kirtley, and yes, even Annika—resurrected from the ashes of my libido after detecting the presence of the impressive Ms. K—I have a whopping fire blazing in the keeping room, my clammy sleeping bag airing on an ornate cherry side chair before the hearth.

Towel hooked across my hips, I rummage in the box for my Laphroaig; and teasing the cork out with my teeth, pull a second chair as close to the flames as I dare. I take a swig. Another. Hot baths are nice but booze is better, and the chill finally starts to recede. It's maybe four o'clock, but wrestling with the elements has made me sleepy.

I must have dozed, because some time later I wake to the buzz of Rachel's drier wherein I had tossed my clothes. Only then do I rise and stretch, heading to the table to unpack the rest of the box. My cataloguing work, half a cherry pie, the precious diary. All a tad damp, but otherwise unscathed.

Warm, dry, and sufficiently power-napped, I grow antsy. A day and a half hunkered down in a soggy tent will do that to you. And then there's all the emotional upheaval surrounding Clayton's death, the dismal prospect of tomorrow's burial—something I can't possibly hope to avoid—and I'm itching to lose myself in something. Anything.

I opt for the teenage angst of Hannah and crew, and with the house settling around me, cozy with the crackle of burning logs and the muted ticking of the kitchen clock, I find the place marked by my 1955 PeeWee Reese—the card with the corners Dad always figured got curled in the spokes of some kid's bike.

Matinicus, Sunday 26 July

I'm uncertain, now that I come to write of it, just what it was I saw this noon. Did I perhaps mistake the meaning? No, a kiss is yet a kiss, and Weston not one to curry favor where none is truly sought. Nonetheless, it quite astounds me that he should waste himself consorting with such as Sally Young. Still, men are weak creatures, and Weston so easily taken in.

It was after the churchgoing and our noon dinner, Weston not being present at the meal for reasons I knew not. As the winds from the southwest were sure to bring rain, and I in need of wild mint and chamomile before the damp took hold, I made for the woods with basket in hand. For it is here I often find pink root for the easing of Mary's worms, and Goldthread for the painful throats that afflict us all. I had scarcely reached the place of the whispering trees when I heard familiar voices approaching along the path.

Tucked between tree and bush as I was, they took no notice of me, a good thing indeed, as I was struck quite dumb. For there before me strolled Weston and Sally Young, her arm tucked in his quite as if she owned it. That he should accompany her thus could be but some act of kindness, repayment of some favor owed the Squire. Indeed, they were still in their churchgoing clothes, Sally's blue petticoat dipping prettily at the hem of her gown, a new straw bonnet atop her curls. That Weston swung a picnic basket spoke as well to some sudden invitation; thus his not informing me of it. No doubt the Squire had just left them to make his way home.

As it was too late to slip away unnoticed, I hid myself behind a maple tree lest they discover me and Weston accuse me yet again of following him about, which I do not.

You have read Charlotte Temple, then? he asked as they passed. I'm glad of it; I quite approve of Mrs. Rowson's writings, as you know. They appeal to the tenderest of sentiments while urging young ladies to caution. Her purpose, like that of the good Nathaniel Cogswell, being the elevation of moral character.

I have heard it is based in truth, said Sally, ducking her head to his shoulder for the briefest of moments.

Sadly so, said Weston. A fiction founded on fact. As Mrs. Rowson herself has said, and I believe I quote her directly, Retribution Treads upon the Heels of Vice; and Conscience shall Sting the Guilty, Putting Rankles in the Vessels of their Peace.

With this, Sally stopped to rest her back against a tree.

But surely, Weston, said she with a pretty flush, when one is in love...

When one is in love, my dear, said Weston turning to face her, one marries. One does not practice seduction upon the innocent. Indeed, he continued, placing the basket at his feet, if I fault anything in our author's depiction, it is of the cad himself. His character was too favorably drawn, in my view; his punishment by far too light.

Then, and I can hardly believe it still, Weston took Sally's hand in both his. When is it you and your father make for Wiscasset? he asked.

In two days' time, answered she, as his brig has made port and he has some business with the Captain. He returns at the weekend, though I shall stay on to visit with my aunt for a week or more.

Then with a quiet word beyond my hearing, and Sally's own answering laugh, he raised her hand to his lips.

I longed to flee, but found I could not. For see I must, and as they continued on, Weston keeping hold of that hateful hand, Sally leaned herself against him, her head upon his shoulder.

I drew back through the trees then, unable to bear more, and ran for the farm hardly caring if I was seen. I was fairly panting with fury on reaching the parlor, and cast about me for something to smash. For it is at such moments that the breaking of some little thing is all that will calm me. Whirling about, quite beside myself still, my gaze fell on the corner cupboard crafted by Isaac for the Willowware Patience so loved.

Perfect Patience, thought I, taking up a dinner plate and smashing it to the floor. Perfect Sally.

I felt such joy at the sound, I plucked up another. A kiss from those lips to that hand! I raged and smashed the second.

I was holding yet another aloft, ready to let fly, when I turned to see Mary quite still in the doorway, her eyes wide with terror at the sight of me.

And so I screamed loud and long, in glee as much as fury, at which she dropped her bucket and ran, the lobster shells she uses in her play spilling across the floor.

Laughter took me then; I was helpless against it as I made for my chamber bent on destroying the shirt I fashioned for Weston. But as I reached to my basket a calmness stilled my hand, and I at once understood. For the fault lay not with Weston, I realized, but with Sally who practices her arts shamelessly upon him. It therefore falls to me to show him the fool he makes himself by wasting his attentions on one so flighty and frivolous as she.

I am quite content now and determined in my course, knowing she'll be gone for some weeks to come. Time enough and more for turning him from her forever.

EIGHTEEN

Matinicus, Wednesday 5 August

Lydia Tolman lives.

What—that's it?

I stare at the single line, trying not to be freaked by the thumping that's started up above me. *Ignore her and she'll go away*—works with most women, why not a little ghostie girl? Just to be safe, though, I rise, toss another log on the fire—a purely defensive move designed to reassert my first floor sovereignty. Not having been in the house after dark since our initial, disconcerting pseudo-introduction, I can only hope she shares my notion of our respective territories.

Fortifying myself with another wee dram, my fire roaring to life, I resettle and page back in hopes a reread will help me suss out the odd sense of disconnect I've been left with.

Voilà. Seems more than a week has passed between Hannah's discovery of Weston and Sally trading seduction techniques and that subsequent and cryptic one-liner about what's-her-name—a first for a woman who writes daily, passionately, holding little back. Wrote, I remind myself. Past tense.

So how come? And who the hell is Lydia, anyway? I put my glass down, belch, force myself to concentrate. Ah, Lydia—the chick Hannah doesn't like; the one in labor during Sally's little soiree. Almost died in childbirth, did she? Bummer. I have to admit a bias toward my authoress, spunky little thing that she is. If Lydia's on her shit list, she's on mine too. As is Weston. Never did trust that pedantic little fucker.

I grimace toward the pitter-patter of little feet running crazed circles above me—that awful room, I suddenly realize, being directly overhead. Hell with it, I decide. Two can play this game.

"Time for bed, kiddo!" I yell, feigning the basso profundo of parental authority. "Knock it off."

Amazingly, she does. Then again, she could be kneeling on the floor, her X-ray vision focused full upon me—a train of thought I try not to examine too closely. Instead, fortifying myself with another sip, I turn the page.

C'mon, Hannah; don't fail me now.

Matinicus, Thursday 6 August

This day brought nothing but trial, beginning with the news of Sarah's lying-in, which has finally begun. I spent the morning at her side doing what little I might, as Mistress Wivell will come only at such time as the pains are full upon her. I could be but little help; still I think she was glad of my company.

The negro was splitting birch in the dooryard on my return, despite the continuing rain. He's a sly one for sure, keeping his eyes from me as if feigning ignorance of my movements. But he fools me not; the man watches all.

My mind being full of the spinning and churning earlier left undone that I might go to Sarah, I did not hear Lydia Tolman's stomping approach 'til I'd all but reached my doorway.

I find nettles in my baby's quilt! accused she, thrusting the same at me. What other poisons did you fashion into it to cause the sickness we've had upon us?

With these words, she threw it to the mud. Such a lovely quilt, too.

In my shock a small laugh escaped. But you're quite mistaken, I cried. I wish you and your daughter only well.

You fool no one here, Lydia sneered. We know of your doings at Vinalhaven, how even your family wanted shed of you.

Pray come into the house where it is dry, Lydia, said I, opening the door.

And these poor girls, continued she—determined to rage there upon the stoop even though the black has stopped his work to openly regard us—so unkindly kept from those they have long known, not permitted to join in knitting with the others at my home. You think we believe your excuses? The sailor who bides with us is hardly the threat you take him to be. He's but a meek fellow, and though his memory yet eludes him, clearly a gentleman. No, 'tis purely from spite you do this.

I made no reply. 'Tis true I've forbidden the girls to go. Why should I allow them such companionship when I myself am excluded? It is rather Lydia who is the spiteful one.

She was quite upon me then, her dripping face not inches from my own.

You'll have much to answer for when Isaac returns, Hannah Burgess. For his ship has been sighted at last and not but two days off. He shall soon be home and all things put to rights.

I gape at this news. Isaac home? It cannot be. For Weston's birthday shirt is finished, the day itself tomorrow. And Sally's visit to Wiscasset extended in the bargain, though I'm certain 'tis but a ruse designed to increase Weston's ardor.

Lydia was gleeful at my distress, her look knowing. The arrow having found its mark, she backed from me and turned for the path through the woods toward home and babe, the quilt that was my gift to them both lying muddied in the dooryard.

'Tis the black's fault, this Atticus—the man himself staring at me hard, taking my measure anew. I slammed the door on that look, cursing him for his trouble. I must find some way to be rid of him, and soon. For prying eyes are upon me here, just as they were at home.

Matinicus, Friday 7 August

If writing of such wondrous events means breaking their joyous spell, so be it; I'm far too happy this night to care. For all my wishes were gratified this day, even to the ache of a woman who's been with the man she loves.

It being Weston's birthday, our noon meal was in the vein of a celebration. I cared not that it cost dear; 'tis I who have the keeping of the store account and the others can do without their little sweets if I so choose. Indeed, the Squire himself could have found little fault with our table; for when Weston arrived from the schoolroom with Seth and the twins, the hearth was festooned with blossoms and boughs, our table dressed with the Willowware. At its center sat a corned beef with long sauce and vinegar, a pot of beans. And not one sweet but two: an Indian pudding with molasses cream and the soft gingerbread Weston so loves.

Why Hannah, laughed he. It looks to be Christmas. Has Isaac returned, then?

No, I say, with a warning glance to the girls who have taken to whining at the mere mention of him. 'Tis a celebration of another sort. Think, I teased. Is it not your birthday?

Is it? Why yes, I believe it is. He looked pleased to be so remembered, growing playful with the girls until we settled to make our prayer, at which time Lavon came in, helping himself to the food before the Lord had been properly thanked. Still, I bit my tongue rather than argue on such a day; and Weston, his spirits being quite high, drew the boy out in hopes of luring him again to the schoolroom. Wasted breath, to be sure.

Dare to be honest, lad, and fear no labor, quotes Weston at the last. The business of fishing requires as much learning as any other if success is your goal.

'Tis not labor I fear, answered Lavon while making free with the pudding, but the learning that keeps me from it. As for honesty, he said, sending a dark look my way, you'll find little of it in this house.

But I would not be goaded; the secret I held was too important to spoil with ugly words.

Instead, they began a lively debate as to exactly when Isaac might reappear, I myself remaining silent as my thoughts on the subject would surely shock them all.

After the meal was finished and the children sent to gather berries for drying, Weston and I sat before the hearth, he with his Thomaston Register and I with my mending, until such time as I knew all to be well away. Only then did I make my way to the cellar where his birthday shirt was hidden away, calling to him for help in moving a barrel of meal. A ruse to entice him to join me.

Stepping within, he glanced about in some confusion, for the light was low and I was in shadow.

Hannah? he called. Hold a moment, while I light a lamp.

I have something for you, I said, the package I'd wrapped and fastened with string secreted behind me. Then, as he held the light aloft I stepped closer, a shyness I did not expect coming over me as I presented my gift.

Why, Hannah, he began, a smile in his voice. What is this?

I thought it unwise to make the gift with the children present, I explained as he set the lamp on the barrel. Open it, I laughed, stepping closer.

He nodded, glancing uncertainly at me. And when he saw the shirt, the blue fabric so handsome and finely cut, the color rose to his face. He shook his head.

Dear Hannah, he protested. It is too much. I cannot.

He made to return it but I stepped away.

You must try it. Go on, I shall turn my back.

But still he hesitated.

Don't be a child, Weston, I said with the tone I use upon the girls. 'Tis but a shirt. And as the fit may need altering, I must see it upon you.

Feigning impatience, I turned away, imagining the sight of his fine, broad chest as the worn cloth slid from his arms, replaced with new. I turned as he was fastening the sleeves, his chest still bared; and I stepped close, running my hands along his arms to take their measure. It was magnificent on him, and I told him so.

You are a fine man and strong, I said; and kissing his chest, wrapped my arms about his neck that he could not push me off.

He stiffened at my touch, gasped at the press of my lips to his breast.

Weston, I breathed, only then knowing the deepest craving of one for the other, moving against him as my body instructed. The distasteful things endured at Isaac's hand necessary now to my very existence. Was this my plan all along? I no longer know.

No, Hannah.

He pulled my arms from his neck; and with the strength of a man at war in his soul, pinned them at my back even as I ran my tongue at the pulsing beat of his throat, his taste sweaty and salt-laced.

Stop, he said, a shudder taking him. Isaac will be home to you soon, this very night perhaps. We must put all thought of this from our minds.

It is you I love, I told him, smiling up into that face.

I stepped back, then, watched his eyes grow dark and smoky with need as I slipped free the fastenings of my gown, the buttons of my chemise.

How can this be wrong when fate has brought us to this pass? I whispered, surprised at the voice that escaped me, as it was one I did not know.

I betray Isaac's trust, he moaned even as he reached for me, his hands fumbling beneath the fabric of my dress. Laughing, I slid his fingers to that place I would grant him entry, closed my eyes in pleasure at his touch.

My husband is dead, I whispered.

He was on me then, all heat and need where reticence once reigned. Hoarse and urgent, whispering instruction in how to please him, Sally Young banished from his thoughts for now and evermore.

But that is not the whole of it. For once the household grew quiet this night, Cousin Burgess having come to us at half after nine with news that the vessel thought to be Isaac's was instead a sister ship Boston-bound, Weston drew me into the dark of his chamber where I lay with him not once but twice more.

My happiness is complete. Isaac is most certainly lost, my freedom gained. Freedom that I might marry Weston. My Weston.

His smell is upon me still.

Holy crap.

I feel vaguely guilty, a voyeur cut loose from some sleazy nineteenth-century peepshow. Surprisingly, or maybe not, the old me has grown, shall we say, *alert* as a result of the scene I've just witnessed—the pages fairly smoking with a secret I can only hope my smitten Hannah took with her to the grave.

And Weston—well. I always figured him for a louse. Knew he wasn't above using his position to score a little poontang—takes one to know one, after all. Odd feeling, staring yourself down like this. It's like I'm in some kind of time warp. Past is present, present is past; and teachers of the young are lechers all.

The rain's taking on monsoon-like proportions—the noise of it obscuring even the wind.

Time for some sustenance, I decide; and rising in my toasty and toasted state, I grab the pie and wander through the darkened parlor toward Rachel's studio in *naught but my towel* as Hannah might say—a place I've taken to visiting a few minutes each day for no reason other than it makes me feel good. Passing the corner cupboard, I elbow the door shut yet again, latching it this time for good measure. Seems every time I pass through here the damn thing's swung open. Some slick little ghost-trick, no doubt.

Onto the studio, where stacks of unframed paintings line the walls—evidence of Rachel's amazing artistic juice. The room itself is filled with all manner of painterly paraphernalia: sponges and palettes and brushes, rolls of paper toweling, tubes of color parked everywhere. That fancy horizontal easel she bought just before my last visit currently sits angled before the front window, the better to catch the morning light. No curtains, of course, which given the day, means a rainy, windswept view of the ever-expanding mound of shells just outside—about four feet now would be my guess. A little over the top as practical jokes go, but damned if I'll be the first to blink.

Tonguing some pie from the pan, I plunk my derriere on Rachel's stool and give it a whirl—my thoughts returning to the diary, pinging pretty freely along till I stub my mental toe on the incendiary nature of chick rivalry. Hannah and Sally; that weird little scene with Lydia. Men might be responsible for most of the rape, pillage, and other warlike action down through the ages; but the petty resentments, accusations, and cruel tit for tat women inflict on each other are the stuff of legend. I'd love to know the deal here—not just the history between Hannah and Lydia, but the story behind that tantalizing reference to Hannah's past. What I need is that letter she got from her father—the one that so upset her. I know it's not tucked in the diary; I've already checked, and I'm at a loss as to where else it might be.

I slide from the stool, finger up another bite as I step to the hall, cock my head toward the second floor. No knocking or thumping—not at the moment, anyway—no tripping along the floorboards, but there's...something. The heaviness in the air might be nothing more than the steady dive of the barometer, of course; then again, it might just as easily be the gathering of Her Spiritness, the better to scare the bejeezuz out of me.

It dawns on me then that I haven't a clue as to when this kid actually lived, or whether she was even of the Burgess clan. She could have been a guest, the child of a servant. But why, then, does she haunt that unhappy upstairs room? The other question, of course, is why I care. No doubt it's a testament to how pathetic my own life has become that this kind of thing is starting to consume me.

People who believe in all this spirit stuff, and heretofore I was not one of them, claim the presence of something or someone like this implies unfinished business of some sort—a great wrong that needs righting, say, or a warning of imminent danger. Do I believe any of this hogwash? Not really. Still, there's no denying the second floor's a happenin' place, and as I wander back to the keeping room ready to call it a night, the house seems to shift and settle around me.

Here's the question, though. If ghostie girl's so desperate to communicate, why's she chosen me?

NINETEEN

Gotta say I'm impressed.

As it happens, services for the Matinicus departed involve none of the usual falderal foisted on the rest of us by the megalithic funeral industry—things like viewing hours, recycled flowers, or dreary organ musak wafting from hidden speakers in suspicious-smelling rental chapels. Nor, I should mention, was Clayton embalmed, which is why he was delivered to the dirt not an hour after Josh fetched him home from Rockland this afternoon on the *Mary Kate*.

No over-priced professional strangers gonna bury our dead—nosuh. Got it straight from Gail. Out here, and much as they always have, folks come together to dig and bury, saying a few words over whomever before slapping the dirt from their hands and heading off to work or home or, in this case, free beer at the Hatch.

The monsoons have finally abated, it's crisp and clear—not a cloud in the sky. One of those handful of pristine summer days that always seem to tail a spate of lousy weather. Looks like the whole island is here, too, which is to say forty or fifty people of varying ages peppered with a few of us summer folk, among whom are Kirtley and myself—she alluring and demure in a black knee-length skirt and a sheer blue top which unfortunately does nothing to hide her amazing bod as she weaves sylphlike through the throng. My blood's been thrumming since I caught sight of her at the service, having arrived in my usual tardy fashion after waking late to the damp and chill of the keeping room floor. Not only that, but last night's perusal of Hannah's diary has left me in a state of lingering arousal I recognize as the familiar longing for that which can only end badly. Not a good sign.

I didn't greet Kirtley at the cemetery, nor she me, but the charge between us could have melted every plastic flower within twenty-feet—this despite our not having spoken since the afternoon she breezed oh-so-casually into the dugout, shattering my studied sang-froid.

Hoping to avoid any further assaults on my weakening willpower, I hung back as small groups peeled off toward the harbor. Besides, I figured, high time I paid my respects to Ben—something I'd been putting off for weeks—but after fifteen minutes I still hadn't found any gravestone with the name Leland on it.

"Wasn't buried here," Al tells me when I show up at the Hatch maybe half an hour later. "Rachel asked, but much as we all liked the boy, if you're not from Matinicus or married to someone who is, you get planted somewhere else," he says, slapping a mug down and pouring me some coffee. "Non-negotiable. You gonna eat?"

Three choices on the sandwich board today: Yaz, Little Joe, and The Oil Can—named for mediocre pitcher and rage-aholic Oil Can Boyd—the tamer gustatory version being your basic tuna, tomato, and cheese melt on rye, which is what I go for. Free dessert if you get the nickname derivation right.

"*Oil* is Mississippi slang for beer, of which the man was overly fond," I tell Al. "I'll take the pie, whatever it is." Gail could fashion one from seaweed and it would somehow still taste like heaven.

"Got word this morning," *Hombre* says from behind me. "They're callin' Clayton's death accidental. No evidence it was anything else is the problem. Probably just flipped a coin. Heads he lost his brains on a rock; tails he got nailed by a tire iron."

It's the first I've heard of this, and I have to say I'm relieved. The last thing these people need is a bunch of cops swarming all over the place. God only knows what they'd find. Half the island could be led away in cuffs.

"They can put any name to it they want, but it ain't like no accident I ever saw," Gail insists, slamming the Philco shut. "Head was crushed like a melon."

"Someone's breathin' easier; that's for sure," *Hombre* growls as I swivel to join the conversation—the Old Gil keeping tabs on Kirtley in our peripheral vision as she sips a beer on the deck.

Cheryl snaps her Bic at a Salem—a strangely subdued Cash hanging behind. Can't be lost on him that if he'd lost last week's fight, he might be the one we buried here today. That or he's trying for invisible should anyone be thinking of nailing him with this.

"John best not be expectin' nothin out of all this," Cheryl says. "Uncle or no."

Josh shakes his head. "And him with the nerve to show up here."

"John was here?" I ask, surprised.

Cash snorts. "You was standin' right next to him, you dub."

No kidding. Amazing I could miss a guy with one arm, or maybe not—my attention being so thoroughly focused elsewhere.

"Don't make sense he'd come for the burial if he was the one did it," Josh says.

"Why not? Man always did like to gloat." Cheryl sends a plume of smoke skyward. "How the hell did he get on the island?"

"Fuck if I know," *Hombre* tells her. "Boat ain't in the harbor. Could be he anchored out down to South Sandy, walked up."

"Anybody talk to him?" Al asks.

Hombre shakes his head. "Couple of us headin' over to Clayton's, though, make sure he ain't cleanin' the place out. Could be a couple hundred grand out there, way Clayton squirreled shit away. Never did no business with banks."

Or the IRS, I wouldn't imagine.

It's Tiffany who brings me my sandwich, and she looks none too happy about it either.

"Hey," I say, shooting her my sunniest Jeff Bridges in hopes of dispelling whatever teenage gloom has her in its grasp.

"Hey," she says distractedly, eyeing the dwindling numbers on the deck before slipping into a broad grin.

I turn to see Kirtley grinning back—some private joke, looks like—before she cocks that gorgeous head and raises her beer toward me in greeting. I manage a brusque nod before turning back to my lunch—a remnant of my eight-year-old self, so flustered by Mary Garver's brilliant smile during recess, I pushed her to the dirt then ran hard as I could in the opposite direction.

Thus began my schizophrenic dance with the opposite sex.

I bury my confusion in a bite of the gorgeous wedge of lemon meringue Gail's just placed before me. Tangy enough to pucker the lips—the way it was meant to be. I'm forking up a second bite when Cash and Ivan are suddenly beside me.

"Headin' out to *Bounder*," Cash says, laying a hand to my shoulder. "Her invitation. You comin'?"

There's only one *her* he could possibly mean.

Oh, man.

This is the worst thing I could do at this juncture; I know it even as we row out, maneuver Cash's skiff among the others already streaming from the wide stern—every one of us here hungry for a glimpse of the place Kirtley calls home.

I know just two things about sailboats. The pointy end tends toward the wind; and once it starts that complicated dance there follows a lot of frenzied yelling and pulling on ropes. But even a dolt like me can tell this one's exceptional. Stepping to a teak deck sporting hundreds of feet of gleaming stainless steel and more dish antennas and receivers than UMaine's three-floor Comm Center, it's clear I've entered the rarified world of Newport, silk ascots, and oyster shooters. Everything around me screams luxury, elegance, major-league moolah. Three mil to be exact—Al got it straight from Kneeland himself last summer, first year he had the thing.

I could spend an hour up here taking in all the sails and lines and shiny instrumentation, but based on the laughter drifting up the companionway, all the action's below, so that's where I head.

The main cabin, what I would call the living room for want of any nautical terminology beyond the occasional quick read of a Patrick O'Brian swashbuckler, is a study in sleek and open with lots of windows for natural light. And, as it turns out, enough headroom for even me.

The kitchen, defined by a long swath of Corian countertop just to the left of the steps, boasts as many amenities as my loft—four-burner stove with oven, microwave, a glass blender behind which a barefoot Kirtley is busy churning out frothy pitchers of piña coladas, all relaxed-looking in cut-off jeans and skimpy halter top now it's time to get down. Tiffany's beside her, of course, chewing on her ear as the blender grinds away. The whole place smells of coconuts.

Josh appears at my elbow just as I'm mulling a hasty retreat to the emotional safety of the skiff. "You ever have one of these things?" he asks, considering the frozen concoction in his oversized paw.

I admit I have.

"Not half bad, really. Kinda sweet."

We nod over this for maybe twenty seconds until he wanders off to join Cash and a couple others in front of an enormous flat-screen TV. Never mind it's not on; it's merely something to focus on amid the stunning totality of all this: couches and swivel chairs done up in cobalt blue ultra suede, glass-topped tables, fine watercolors, and a bank of electronics that could rival a submarine—all of it subtly lit by recessed lighting. All about me guys imbued with the smell and dirt of workboats wander in a kind of shocked awe. Me? I zero in on the quality of the various woods. Teak and holly floor—real Burma teak, too, Techtona grandis, not one of those tacky impersonators from Rhodesia or the Amazon. Light ash paneling with cherry inlays that must have taken hundreds of man hours to execute. You get the idea. It's no wonder Kirtley spends so much time down here; I could live on this thing, too, long as there wasn't any actual sailing involved.

I pause by a table of pretzels and nuts and other assorted munchies, pluck a handful of cashews and peruse the place. What to do? I've yet to greet my hostess, whose dewy gaze I've felt graze me more than once, but she's paused in her blending frenzy to explain the boat's water desalinization system to several of the boys. I decide to poke around.

Heading forward, I stumble over a four-inch threshold into what looks to be a guest cabin, one complete with bath—which, when floating, Mr. O'Brian informs me, is termed a head. There's another small room tucked up here as well, this one stuffed with sail bags; and after I've checked that out I end up back with Cash and Josh who've moved their act to a built-in desk positioned beneath a mind-boggling array of screens.

"Check this out," Cash breathes.

The electrical panel has maybe forty switches—radar, GPS, autopilot, computer, something called a chart plotter—all carefully labeled. Allan, it appears, was a neat freak. I fix on one that actually reads *garbage disposal.*

"Single sideband," Josh says approvingly. "Weather fax."

Cash snorts. "Lot of fuckin' good it did him."

"About seventy thousand dollars," Kirtley says from behind us. "All upgrades." Arms crossed, she nods toward the wall. "Allan bought only the best."

Cash nods like he sees this kind of opulence every day. "Thing must be pretty tricked out if you sail it around by yourself."

"Electric winches," she shrugs. "A five-year-old could sail this thing."

I leave them debating the pros and cons of stuff like roller-furling rigs and lazy jacks, and wander toward an etched glass door I'm brazen enough to open, stepping into what is clearly Kirtley's private cabin—the silk blouse she wore to this morning's service draped casually over the arm of another blue suede chair, skirt tossed to the quilted king-sized bed. The end tables flanking it are in cherry, same with the built-in dressers and bookshelves— these last filled with sailing tomes and stacks of magazines. Riveting stuff like Journal of Polymer Science, Plastics Engineering, Cambridge Chemical Journal.

Sticking my head around the corner, I note an even larger head with another yard or two of Corian, a wooden bathtub of inlaid black cherry.

Oh, my.

"Get off! You ain't the boss of me."

I glance around at the sound of Tiffany's angry protest, Ivan's answering snarl, only to find Kirtley's trailed me here and stands with her back against the door jamb, hands tucked behind her as she takes in their little scene. Ivan's ready to leave, it seems; Tiffany most definitely is not. He keeps pushing her like this, she'll probably deck him.

"Short fuse tonight," I observe.

"Seems our girl's managed to get herself pregnant," Kirtley says quietly, smiling indulgently at Tiffany's imploring look. "Amazing in this day and age."

I'm stunned to say the least; wild to ask how she knows this. But rather than reveal such prurient interest, I go with domestic—nodding toward the open head door.

"Simplicity pattern by Corian, right? Got the same stuff in my place," I tell her, as if we've met here with nothing more on our minds than trading decorating secrets.

She fights a smile, glances back to where Tiffany has surprisingly acquiesced, preceding Ivan up the companionway in a red-faced huff.

"I only invited the others to get you out here," she says, still facing the room. "But then you already know that."

"Nicely done," I venture, relieved we've backed away from the jarring image of Tiffany hipping a slobbering, Rubenesque baby Ivan around the island a year from now.

"Getting a man's attention has never been a problem for me before. I was beginning to think you might be gay."

I should be so lucky. "Challenge is good," I say, and suddenly I'm back at the Hatch the first night she breezed in, the look of utter abandon on her face as she gyrated gloriously atop Al's pool table. "So what do we do now?"

She turns, nails me with a look. "We could fuck," she suggests with total innocence. "Isn't that what this is all about?"

Amazing how much she reminds me of Annika just now—so confident, so single-minded in her pursuit of pleasure. No question it'd be a train wreck, but man, what a ride.

C'mon, Gil-boy, urges the old me from where he's lazing on the bed, fingers laced comfortably behind his head. Oblige the lady. You know we want to.

"What about Clayton?" I ask. I mean the man's been dead all of a week. "You two do a lot of sailing—you know, in the biblical sense?"

"Clayton was a lot of fun but now he's gone," she informs me, "unfortunate as that is. Makes your point rather moot, wouldn't you say? And no, since you asked; we didn't fuck. It was all oral."

I just about choke, though that's hardly my only physical reaction, if you know what I mean. Her look is so full of sexual promise I can feel it surging through my veins. I'm like an addict contemplating his first fix after a long stint in rehab, no longer sure why he even bothered.

"A kiss, at least," she says, stepping closer. "Wouldn't do to insult your hostess, now would it? Besides, I can do a lot with that after you leave."

Oh, don't I love the nasty girls.

Cash pokes his head in just then, saving me from myself. He glances from Kirtley to me and back again. "Right," he says. "Train's leavin', you want a ride."

TWENTY

What can I say? I could plead the intoxicating promise of that proffered kiss, coupled perhaps with the stress of Clayton's death. Maybe even Weston's steamy little tryst with Hannah—the boner I got just reading about it a testament to my sorry state. But it was inevitable, really. I see that now.

Al keeps a small skiff tethered to the Galley Hatch wharf, its use free for the ferrying of provisions from store to boat. The fact it was me lugging my pitiful self back out to *Bounder* sometime after eleven was no doubt stretching this largesse, but I'd long since lost the battle by then—suckered by the sweet rush of anticipation. The old me was gleefully in charge again, a grim urgency to his strokes as he labored to get me out there before I came to my senses.

Truth is I'd have swum if I had to.

Some three hours later I'm slinking back along the moonlit road toward home, spent and exhausted, gauging the extent of my wounds—a couple rope burns from our foray into nautical knot tying, some nasty black and blues I'm going to have a hard time explaining. Upside is that the place she bit my lip clean through has finally stopped bleeding. Hurts like hell, though.

"Who the fuck's out there?" The drunken growl nearly drives me out of my skin. About twenty feet to my left, I figure, though it's too dark to say for sure.

"Just me," I call out. "Hodge."

"Hah! I know where you been, you ole Tomcat. Oughta shoot you just on fuckin' principle."

It's then I catch the wink of moonlight on the RV, Cash's dark outline rocked back in a deck chair—my eyes locking onto something smooth and steely resting on his knee. I grow absolutely still, fighting the urge to bolt.

"Got a beer here with your name on it," he says almost grudgingly.

I sigh, wondering if I've got the energy to make it over. Might be easier just to let him shoot me. At least that way I'd avoid the inevitable bout of self-loathing I know awaits me in the morning.

"We was friends, you know," he says as I approach.

It's a pretty safe bet he's not talking about me, so I take the three steps to the deck as if they're twenty, collapsing into a molded plastic chair he's nudged forward with his foot. I know just enough about guns to recognize one when I see it, and I shoot a sidelong glance to his lap to confirm my earlier impression. Yup, and she's a big one, too.

"'Course they all think it's me," he says, arguing with himself. "Who the fuck else would it be?"

I nod as if this makes complete sense. He smells strongly of pot and booze and polyester resin, as if he spent the better part of the night in his shop laying up fiberglass. It's like sitting next to a smoldering tire.

I yawn and make a stab. "Is this about Clayton? 'Cause last I heard, everyone thought it was John."

He whirls on me then, all recognition gone, as if I just now dropped from outer space onto the seat beside him—his eyes, wild and bleary with drink or whatever, twitching out some hinky Morse Code that we might better communicate. Constant exposure to long-chain hydrocarbons will do that to you.

"Somethin's seriously fucked up," he whispers hoarsely. "It's in the fuckin' air, man. Gonna get us, we don't do somethin'." He grabs my arm hard and I wince. "You gotta teach me some of that karate shit, case they come in the night. We'll do it tomorrow."

Right. I look around for that beer, any intoxicating beverage for that matter. If my mouth is working, I reason, I can hardly fall asleep.

"You and that...what's-her-name. Grab it while you can. That's what I'm gonna do, grab it while I can—'fore this whole place ends up in the shitter."

I shudder, though whether it's the sweat that's finally dried to a salty chill or the image of a naked, mud-caked Cash grinding up the trails on his Yamaha Grizzly, I can't say.

He pauses for a belch. "Clayton had a thing with my ma."

"I heard," I say, squeezing the bridge of my nose, so exhausted I can barely focus. Suddenly all I want is to lie down. Anywhere will do. The plywood under our feet is looking pretty good, except for the fact it's bowing dangerously beneath our combined weight—something that seems to concern Cash not in the least.

He grunts. "If I was gonna kill that asshole, I'd a done it back then. Threatened to a hundred times, but I'd never—not an island guy. Not even him." He strokes the thing in his lap absently, as if petting a cat.

"I believe you, man; I do." Boozy paranoia and loaded firearms do not a good combination make. "How about you put that thing down and fire up that doobie behind your ear instead? You're making me nervous here."

He looks down as if he's never seen the thing before. "This? Shit, ain't even loaded."

A yawn escapes as I massage my shoulder—slammed into the floor when Kirtley and I tumbled from the bed mid-flagrante. I mean you gotta ask yourself.

Cash shoots me another sideways glance as he lights the joint, inhales sharply. "Christ," he says, passing it to me, "you're in worse shape than me."

I snort agreement, wince as smoky heat meets the corner of my mouth.

"You get jumped or what?"

I have to chuckle at this. Whether I was jumper or jumpee remains unclear, but I wasn't on *Bounder* two minutes before Kirtley and I were on each other. Sexual fantasy being the unparalleled aphrodisiac it is, in my mind she became Hannah and I Weston—all my ranting about the guy notwithstanding—the two of us secreted in the cool, dank privacy of the Burgess cellar where we enjoyed activities still considered illegal in many states. And with great zeal, I might add.

The discovery of the hard edge of a man's slipper beneath my shoulder as we slammed to the floor might have given a less intrepid guy pause, but I was too far into my mission by then to do more than fling the thing toward the door. In the end, I expect I pleased the lady quite well—Grand Slam at least, though keeping count is not my thing. I know we first rounded home plate, tumbling and scratching, around midnight—keeping it up for some time. Beyond that I'll say nothing but that we seem extremely well-matched in the sexual arena. Twisted peas; bent pod kind of thing.

I glance over, hardly surprised to see Cash has nodded off—head canted back, mouth open, hands palm-up in a sort of modified Lotus position. The breeze sighs through the overhead bough of a maple, parting the leaves and throwing a shaft of light onto the striations of scar tissue on his right arm— scars, I realize now, that travel up his neck and along his acne-pocked cheek beneath the raging Fu Manchu.

He's snoring when I relieve him of the still burning joint, take another hit and let it settle, images of Kirtley's sweat-slicked body stirring me to life. Question is, will I go back?

Man, I hate questions like that.

TWENTY-ONE

I'm up early despite not having slept well—unusual for me. You'd think the way I slunk in here last night I'd have snored my way through lunch. But no. Rising at an unheard-of six a.m., I itch to throw myself into something. Anything physical will do; the more exhausting the better. Sheer avoidance, of course. I've failed some test here and I know it; I'm just not ready to face it yet.

Instead, I launch a cleanup of the dugout now the place has dried out a bit. A bittersweet effort, I have to say. I've come to appreciate the comforts of the house, and even, now I've grown used to her antics, the occasional odd company of little ghostie girl. Imagine.

Maybe an hour later, after cleaning and re-staking the tent and setting out my new lime-green, glow-in-the-dark loungers—Doug's idea of a joke, apparently—I sling my rucksack over my shoulder and hit the road for some field work; cutting behind the barn to avoid the road in front of Rachel's where overnight the four-foot mound of lobster shells has halved itself amoeba-like into two distinct piles. Why two, I wonder? Hell, why one for that matter?

It's hot and dry—mid-eighties, maybe—a chorus of cicadas grinding away as I pick up the road a bit farther on. It's here I'm joined by one of those interchangeable black Labs—a portly and gregarious animal content to waddle the middle of the road in lazy pursuit as I head for a stand of silver birch between Rachel's place and the old Tolman farm.

Birch trees are cool—one of my favorites. It's their economy that gets me. Back in Hannah's day, the bark was used for everything from pain relief to tanning leather, the leaves for arthritis, sap for sweetener. Twigs from the silver birch, or betula pendula, are still used to make brooms. It's fast-growing, too, maturing at about forty years as opposed to an elm that might take hundreds.

I note the white papery bark of this bunch which is indicative of relative youth. No sign of pests either, which is good news—none of the leaf dieback or D-shaped exit holes of the birch borer, or the discoloration you find with leaf miner infestation.

The dog flops down in the shade, panting like he's run a marathon, while I pause for photos. I know how he feels. I've been doing this sort of thing long enough to know when my heart's not really in it, but it's a penance thing today, and I plan to push myself 'til I'm done in by the sun, the bugs, or the poison ivy.

About an hour into all this, we take a break. Wouldn't want old Porky here to die of heatstroke. We're sitting against a tree, sharing my water bottle, when I spy a couple wild clumps of chamomile and mint in the brush about ten feet away, beyond that a patch of St. John's Wort and the broad, hairy leaves of comfrey. Interesting. I've come across a few domestic grains like barley and buckwheat in my wanderings around the island, some flax, but all this in such proximity looks suspiciously like the remains of an old herb garden. Old enough to have been used in Hannah's day? I wonder.

At one time there were maybe a hundred homes here, and I have to be careful in my wanderings lest I take a tumble into one of the crumbling foundations, camouflaged as they are by the lush undergrowth. I've stumbled across any number of these things, even a derelict well shaft or two—though these last have for the most part been covered with plywood, or at least marked in some manner.

The pooch has been pawing at something in the dirt—a small stump of vegetation, maybe—determined to tease it out and make a meal of it. I lean closer, spy the tail of some kind of material. Curious, I wrestle it from him, give it a pull. When it comes away with a tear, I realize it's some kind of textile, buried a long time ago from the look of it. I take my spade and spend a few minutes carefully excavating 'til I come away with what looks to be a balled-up dress, stained in places and obviously very old—the outer layer of material brittle and decayed.

Huh.

Probably not something my rotund friend should devour, much as he seems to want to, so I ball it up and tuck it in my sack.

A while later, I'm picking my way along the western shoreline, on the lookout for some cozy spot we can eat my sandwich and maybe grab a power nap to make up for last night's lack of rest, when I nearly trip over Tiffany, tucked as she is in a crevasse of rock—legs pulled to her chest, chin on her knees. Just below her a glorious surf pounds a craggy inlet, a pair of gulls surfing the updraft gazing placidly in our direction.

My new knowledge of her situation leaves me oddly tongue-tied, and I consider a retreat—I know a private moment when I see one—but Porky has other ideas. Turning up the waddle, he whines his way among the boulders with surprising grace.

"Hey, Tiffany," I offer, feigning surprise.

I catch a slump of shoulder before she turns, forcing a smile. "Hey, Hodge. Hey, Maggie; hey there, girl."

"Let me ask you something," I say, claiming a sun-warmed rock a couple feet away as she begins a distracted kneading of the dog's ears. "Am I running into the same pooch all the time out here, or are there like twenty of these things?" I unwrap a PB&J and extend half. "Lunch?"

She shakes her head, continues with the ears. "Somebody dumped a litter of pups on Markey Beach when I was little. Thirteen of 'em, I think, but a couple died before they were found. The rest are just all old and fat and wobbly now—aren't you?" she teases, burying her face in the warm fur. Coming up for air, she stares off, heaves a distracted sigh.

"You okay?" I ask, eyeing her as I take a pull on my water bottle.

"Bad day," she mumbles. "Bad life, actually."

I feign innocence. "Guy trouble?"

Secrets between chicks are sacred things, and no matter how conflicted I otherwise am about Kirtley, betraying this confidence isn't something I'm willing to do—never mind she did it first. And while there's no reason this kid should open up to me, suddenly and for reasons I don't begin to understand, I want her to. Very much. She looks so heartbreakingly vulnerable right now, it's making me nuts.

I try again. "Anything I can do?"

The hormones must be flowing my way today because she cocks her head with a flash of the old attitude.

"I need to get hold of a pregnancy test." Daring me with those eyes. "You do that for me?"

We meet the next morning at Rachel's. Tiffany's adamant this bit of alchemy be performed here; too much of a chance Gail might walk in on her at home. Meanwhile, I had Doug pick up one of those do-it-yourself pregnancy tests in Rockland, bring it in on the early flight. Gave him some line about how I use the chemicals for identifying certain tree diseases. Complete bullshit, of course. Amazing what I can get away with in the name of science.

Tiffany's all business, grabs the box almost angrily and heads right to the bathroom. Scared, I figure. And who can blame her?

Ten minutes, she tells me, slamming the door, so I wander to Rachel's studio, park myself on the stool for the duration. I've been here maybe five of those ten when it hits me how still the whole place has gone, almost as if it's holding its breath. Crazy, I know, but I've hung out here long enough now to have a sense of little spirit girl's moods. She's focused hard on something—riveted—and I doubt it's me. Tiffany, then? And what's with the sudden smell of lilac?

The ring of a phone on the wall just inches behind my head about jolts me out of my skin. Half a ring, really—the sound shrill and decidedly out of place in a house posited so resolutely in the past. I whirl and stare at the offending unit, wondering a little uneasily why it's chosen just this moment to ring.

Some friend of Rachel's? An art client, maybe? Rachel herself trying to reach me? This last's enough to decide me. Should it ring again, I'll answer.

It obliges and I grab the handset—a cordless number peppered with fingerprints the color of salmon and burnt umber.

"Hello?"

Nothing but the sound of far-off static, the kind you get with a bad long distance connection. I try again.

"1799 House—home of Rachel Leland, artist extraordinaire."

A low hiss undulates eerily over the line, rising and falling behind all the static in a kind of otherworldly techno-speak that causes my hackles to rise—much as they did that night I tried sleeping upstairs. No. Uh-uh. I'm not playing this game. Slamming the phone in its cradle, I hoof it back to the kitchen just as Tiffany's exiting the bath, a stricken look on her face.

"Fuck," is all she can manage, and even this is barely a squeak.

Oh, boy. I pull her in for a hug; pat her back which has grown rigid with shock. It's without a doubt the most emotionally intimate moment I've ever shared with a woman. Depressing, when you think about it.

"Ivan doesn't know, I take it?"

She shoots me a look. Guess not.

"He's so lame," she complains, drawing away. "Went off on Cash last night after we come in from *Bounder* 'bout how he wasn't gonna stern for him one more day. Sayin' if he has to do all the work anyways, might as well buy his own boat. Like he's got any money. Can't even pay for his beer.

Don't need him goin' all macho on me, makin' claims—specially not now."

I wait a beat, let this settle. "Any idea what you want to do?"

"Kirtley says I should have an abortion."

Ah, yes. I think—noting the interesting little flip my stomach does at the sound of that name.

"Otherwise she says I'll just end up some loser like Gail, stuck out here running the store for the rest of my life."

This stops me. "She actually said that to you? About Gail?"

"She's just being honest. I like her; she talks to me like I have a brain. Plus, she listens—not like Gail and them." She shoots me a sideways glance. "Gail's not really my aunt, you know. They just say that."

Do I hug this kid again or kick her in the ass? "Does it matter?"

She shrugs. "Kirtley says an abortion's really easy. You go over to Rockland for the day and zip-zip, it's done."

Zip-zip, huh? Far be it for me to muddy the procreational waters—God only knows how many potential Little Gils have been quietly and surreptitiously zipped—but I sense reluctance, an ambivalence far more complicated than simply whether or not she's interested in being tied to Ivan and his grody flip-flops for the rest of her life.

The lilac smell's getting a bit much, so I open the kitchen door and we step to the porch.

"I keep it," she says, "they'll all expect me to marry Ivan. Then how'll I ever get out of here, find my mother? She's just like Kirtley, you know—beautiful and smart. Has a great job, too."

I wince. So many levels of meaning here, I hardly know where to begin. Best keep my mouth shut, I decide, considering I'm one of the assholes out there randomly shooting off genetic ammunition for no other reason but that I can.

"Take a little time," I say, gently brushing a strand of hair from her eye. Can't help myself. "It's an important decision; a couple days one way or the other won't matter."

She cocks her head, eyeing me in appraisal. "Who'd have thought you'd turn out to be a nice guy?"

I'm not actually; wish I were, though—if just for this moment. And this better not be some stealth move by the Old Gil determined on notching his way toward sexual conquest—something I've caught him at before—because I'll throttle his ass. Fifteen would be a new low, even for us.

"Whatever you decide," I say, "you need my help, I'm there."

On the rare occasions I do something this stupid—offer to step into the breach on behalf of someone else—I'm invariably gripped with anxiety lest they actually take me up on it. So it's a surprise when in fact I find myself hoping I get the chance.

Maybe an hour later, with Tiffany long-gone and my stomach a-growl, I head for the reassurance of Gail's apron and some stick-to-them-ribs Galley Hatch cooking. Playing grown-up is hard, hungry work; no wonder I've put it off so long.

I'm almost to the harbor road when out of nowhere a car streaks by doing at least forty. Then another. Plumes of dust as they brake and swerve into Josh Philbrick's drive, nothing more than a twenty-foot circle of denuded lawn fronting an exhausted-looking Cape. A scream of despair stops me in my tracks, my heart about going through my chest. Shouts, then. Yelling. Keening sobs. I break into a run, rounding the corner in a sprint.

Man, what a scene.

"For Chrissake, get it off him!" Cheryl screams, trying to push past Cash, who's planted himself firmly in front of her.

My gaze swings from her contorted face to two plastic bags spewing their contents at her feet—a loaf of Wonder Bread, a collar of Bud cans, couple packs of smokes—then left to a truck I recognize but am oddly unable to place, my brain having inexplicably shut down. Nothing really computes 'til I fix on those ridiculous orange flip-flops, the rest of Ivan on his back beneath the truck like he's down there changing the oil. I expect him to scramble out, tell us what's gone wrong, stop Cheryl's screams. But the legs are unmoving; the flip-flops stilled.

"Can't move nothin' 'til Gail gets here, baby—you know that," Cash tells her, using his body to block her view best he can. "Ain't nothin we can do for him, anyways. Come on, now; come away."

Can't be, I think. No way.

The faded blue Galley Hatch pickup careens around the corner just then, sliding to a halt mere feet from me. But I've grown cold and numb and hardly notice.

Flashes then. Gail kneeling by the truck with *Hombre*; Josh staggering a tight circle—face in his hands, Cheryl screaming and pummeling Cash's chest as he holds her back, silently taking the blows. Tears on his face too, now.

"Looks like he jacked the thing up under the shock absorber," *Hombre* says solemnly.

They shift positions slightly and I catch sight of Ivan in the dirt. Eyes empty, body gone slack.

"He was just changin' the ball joint, for fuck's sake!" Josh cries toward the sky, fisting his hair as he turns from one person to the next, explaining to anyone who'll listen. "I left him to go for beer not a half hour ago."

"Jack musta let go," *Hombre* says, pointing. "Looks like the car rolled; brake drum come down, crushed his chest. See where them ribs is snapped and popped through?"

Gail nods, her face a hard mask. Behind her Cheryl continues to sob.

I find myself pulled inexorably forward, everything in slow motion as I reach them—my gaze drawn to Ivan's surprised face, arms splayed wide in mute appeal as if asking how such a thing could have come to pass. His chest where the drum punched through a gruesome, bloody mess.

I stumble to the edge of the yard and hurl—the image of Clayton's slaughtered dog rising before me, hanging mangled and deflated from the barn door. I hurl again, blood pounding in my face as my thoughts coalesce around another, equally urgent alarm.

Oh, God, I think. Tiffany.

TWENTY-TWO

The immortal Yogi said it all—that thing about déjà vu, I mean. Ivan's death brings out the same Coast Guard dog-and-pony-show as turned up for Clayton just last week—same black and orange Zodiacs, identical pistol-packing crew whipping out clipboards for that all-important sign-off down on the dock. Useless bureaucratic rigmarole, if you ask me—impersonal as hell, and somehow very wrong. I mean Jesus Christ, this is just a kid we're talking about here.

Fifteen minutes bearing witness to Cheryl's emotional collapse is about all I can take; nor can I face the shocked, disbelieving crowd gathering at Al's. No telling where that might lead vis-à-vis my libido should I encounter Kirtley just now. I'm feeling crappy enough, thank you, and weak to boot—my moral compass stretched to the max and it's not quite three o'clock. God only knows what the rest of the day will bring.

Eventually, I make my way back to Rachel's where I collapse in a kitchen chair, the unreality of all this finally hitting home. Overwhelmed by the same sense of disorientation that claimed me after Ben died, ditto Dad. Like Ben, Dad was sick, though he wasn't young. Then again, Ivan was young but he wasn't sick. Why the deaths should be linked in my mind I haven't a clue, except that all three came out of nowhere, effectively blindsiding me.

I grab the Laphroaig and head to the keeping room, parking my weary ass on the floor before the cold hearth. I think about Ivan for a while; about Tiffany for considerably longer—the scent of lilac that filled the place when she was here still lingering.

Might walls be like trees? I wonder vaguely, briefly trotting out my early romantic notion that wood—as living, growing matter—absorbs emotion and experience, from time to time releasing bits of this physical memory from some huge, intergenerational store. I nail down my original hypothesis, try and trace the old reasoning, but my three dead guys refuse to let me go. One of my inamoratas, can't tell you her name 'cause frankly I don't remember, insisted that this kind of intellectualizing in the face of emotional disaster was my standard MO; that my refusal to take time to mourn these and other assorted losses accounted for my inability to commit to a woman—i.e., her—lest I incur further such heartbreak. She suggested body work, a concept I immediately latched onto, but the crystal healing and meditation parts were a tad New Agey for me. I dumped her when I got tired of listening to all this crap—not much body work in it at all as it turned out, not the way I define it anyway—and turned my energies instead to researching the latest crop of incoming grad students. Which, I suppose, only proved her point.

God, how grim. I'm definitely in a funk; even the scotch doesn't appeal. Casting about for distractions, my eye falls on Hannah's diary lying not three feet from me at the edge of the hearth. Pure escapism—I know that. Still, anything to keep from having to think, help distract my mind from its current dark drift.

But here's the thing. When I thumb it open, it's clear that a few pages have been torn from the spine. Long time ago, too, from the look of it. I finger the rough edges, page back and forth checking the dates. Sure enough, several days have gone missing.

Huh.

Matinicus, Sunday 16 August

I must warn myself hourly against such despair as has gripped my heart these last two days, for Weston distances himself from me now he has spent his passion. Since the glorious night of our joining, he's barely spoken in my presence except for that necessary to the running of our home; and is careful to keep himself apart from me even when others are about. Surely 'tis the depth of our love that frightens him, time being all he needs to accept what in my heart I already know. Toward that end, our chance meeting in the wood this afternoon can't but help speed his understanding.

Should I need further proof that things turn my way, I find I'm soon to be rid of the black, missing since this noon when the murdered body of Tolman's sailor was found tumbled in a bloody heap from his bed. Many times I warned them; they cannot say otherwise.

But first to the day itself. The pastor, having just returned to his post, kept us overlong at the church with exhortations of sin and damnation, which did little for my spirit but remind it of its thorough dislike of the man. The noon dinner being delayed by this, and Weston remaining behind with the men, it was not until the sun was dipping west that we came upon each other in the woods behind Tolmans'.

I spied him first, dreamy and distracted as he was, Isaac's flintlock slung across his shoulders in casual caress.

Weston, I said, unable to hide my delight. You've been hunting?

He flushed upon seeing me, his expression of surprise equal to my own, if lacking quite the same warmth. It was a moment before he spoke, so taken aback was he.

I've been to shoot the whistlers you asked of me for supper, he said flatly. Do you not remember?

It was then I noticed the birds tied at the feet and slung across his chest.

O, yes, the birds, I laughed. Though in truth my heart beat close to bursting, so desperately did I want to fling myself against him, to tumble to the grass and let passion consume us once again. But such was not to be.

You're breathless, said he. Your color quite high. Have you been running?

Indeed not; I've been greening, as you see. With this I held my basket out, though there was little within that might attest to my efforts.

You keep your hand tucked behind you, he remarked.

There's blood upon it yet from the gutting of the lamb, I said lightly. 'Tis unsightly.

With this I make show of scrubbing it hard against my dress. There, I smile. Better now.

He nodded, making to leave, but turned again to me at the last.

You're no longer angry with me, then? he asked.

This due to my recent and unfortunate fit of temper, my disappointment at his change in demeanor being great as it was.

Indeed no, I laughed. I ask only that you forgive my unkind words.

Not at all. T'was but a mistake. The Lord will forgive us our lapse, I'm sure. There, he said smiling, we shall say no more of it.

I took him to mean our harsh words, of course, and not the other, for the memory of it remains my only joy.

More birds for supper then! chirped he in a tone suggesting relief, hoisting Isaac's flintlock as he turned again to the woods.

T'was but an hour later I heard the men in the door yard, voices raised as they stormed the keeping room, though I had washed myself by then. Messrs. Ames and Tolman, Wivell, and Cousin Burgess, all of them looking quite wild.

Fast behind came Weston, gun and birds in hand, his face paling at sight of them.

What is it? he demanded, dropping the birds by the sink. What has happened?

The sailor in our care has been stabbed! Tolman fairly spat. Murdered! His bloodied body lies yet in my home.

Stabbed? Weston's eyes grew wide. Surely not. Lydia and the child are all right?

Tolman nodded. Aye, he said, though beside herself that something like this should occur with both the babe and herself only steps away. The brazenness!

It was the black, I said. He's not been about the place or his chores all day. My butchering knife I noticed missing this noon, as well.

With this I pointed to the empty shelf on which it is kept.

Tolman regarded me coldly. Do we understand you to accuse Atticus in this, Hannah? he demanded, his tone suggesting subterfuge. It seems Lydia has been spreading her lies to him.

I know not, sir, I said with like coolness, but as you can see the knife is gone and the black missing as well. The rest is for you to determine.

But surely he has no reason for this, protested Weston.

Four reasons lay rotting in the burying ground these weeks, sputtered Mr. Ames. For if he killed the others on the Amaranth, 'twould not do to have Tolman's sailor regain memory of the day, now would it?

Did he not react with fear when first told the sailor was recovering? I reminded all.

He did not do this, Hannah, Weston quite snapped before turning again to the men. Surely gentlemen, it's unfair and precipitous to lay blame when Atticus is not here to answer such charges.

Come, man! exclaimed Cousin Burgess. Who else but he has reason for such a thing?

And us taking him as friend, spat Ames. Him with his pretty story of being wrested from his little ones. Mark me; he'll answer for this when he's found.

A search of the island must be made at once, said Tolman. I've sent to the store for the Squire, but he's about the island seeing to other concerns. He'll hear of it soon enough, I'll warrant.

With the men then forming their parties, I returned to my chores and the plucking of Weston's birds for our supper, happy in the knowledge that the black and his prying eyes will soon be gone.

Matinicus, Monday 17 August

I sit before the fire now, the evening having taken a chill while I await Weston's return. It was at noon he announced his plans to take supper with the Squire this evening. A meeting of some import, I gather, as he took even greater care than usual for his clothing. It pleased me to see the shirt I made him looking so handsome beneath his waistcoat. And while he said little to me as he stood before the hearth giving nervous checks to his pocket watch, I took the wearing of it as a message. Silent testament of his feelings for me, a plea for patience, perhaps. Still, I'm determined to speak my heart on his return. For even Cousin Burgess now agrees that Isaac is unlikely to return, and it behooves us to make our plans.

As Monday is washing day here, I spent much of it in labor with the girls, not reaching Young's for supplies until the afternoon was well advanced. Nor did I know of Sally's return from Wiscasset until I entered the store and found her standing in her usual bored fashion behind the counter. Her frock new, of course, and tightly corseted in the latest style, though I've heard it said that a young woman recently perished from the excessive lacing of one such as that.

We were alone, as it happened, Sally fairly frothing with news of the mainland as I gathered my purchases.

O, the evening assemblies! cried she, all a-twitter. The dresses so smart. Not a calico in sight.

I was able to smile at even such nonsense as this, for I found I quite pitied her mooning regard for Weston now he and I were one.

Imagine, Hannah, a muff and tippet of ermine! And the wedding dresses! I've decided I'll not wear white when I marry, now I've seen the new purple silks as were displayed there. Eventually, that is. I mean. And with this she blushed.

I thought then of the plain muslin of my own wedding, a poor cousin even to the calico Sally so disparages, the memory bringing to mind yet again how poorly father valued me. That hateful, hateful man.

Sally offered yet more in this frivolous vein, but I was weary of her boastful gibbering and paid her little mind until she lit upon happenings closer to home.

And Papa says he's to knit nets for the store now there's no suspicion hanging over him. As he's to leave your farm anyway, that is.

She spoke of the black, this Atticus—taken once more to the island's bosom, now he's been proved innocent of murdering Tolmans' sailor.

Imagine, Hannah, a murderer among us. Is it not delicious? One of the Portuguese fishermen come to the island to steal, no doubt. Papa said there was much in the way of blood. Poor Lydia! Alone in the house with the wicked man, and with a new babe in the bargain.

I asked her to tally my purchases, for I knew all this, even to the Squire's claim that the black was with him at the time of the murder. That the men take this as proof he had no hand in the savaging of the Amaranth is folly indeed, as the one has naught to do with the other to my mind. But the man is sly, and has inveigled his way among them, even to voicing his wish to stay and make his home on the island. I'm to be rid of him here at home at least, as he's formed a friendship with old Wivell who's promised to sell him land on which to build a cabin.

And still, my repeated warnings meet deaf ears. Indeed, it is upon me their hard looks now fall. O, they're polite enough to my face; but I feel their eyes on me as I turn away. They watch me, whisper of me out of my hearing.

Henceforth I shall secret these writings, for someone reads these pages. I feel it.

TWENTY-THREE

Someone reads these pages. I feel it.

Whoa. That's freaky.

"Yo!"

I drop the diary and scramble back—half expecting to see Hannah materializing post-time-travel, barreling toward me in all her magnificent teenage fury to wrest this thing from my grasp.

"Hodge?" Al, all twenty-first century of him, eyes me from the kitchen. "Knocked, but I guess you didn't hear. Surprised you're here, actually; figured you'd be down at the dugout." He slides onto one of Rachel's cherry side chairs, chin nods toward a paper bag he's dropped on the table. "Told Gail I was bringing you lunch."

Lunch. Of course—my plans for it completely derailed when Ivan's body was found. No wonder I'm such a mess. I'm famished.

I grab the Laphroaig and join him at the table, slapping the bottle down in invitation. My turn to buy him a couple drinks, I figure.

"Now you're talkin'," he grins as I pad to the kitchen for a beer, snag a shot glass from the drainer.

"Boy, do I need this." He downs it in a couple quick sips, nods approvingly. Pleased, I pour him another.

The bag holds a cheesy Joe Pepitone—roast beef, coleslaw, melted Swiss on rye—bag of chips, a couple dills. Al waves off my thanks.

"Had to get outta there. All those women cryin' and wailin'—'cept

Tiffany, of course. Ain't seen a tear outta that girl since her mama up and left." He tosses back the scotch. "No deaths out here in maybe three years; then bang—two in as many weeks? I mean, what are the odds?"

Two out of fifty, I think, chewing. That's what, four percent of the population? This keeps up, the place will be deserted in less than a year.

"Other reason I came over, John's on his way from the mainland as we speak. Heard about Ivan; called a meeting in the old store for an hour from now. Cash told me to make sure you're there."

I swallow hard. "Me? How come?"

Al shrugs. "Could be he wants bodies—you know, up the intimidation factor. The more of us there, the less likely John will pull somethin'. Then again, he might just want your take on the guy."

My take? Easy; man's scum. Tried to rape Gail when she was a kid, right? All I need to know. Then again, Cash is big on shows of power. Who else packs two semi-automatics on the nights he patrols the harbor? And yes, okay, I admit to a certain amount of curiosity—a shameless desire to put a face to the brutish reputation—so I agree to strut my stuff with the rest of the boys, though something tells me I'll regret it.

"This is all hush-hush, you understand," Al says. "Gail gets wind John's on-island, she'll take a cleaver to him—no lie." Turning, he chin-nods toward my Pee Wee Reese lying on the table beside Hannah's diary.

"That what I think it is?"

I grin around a mouthful, slide the card toward him.

"You got more of these, too, I'll bet," he says fingering it.

I smile, belch—glad to have something to take my mind off Ivan and the impending confrontation; and upending my beer, head to the kitchen for my rucksack. First thing I find when I tug the pack open is the dress I unearthed out there in the woods and promptly forgot about—balled up tight and smelling of mold and dead animal. I pull it out, along with half a rancid PB&J, and leave both on the counter to dispose of later. Rummaging in the zippered pocket, I pull out two of my favorite cards—my 1949 Gil Hodges rookie and one of my Jackie Robinsons. I carry a couple of these things with me whenever I travel, a kind of good luck charm. If there was ever a time to break them out, I figure, this is it.

"Whoa," Al says when I hand them over. "Robinson's '49 Dodgers card. *Babe Ruth changed baseball; but Robinson changed America.* You ever hear that?"

"I have."

"He and PeeWee Reese were a hell of a double-play combo."

"One of the greatest," I agree. This could be a replay of a thousand conversations with my father. Feels kinda nice. Comforting.

He studies the Hodges a minute, shakes his head. "Any more this quality?"

I nod. "All the Topps '52's, the complete '55 Dodgers. Inherited them from my Dad." I don't mention my 1911 T206 Honus Wagner and the entire 1915 Cracker Jack set. A man can only take so much excitement.

A whistle escapes. "Worth a fucking fortune."

I shrug modestly. As I said, I rarely pull this stuff out, and I've never revealed the extent of Dad's collection, but it's worth it to see Al relax a bit, the tightness around his eyes soften.

"Gotta get back," he says, rising and reluctantly setting the cards on the table. "Delivering lunch only takes so long in Gail's book. I'll catch you at the meeting." He nods toward the diary. "Tell me you ain't still readin' that foolish thing."

"Afraid so."

"Why Rachel and Gail got so frothed up over it, I'll never know. Black spot on Matinicus history's all it is." He throws back the rest of the scotch. "Got to the place where that schoolteacher makes his big announcement?"

Now that gets my attention. As soon as he leaves, I take the diary and what's left of my lunch to the porch, park myself on a step to find out. No more than a half hour, I tell myself. Okay, forty-five minutes, but that's it. Turns out I need less than five.

TWENTY-FOUR

Matinicus, Monday 17 August

Lies! He tells only lies! O, to be so poorly used.

Weston has formed an alliance with Sally. There, I have written it. I surely cannot speak it aloud without losing my reason.

I fell asleep at the fire tonight after last writing in this book, and would have slept the night through but for the quiet latching of the door.

Weston, I said, rising and moving toward him. The Squire keeps you over-long tonight.

He appeared distracted and unaware of the heavy dew collected on his brow.

My mother, I said, reaching a hand to his face, could tell by the feeling on her lashes when it would be thick-o-fog in but two hours time.

He drew back sharply, as if I had put fire to his cheek and not a loving touch.

What is it? I laughed. There is no one to see. The children have been asleep these many hours.

Hannah, said he. Please sit. There is something we must speak of.

He was nervous, I saw, and my heart swelled. For in my foolishness I thought he meant to bring happy conclusion to our courtship.

And you shall sit beside me, I agreed.

If you wish, was his reply.

But once seated, he immediately jumped up. I must at the first beg your pardon, said he. What transpired between us that night weeks ago was my fault entirely. I have felt the shame of it since and can only plead fatigue and surprise, my morals left unguarded after the presentation of your lovely gift.

I felt confused; this was not the start I would have had him make.

I understand, I said. Foolish tongues will wag lest we make our plans now it is clear Isaac shall not return.

His face paled at this and it must have been then I first knew, for my heart began beating so.

There was no love in the look he sent me, but pity. I'm to marry Sally Young, Hannah. The Squire has just this evening given his consent, if a bit reluctantly.

I stared stupidly at his face, one I love still. Marry Sally Young? I thought. Marry Sally?

You cannot, I said simply.

Reclaiming his seat beside me, he took my cold hand in his.

Dear Hannah, he sighed, forgive me. A man, it is clear to me now, should accomplish a marriage early in life so as to avoid such temptations. Surely you see we can't go on like this and remain honorable?

I was speechless at this.

Being here with you these last months was in some ways a playing at marriage, he continued. Selfish of me, I know, but it was perhaps what I needed to prove myself suited to it. For that I thank you.

You're quite welcome, I'm sure, I said stiffly.

Hannah, he began.

You do not love her, I said, the heat rising to my face, for I knew in my heart this was true.

On the contrary, I'm quite fond of her. She is lovely and admirable in manner.

Well, I wish you joy of her, with all her pretty pouting and tossing of curls.

I rounded on him then, for to have all my hopes crushed by such a simpering fool as Sally Young could quite drive me mad. Surely she knew of this when I saw her at the store. How she blushed with all that talk of wedding dresses. Rich, is it not, that I should have felt pity for her?

Do you not remember the things you whispered to me that night? I hissed. What a lucky man Isaac was, you said, to have a wife so receptive to a man's touch. Do you think your Sally with her giggling, girlish ways will rise to you in the dark as I did, bury her face between...

Enough! he cried, jumping again from his seat.

O, I laughed. Enough is it, now you've had your pleasure of me?

Can you not imagine what it's like, said he as he paced at the hearth, kowtowing to these men day after day, considered one of them yet not? Forced by your relative stations in life to call them Sir and Mister when they refer to you by your Christian name as they would some servant? Indeed, had Sally not threatened to remove herself to Wiscasset for all time should her father not consent to our union, he would no doubt have denied me.

But I am soon to be free, I reminded him. We can leave here; and you will kowtow to no one.

Let me be plain, Hannah. Even were you free—and you are not—he said, holding up his hand to forestall my interruption, I could not marry you. Taking Sally as my wife elevates me where marrying you would not. I'm sorry to put it thus, but you would have the truth of it.

It is the money you want, then, her horses and fancy house. Not her.

She's not unpleasing to me. She's quite biddable and will be easily schooled.

And I am not, I say.

No, he laughed. You are not that.

I'll tell her all, I fairly spat, for I was desperate. 'Tis doubtful she'll have you then.

Consider carefully, Madam, said he coldly. It would hardly be in your interest to do so. You must realize you carry more fault in this than I, what with your constant attempts at seduction, the ways in which you attend me. It is quite remarked upon.

He straightened himself then, smoothed his coat. We'll speak no more of this. Sally and I will be married within the month, and that is an end to it. There's to be a gathering at the Youngs' Saturday evening in celebration, to which you will no doubt receive invitation. I would ask that you not attend if your feelings on the matter are not altered by that time.

He made then for his chamber, thinking to turn again as he reached the door. One further thing, he said. I'll thank you to cease making free in my chamber during my absence, handling my belongings. It's an indignity I'll no longer bear.

You're quite mistaken, I'm sure.

It will cease immediately. With that I shall say goodnight with hopes the morning will find you reconciled.

Reconciled? How little he knows of me. How can I be reconciled to the loss of the only man God has given me eyes for? And those words, the haughty tone. How they remind me of father. Perhaps Weston shall himself pen me a letter seeped in the puss of hatred and shame now he has found his fortune in Sally.

Still, all is not yet lost. This marriage is still some time off; much might happen in a few weeks' time. For as Weston himself has said, I am not so easily schooled.

TWENTY-FIVE

The old Young Store looms large in my imagination, of course; and as I step through the door for the first time, I'm half-expecting the 1829 version of the place—Hannah and Sally glaring at each other across the counter, cigar smoke wafting through the room as a distracted Squire conducts business at some long table overlooking the harbor. So it's a shock when the interior proves little more than an open shell complete with crumbling loft. Gone are the shelves of domestic goods, the sawdust-covered floor, the barrels of molasses and sugar and grains that dominated back in the day. Even Sally's counter, I'm sad to see, is no more. Instead, a scarred-up picnic table littered with Styrofoam cups sits shoved to the wall, a couple broken lobster traps beside it. I catch an oily whiff, trace it to a lawnmower parked in the corner by a couple gas cans, a scattering of oily rags. Communal storage, I figure.

The antsy blue-jeaned throng milling about in lieu of Squire Young, et al look to be the same bunch Cash summoned to his shop just after Clayton's body was found—minus Ivan, of course—with a half-dozen bleary-eyed sternmen, lured no doubt by the promise of beer, thrown in to pad the numbers.

Spying the cooler by the door, I snag a Rolling Rock, pop the top and make my way to where a large dockside window offers a drop-dead view of the harbor—the talk around me mostly of Ivan, Cheryl's emotional collapse. I nod to Al, seated with Josh at the picnic table; nod again at an amped-up Cash deep in conversation with *Hombre*. Such requisite social niceties dispensed with, I relax against the wall with my beer and try for invisible while we wait for the one-armed John to appear.

Just why Cash wants me here remains a mystery. I try sussing it out yet again, but my focus keeps slipping, stuck as I still am between centuries. Instead, I lapse into a kind of reverie—a merging of realities in which a flushed, determined Hannah storms in, impatiently picking her way among us to confront a gussied-up Sally with the not-so-honorable side of Weston Philbrick; and sending her, skirts a-flying, for the solace of her father's arms. It's an arresting image. Imagine, I think, Hannah taking her revenge right here in this very room, perhaps on this very spot—and for the briefest of moments I sense her energy, her calculated rage.

I'm pulled from this tasty little daydream by the throaty sound of an engine—the sight of *Jaws* steaming full-bore around Indian Ledge drawing everyone to the window. Last I saw this thing, the gorilla driving it had his paws deep in one of Cash's traps. I wonder briefly if John has brought him along for steroidal support, but he looks to have come alone—something which, for some reason, does little to cheer me.

"Why the fuck's he gotta do this now?" Cash complains to no one in particular. "Like we ain't got enough shit to deal with today."

"Didn't say," Josh shrugs. "Just that he got word 'bout Ivan and was comin' out. Wasn't exactly askin'."

"Nobody goes out to meet him, you got that? Man comes to us," Cash growls as the boat slows, stops, and John—big, wide and all muscle—deftly ties off to the wharf.

Nobody moves. I, myself, am quite rooted in place, gaze riveted to where the lower half of John's right arm would be if he still had one. No prosthesis, either; just that stump bumping along a couple inches below the sleeve of his green tee as he quickly one-hands it up the ladder. And if he knows we're watching, he doesn't let on. Not so much as a glance toward the building as he stomps toward us.

Heads turn as one as we track his movement along the side of the building 'til his bulk fills the doorway. Up close he looks like some blown-out, psychotic Opie: wild red hair peppered with gray, face full of freckles, steely blue eyes. I lock on the enormous red lobster plastered across the front of his tee, the words *Red's Eats*.

He takes his time sizing us up, those iron-hard eyes eventually settling on me.

"Who's this dub?" The voice is deep, gravelly; something wheezy going on in his chest when he talks.

"Lawyer," Cash snaps.

Lawyer? I glance to Al for clarification but he's clearly as bewildered as

I am.

"Ain't no law out here but us, boy," John snaps. "Besides, this here's a closed meetin'. No outsiders."

I agree. My presence is definitely not called for. What I should have done after Al headed back, I realize now, was get good and toasted, then curl up for an uncomfortable couple hours on Hannah's horsehair sofa. Or Rachel's—whatever. Frankly, I'm having trouble keeping it all straight— past and present; life and death. The stabbing of Tolman's sailor coming so close on the heels of Ivan's own demise, I feel trapped in a time warp of death and deceit. Coming face to face with a guy who would calmly chew his own foot off if it came to that isn't making things any easier.

I start to excuse myself, but Cash slaps a hand on my arm.

"Hodge stays."

They stare each other down for maybe ten seconds before John finally lets loose a gut-shaking guffaw. "Okay, then, *lawyer*—maybe you can tell me which one a these A-holes is gonna pay for my traps—ones they cut a few weeks back. About ten grand, I figure."

"Nobody here knows nothin' 'bout that," Cash shoots back, his eye starting to twitch now. "What we remember is that moron you set to poachin' from ours."

"Well, you ain't seen him back, now have you?"

"What is it you want here, John?" Josh asks quietly from his perch against the wall.

John swings his gaze, considers. "Heard some talk you boys thought it was me killed Clayton, which I didn't. Man slipped on the rocks is what I heard. And now, what with the boy dead, figured it was time to set things straight 'case you're thinkin I had somethin' to do with that, too. Which I also didn't."

"Seems you heard about it awful quick," *Hombre* suggests.

"I still got friends out here, 'case you forgot. I keep tabs. Seems to me if you're lookin' to lay blame, you best look to your own. The boy quit on this one yesterday," he says, chin-nodding toward Cash. "Anyone got a problem with the kid, it'd be him."

Cash lunges, but doesn't get a yard before Josh and *Hombre* latch onto him, drag him back. "You motherfuckin' piece of shit!" He spits.

Having made his point, John spreads his hands in a gesture of reconciliation. "Me, I'm just an old fisherman with a bad heart. All this stress ain't good for me. I'm thinkin' it'd be good all around if we call a kind of truce for now, 'til things settle. Then we'll see where we are. Maybe the lawyer here can come up with somethin'."

Cash is still glaring but Josh purses his lips, nods slowly. He's the only one in the bunch with any real sense, I've come to realize.

John heads toward the door, then turns, points to me. "You're alright. Only lawyer I ever seen could keep his yap shut longer than thirty seconds."

TWENTY-SIX

Dad died battling ALS, Amyotrophic Lateral Sclerosis, the disease that claimed Lou Gehrig—ironically enough one of the old man's favorite players. Like Gehrig, he was quiet and self-effacing; never talked about his illness, even to me. First I knew anything was wrong was when he stopped his treks from Long Island to the Bronx to cheer the Yankees to victory, claiming baseball had become more about egos and outrageous salaries than the sport itself. Depressed him, he said. It was mom who clued me in; physical stamina, she told me, was one of the first things to go. Three long years he suffered, though he didn't admit to what he called "discomfort" 'til maybe the last few months. And let me tell you, pain management a decade ago was nothing like today, what with all the new chemical cocktails and morphine pumps for self-propulsion into la-la land.

After nearly forty years together, those two were like some finely tuned machine—totally in synch; so when mom died of a massive coronary three months to the day after scattering his ashes over his favorite fly-fishing spot in Shinnecock Bay, it surprised no one. Certainly not me.

I stretch, sigh, take another pull on my Heineken. It's been a long fucking day. Between Tiffany turning up preggy and then our finding Ivan that way, I'd about had it by noon. And that was before Weston dumped Hannah and John showed up. Afterward, it was all I could do to drag the cooler and one of my new glow-in-the-dark loungers to the long flat rock where the dugout drops to the sea—the drama of a crashing surf the perfect foil for my churned-up frame of mind. I don't get in this kind of funk often, but when I do, I know to just sit back and pop a cold one, 'cause I'm about to whip myself with every stray problem I can drum up—my time-tested equation being conundrum times helplessness equals pissy mood.

I'll blame Al; he's convenient—all that back-and-forthing about the ball cards reminding me too much of Dad. Clayton or Ivan maybe, since they're not around to argue the point, damn them. Tiffany would work, too; or the all-too-delectable Ms. K. Then there's John's little surprise visit, which raised more questions than it answered—giving a stir to my own vague suspicions.

The possibility of modern-day foul play threatens overload; the past feels far more manageable just now. If Atticus didn't kill Tolman's sailor, I wonder, who the hell did? And this obsession Hannah has with Weston. Enough already. He's moved on, the miserable prick—believe me, I know the signs, having employed many of the same tactics myself. Well, hell with them. I won't read another word. Leave it to me to find some two-hundred-year-old bodice-ripper such compelling reading.

I toss my empty bottle into the sea, reach to the cooler for another and pry off the cap—continuing my mental rant.

Why do they still use pine coffins out here, anyway? Mahogany's better looking, if less easy to slam together. Then there's Cash. No way he'll find another sternman so late in the season. He's just dumb enough to try it alone out there, too—wind up as the island's next statistic. Next pine box.

I shift uncomfortably at this, slap at a mosquito, take an angry pull on my beer.

And Cheryl—man, she'd make a great grandmother; too bad she'll probably never get the chance. Speaking of which, is Tiffany avoiding me again just 'cause I know her little secret? What's more, why do I care? I counsel kids all the time; it's part of my job description. They're generally in the midst of some crisis or other—several have struggled with pregnancy—and I've never internalized any of it. I just give out the pertinent informa-tion, pat 'em on the back, and send 'em on their way. They know where my office is, right? If they need me, they'll find me. So why is this any different?

Let it go, I tell myself.

Who the hell buries a dress, anyway? Before heading to John's little party, I took the thing to the barn and fanned it out on the dirt floor. The stiff brown stains on the skirt gave me the willies, frankly—convinced as I suddenly was that it belonged to ghostie girl. Couldn't get out of there fast enough.

Pinging along like this, I bump headlong into the concept of work, supposedly the reason I'm out here, after all; but the idea holds little appeal. I have a sudden glimpse of this whole cataloguing mission as nothing more than self-indulgent hogwash. I mean who gives a rat's ass if some dusty academic produces yet another obscure botanical write-up of an island nobody's ever heard of? Sure, I could sex it up, tie the whole thing to some nonsense about the interdependence of all this biodiversity, play around with some metaphors to island life which just happens to be in rather rapid decline at the moment. In the end, though, who really gives a shit?

Must be a hole in this bottle, 'cause it's empty. I throw the cooler open, grab another. It's then I hear someone coming up behind. Good thing, too. I can't take much more of myself.

"Grab a lounger and join the party," I call, not even bothering to turn around.

"Most men call the next day, send flowers—something," Kirtley informs me, parking her tight little derriere on the rock beside me.

Should have known; she's the only one who could possibly make all this worse.

I raise my beer, note the uptick in my pulse. "Good opener."

Faded jean short-shorts, thong sandals—her minimal bikini top barely cupping those nut-brown nipples, leaving the beautiful perky rest of her to goad me.

A gentleman would give her a hug, a kiss—something to acknowledge the change in our interpersonal status—but instead I reach to the cooler, toss her a Heineken. Single-handed catch, too, wouldn't you know.

Prying the cap off, she slides out of the sandals and cranks back on her elbows, downing half the beer in a go. A woman of large appetites, as I well know.

I pull my thoughts back, point with my bottle to the ledge below us. "Wild orchid," I say. "In the rocks there. Green Wood variety—Habenaria clavellata." I belch. "Twenty-two varieties out here, according to a guy I know." Knew. "So far I've found nineteen."

She nods. "Thought you were into trees." She draws again on the beer, then tilts her face toward the sun, extending those amazing legs in a long, lazy stretch. Legs that can wrap around a guy like...

"Vanilla bean comes from an orchid," I blurt, cutting off the thought. "You know, the stuff they make vanilla extract from? Cakes and cookies, like that?" Rambling like some pimply-faced teen, determined to keep my eyes from the way she uses her bottle to cool the creamy valley between those breasts. I could tell her that the term *orchid* itself derives from the Greek for testicle; she'd have a field day with that one, for sure, but it would sort of defeat my purpose.

Instead, I fix on the gold of her anklet twinkling in the sun, the little charm resting against the delicate round bone on the side of the foot. Tibia? Talus? I used to know.

"What *is* that thing, anyway?" I ask, pointing with my bottle.

She glances down, wiggles the foot. "Miniature of *Bounder*, believe it or not. Allan made a point of labeling things that belonged to him. *This is mine.*"

"Somehow I can't imagine you belonging to anyone."

She shrugs. "I let him think what he liked." She laughs at my look of surprise. "Come on, Gil, you're a sophisticated guy; you know how these things work." She shakes her head, throws back the rest of her beer. "We both got what we wanted."

Some women fake orgasms; others fake whole relationships. A quote I once read—interview in Rolling Stone with some actress, I think. I considered it pretty pithy at the time. Now it just seems sad.

I take a swig of my own to cover my reaction. Once again I'm feeling pulled into something I didn't ask for, this bit of depressing news further complicating my already sucky day. I cast about for a change of subject.

"How's Tiffany holding up?" I ask.

Kirtley shrugs, glances off over the water. "Still on the fence about this pregnancy thing. She puts the decision off much longer, there won't be one to make."

I eye her over my Ray-Bans. "I meant Ivan—the kid who died today?"

"Come on. He was a controlling little prick; she couldn't stand him most of the time."

"Not so sure about that," I hedge, though it's a relief to be back in familiar, if vaguely disturbing territory.

"Liar," she says, smiling around a sip. "It was all about fucking, learning the dance. You remember fucking, don't you, Gil?"

Amazing—this quick-change to sexual vamp, I mean, and the effect on me is electric. Suddenly I'm acutely aware of the lap of water against rock, the slippery ropes of seaweed undulating in the current beneath us.

"Besides," she says, "what would you know about it? This is *chick stuff*, as you men like to say."

Obviously. Still, I can't help wonder at all this female bonding. Why would a woman of Kirtley's obvious savoir-vivre bother with a kid as rough around the edges as Tiffany? A teenage pregnancy of her own, perhaps? And what about me? Has Tiffany somehow become every child/woman I've ever wronged? Some pathetic attempt to put it all right?

Lying back, Kirtley slips off her non-top. "Mind if I sunbathe?"

"Please," I say, strangely miffed. I want her to leave and I want her to stay. Boy, do I want her to stay. The Old Gil concurs, which makes it at least two against one, considering Mr. Johnson is weighing in now, too.

The shorts are next. No panties, no bikini bottom. Nothing.

"A nice guy would shed his inhibitions and join me," she says, giving that body a long languid stretch.

Before I can respond, she snakes a silky leg onto my lap, begins a rhythmic massage of my crotch with her heel—all the while gazing demurely out to sea.

I should stop her, I know. Instead, I decide to ignore her. Stupid plan. I can run but I can't hide, if you get my meaning. She's right about those toes, by the way; less than thirty seconds later they've got my shorts unbuttoned and are making a first run at my zipper.

I try concentrating, mentally flipping through the '55 Dodgers' pitching staff in alphabetical order—Don Bessent, Joe Black, Roger Craig, Carl Erskine, Jim Hughes, Sandy Koufax, Clem Labine, Tommy LaSorda.

Oh, Jesus.

Billy Loes, Russ Meyer, Johnny Podres, Don Newcombe, Billy Loes.

It's no use; she's got me and she knows it. Snagged again on the rusty hooks of passion and danger.

Suddenly, I'm beyond pissed—at Kirtley for being so right on; at myself for not having the self-control to walk away from her. The triumph in her eyes is the final straw. I'm so fucking frustrated by all that's gone on today, I could explode with the need to tear into something. Might as well be her.

I'm on her, then—so hot for it suddenly my hands are shaking as they find her. She's wet already; no foreplay for this chick but the charge that comes from stripping me of my willpower. I know you, her look says. You're just like me.

What happened on *Bounder* was kiddy stuff compared to this. I swore off angry sex when I walked away from Annika, but I apparently didn't learn anything, 'cause here I go again. It comes back fast, too, like riding a bike. Absolutely nothing sentimental about it. No romance in the way we wrestle to the ground and grope for purchase—not so much kissing as chewing. Anyone could come along and see us, of course, which only increases my urgency.

Eventually we make our way into the same crevasse of rock where I spied the orchid, Kirtley's naked back smashing it against a jagged edge, drawing blood. This brings a half-lidded smile, a moan of pleasure.

Another minute and she pulls back—eyes flashing, breathless. "Hurt me," she demands.

Hurt me? Even at her nuttiest, Annika never asked for outright abuse. Not during sex, anyway.

She slaps me when I don't respond, startling me. Grinning, she hits me again—harder.

"Hurt me," she repeats, as if it's the most reasonable thing in the world.

"It gets me off."

I shake my head, wrestling one of her legs over my shoulder, grinding into her harder, deeper. Feels fucking great to me, but it's apparently not what she has in mind.

"No, you asshole!" she howls in frustration. "Hurt me!" Then with a guttural growl, she bites down on my tongue so hard I'm sure she's bitten it off.

I scream, though most of the sound's lost in my throat since our mouths are still locked in combat. I immediately go limp which makes it considerably easier to withdraw. The little guy back in his shell, never to be seen again. And who can blame him?

"Hesus hucking Heist," I manage—doubled over, fingers oh-so-gently probing my mouth. Strings of blood drool from my chin, but the muscle's still intact, thank God. I've managed to bullshit my way out of a lot of things over the years, but even I couldn't explain a severed tongue.

"Enuh," I say thickly, backing away. "Hiss is issane."

"Where do you think you're going?" she laughs as I grab for my shorts, inexplicably drifting atop a creeping juniper, and stumble into them.

"Come on, I'm sorry," she giggles as I turn, starting up the path toward Rachel's. "Come back and play, okay?"

Ice, I think, flipping her off as I continue toward the house. Sucking on some cubes might bring the swelling down, staunch the bleeding.

That or the pain will kill me.

TWENTY-SEVEN

Turns out my instinct to avoid Ben Leland's memorial service a few years back was a good one. Burying a kid is the absolute worst. Pure unremitting agony in the faces around me—Cheryl's so swollen and contorted she's all but unrecognizable, Tiffany's pale and stony as the two stand arm in arm during Ivan's brief service. Cash stands slightly behind them, as does Kirtley—demur in the same black skirt and silky top she wore to Clayton's burial. Everyone grim and stunned as this poor kid is prayed over. Sixteen fucking years old.

Seems Ivan was more Burgess than Ames—genealogically speaking, that is. Related to Clayton, ditto Big Bad John. But while Clayton and Ivan both descend from Isaac's youngest boy, Seth, John comes down from the surly adolescent Lavon. What a surprise. All this according to Gail, which explains why we're standing in the misty rain watching Ivan's pine box being lowered into the dirt four spots down from Clayton and a mere three rows behind the lichen-covered gravestones of Hannah's various stepsons. As if all this weren't disorienting enough.

Services out here are blessedly short, and once the crowd begins peeling off, Cheryl sobbing against Cash's chest, Tiffany's left to stare blankly at the mound of dirt under which Ivan now lays. Impossible to read her expression, mostly because she refuses to meet my eyes—embarrassed as she no doubt is at having confided in me now that things have grown somewhat more complicated. It's then that Kirtley moves in—this other Keeper of the Secret—sliding an arm around Tiffany in comfort, the kid's head falling to her shoulder as they begin the slow walk back to the harbor.

Girlfriendship is a magical thing, I've observed. Nothing remotely like it in the male kingdom—not in my corner of it, anyway. Sure, I've got any number of pals—guys I can call up when I want to beat somebody's ass at squash or feel the itch, under the guise of wanting to grab a beer, to ogle the latest influx of coeds strutting their stuff in town. But this kind of soul-baring? Definitely not on the program.

This bothers me for some reason. Annoys the shit out of me, actually—the sight of Kirtley setting my tongue throbbing anew and pissing me off all over again. Not to mention I've been off alcohol since my recent bloodletting—stings too much—so I'm irritable as hell, anyway.

"Heart attack's a heart attack, right?" This from Al, who's appeared beside me.

"Pretty hard to fake," I agree. "You're thinking Uncle Clunk? That guy who died when I first got here?" I have to say the thought's started skulking along the back of my mind, as well—John's visit having stirred things up for me, started me thinking about all this in a new way. I mean two unexpected deaths in less than a month is weird enough, but three? Pretty much a statistical impossibility in a population this small.

"Never felt right—that whole thing," he says, looking over the crowd. "Guy wasn't that old, no history of heart problems. Had some cholesterol thing, but who doesn't?"

"Would give all this a new spin, certainly."

"Heart stopped—seemed pretty straightforward." He shrugs. "Gail maybe got it wrong." He nails me with his eyes. "And don't you never tell her I said that."

I gaze off. "No autopsy, right? He could have been strangled, then—smothered, maybe."

Al nods. "Tough to do when you only got one arm."

"But not impossible."

"True."

"He could have sent someone else," I suggest.

"Not John. He's a hands-on kind of guy."

We consider the muddy, churned-up earth. "Why bother to come out here at all the other day?" I ask. "He could have accomplished the same thing with a couple phone calls—deny the murders, offer a truce."

"No idea. Don't trust him for shit, though."

"What about the others? They think he did it?"

"Some of 'em are leanin' that way. Pickin' us off one by one, like he promised. All that talk about a truce meant to throw us off. Couple others think it could be Cash, specially since Ivan quit on him the day before. No one's mentioned Clunk, at all; we're the only ones seem to think he might be part of this."

"But we agree none of it was accidental."

He shoots me a look. "Clayton slips on rocks he's been crawlin' around all his life, and Ivan's chest gets crushed by a truck that chooses just that second to fall? Don't hardly think so.

And then there's Clunk, all alone in his backyard. God only knows what happened to him.

"Thing is, John's pretty specific when it comes to retribution. Lest the point get lost, you know? Clayton I can maybe see, what with all this fishin' nonsense. Wouldn't matter he's family—not to John. Ivan, even, if he's lookin' to get at Cash, which he just might. But Clunk? He didn't move out here 'til after John left. Far as I know, they never even met."

Huh. "Different killers, then?"

"That, or some other guy on a fuckin' rampage."

"Any ideas?"

Al shrugs. "There's people had problems with each of 'em, except for maybe Clunk. Grudges last for generations around here; these are patient people." He squints, scratches the back of his head. "Should probably tell you a couple of the boys are looking at you pretty hard, too."

Our eyes meet. "You aren't serious."

He glances off. "Can't see it, myself; but some of them out here ain't got two brain cells left to rub together—you know that. New guy's an easy target." He shrugs. "Thought I should mention it."

I'm too stunned to respond.

"Okay, then," he says.

"Right," I nod.

"Talk to yuh."

I remain rooted in place long after everyone else has drifted off—head down as I try and get my mind around all this. The rain's more insistent now, my jeans and sneaks wet through, though I hardly notice. They can't seriously think it's me, I tell myself; I'm just some fucking tree guy whose biggest, perhaps only claim to fame is a passing resemblance to an aging movie star fewer people remember every day.

Only way to convince them they're wrong, I reluctantly realize, is to point them in another, more fruitful direction. I run through our list of possible killers, taking Clunk out of the equation for a minute. There's John, of course—revenge being the powerful motivator that it is. Then again, at least half the island had it in for Clayton, including Cash. And what about Ivan? Cash finally lose his hair trigger over the kid's sucky work ethic? One of his drug connections get pissed and decide to make a point? Maybe Gail found out Tiffany was pregnant and simply offed the kid on principle. Tiffany herself? No. Definitely not.

I must be pacing, 'cause when I look up again, I'm standing before the still-raw mound of earth marking Clayton's grave. Dead guy number one. Or two—depending.

"What really happened to you, man?" I mutter. But these deceased twentieth-century Burgesses—their plots dotted with a smattering of American flags and war memorials, bouquets of dirty plastic flowers—prove as reluctant to offer up answers as their living counterparts.

I'm muddling through all this, wandering forward a few rows 'til I find myself smack in the pages of that damn diary. Slate headstones, many split with age. Lavon is here, just as Gail promised, buried with wife Phoebe—three sad, tiny headstones planted before them. Buried beside him is little brother Seth—entombed with three consecutive wives from the look of it, lucky bastard. Patience, Isaac's first wife, lies with her stillborn baby according to her epitaph. I can't find any of the girls, but they could easily be buried with their husbands' families. No graves for Isaac or Hannah either, adding yet another mystery to the growing pile.

It's when I look back that I spot it—a small headstone overgrown by one of the lush French lilacs that abound here. The sight stops me, not sure why except it appears more ornate than others dating from the same period. I crouch and peer at it, despite the fact the rain has become a steady downpour. Slate headstone, very old, lovingly adorned with cherubs and ornate curlicues—embellishments that seem oddly out of place here. I lean in, wet fingers gently tracing the inscription through the lichen—the letters still remarkably clear, protected from the wind and salt air by the teeming lilac hovering over it.

A lilac which has grown suddenly fragrant.

Impossible, I tell myself. The smell's nothing more than a mental feint, the same knee-jerk reaction that makes you feel heat when you stand by a cold stove. Nonetheless, the blood begins to pound as I read, my damn tongue starting up again.

Mary
Dau. Isaac and Patience Burgess
August 22, 1829
ae 3 yrs, 4 mos
Sweet Angel Gone to God

TWENTY-EIGHT

It doesn't come together for me 'til I reach the house. First thing I notice is the front door flung wide, hinges screaking eerily as it plays back and forth in the wind. My immediate concern is just who might be waiting for me inside, but then I notice the shells, or rather the lack of them, as they seem to have disappeared from the road. This, at least, is good news—or so I think until I step tentatively into the rain-soaked front hall to find that sometime during the hour and a half I've been gone, the mounds have simply reformed themselves rather messily just inside the parlor door. The now sodden, fishy smelling parlor. I try to convince myself someone did this—some living, breathing, really pissed off person, that is—but I don't for a second believe it.

A glance to the wet shell and leaf-strewn settee tells me it's probably ruined. Rachel is going to kill me.

Furious, still a-drip, I glare toward the second floor. "Enough!" I yell. "What the hell do you want from me?"

Nothing. Not a snigger or a sigh or a whimper. No patter of little feet. Just the sound of the rain and wind, the knocking of the door against the wall behind me.

Something tugs at me then—something I've read somewhere about lobster shells in the parlor. But where? Then I remember. The diary. Just after Hannah stumbled on Weston and Sally wooing and cooing in the woods, she roared back in here and started smashing up the china. Terrifying Mary, who dropped her bucket of lobster shells and ran. The shells spilling across the parlor floor.

Lobster shells on the parlor floor.

Holy shit. Sometimes my stupidity amazes even me. Turning my gaze to the stairwell, I reach behind me for the door, snick it quietly shut.

"Little ghostie girl?" Then tentatively, almost feebly. "Mary?"

A few floorboards creak deep in the shadows above me.

It's gotta be her; too many things fit. According to her headstone, she died in August, 1829; same year—hell, same month of the current entries in the diary. A diary originally left out for me. I get that she wants me to read the thing, I do; I just don't get why.

Still, instinct tells me I'm onto something, and I make a beeline for the keeping room where the diary's lain untouched since the day Al dropped by. I know, I know; I swore off reading anymore of the damn thing, but I can't help myself—wild as I am to find out just what happened to this child.

Shedding my gear, I settle at the table and greedily grab it up, forcing myself through a couple entries full of domestic minutiae—hoeing, chopping, milking, weeding—all of it peppered with a litany of complaints. How the whir of the flax wheel gives her a headache; how Lavon has for all intents and purposes moved out, returning only long enough to make off with half a barrel of freshly brewed beer. Not a single mention of Weston or his upcoming wedding to Sally—odd, considering he's been at the epicenter of all Hannah's obsessive pourings-forth. Nothing more about Atticus or the unsolved murder, either—also weird. Plus, the writing here seems disjointed and flat, as if she's just going through the motions. Where's the fire, the sass?

I have the sudden image of Hannah, sitting angry and isolated in this very room—at this very table, perhaps; it's certainly old enough—filling page after page with this drivel. Is Mary playing at her feet? I wonder, glancing down. The girls out milking cows and beating rugs in the dooryard? Finally I spot it, the first mention of Mary taking sick. It begins the entry dated two days prior to her death.

Matinicus, Thursday 20 August

A chilling mist has been upon us for days, the firewood being too wet to light.

Mary continues unwell. She took but a little gruel this morning, a bit of cracker in the afternoon. There are chores to be done, but the twins have yet to make themselves busy, dawdling about the upper chamber as they've been, keeping anxious watch over their sister.

If my troubles were not great enough, I found the negro crouched in Mary's chamber earlier, making free to examine her feet and hands. I care not that they have become great friends; I shan't have him slipping unseen about the place, this man with his prying ways. My demand that he leave off and quit my house at the instant earned me nothing but one of his hard looks until I took up the broom and beat him into retreat. And bringing her food not an hour later, I found a crude doll fashioned from a bit of cloth and cornhusk tucked between her sheets. Left by the black I'm sure, as it was not there earlier in the day.

Mistress Wivell stopped in the afternoon, the gout in her feet making the climb to the upper chamber arduous. Her tone with me was for once gentle, approving of the care I give the girl, though even a child knows to apply burdock steeped in vinegar for headache. Mary had a violent fit of cramps and vomiting while she was here as well, which altered the woman's thinking as to my concerns. For she had at first dismissed my alarm, something she clearly now repents.

The tongue swells, she nodded. Did you notice?

I did, I told her.

And there seems some paralysis on the left side. It began with headache some weeks ago, you said?

Indeed, said I.

It grieves me I did not come sooner, Hannah. It truly grieves me. The symptoms confused me, you see. Confuse me still, truth be told. I'll return on the morrow to see how she fares.

I smiled my forgiveness, a generosity, I think, considering she has never once ventured to make me friend.

Others have been stopping, too, now we know it is not the pock. It is only their arrival that stirs the twins from their vigil, for I send them to do what conversing is necessary, accepting gifts of food in my stead.

Lavon spares us some little time as well, now Mary has worsened; and Weston himself sat with her this evening upon returning from the Squire's, Sally's scent lingering unpleasantly about him. Later, upon descending from her chamber, he joined me before the hearth, something he has not done since the night we argued so bitterly.

Are you well, Hannah? asked he with much of his former gentleness. Is there anything you require?

I shook my head, gestured toward the open door through which the Squire's man could be seen chopping wood despite the rain, and a woman not of my acquaintance pulled milk cans about. As you can see, I said, I already have much help.

Your concern for Mary is greatly remarked upon, he told me. Your care of her, so loving and constant, without reproach. You could not do more for her were you truly her mother.

I nodded.

Mistress Wivell has herself said there is nothing more that even she might have done, he told me. Then, his face a mask of sadness, he placed a hand on mine. It is best we prepare the other children, Hannah. I will stand with you in this.

Thank you, I said, smiling meekly to my lap.

It was a start.

Matinicus, Sunday 23 August

Mary departed this life yesterday eve. We had the burying this morn.

Odd that the death of a mere child should so alter my lot here. Immediately upon her passing, the house was filled with women who made busy washing the body and putting on the grave clothes, the twins having chosen a favorite frock and cap. All of them kindly overlooking my having let the house go in caring for she who was slipping away, fluttering about me quite as if I were Sally Young and they my handmaids.

Likewise, at the burying ground they gathered 'round me in comfort, even to Lydia and Sarah, their babes in arms despite the continuing rain. Women are as one at such times, my mother once told me. Petty grudges put aside. Where life divides, death unites.

Much was made of my stoicism. The tears will come later, they assured me with pats for my arm. It is good you are strong for the others just now. With this their eyes found Seth clinging fast to the leg of Lydia's glowering husband; the twins, weepy and red-eyed as they hung on Sarah's skirts.

They have lost much since winter, these women whispered. Mother and brother. Baby sister. They said naught of Isaac, of course, no doubt convinced any mention of him or his ship might topple me to my grave as well. Yet with my arm tucked in Weston's, his absence from Sally's side clearly leaving her in pique, I felt quite better than I have in weeks. I would have smiled for sheer joy but for the impression it would have given.

As 'tis, I flaunt convention with my refusal to wear the black of full mourning. 'Tis not fair—the child was not mine, after all. Six months it is expected of me before I'm allowed the muted colors of half-mourning, and then those for yet another half year. Why should Sally attend the burial in summer colors and ribboned cap while I appear the dowager? Thus it was I chose the indigo. In private I shall continue to dress as I think fit, as well. No doubt they'll think it distraction on my part; too stunned by grief to know what I do.

The pastor spoke of God's grace easing pain with time, though I have never found it so. Time is rather like the sting of salt on a wound, affording sharper insight as to how the pain was inflicted and why. Instructive, perhaps, but hardly easing of the injury itself.

Throughout, the negro watched from beneath the rock maple where his fellow sailors now lay, Lavon silent at his side, braced against the massive trunk. The two of them watching me as, one by one, the men came to express condolence.

Mr. Ames was the first, approaching shyly, hat in hand.

T'will be hard on ye until Isaac's return, he said with reddened face, though his eyes did not collude with mine in this lie of happy reunion. I'll be by to help as best I can; ye can be sure if it.

I had hardly thanked him when the Squire pushed forward and took my hands in his.

Hannah, said he. Have no care about the store account. We'll accept no payment of any kind for the present. And Sally will, I'm sure, grant you full use of Weston's company as long as you have need of him.

Polite laughter as he turned to seek out Sally's face, which appeared quite ashen. Is that not right, my dear? he asked.

Of course, Papa, she allowed, though the gaze that met mine was hot and angry.

It is now quite late, and still the girls cry in their chamber above. Refusing comfort from me as they have from the first, even now taking solace only in each other, the burying of damp cheek in shuddering shoulder.

It appears Weston shall be the only one to sleep hard this night, his snoring heavy through the mutual wall of our chambers. I shall lay my head at the place beyond which I know his to be, conjuring ways to postpone this wedding yet further.

TWENTY-NINE

I gotta be missing something here, I think as I heave shells to the yard. If Mary died of some virus, say—an all too common occurrence back then—why all this lingering about? The ringing of phones, the pattering of little feet? Why isn't she Resting in Peace, so to speak, like any well-behaved, dead three-year-old would do?

I mop the floor, towel off the settee best I can, then close and lock the door to that damn corner cupboard yet again. This time I pocket the key rather than leave it in the lock. Let my restless little friend figure a way around that one.

Still I linger—uneasy, churned up. Going back to the dugout isn't an option tonight, and it's not just the weather or the fact a couple of the guys might be lurking about waiting to grill me about more current events. I'm simply loathe to leave Mary just now—weird as I know that sounds. Not that she needs me, understand; she's been banging around here quite capably for a couple hundred years now.

Still.

I decide on a fire in hopes it'll dry the place out a little, suck some of the moisture out of that cement-like sofa. Then I opt for a hot tub, throw in a long squirt of something called Sweet Almond Bath Oil, soaking 'til the tension starts to recede. Toweling myself, I grab the Laphroaig and head for the hearth. My sleeping bag's back at the dugout, of course—no doubt working on a new crop of mold spores—so I spread my towel before the fire and take my first tentative sip of single malt post tongue-chomping. Still a little tender, but I can live with it.

The liquor hits me immediately, not surprising considering I haven't eaten since morning. I crank back on my elbows, happy to settle for my peat-infused concoction of barley, water, and yeast. Sounds like food to me.

I don't want to think about John or whoever skulking about the island killing people, so I don't. I likewise veer from the uneasy feeling of being under suspicion myself. Instead, I lay back and consider my bottle—that little HRH Prince of Wales coat of arms on the label. Like Chuck, my favorite is the mildly smoky Fifteen-Year-Old, forever distilled on the southernmost island of the Inner Hebrides—a place not unlike Matinicus itself. Gruff, independent people; rugged, uncompromising landscape. The kind of place you might inadvertently unearth an old, bloody dress.

It's my last cogent thought before I begin to drift, lulled by the liquor and the warmth of the fire. Next thing I know, I'm jolted from sleep—some dream about Mary loosing her shells across the parlor floor, Hannah smashing china she keeps pulling from the cupboard. That missing letter, the one from Hannah's father that's been eating at me? I know where it is. The damn thing's been staring me in the face all along, Mary all but jumping up and down trying to show me the way.

Bolting upright, I stumble to the parlor while above me little feet thunder back and forth in frenzied anticipation. I glance uneasily toward the ceiling as I fumble with the key, then turn my attention to the cupboard door when the lock proves stubborn. Nothing but china and knickknacks visible through the glass—probably why I never bothered to search the thing before. And sure enough, once I get it open, I find another shelf recessed a couple inches below the level of the door.

Feeling my way along it, I pull out a handful of receipts, a teacup missing its handle, an old brittle newspaper. Beneath all this is a flat, five-by-seven manila envelope, clasp tightly shut, my fingers tracing the unmistakable outline of the folded four-by-four square within.

Returning to the keeping room with my prize, I take my seat at the table and pull the fragile folded letter from its modern-day manila sheath—heart pounding as I stare at the words before me, the address written in a faded, flowing script on the front of the square:

Mrs. Hannah Burgess
Matinicus

Unfolding it carefully, I lay it on the table and begin.

20 June, 1829

My dear Hannah,

I open with wishes for your good health and that of your young family, as well our prayers for your husband's safe return from the summer's fishing. No doubt you've heard that Joshua and Matthew signed on to the same vessel at the last moment, but then your brothers have from the start insisted they would have nothing of the farming life. God grant them all safe return.

Harvest promises fair this season; your garden and that of your mother full of beans and peas, and the squash coming nicely. Of the five cows that calved this spring, four still live, our only loss since you left being Betsy, the mare who pulled our sleigh over the ice the year the bay froze solid, do you remember? Taking us from Pulpit Harbor across to Fletcher's Beach where you children played much of the day. That was a time.

Hannah, dear, I deeply regret the angry words at our parting. Your mother and I both hope the passage of some time has cooled your anger. It was never our plan to be rid of you, as you claimed, but to protect you from almost certain violence and to put the incident at the creek behind us. We kept you with us as long as we dared, never once holding with the others that you were in any way responsible for poor Martha's death. Whatever happened that day, a young girl drowned, good neighbors lost a cherished daughter, and the town a fine young woman of much promise. You grieve as deeply as anyone, we are sure.

No doubt the matter of the Calderwood's goat unduly biased thought against you here. The theft of the man's arsenic was hard enough to obfuscate, our care to keep suspicion from you perhaps giving the impression of a willingness to collude with you in such pranks. Still, I shall always believe it was this episode that predisposed others to think you capable of far crueler things.

While in no way admitting any guilt on your part, we've offered what small solace we are able to Martha's family. Your mother leaves produce from your garden and what small gifts we can manage at their door almost daily, one she remains convinced will someday open to her again in friendship. I, myself, am less hopeful, though Martha's father did agree once you'd left Vinalhaven to take the matter no further. In this regard, your mother wishes me to relay that she burned the hair ribbon found in your apron pocket that terrible day; no more shall be said of it.

It is not my wish to paint a dismal picture of our situation here. On the contrary, your little brothers and sister are happy enough on the farm, and I do well enough on my own, as you know. It is your mother who suffers most for the lack of society, yet she complains not at all, convinced as she is you will find the happiness on Matinicus that long escaped you here. Isaac is a good man, a friend of some many years, and it shames me I never shared with him the specifics of the incident at the creek, though I'm certain some word of it must have reached him.

Hannah dear, I think it best you not visit for a while, allow the general feeling here to cool. And, please, no more letters to your mother, as your pleading and accusations toward me vex her so.

You must, for your own sake, learn to throw off the resentments that have o'ershadowed you for so much of your life. This constant belief that all are against you, so inexplicable to those who love you, serves no good. We can but hope the keeping of a home and family will right your mind.

I close with hopes of your continuing good health and the growth of happy spirits, and remain your loving father,

Hiram Carver

I sit for the better part of a minute, stunned into absolute stillness by the thing on the table before me. This can't be the letter Hannah referred to in the diary; where's the despicable, unfeeling monster who forced her into the arms of a guy twice her age? The cold, vengeful father she hated to her very core?

My eyes go to the ceiling where the silence has grown positively thunderous—as if the kid's exhausted herself with all this jumping up and down to get my attention. Well, she's got it now. There's nothing for it. I have to know how this thing ends. There'll be no sleep for me 'til I do.

THIRTY

Matinicus, Monday 24 August

 We've argued yet again, Weston and I, as he stubbornly refuses to postpone this wedding, despite the great need I have of him now that both Lavon and the black have left me. It is Sally who presses him, I know, fearful as she is to have him near me.

 Be reasonable, Hannah, Weston said. There is little I can do for you, and certainly nothing that necessitates the putting off of my marriage.

 It's your company I require, I told him. Sally shall have you to herself soon enough.

 But he turned away with a scowl; he loses patience more quickly now, I find.

 Listen to us, I laughed. We quarrel as would an old married couple.

 But he did not respond, being not of a mind to take my wit, so I tried a different tack.

 'Tis far too big a house for one, I pleaded. I quite rattle about in it, no longer having even the children to care for. Now that the burying is over, it seems all have quite deserted me. The twins gone to Sarah, spirited away by Lavon without so much as a word. And Seth to Cousin Burgess and his wife, though they have five of their own to raise.

 And whose fault is that? Weston protested. 'Tis true you were kind enough to Mary during her illness, but otherwise you've offered these children little by way of motherly feeling or consolation; indeed, you seem to have no natural sense of it. Is it any wonder they seek it elsewhere?

And what of me? I cried. Who consoles me? My daughter dead, my husband lost at sea.

A husband you love not, he snapped, as you never cease to remind me.

It is the black, I fumed. Your good friend Atticus has turned you against me, and for no reason but to keep suspicion from himself.

Suspicion of what? Weston laughed.

'Tis certain he killed Tolman's sailor, I said, as he did the others. I feel it to my bones. No one else had reason for such a thing. But he's far too sly and practiced at deception to leave any mark of his guilt.

The Squire was with him at the time, Hannah. If that is not proof enough of innocence, then all here might be under suspicion. Even you, for did I not come upon you in the woods the very day the sailor was stabbed? And was there not blood on your hands?

The gutting of the lamb, if you remember, I said.

My point is that even the most innocent of behavior can be taken wrong by those with reason to do so. It distresses me you can find no kindly feeling for the man, considering his plight and all he did for you and the children while living here. You blame him for all manner of things, a fact which might, as you point out, indicate some covering of your own trespass.

I glared, speechless at being so treated in my own home.

He stood, then, made a mockery of a bow.

I think it best I make other arrangements for my board until Sally and I are wed, he announced. You'll agree 'tis quite impossible to continue in this manner. I shall be gone within the week, troubling you no further.

If you wish, I said coldly.

Even Weston would desert me now, it seems. He knows not what he does.

Matinicus, Thursday 27 August

Weston has himself fallen ill. We fear it's the very sickness that took our Mary, his symptoms being much the same. Violent cramps about the stomach, vomiting, and the loose stools that plagued her to the end.

Mistress Wivell has been to cluck over him, though her ministrations offer no more relief than do my own. Indeed, for quite two days I've nursed him as would a loving wife, his gaze in this weak and palsied state entreating such gentle care as only she who truly loves him might give.

Your Sally would hardly do for you so, I said with a kiss for his brow. Tears coursed his cheeks as my hand found him beneath the blanket, rousing him to desire and quick release.

There my darling, I breathed at his ear. Is that not better? I kissed his mouth sweetly though he closed his eyes and turned his head from me, shy as he is in such things.

'Tis not too late even now for him to accept the truth, that we are wed in the eyes of God. For it is the Lord who has intervened, revisiting on Weston the pain he has brought me that he might see his error. And repent he shall, or God may take him and be welcome.

It was hardly a surprise when Sally herself knocked at my door this noon, beribboned and parasolled against the sun. It was her first visit since my taking up residence here. And while her manner toward me has ever been one of condescension, I greeted her pleasantly, inviting her to take tea in the parlor as if colluding in some fiction that it was me she was calling upon. Never has refreshment been so prettily refused.

Seating herself, removing gloves better suited to the parlors of Wiscasset than the dusty roads of this miserable place, she chatted first about the weather, and once finished with that exhaustive subject spoke of her upcoming wedding and honeymoon, a trip to be made by steamship to enjoy the cultural diversions of Boston. A gift from her father, as are all things.

You will of course postpone, I said. Should Weston recover as we all hope, he'll be ill for some time.

Sally blanched at this. Surely not, she whispered.

Indeed, he is weak as a babe, unable to do even so much as bathe without assistance.

She was plainly furious at the intimacy this implied, but was too much the lady to express it.

You'll excuse me now, I said, for I must rest when I'm able. Weston's care has consumed much of my effort these last days.

I wish to see him, Hannah, she announced, rising. As I'm sure he wishes to see me.

That can hardly be the case, I said, as he is sleeping. With this, I made toward the door to show her out.

I'll look in upon him, then, if you'll direct me.

I think not, for your own sake. Mistress Wivell has not ruled out contagion. The very house may itself be unclean. Thus it is I've sent the children away.

Though you, yourself, do not appear ill, she said, looking about her with uncertainty.

It is thought I might be immune, I told her, caring for Mary as I did. You forget, as well, that Weston and I have lived together under this roof for some months now.

I glance to my hands, twist my wedding band. Quite, I said, raising my eyes once more to hers, as man and wife.

Small patches of red rose to her cheeks at this.

You lie, she hissed, proceeding then to pronounce me all manner of evil things which I'll omit mention of here; but when I shut the door upon her, she was quite sobbing in the yard.

T'was the first thing to bring a smile to my face in days.

Matinicus, Friday 28 August

That black devil plagues me still, the stupid meddling brute, daring to enter here and wrest Weston from my care! I who am wife to him in all but name. The man risks much who angers me so.

I was newly in from the milking, the cows caring not that I have been abandoned here without help or aid, pulling the cans to the buttery when I heard a low murmuring from Weston's chamber. I went at once, thinking him to have wakened, and instead found the negro, shirtless and intent in whispers over our love bed.

What do you here? I demanded. Leave this house at once!

He ignored my words, as always, my pounding about his naked shoulders nothing to him as he spooned some vile concoction from an ancient urn to my slumbering Weston's lips, much of it wasted down his chin.

Do you not see he sleeps? I hissed. Leave off at once! It is I who have the care of him, not some filthy slave with no knowledge of such things.

Plantain, horehound, and golden rod root boiled down, he said, his gaze fixed on Weston's face as he continued the useless spooning. Rum and lye added in.

Whatever for? I demanded.

Against the poison, he said, corking the urn and wiping Weston's lips with the back of his hand. Mistress Wivell, she mean well, but I spec she don't know poisons.

With this he spared me a look that might wither stone.

I suspicioned it with the little miss, he said, not bothering to hide his disdain, knowing it was you hurt her arm.

You know no such thing, I spat. It was Seth, as I have all along said.

I be too late with her, but not mister Weston, he grunted, cradling him and standing, Weston useless as a rag doll in his arms. Not if ole Atticus can help it.

You accuse me of poison? I laughed. If I'd poisoned him he'd long be dead, and neither of you here for the telling of it.

He answered not, but made for the door and the keeping room beyond. And thus it was he carried Weston off, leaving the door to swing wide in his wake.

Bring him back! I screamed, throwing the beans still hot from the hearth upon his scarred and leathery back where they hissed and steamed and burned him. You shall live to curse this day!

Even now, I shake so with fury I can barely put down these words. Such lies, such ingratitude for all my efforts and love so freely given.

They shall pay. They shall all pay.

Rattled, I stare at the date of this next, and apparently last, entry—then glance at my watch to be sure. August 31. Same day, almost two centuries later.

Freaky.

Matinicus, Monday 31 August

I am desperate for news of Weston. Three days since the negro bore him off, and still no one brings word, those that pass the house looking askance if they look at all.

I must learn where he's been taken, assure myself that he fares well. Wivell's, most likely. The Squire's, if Sally has her way, unless her feelings for the man have altered now she knows how things stand between us. Neither place one to which I might readily be admitted. Still, I must find a way.

The house is silent around me now but for the noises that continue from Mary's chamber. And though I've searched, I find nothing to explain them. A loose board most like. Must I attend to even this now?

More on the morrow, for I must tuck these pages away to answer an impatient pounding just now upon the door. News of Weston, most like. Finally.

THIRTY-ONE

I find Gail in the usual place, her back to me as she scrubs at the grease board. It's mid-afternoon and we're alone as I slide onto a stool, toss the paper bag on the counter.

"Hannah did it all," I say flatly. It's not a question.

Her head snaps around, that hard gaze giving up nothing as she towels off her hands. "Just figured that out, did you?"

I ignore the dig, preferring to wallow in the irony. Guy like me duped by a chick two hundred years dead. And here I thought it was just the living, breathing ones I was having trouble with. Head up my ass as usual, practically tripping over clues and inconsistencies in my rush to empathize, see Hannah as some helpless pawn in the marriage game—understandably resentful at the turn her life had taken and yeah, okay, maybe not the best stepmother in the world, but not vindictive. Certainly not murderous.

"Found this about a week ago," I say, chin nodding toward the bag. "Half-buried in the woods between Rachel's and the old Tolman place. I think it's the dress Hannah wore when she stabbed the sailor. Wasn't sure what to do with it."

Gail picks it up, tosses it to the garbage, goes back to the grease board. Problem solved.

"Diary ended pretty abruptly," I continue, determined on answers this time. "But then you know that. Nothing after Atticus took Weston away. Someone showed up that last night, but I don't know who. It's like getting to the end of a book and finding the last chapter missing."

"They'd come for her," Gail says, her back to me as she writes. "We have to do this now?"

"Afraid so." There's a reason Mary wanted me to know all this, and I'm going to find out what it is. Something tells me solving this one little mystery is the key to everything else.

Gail sighs, wipes her hands. "Okay, but make it quick. Pizza Night tonight." She pours two coffees, slides one my way. "Got a deejay coming out. Al figures if people don't blow off some steam and quick, the whole place is going to implode. Probably right."

She leans into the counter and sips her coffee with the weary look of a woman long used to the antics of the drug-addled and gun-happy. It's beyond me why the place hasn't been overrun with cops, frankly. Anywhere else in the country, three untimely deaths in less than a month on an island of a mere fifty souls would raise at least a couple eyebrows, result in some kind of investigation—perfunctory as it might be. I ask her about this.

A snort of derision. "'Case no one's filled you in," she says, "Rockland police think we're all a bunch of drunks and inbred rednecks, though they do appreciate us takin' the more violent types off their hands. Probably got half the city lockup livin' over to the Sands right now, sternmen are that hard to find. I did call in the Coast Guard a couple years back when the guys got into some brawl up to Markey Beach, started cuttin' each other up. Kid I spoke with laughed, said if they were lucky we'd have killed each other all off by the time they got out here." She shrugs. "Better that way, anyway. You see Clayton or Cash bein' grilled by some kid fresh out of school? They'd cut him up, use him as chum, send a thank-you to the state for savin' them some money."

Okay, so no cops.

"Besides, my worryin' about it won't change a thing. Somebody'll figure all this out; then we'll deal with it in our own way, like we always do around here. Bad things come in threes is the way I see it; let's just hope it ends there."

A little cavalier under the circumstances. Then again, I wasn't raised on an island where public brawling had been elevated to something on par with, say, the World Series, but without all those pesky rules.

"So," Gail says. "Hannah's diary. What do you want to know?"

"Everything you can tell me. Starting with Mary."

She eyes me over a sip. It's the first real interest she's shown since I walked in. "Why her, exactly?" she asks. "You seen her?"

Wait—is she telling me she knows about ghostie girl? I find myself hesitating—protective suddenly, loathe to expose her filmy little presence if I've misunderstood.

"She's not happy," I say, making a cryptic stab. "I can tell you that."

"Nor would you be if you'd been poisoned by your stepmother." She sips, waits a beat. "Never seen anything, myself; I think Rachel might've; she never said. There've been rumors forever, though."

I think of the painting in Rachel's bedroom, the one I saw my first night here. Something heartbreaking about that tiny figure bent to the corner, face in her hands. Such hopeless despair. No way Rachel could've painted that if she didn't know, hadn't seen.

"They used arsenic for all kinds of things back then—insecticides, mostly. Small doses were even considered medicinal." Gail shakes her head. "Made a great poison, too, if you knew what you were doing. Excruciating, gruesome way to go. And slow. And there was Hannah, coolly spooning it into Mary day after day. A real piece of work, that one."

"Atticus knew," I say.

Gail nods. "Saw through her pretty much right away. And she couldn't have that, not after she and Weston started up. Those prying eyes, as she put it. She figured the murder of the sailor would do the trick, was convinced everyone would assume Atticus had done it. Never figured on his having an alibi. Once he was in the clear, he got out of there pretty fast."

"If he'd stuck around," I say, "Mary might have lived."

"I doubt it. Hannah would have just found another way to rid herself of the girl. The women who dressed her for burial found a lot of injuries, broken fingers and toes, things small enough to be put down to accidents except there were too many of them and too recent. There was some talk, apparently, but nothin' was done—times bein' what they were."

I'm about to ask how she knows all this when the kitchen door slams and Al shuffles in with a box of beer for the cooler.

"I think she killed the girl to keep from bein' found out, myself," Gail says. "That and win sympathy from Weston. She kept tryin' to find things that would force him to postpone marrying Sally."

"Only he wasn't coming 'round the way she wanted."

"Exactly. So she pulled the same thing with him, only Atticus came to the rescue this time. Town was horrified once they realized what was going on. Went against all their notions about women as the fair and gentle sex, the sacredness of motherhood, like that. Even worse, it was one of their own doin' all the killing."

"Tiffany around?" Al calls over. "Got some beer in the pickup needs unloading. Hey, Hodge," he adds, shooting me a grin. "Got a little chili left, you want a bowl."

I wave off the offer as Gail rises, pulling her elbows from the counter. "Saw her long enough to argue about Kirtley Kneeland again," she scowls.

"I want that woman off the island, Al—I mean it. I don't trust her. I told Tiffany I catch them skinny dippin' together one more time, I'll whip her ass all the way back here."

"Which means she'll be at it again first chance she gets," Al laughs. "Let it go, why don't you? She'll be off to your sister's in another week anyway; start up with school again."

Wouldn't count on it, I think. School's the last thing on that kid's mind just now.

"I left it up to you," Gail says, "you'd let everything go. It ain't doin' her any favors, either."

"Gail, honey, wouldn't kill you to show her a little affection once in a while."

"Girl's got trouble with right and wrong, Al—always has. You been soft on her since the day Deb dropped her on our doorstep ten years ago. And we been payin' for that one ever since."

A little harsh, I think, rising to lend a hand with the beer. Resentful even. Gotta be tough raising somebody else's kid, but still.

Later, heading out, I decline an invitation to join tonight's party. Best to keep a low profile, I figure, 'til I'm off the current short list of murder suspects.

"By the way," I ask, turning at the door. "Did Weston make it?"

Gail nods. "Married Sally a month later. Six kids—all boys. Every Philbrick on the island comes down from them."

Why aren't I surprised? Mary and the sailor dead, Isaac's family scattered to the winds, but Weston gets off scot-free. "Let me guess," I say. "He denied sleeping with Hannah."

She doesn't bother looking up. "Swore up and down he never touched her."

Of course he did, I think. It's exactly what I'd have done.

THIRTY-TWO

It's like a sledgehammer to the chest.

Gail.

Only yesterday she and I were dancing around the subject of ghostie girl; just last night she and Al hosted another hopping dance party—the hooting and hollering echoing all the way to the dugout. This morning she fired up her ovens for another round of Saturday baking and opened the Galley Hatch for lunch. None of this is in dispute. But then it gets weird, because sometime after that—a line of pies still cooling in the kitchen, her dishtowel hanging neatly over the handle of an oven door—she simply went missing.

Disappeared. As in off-the-face-of-the-earth.

At first Al's just confused, wonders if he forgot she was headed off somewhere—"No secret I don't always listen close when she talks"—but, and this is where I wandered in, he can't for the life of him figure where that might be.

I hang around; dinnertime comes and goes, and by now he's really getting worried. Hell, we all are—except for Tiffany who's M.I.A., as usual. Al makes the calls—one to Doug to see if Gail might have flown over to visit her sister in Rockland; then, just to be sure, the sister herself. He tries her women friends on the island. No one's seen her.

By now word has spread, and some of the guys show up. Cash, Paul—a.k.a. *Plan Bea*—and Josh. Even *Hombre*, with a trio of blown-out sternmen from the Sands—all mutual hostility suspended as we fan out across the island for the next couple hours, flashlights in hand.

No luck.

Next morning, our numbers have swollen to maybe twenty—a larger group with an organized plan. And a dark fear in the back of our minds. We break into pairs, slog through the woods calling her name. But this is a big island—almost seven hundred acres—much of it wooded. And at ten that night, grim and exhausted, we've still found nothing.

I offer to stay the night with Al, but he's having a hard enough time holding it together for Tiffany, and hardly needs me to worry about as well. So I head back to the dugout, pull my sleeping bag from the tent and stretch out beneath a blanket of stars. Frustrated, consumed with worry, determined that if Gail's injured somewhere out here, helpless to do anything but stare up at the sky, I'll goddam well keep her company.

So many things go through your mind at a time like this. I run through our last conversation looking for answers—Hannah's deluded obsessions, Mary's gruesome death, Gail's own oddly reconciled attitude toward the current crop of murders. Ironic, considering.

My gut tells me it's one guy doing all this. Gotta be. A bunch of organized killers with this twisted an agenda would be hard enough to find in the general population; impossible for a group this mutually suspicious. And I swear if he's hurt Gail, whoever he is, I'll kill the bastard myself.

I toss and turn about all this for a couple more hours, and just after dawn decide to strike off on my own—arming myself against God-only-knows-what with a rucksack of cataloguing work I know I'll never touch.

Maybe an hour later I find her.

Lucky me.

Wouldn't you know but it's a brilliant day, clear and crisp, with long shafts of sun striking through the trees. I'm working my frustrations out hacking at a tangle of spruce deadfall somewhere close to where I found the dress, sweating profusely as I whack my way deeper into the woods along an old, unused footpath, when it suddenly opens to a clearing I remember coming across before. The remains of a crumbling foundation, a derelict well that's of an ancient square-sided design—nothing more than a deep, gaping shaft, really, set flush to the ground. Dangerous as hell, of course, and like every one of the old wells I've encountered here, normally covered with a broad sheet of plywood weighted with rocks.

Only it's not anymore. A corner of the plywood is instead jammed skyward as if something landed hard on it, punching through.

Strange the way we delude ourselves. On some level I know what I'll find even as I approach—slowly, heart thudding, all too aware the shaft walls could already be giving way beneath the innocuous looking ground cover. Still, I tell myself it's probably just kids messing around, or one of the old dogs, maybe—the plywood looks too worn and desiccated to hold a five-pound cat, let alone one of those ample canines.

I stretch my neck over the rim, peer cautiously into some thirty feet of inky darkness. At first I see nothing; then the soft lump of a human body takes shape, the glint of that cropped red hair. No movement, a low buzzing of flies.

I'm momentarily paralyzed, can't do anything but stand there fighting the urge to vomit as I call her name. Choke it out again. By the third time I'm yelling, near panic, though it's clear she's beyond responding. It's then I turn and break into a run; stumbling back along the path—trying not to feel, trying not to think, and failing at both.

I'm filling everyone in as the recovery begins. It's obvious my being the one to find Gail has done me no favors here, Cash's jaw working as he pushes roughly past to shimmy down the well shaft—rope looped around his waist as Josh and *Hombre* lower him into the hole.

Al's trembling beside me as Cash reemerges clasping Gail against his chest in a parody of a lover's embrace, the others smoking and talking quietly from a respectful distance. I place a hand on Al's shoulder to steady him, forcing myself to look. Despair, disbelief at what I'm seeing, the renewed urge to hurl. But I won't this time, not like with Ivan.

Her face is a raw, bloody mess—front teeth broken off, jaw and nose smashed, left eye caved in—as if someone had taken a two-by four to her. More than once from the look of it.

The island's remaining EMT, a retired New Hampshire firefighter and island transplant named Bill Cutler, seems competent enough as he takes down Gail's basic information. Nervous, though, and obviously uncomfortable discussing her injuries—a dangerous posture to take with this group.

"She's my wife, dammit," Al spits. "I want to know what killed her."

Not to mention who, I think.

Bill fiddles nervously with his pen. "Hard to say without an autopsy, Al. She hit her head at least a couple of times going down. Might have been that. Well runs twenty-five, thirty feet so she probably had any number of internal injuries. Looks like she broke a wrist and both legs; so climbing out wouldn't have been an option—assuming she was conscious, which I doubt."

Al tenses. "You doubt," he spits. "Might have been. Probably. Anything at all you're sure about? Look at her face! You think that happened fallin' down a well?"

Cash grinds out his butt and moves forward, the rest of the guys falling in behind. "Some sick fuck did this to her," he says. He's glaring at Bill, but the look's meant for me. "Lured her out here, prob'ly, then beat her to death."

Al flinches beside me.

"How long's she been dead?" Cash demands.

To his credit, Bill's reluctant to say what I instinctively feel—that Gail lay in that damp, miserable hole for some time before she died, no doubt in excruciating pain.

"Twelve hours, maybe less," he finally admits, not meeting Al's eyes.

There's some angry mumbling as Al processes this, his head dropping a moment. When he looks up, it's to take me aside, the trembling hand he uses to rub at his forehead reminding me strangely of Dad in those last, awful months.

"Didn't have time to look for Tiffany when you brought news," he says quietly. "Somebody's got to find her. I'm not leaving Gail."

I nod my understanding, shoulder my pack, and take off without a word to anyone—adrenaline pumping as I weigh the options. I end up jogging the half mile to Markey Beach on a hunch—bad one, it turns out, despite the stellar day. It's then I remember stumbling across her tucked in the rocks somewhere along the western shore. It was the day she told me she was pregnant. A special spot, maybe? Most kids have them; places they go when life seems too much to handle.

Twenty minutes later I've managed to find the path I took that afternoon, struggling for a way to break the news once I get there. A couple years back I was the academic advisor to a kid whose father died in a commuter pile-up outside New York City. The Dean of Students was out of town that day, so it fell to me to break the news—something I'd been able to do with my usual astounding level of emotional detachment.

Somehow I know it'll fail me now.

I finally stumble on the spot, but this, too, is a bust. No Tiffany nestled in the rocks. No sign she's even been here.

The harbor, then, for a quick scan of the dock. A jog up to the Galley Hatch. Nothing.

Only then do I happen to turn my gaze to the harbor. I know something's different, but I'm so rattled by this time it takes a minute to compute. There, in the middle of the harbor where *Bounder* usually sits is, well, nothing. She's gone—two dinghies tethered to her mooring ball bobbing gently in her place. One I recognize as Kirtley's sleek white zodiac. The other I know just as well.

The battered skiff belonging to the Galley Hatch.

THIRTY-THREE

I'm straddling one of the loungers the next afternoon, a sandaled foot parked on either side of the thing—driftwood, shells, and some thread I found in the house set out on the webbing before me.

This particular knot's a bear, so I don't bother looking up when I hear company coming through the woods. Cash et al, no doubt—all that testosterone about to hit the fan. Just one set of footsteps, though, I quickly realize—the tread light. Female, I figure. Hoping it's Tiffany; knowing it's not. Call it instinct.

"Knock, knock," Kirtley says, much as she did that first day.

Bound to happen, her showing up like this—they all do once you stop paying attention, I've noticed. Chinos today, and a polo shirt. Boat shoes. Going all conservative on me with the yachtie look. But I'm not fooled, having already filed her away with the likes of Annika under Women Determined to Hurt Me.

"Gil can't play today," I say, eyes glued to my little project. "Tongue's still healing." But the uptick in my pulse has caused my nearly-finished knot to slip off the shell. "Damn," I mutter.

"I feel like such a shit," she says, seating herself on the other lounger. "Really. I was thinking we might start over."

"Were you." Focus, I tell myself. Ten-year-olds can rig this thing in their sleep.

A sigh. "You might at least offer me a beer."

"Help yourself," I say, nodding toward the cooler. Another knot down.

Only—what—thirty or forty to go?

She uncaps it and takes a long draw. "God, I needed this."

I sneak another peek. Freshly showered, all dewy and damp—as if she's just come off hours of world-class sex. Nothing like four or five orgasms to calm a girl down, stir up that rosy glow.

She meets my eye, grins conspiratorially—only then noticing I'm actually in the middle of something here.

"What's this?" she laughs.

"Wind chime. Never made one before—figured it was time." And coming along quite nicely, thank you. A frivolous way to spend my time considering everything's crashing down around me, but I find I no longer give a shit.

"A little weird," I say, carefully tightening my next miniscule knot, "your sailing off with Tiffany like that yesterday, what with Gail missing and all."

In all fairness, Kirtley could hardly have known I'd already stumbled across the body or that Al was desperate to locate the kid. But I'm still annoyed and itching, for some reason, to irritate her. "You do know she's dead, right?"

"We weren't out all that long; I thought it would help take Tiffany's mind off everything for a while. And, yes, of course I know." A pause. "That woman never did like me—no idea why."

She seems genuinely puzzled by this. I smile, shake my head, carefully looping another shell with thread. "All those tequila shooters, I imagine. The table-dancing and indiscriminate sex. Just a wild guess."

She grins over. "You're crazy if you think Tiffany hasn't done all that and more. She got pregnant on Gail's watch, after all. I'd have put the kid on birth control at ten." She takes another pull on the beer. "Wouldn't surprise me if she decides to have this baby, by the way, now Ivan's no longer in the picture."

"Uh-huh." Another knot down. I pause to look up, casually scrutinizing the tree line for glowering faces. Nothing. They're out there, though—I'd put money on it.

"Deep down she's glad he's dead," Kirtley says. "She just can't admit it."

"Talking about Tiffany or yourself here?" I ask, raising my work for scrutiny.

"Oh, come on," she laughs. "You're telling me you've never once been involved with someone you wished would just drop off the face of the earth?"

Annika, I think, immediately jolted by the thought. Not literally, of course—or so I tell myself. But I remember some pretty hairy weeks there when I'd have given just about anything to have her disappear.

"Thinking's not the same as doing," I say. "You'd have to be a monster, or a psycho. Maybe both."

"So which is it here—monster or psycho?"

Good question. "Some of them think it's me," I say, reaching for a beer. Fingers need a break, anyway.

"You!" Half laugh, half bark.

"Makes a certain kind of sense from their point of view. I show up and people start dying. Same with you, I might add."

She bolts upright—her face filling with delight.

"Relax," I say. "Can't be either one of us."

"Damn." She tucks her knees to her chest, pouting. "Why not?"

"Couple reasons." I might be piss-poor at this detecting business, but scientists are trained to weed through seemingly unrelated bits of information and toss out things that don't fit. So I've managed to cross a few people off my rather lengthy list of potential murderers. Kirtley was right up there, albeit briefly—I mean who knows what really happened to her husband—'til it dawned on me she had absolutely nothing to gain from any of this. Motive and opportunity, right? It's what the cop shows tell us, anyway. Which means that whoever killed these people had to have an islander's knowledge of their lives—habits, schedules, not to mention who else was likely to be around at any given moment. Couldn't pull it off otherwise.

Chick's a fucking squirrel, but there's no way she killed these people. Which brings us back to John or maybe Cash, but I don't know—doesn't feel right somehow.

"Delicious, isn't it?" Kirtley purrs. "I just love a good mystery."

I cock an eye. "It doesn't bother you that these people are dead?" Because it sure as shit bothers me. The first deaths were bad enough, but this is Gail we're talking about, the closest thing Tiffany's got to a real mother—something she desperately needs right now.

"Life, death," Kirtley says. "We're here for a while, then we're not. Allan for instance. Healthy guy—nothing physically wrong with him except a couple weak joints, the occasional erectile dysfunction. Falls off the back of a boat one night, and just like that it's over. Ironic, really, considering I used to fantasize about it all the time—getting rid of him, I mean."

You and about twenty million other wives, I think, setting my beer down while I rummage among the remaining pieces of driftwood for one the size of a toothpick.

"Something with the boat would be the most obvious choice, don't you think—sailing being the inherently dangerous sport it is. You'd have to wait for the right opportunity, of course, but then who was to know, right?

"Imagine, he's leaning out over the open stern and all you'd have to do is give him a little shove. It would be such a rush, wouldn't it? Knowing you had ultimate power over whether he lived or died?"

My hands go still. "You're putting me on."

"Am I?" she teases. "So suppose you do it—on a whim, say, to get back at him for all the drunken raging, the verbal abuse. A decision, then—go back and pick him up?" She looks over and meets my eyes. "Or no?"

She waits a beat before glancing off over the water. If it's about getting my attention, she's sure as hell got it now.

"So say you decide to just keep sailing. For a minute he's too shocked to do anything but tread water; then he starts yelling, screaming, pleading. No other boats out there, nothing at all. No chance he'll survive. All he can do is watch as you sail away with his life—literally."

She grins, the beer gone, and waggles the bottle at me. "Mind?"

"Please," I manage, watching her fish out another. "And what would you do then—you know, afterward? Go below and have a nap? Make dinner?"

"I'd masturbate," she says with a slow smile. "I could show you."

She's playing me, of course, no doubt on the prowl for another round of sexual bloodletting. A month ago the comment might have intrigued me—okay, no might about it. But not anymore.

I throw back the rest of my beer and stand, tired of waiting for a contingent of the high-strung and gun-happy to find me. Time to take the party to the boys, convince them to call in the cops instead of simply waiting around to see who's gonna to be next.

"Hang out if you want," I tell her, donning my cap and slipping into my shoes. "I've got an appointment with the disgruntled masses."

Town wharf's the logical place to start, and though most of the guys headed back out after we finished up with John, I figure I'm bound to run into at least somebody I can try and reason with.

Wrong. Other than a truck or two tearing past as I make the dock, guys who used to grant me a minimal island wave—hands on the wheel, couple fingers flipped up as they pass—are shunning me now like I'm just another scumbag tourist. The place is deserted but for Tiffany's skinny frame parked at the end of the jetty, back against a piling as she stares out to sea.

Ka Ching and *Hombre* are still out, I'm relieved to see—the two guys most likely to come at me swinging before I get the chance to open my mouth.

"Hey," I say.

Startled, she whirls to face me, almost physically flinching as I settle a couple feet away—tucking her knees to her chest in some effort to ward me off. At least I read it that way. I haven't seen her since we found Gail, and it's possible that she, too, blames me. If I hadn't found her, she wouldn't be dead—something like that.

"I'm so sorry," I say, and simply leave it at that, refusing to insult her with a bunch of bullshit about how everything's going to be alright. We both know it's not. I'm praying she doesn't ask me anything tough, like whether Gail suffered, but I needn't have worried.

"This place is so lame," she says, rocking herself now. Self-comfort, any child knows, is better than no comfort at all. "I can't wait to get the fuck out of here."

Teenagers are so marvelously self-absorbed, never more so than when some life-altering change is staring them down; so it's frankly a relief to see her managing some semblance of normalcy with everything else that's going on. I glance away to hide my smile, something she surely wouldn't appreciate.

"Don't blame you," I say. "Keep in mind, though, that our problems have the habit of following us around."

She narrows her eyes. "What the hell does that mean?"

"Just that you've got some decisions to make, and soon. Leaving Matinicus won't change that."

She bites savagely at a nail. "I know, I know—alright?"

"You could always talk to Al," I rather stupidly suggest—the stupid part hitting me immediately.

"You crazy? He'd tell Cheryl for sure. Bad enough she calls me like every day, inviting me for dinner and stuff just so's she can talk about Ivan. Like I don't feel shitty enough already. Kirtley's right; I tell any of them I'm pregnant, that'll be it. I'll never get out of here."

Oh, her. "Nobody's decision but yours," I say. "Kirtley's going to sail away one of these days, though—you do know that, right? She's got her own life to live, and I can guarantee you it won't be here. You're the one who has to live with whatever you decide."

"I wish you'd all just get off her case, okay?" Rocking harder now. Antsy, nervous—like she's holding something back.

"What is it?" I ask, ducking my head to meet her eyes, but she looks away—blotches of color creeping into her cheeks. "Tiffany?"

"Gail didn't understand about Kirtley; that's the problem. She's had it tough; you don't know. Her husband was a real creep."

"And?"

"And Gail found out I snuck out to meet her a bunch of nights; said Kirtley was trash and I was starting to act just like her. Made Kirtley sound like a real skank. God, I hated her sometimes."

"All teenagers hate their parents," I assure her. "It's some kind of law." I've seen this reaction before, of course—kids so shocked and disoriented by a parent's death, they channel it into some kind of self-flagellating rage, trolling through a lifetime of guilt and mutual accusation for some sort of justification. Otherwise, the world would look like the frighteningly random place it actually is.

"Me and Gail had like this huge fight about it the day she...you know."

Oh man, I think. She's blaming herself for all this now, too?

"Gail got super pissed when I told her about how Kirtley thought it was a great idea for me to go find my mother myself. She was like spitting, she was so mad. Being with my mother is like all I've thought about for a really long time, and Gail made fun of it like it was nothing. Then she said she was going to find Kirtley and tell her to get off the island; have the guys make sure she did. Man, I like panicked; Kirtley's my best friend, you know? She gets it, how hard it is living out here away from real stores and movies and how it really sucks with all the fighting? I told her about John and the lobster war and stuff, and how the cops and the people over in America don't care what goes on out here, which is why Cash and them get away with selling a shitload of drugs. She understood about it all."

Fuck me, I think. No—fuck me twice.

"When did you tell her all this?" I ask, somehow managing to keep my voice neutral.

"We were on *Bounder*—the day they took Uncle Clayton away. Why?"

We in the science biz have what we call a precipitating event—that one, single thing that sets everything else in motion. Kind of a domino effect. Can be some huge, tectonic event, or something as small and insignificant as a few lines of seemingly innocent conversation.

"We talked about all kinds of stuff, the way girlfriends do, you know?" Tiffany says. "I told her about that black sailor being my great-great-great grandfather? She thought it was really cool that I'm part black; that's what I mean about her. She totally doesn't judge anybody."

I'm momentarily derailed by this—could she actually mean Atticus?—but I can't spare the brain cells on it right now.

"Just so I understand," I say. "The day Gail disappeared, she was going to tell Kirtley to leave the island? Was she planning to confront her that day, do you know?"

It must be something in my face, 'cause the kid gets that deer-in-the-headlights look. "That's what she said—why?"

"Nothing, really," I tell her, scrambling. "I'm just trying to figure who knew what and when, is all. Kirtley might have mentioned something important to someone sometime."

Tiffany's a real smart kid, but she's no match for my twisted bullshit, so she lets it go. Good thing, too, cause the ante's just been upped, what with Ka-Ching steaming round Indian Ledge, swaying under a full load of traps. I need to know if I'm right about Kirtley, and I need to know fast. Getting into it with Cash will simply slow me down. Problem is, the only guy on the island with the answers I need has gone into seclusion.

He'll see me, though. He's got to.

THIRTY-FOUR

Tiffany rested her chin on her knees and closed her eyes, glad Hodge was gone now so she could concentrate, figure the stuff she needed to pack. Kirtley's empty dinghy was tied to the dock, so she must be off getting all the stuff they'd need for their trip, which was going to be a real lot. Bermuda was a long way; took like a week to get there, Kirtley said. Another day or two and they'd be out of here—just the two of them. It was going to be so cool.

When Kirtley invited her to come along, Tiffany thought she was kidding. Like maybe Hodge was right and she really was leaving soon, was maybe just saying this to bring the subject up in a nice way. But she'd been serious. Tiffany still couldn't believe it. Her dreams coming true at last. She'd begun to think she'd never get out of here—away from Ivan and Gail and them. Just goes to show how even really bad things can lead to good in the end.

She didn't really know where Bermuda was exactly, but it looked cool from the ads on TV. All those long, sandy beaches—really fine sand, too, not like the sharp chunky stuff here that got stuck between your toes. And the water was warm, Kirtley said, warm as the air. God, she couldn't imagine.

She didn't have the right kind of clothes, of course—*Cruise Wear*, Kirtley called it. Special clothes just for being on boats. But Kirtley told her not to worry, they'd buy some when they got there. A bikini, even, if she wanted one. Gail had never let her wear a bikini, said they were cheap.

But it was just a vacation—a break, Kirtley called it, before Tiffany got serious about finding her mother, which was even more important now she was going to be one herself. Which she was, never mind she hadn't told Hodge she'd already decided. Less people that knew, she figured, the better—at least 'til she was out of here. And she'd be a good mother, too—not mean and sarcastic all the time like Gail, who'd never really wanted her around even in the beginning.

Tiffany sighed, thinking about Gail. She knew you weren't supposed to say bad things about the dead, but if you asked Tiffany, Gail definitely got what she deserved. She'd never forget the huge fight they'd had the first time she said she was going to find her mother, even if it meant going places as far as Europe or South America—Africa even. Gail just laughed, said it showed how stupid Tiffany was that she didn't even know she couldn't get out of the country without a passport, which she didn't have.

But Gail was the stupid one, 'cause when Tiffany asked Kirtley about it, Kirtley said she didn't need one—that she could get into Bermuda with just her birth certificate. Only problem was, she'd have to search through all Gail's stuff to find it, which would give her the creeps, considering.

Other things worried her, too—things she hadn't told Kirtley in case she changed her mind and sailed off alone. First was that no one could know where they were going or even that they were leaving. Kirtley'd been definite about that. Had to be a secret. Probably she didn't want her creep of a husband to find them, which Tiffany completely understood. But that meant Tiffany couldn't tell anyone—not even Al. She felt kind of bad leaving him with Gail being dead now and all; he'd always been okay to her, and he'd have nobody after she left except maybe Hodge, and he was just a summer guy.

She'd write him a letter from Bermuda, she decided—yeah, that's it; let him know she was okay and just taking a break. He'd worry when she didn't turn up for school, of course, but she couldn't help that. Later, when she was settled, she'd write him another letter, tell him about finding her mother and about the baby. He could come visit them, maybe.

God, she wished she could see their faces—Cash and Cheryl, Josh and all them—when they found out she was gone. Tiffany, who they all prob'ly figured would take Gail's place at the store for like her whole life, just up and leaving without them even knowing.

And Mr. Kneeland—won't he be surprised when he flies in to meet Kirtley and *Bounder* is gone. Well, fuck him. The prick. Men like him who treat women bad deserve just what they get.

THIRTY-FIVE

I swing by the Galley Hatch twice after leaving Tiffany, and both times it's locked up tight—no sign of Al anywhere. I keep hoping I'm wrong about Kirtley, because the other option sucks. Self-descriptors like mind-boggling stupidity and can't-deduce-worth-shit come to mind. Ironic, isn't it? Just hours ago I was so certain of Kirtley's innocence I actually proclaimed it to her face. No wonder she was so amused.

I try the Hatch again at dusk and, peering into the shadows, finally spot Al parked on a stool—head in his hands, a bottle and shot glass on the counter before him.

I twist the knob. Still locked. "Al!" I call, rapping once on the glass.

"Fuck off!" he growls, not even bothering to turn. "We're closed." His voice is thick, anguished.

"Let me in. We need to talk."

"I said fuck off!"

"I've got news," I say, feeling the lie sink it's teeth. Anything to get in, I figure; I can wing the rest.

He swings his gaze, weighing my words. Maybe ten seconds later he drags himself over, looking hunched and beaten as he unlocks the door—the limp worse than ever as he shuffles back, pours himself another shot of Jack. He doesn't offer and I don't ask.

"I'm gonna kill that fucker," he growls. "Get my hands round his rat-bastard throat and squeeze till blood squirts out his eyes. Rip his other arm off and make him eat it."

"It wasn't John," I tell him, sitting.

"Hell it wasn't. Some fuckin' truce, huh? Only thing happened was we dropped our guard, let him slink back out here like the slimeball he is. Probably stuck in his craw all these years—Gail kneeing him in the balls like that back when they was kids, not lettin' him have his way with her. Figured long as he was out here pickin' off the others, might as well do her, too."

He flicks a cold gaze my way. "Now the boys, they're not so sure. They want to know how it is you found Gail back there in the woods when nobody else could. And how you turned up at Josh's place so fast right after Ivan was killed. I swear, Hodge, I find out it's you who done this, I'll come after you myself." He throws back the booze, pours another. "But 'til we know for sure and make it right, fishin' stops and the traps get pulled. Gonna be a fuckin' war zone around here, we don't get to the bottom of this and fast." He glares at me again. "You want to save us some time?"

I shake my head. "It wasn't me, Al," I say quietly. "I loved Gail, too."

His face crumbles at the sound of her name, the last of his rage-fueled bravura spent in a long sigh. He tosses back the shot, pours another. "I'm not lookin' for company here, Hodge. Tell me this news you got and get lost, okay?"

"I ran into Tiffany on the dock this afternoon," I hedge. "I get the feeling she thinks Gail's death is her fault, somehow."

"Of course she does," he snaps. "She's a teenager. Everything's about them."

"Remember the afternoon I was helping you offload beer and Gail was ranting about wanting Kirtley off the island? Tiffany says they argued about it the next day, too—the day Gail disappeared; that she was heading off to confront Kirtley. That true?"

"How the fuck should I know?" he says, face buried in his hands. "Those two were always fighting—typical mother and daughter shit. I stopped listening years ago."

I force myself to focus. "How much do you know about Kirtley, Al?"

"Kneeland?" He drops his hands and glares, thunderstruck. "What the fuck, Hodge. I heard you two been doing the horizontal mambo, but you're askin' me this shit now? Now?"

"It's not about that. Hear me out, okay? You know anything about her past—where she's from? How Allan met her, anything? It's important."

He shakes his head, throws the liquor back. "Lived all over the world, he told me once. Said her father was in the Foreign Service or something. I could give a shit."

"How'd they seem together—you know, as a couple?"

"Never said much to each other that I saw. Kirtley was really into partying; Allan would just hang back and watch, like she was his little performing doll. Whole thing felt a little off to me, you want to know the truth. Somethin' weird there. He's got a couple grown kids he never sees. I got the feelin' they don't like her."

"When was the last time you spoke to her?"

"You mean like a real conversation? Hold on, I gotta think." But the liquor's kicking in now, and this takes him a minute. "Back before Ivan, probably. Yeah, she was in for supplies, and the two of them—Josh and Ivan—were talkin' here at the counter figurin' a time for workin' on the truck."

Bingo.

"You're gonna tell me what this is about now, right? 'Cause I really ain't in the mood."

Bad idea. Not only that, it's a stupid one. If word gets out before I've got some concrete proof linking Kirtley to all this, she'll bolt. Probably end up doing the exact same thing somewhere else.

"Hodge," he pleads. "I'll go out of my mind, I don't do something here. Tell me what you're thinkin'. I can help."

Right. I tell him and the first thing he'll do is warn Tiffany. Who'll never believe him. And where will she run with this ridiculous accusation? You got it. Then again, Al doesn't want the killer to slip away anymore than I do. Question is, how much is he willing to risk to catch her? I decide to chance it.

"We've got trouble, Al."

"No shit."

"No, I mean it's not John who's been killing people. It's Kirtley."

"Kirtley? You're nuts." Instant sobriety—quite a feat, considering. "But she's a woman."

"Right. Remember Hannah Burgess? She killed three people, and those are only the ones we know about." And then I lay it all out—how long Kirtley's been pumping Tiffany about the island, the kid happy to tell her about the mess with John and how the cops turn a blind eye to pretty much everything out here. Easy enough for her to stay below the radar, too—what with everyone at each other's throats anyway. Kirtley was the last to see Clayton alive, I remind him. Overheard Josh and Ivan setting a time to fix the truck. And Gail had been planning to confront her the day she disappeared.

"It's a sure bet she killed Allan, too," I say. "God only knows how long she's been at this." Traveling so much as a kid? Sailing from port to port on *Bounder*? It doesn't bear thinking about.

A slow nod. "Her story kinda bothered me from the start, now you mention it—that business about him falling overboard for one thing. Guy was into safety big time; told me he always clips into a safety harness when he's doing off-shore runs. So this one night he doesn't? And then her turning up here of all places after he died. Why? I mean this place ain't exactly hopping." He glances to me, then. "What she did to Gail, Hodge; it was so..."

Brutal? Sadistic? "I know." This is a woman who loves to kill.

"Why us? That's what I don't get."

I have no answer for this. Could be there isn't one—not in the usual sense. Hannah, warped as she was, at least had some kind of reasoning for the things she did. Twisted and self-serving, yes, but reasons nonetheless. Nothing compared to this.

"We could be talking serial murder here, Al; killing for the thrill of it. The usual rules don't apply."

"Serial murder—you mean Ted Bundy, like that?"

I nod. "Which makes Kirtley far more dangerous and unpredictable than someone who's just got some axe to grind.

"We need proof she killed Allan," I tell him. "He's the only one we can really connect her to, the only one she might conceivably have a motive for. Prove that, and we might convince the authorities to look at her for the other deaths."

Easier said than done, of course. The guy's been dead for months. No body, no murder weapon, nada. If I'm right and Kirtley's been at this a while, she's long since learned to cover her tracks. "On the boat, maybe, something he left behind that could trip her up. Financial stuff, a diary—I don't know."

Al slaps the counter. "Ship's log! Every boat's got one. It's like a brag book for captains. Allan would've used it to keep track of their position, the weather, how fast they were going, like that. A lot of 'em make comments about what was going on onboard, too. What they had for dinner; mood of the crew, shit like that. Might be something in there we can use."

Possible, I guess. From what little I've seen of *Bounder*, Allan was a careful, organized sailor. Big ego, too, so maybe recording everything he did was part of his routine. But finding this log and getting a look at it, assuming it even exists, is another thing altogether.

"Something else Tiffany said," I tell him. "The black sailor—the one she said was her ancestor. Was it Atticus? The guy from Hannah's diary?" Crazy, I know, but it feels important somehow—I just don't know why yet.

"What the hell...," he begins, but something in my look checks him. "Yeah, okay, same guy. Settled on the island, even saved enough to buy his family free. This is all according to Gail. It was Tiffany's great-grandfather Tolman married one of his descendants back in the forties, had Tiffany's grandmother, Molly, who married a Burgess. They had Tiffany's mother,

Deb. But all that was too long ago to figure in any of this."

"Probably right," I murmur, trying to tease some thread of continuity from all the serpentine connections.

"I've got to warn Tiffany," he says, rising.

"It's over if you do, Al; you know that. And she won't believe you, anyway. Besides, Kirtley's had a hundred chances to kill her if that was the plan."

"Bullshit. Woman's no fool. Four murders in one place? She's gotta know she's pushing it. Tiffany's just a loose end to her, nothing more."

"We don't know that. She's got no clue we're on to her, so why not go for five or six? Plus, she needs Tiffany's knowledge of the island—uses it to choose her victims. Trust me; Tiffany's in far less danger than the rest of us." I let that sink in. "Two days," I plead. "We've got to stop Kirtley without tipping her off. God knows what'll happen if she sees it coming."

"We should bring the others in on this."

I shake my head. "Fewer people who know, the better. I doubt they'd buy it anyway. Sounds too much like I'm shifting blame to cover my ass. Besides, what if we're wrong about this?"

"We ain't and you know it." He glares at me, deciding. Clearly doesn't like what he's about to say. "Two days, no more. Which means we got to get that logbook right off." He shakes his head in frustration, pounds a fist into his thigh once, twice. "I'd go out there myself except for this damn thing."

"Better I go alone," I tell him. "I know the layout. But I'll need some time out there without Kirtley around."

He nods. "She flies to the mainland about once a week, according to Doug. No idea why. Comes back a couple hours later. Don't think she's been yet this week, so it could be any time. I'll have him call when she gets on the plane."

"He'll do that?"

"That and more. Man owes me. You okay with this end of things?"

"Piece of cake." Pretty cocky considering I've little idea what I'm looking for. Some kind of journal or book of indeterminate size located just about anywhere. And that's assuming it's even onboard.

I glance back when I reach the door. There's a touch of hope in Al's eyes now, but my attempt at a high-watt Jeff Bridges falls miserably flat.

"Don't let her hurt my girl, Hodge," he says quietly.

The look I send him is a promise—one I'm praying I can keep.

THIRTY-SIX

The twilight breeze is light for a change, filling the dugout with the heady sweetness of evening primrose. Amazing stuff, this. Blooms only at night, a kind of olfactory advertisement for its profusion of medicinal wealth—everything from the treatment of heart disease and multiple sclerosis to eczema, cirrhosis, and whooping cough.

Pharmacy in a flower, I think, rolling the canary yellow blossom between my fingers. Now if it could only push back time, bring back the dead; then we'd really have something.

Not quite twenty-four hours since my talk with Al, and so far Kirtley's made no move to leave the island, putting our plan to search *Bounder* on hold. The waiting's driving me nuts. I can't shake the feeling I'm staring at some key piece of the puzzle and just not seeing it. Forest for the trees kind of thing. Which means I could also be wrong about the danger to Tiffany. And I mean way off. Calculated risk, I know, but is it really mine to take? And is it worth it? No matter what the outcome of all this, Gail's never coming back. Clayton and Ivan and Clunk? They'll all still be dead. I keep telling myself there's no other way—tip Tiffany off and Kirtley will somehow know. I just pray I'm right. Anything happens to that kid, I'll never forgive myself.

I crush the petals, toss them aside. When I glance up, Cash is standing maybe six feet away—fat doobie tucked behind his ear, gun jammed in the waist of his jeans. I knew someone would show up sooner or later, and I'm almost glad it's him, though his clothes reek of weed and old bong water—that and something fried from God only knows how long ago.

"What's up?" I ask, cursing myself for not making better friends with Rachel's rifle when I had the chance. Are we really going to fight, I wonder, or will he just shoot me and be done with it—assuming he's remembered to put bullets in the thing this time?

"Time you and me had a chat," he says, his tone flat.

I sweep my arm toward the other lounger and lean back, pulling my cap down and braiding my fingers atop my chest. Behind me, the shells of my wind chime click softly in the breeze. "Chat away."

He doesn't move.

"Nice sunset," I offer after maybe fifteen seconds of such pseudo-intimidation.

"Fuck the sunset."

Right, then.

"Ivan was a good kid," Cash snarls. "Fuckin' lousy sternman, but a good kid."

"You're looking for volunteers, that's why you're here?"

"And Cheryl ain't never gonna be the same."

"No way she could be."

"Whoever done this ain't gettin' off the island alive, and that's a promise."

I glance up. "That night I stopped by your place? You were convinced the others had you pegged for Clayton, remember? I heard some of them were looking at you pretty hard for Ivan, too, what with the way he quit on you. You're telling me that's changed?"

"Bet your ass."

"Little premature, don't you think?"

"What the fuck you mean?" He's gone all twitchy, I notice—not a good sign.

"C'mon, Cash. I can't think of a person out here you don't have some kind of hard-on for. You were pissed at Clayton for naming his boat after your mom, and at Ivan for being so damn lazy. So what did Gail do—cut off your beer credit?"

This sets him back. "You're the one found her," he reminds me.

"True. But I haven't been around long enough to hate anyone here, and certainly not Gail. I've got a soft spot for people who feed me, and her pies were the best. Chili was killer, too." I flip the top of the cooler back, grab a Heinie. "Help yourself," I say.

He ignores the offer, but parks himself on the other lounger. It's something.

"Al says it ain't you, but I'm not convinced."

"Well, I am." I say, prying the cap off my beer. "But relax; it's not you either."

"Glad we got that straight," he says, cracking his neck left, then right. He fires up the bone, holds in a hit. "You think you know who it is, though, don't you?" he squeaks, squinting through the smoke. "You got that look."

I nod.

He takes another toke on top of the last one, then passes the joint to me, the two of us doing the intimate little finger dance known to stoners everywhere. "Ain't gonna tell me, though."

"Not 'til I'm sure," I say. I take a small hit, finger dance it back. "I need a day or two to line up proof."

Who am I kidding? I mentally click off the crimes I'm hanging around just waiting to commit—slip aboard *Bounder* uninvited, find and filch Allan's log, and peruse its pages for something implicating Kirtley. That's assuming I can even get out there. "Could use your help with something, though," I say.

"Yeah, what's that?"

"I'm gonna need to row out through the harbor at some point," I tell him. "Would help if I don't get shot."

"Temptin' target that you make just now."

"That's what I'm thinking."

He considers over another toke. "I'm doin' this for Al, you understand—not for some shit-for-brains, punk-ass guy counts trees for a fuckin' living. Want that understood."

"Understood," I say, my eyes on the shifting colors of the sunset. "Cash is King, right?" I grin, glancing over, but he's already gone, vanished but for the sweet, lingering waft of marijuana—as if, like Captain Kirk, he simply beamed back to the sixties and the starship Coachmen Cadet.

I'm hanging out in Rachel's studio next morning, stool cocked against the wall as I semi-doze in a warm shaft of morning light, when the wall phone against which my head has recently come to rest chirps twice—jerking me awake and tumbling me to the floor where I land ass-first on an unopened twelvie of paper towels. Bounty—the quicker picker-upper.

I'm still half-asleep as I grab for the handset. Another round of wraith-like communication from the netherworld? Last time this thing rang, I pegged ghostie girl as my caller—the crackle of static hardly surprising considering the distance between centuries. No static this time, though; seems the time-space continuum is working in our favor.

I hesitate.

Hesitation on the other end, too.

"Mary?" I croak.

"Who?" Al barks. "Listen, glad I caught you—saves me a walk. Doug just called. Kirtley's boarding the plane as we speak." A pause. "I got Tiffany running deliveries on the other side of the island for the next couple hours. You still up for this?"

I flash to Gail—the incredible pain she must have been in, the utter despair she must have felt as she lay dying at the bottom of that well.

"Damn right."

THIRTY-SEVEN

The first time Dad took me to Yankee Stadium, I'd just turned eight. June 24, 1970. Night game, too, the second in a double header against the Cleveland Indians. A truly magical night made all the more so when Bobby Murcer, Yankee Numero Uno, tied the league record for four consecutive home runs—the stadium erupting with that final homer as if everyone there had punched into the stratosphere with him.

Dad turned to me, then—his face still full and lit with ruddy good health. "Remember this night, Gil," he grinned. "Murcer never chokes; once committed he never backs away from the plate." Even at eight I knew what he was telling me. He might just as easily have said *never do anything halfway*, or *never love with half a heart*, but that wasn't him. He believed in baseball as metaphor for life. The Game could teach you all you'd ever need to know about making hard decisions. About, well, being a man.

It's an old memory—one I haven't dredged up in years, which is maybe why it feels so powerful right now, why I can't get his words out of my head as I row out to *Bounder* some thirty minutes after Al's call. Praying Cash's dispensation against a bullet in the back was the real deal. Could be I'm sticking my neck out like this to prove I really was listening that night thirty-five years ago, that I can actually care enough and do enough when the chips are down. A real departure for me, I have to say. Part and parcel of my admittedly irresponsible lifestyle is the tendency to bolt when things get dicey. Complications of the emotional sort? I run for the hills.

Until now.

Most of the lobster boats are out this morning, and good thing, too. Far as I know, Al and I are the only ones who know what I'm up to out here, and in an attempt to keep up the ruse, I take it slow—tooling around the harbor for a bit as if I've no particular destination in mind. Hate to waste precious minutes like this, but no doubt there are at least a couple pairs of eyes trained on me, and I want them to grow tired of this aimless little exercise before I actually tie up.

Get in, get the log, get out. Simple, right? It's what I tell myself, anyway, as I climb the stern and slink across the open cockpit, which is when I come face-to-face with the closed companionway and, more importantly, the padlock. A bad moment indeed.

Of course she locks the thing, I scold myself as I crouch to examine the setup, see if there's any way around this. It's then I see. Kirtley can be as lazy as the rest of us, it seems. Padlock's in place but not snapped shut.

First thing that hits me after I descend the companionway and carefully re-close the hatch is how unnaturally tidy the place is. Not a dirty coffee cup or toast crumb to be found. Nothing like the way I leave my loft in the morning, that's for sure. Galley's immediately to my left, so I start there. I open the oven; glance in; close it again. No ship's log in there. I check a couple cabinets. Turn the water on; turn it off.

This is ridiculous. I throw myself into one of the blue suede chairs, toss my cap to the side table and try not to panic. It's my first time burgling the home of a stone-cold killer, and I'm at a loss. There must be hundreds of places on a boat this big to hide something like this. And the fact I've got no plausible explanation for my presence here should Kirtley unexpectedly return continues to nibble at my resolve.

Room by room, I tell myself. A section at a time, just like any other cataloguing job. And so I rise, having wasted far too much time already, and spend maybe fifteen minutes sifting through the main cabin—shelves and drawers, the cabinets that line both sides of the room. More storage in this one room than many of the places I've lived. And nothing about any of it offers even the whiff of potential.

C'mon Gil, I urge; think outside the hull. If I were Allan, where would I keep my log or brag book or whatever? Has to be readily accessible for one thing, since according to Al, I pore over it at length each day. Close to where I can sit comfortably and write, too—with a table for my snifter of cognac or whatever. And someplace I have access to all the technical data Al tells me fills these things. Wind speed, compass headings, stuff like that.

I hone in on the navigation area with its chart desk and wall of instruments, seat myself in the black leather comfort of Allan's swivel chair. Precious minutes tick by as I poke through the various cubbies, the twin columns of vertical drawers flanking the desk. It's then I realize the top is little more than a hinged lid which I lift, revealing a bonanza of nautical charts and assorted boat papers. More importantly, tossed casually on top is a spiral-bound, brown leather book about the size of a magazine. The cover reads *Bounder, 2004-2005.*

Bingo.

I spend about ten seconds admiring my detecting skills then flip the thing open. Before me is a record of voyages—dates, positions, cryptic technical notes I don't even pretend to understand, so I tuck the thing under my arm for later perusal. Not the kind of thing Kirtley will miss, I figure—not for a few days anyway.

I've got maybe half an hour left, so I decide to go through the rest of the boat for any other possible evidence that Kirtley did Allan in. The etched glass door to her cabin is open; the room beyond neat as a pin. Bed made up, nothing out on the cherry dresser or twin end tables. Fingering one of two identical sliding doors open, I find myself face to face with a double rung of men's khakis and polo shirts, a floor full of shoes. Creeps me out.

I perch on the edge of the bed, distracted by the memory of a sweaty froth of fragrant sheets as I slide the night table drawer open. The gun that greets me is hardly the size of Cash's, but then how big do these things have to be, after all? Betcha anything it's loaded, too—a realization that hits hard. Last time here I was in full passionate thrall, lost in a level of steamy raunch that would've made even Annika blush. Kirtley could've pulled a Howitzer out and I'd have gladly humped it.

Could be she used the gun on Allan, then rolled him overboard. Would nudge her odds of success up considerably, I should think. Useless as evidence, of course. No body. But scrub the boat all you want and there'll still be some sort of blood DNA, right? Which TV show was that again?

I move around the bed, open the drawer in the second night table. Another gun, I'm thinking—his and hers kind of thing. Instead, I find a man's watch—Rolex, no less. There's also a wallet, a couple spools of dental floss, wedding band and massive black onyx Lodge ring. I flip the wallet open to find the cash and credit cards gone, hardly a surprise. A girl has to eat, after all. The name on the driver's license reads Allan M. Kneeland. Age fifty-six, according to this.

No doubt he stashed all this here when he was sailing, but like the clothes it feels wrong. Anyone other than Kirtley, I'd figure it for sentimentality, a reluctance to let go. But not this chick. She keeps his stuff around to savor the memory of what she did to him. Don't ask me how I know this, but I do.

I paw briefly through her dresser drawers; finding nothing, of course.

Ditto the head with its cherry tub and Corian countertops, though I'm not sure what I thought I'd find in here—a bottle of prescription anti-psychotics, maybe? The whole place is almost obsessively clean, reminding me strangely of that fifties cult classic *Invasion of the Body Snatchers*—the pod people who retreat to their homes at night and do nothing but stare at the walls.

I almost skip the guest cabin, which I know to be uninhabited, but decide for the sake of thoroughness to give it a go. The door to this one is shut, and when I open it, I'm stopped cold. No pod person here. The bed is a crumpled mess, a damp towel dropped to the floor. Hair scrunchies and a familiar tank top tossed on the dresser beside scattered cosmetics. The air feels moist, smells of shampoo and bubble gum.

Tiffany, I realize. The kid's been crashing here. Christ.

This changes everything.

I avoid the Galley Hatch after rowing back in, hoping to isolate Al from any nasty repercussions should Kirtley somehow learn of my snoop through her stuff. Instead I tie the dinghy up and head straight to Rachel's, returning to the Hatch a couple hours later.

Al opens the door from behind a hand-lettered sign that reads *Closed 'Til Further Notice*, and I'm hit with the smell of fresh-brewed coffee, which we drink while I fill him in on what I found—everything except the part about Kirtley and Tiffany playing roomies. No power on earth could keep him from yanking Tiffany out of there if he knew, and who could blame him? That would be it, though. Should Tiffany suddenly drop off her radar, Kirtley'd be out of here like a shot.

Al knows a lot more about boat stuff than I do, so I was hoping he'd have some luck deciphering the log. Unfortunately, nothing leaps out. True to form, Allan was religious about recording position, weather, and sea conditions—not just once but several times a day. But there's little else; and not a domestic entry of any kind. No *The wife's been looking at me a little funny lately* or *Wonder why she's been cleaning that gun so much.*

"All that and we ain't got squat," Al says. "Damn."

"Yeah," I say. "Damn"—the slow prickle of realization that's making its way along my scalp the same sick feeling I got two or three years back when I realized I'd left my wallet atop a gas pump twenty turnpike miles behind me.

"What?" Al asks.

"Jesus Christ, Al. My ball cap—I left it on *Bounder*."

He looks stunned. "Hodge, no. Tell me you didn't. Shit."

We turn as one to the window. Sure enough, Kirtley's sleek white Zodiac bobs gently from *Bounder's* stern. By now she'll have found my cap;

it's the only thing in the room even hinting of human habitation.

"Alright, okay," I say, trying not to panic. "Maybe it's not so bad after all."

A choked laugh from Al. "How do you figure that? The whole point was to stay below the radar with this, case she goes nuts and kills someone else—Tiffany, for instance."

"So she finds my cap out there, so what?" I say thinking out loud. "That only proves I was there. Could have been for any number of reasons, right?" I'm punting here, but a plan's taking shape as I work my way through this.

"Could be she won't know the log's gone," Al suggests. "Might not even know it's there. Think about it. No entries since—hold on." He flips through to the log's end. "May 10—right here," he says, stabbing the page with a finger. "That's more than three months ago—probably the very day she killed Allan. Last known position thirty-eight degrees, forty-five minutes north; sixty-six degrees, fifty-two minutes west. Somewhere between here and Bermuda, sounds like."

"She'll still know I was there."

"And want to know why," Al says, finishing my thought.

"I have to go back," I say, my gaze drawn to the window again. "Now. Convince her I was there looking for her, hoping for a little nookie."

Our eyes meet. "You gotta be kidding."

"Only way," I tell him.

A slow nod. "Keep your friends close and your enemies closer, right? But could you—you know—do it? Knowin' who she is? What she is?"

"I should go," I say, avoiding his question, "Have to make it look like I've been haunting the harbor waiting for her return." I nod toward the log as I rise, make for the door. "Stick it someplace safe, okay? I won't be long."

"Gil," he says, and I turn. "Watch out for that inside pitch."

THIRTY-EIGHT

I take the ladder to the skiff, rowing out through the harbor in the same aimless fashion as before, pretty much for the same reasons. And wondering how the hell I'm gonna pull this off. Most of the boats are in for the day, and while I get a few hard looks from guys off-loading their catch or cleaning skids, it's Kirtley I'm really concerned about. Looking anxious or uneasy could sink me, so I try for relaxed, self-confident. A bit of the horny male thing thrown in. Give her the impression I've got just one thing on my mind—same thing I was looking for my first time out. My cap tossed to the table as I settled in to wait—something I'd hardly do if I'd slipped aboard for a quick toss of the place, right?

I pull alongside, grabbing the stainless steel rail for support.

"Permission to come aboard?" I call. Another nautical insight courtesy of Patrick O'Brian.

She appears some thirty seconds later, lounging against the side of the companionway. Jean shorts cut maybe an inch below the crotch, same minimal top she wore the afternoon she tried to sever my tongue.

"Mr. Hodges," she says, her gaze cool. "What a surprise." Eyeing me as she sips from a tall glass. Iced tea? Diet Coke?

"I was out here earlier," I say shooting her my most sheepish Jeff Bridges—loveable, goofy and heretofore never known to fail. "Waited a bit."

A flicker of surprise at that. Admitting the deed before it's thrown in your face always catches them off guard.

"So I gathered. You left your hat."

"Standard operating procedure," I tell her as *Ka-Ching* slowly motors by, Cash's glare boring into my neck. "Makes a kick-ass calling card; plus it gives me a reason to come back."

She takes a long sip, not quite buying. A stab of alarm as I wonder what other stupid-ass thing I might have done to give myself away. I flash to the guest cabin door; did I remember to close it? A bead of sweat traces the back of my ear as I grapple with the mental mud of stress-induced memory loss.

Finally Kirtley shrugs. "Fortune favors the bold, right?"

I think of Gail. I think of Josh and Ivan. Then I think of Tiffany and widen my grin a notch.

"Tongue's healed," I tease. "I could come aboard and demonstrate." God forbid she takes me up on it. Got a feeling if I kissed those lips right now I might just flash freeze.

"I'm in the middle of something," she tells me. Waits a beat. "Hold on." Then she's gone.

I think of the gun in her bedside drawer. Even she isn't brazen enough to shoot me out here in the middle of the harbor, right? Not with a bunch of lobstermen looking on. I glance around for potential witnesses, hard-pressed to think of one who might actually give a shit.

When I swing my gaze back, she's there in the companionway, my cap in hand. "Later," she says, tossing it to me. "About nine. I'll come to you."

"Can't wait."

I row away—slowly, lazily, like I haven't a care in the world—but inside I'm a mess. Heart ramming my ribs, sweat glands in overdrive. Who knows if I really pulled it off; but I probably muddied the waters enough to buy us a little time. It's later tonight that's the problem now. How the hell do I handle that?

I spend the rest of the afternoon with Al, making our way through the log one entry at a time in hopes we've missed something—anything that might confirm what I know in my heart. Unfortunately for us, the late Allan Kneeland was all business when it came to his boat. The only references we find to Kirtley, whom he refers to simply as "K," are notes about the watches she took each day—sails flown, direction and speed of the boat, how much ground she covered, like that. The last entry, May 10th, appears to be just another day at sea—Allan's notes, like most of the others, made at about seventeen hundred hours, or five in the afternoon. Which gives us squat.

A couple hours of this and we hang it up. Al trots out the chili; I pop a couple Rolling Rocks. Reminds me of some of my great one-on-ones with Dad—a feeling I savor all the more 'cause I've no idea what's coming next.

I'm certain of just two things—I've got to somehow smuggle the log back to *Bounder* before Kirtley realizes it's gone, and my performance at tonight's little soiree better be world class. Anything less will prove me the liar I am.

One thing leads to another, and I don't head for the dugout 'til almost dusk. Probably why I don't see the damage till I'm on it. First thing I notice are all the papers fluttering around me in the updraft. I snatch a few mid-air. A torn page of cataloguing notes, part of a class outline, a few pages ripped from the only textbook I brought to the island.

It's like a bomb went off out here—both loungers mangled, my half-full cooler overturned, smashed beer bottles everywhere. Tent's still standing but empty.

So where's my stuff?

Numb, I follow a trail of papers to the drop-off, knowing even before I peer over the edge what I'll find. Still, the totality of it all takes a minute to register. My clothes, my sleeping bag, the bulk of my papers and cataloguing work all flotsam now—bobbing together in the salt water, rockweed, and bird shit of the tidal pool below.

Un-fucking-believable.

Light's fading fast, so I scramble down, start dragging what I can from the water before the tide turns, sucking everything away. I toss sodden clothing up the rock face; a good wash at the house and most of it'll be fine. My books and papers are another matter—ruined probably, but I'll make the effort anyway, dry them out by Rachel's fire and salvage what I can.

Five or six trips later, the anger's kicked in. Fuming, hands on hips, I mentally tick off the possibilities while staring at the sodden pile of my belongings. Kids? I wonder. No. Too personal, too in-your-face. More likely Cash and friends, all juiced up and done playing nice.

Looking down, I notice the smashed shells and driftwood of the wind chime at my feet.

Fuckin'-A.

Turning, I punt the mangled mess into the sea, the force of the kick spinning me round.

It's then I catch sight of Kirtley tucked in the shadows—arms crossed, back against the trunk of a half-dead spruce as she takes it all in. No idea how long she's been there, and at the moment I don't give a shit, what with the emotional sucker punch I've just taken. An entire summer's work—gone.

"You're early," I say, lobbing chunks of beer bottle into the surf. "Boys got a little wild last night; haven't had a chance to pick the place up. How 'bout we do this another time?"

"You've got something of mine," she says, pushing from the tree and starting toward me. "I know it's not here, so where is it?"

I turn, stunned. "*You* did this?" So much for that elaborate ruse back at the boat. Could be time to ditch the aging movie star shtick.

"Cut the act. You took Allan's log; I want it back. Simple as that."

Whatever for? I've read hundred-page weather reports that were more revealing. She'd know that, too, if she'd ever really read the thing, which tells me she hasn't. Gives me an edge. Not much of one, but I'll take it.

"So you killed him after all," I try. "All that talk the other day; I thought you were just putting me on. Laugh's on me, right?"

She picks her way toward me. "Poor man had a fall, is all. Tripped and went splash one perfectly lovely afternoon. Lot of yelling and cursing—very entertaining. I saw him get picked off by a shark as I sailed away. Did my heart good, I have to say."

She's having fun now, her voice playful as she watches my face—needing my reaction to feed whatever thrill this gives her. I can't imagine I disappoint.

"Afternoon? I thought you told Clayton he went overboard at night."

"Did I?"

"That what you told the Coast Guard—that he went over at night?"

"I might have forgotten to call them at all, actually; I really can't remember. I was in shock, as you can imagine."

"I'll bet."

She's working me toward the water, but instinct tells me to circle back toward the tent. I'll need every advantage to get off a good kick, and having some even ground would be a decent start. It's just about dark, the half moon ducking in and out of the clouds, so the light isn't good—though that's less of a problem than the fact I haven't practiced any Tae Kwon Do since I came out here.

"Where's the log, Gil?"

"I have no idea," I say, edging closer to the tent. "You could have just asked, you know—saved yourself all this trouble."

She smiles, matching me step for step. "It was kind of a kick when I thought you suspected; added a level of danger I found...exciting. But searching my boat? Taking my property?" She shakes her head. "Pissed me off."

I look around. "Apparently."

It's then she pulls the gun from somewhere at her back, holds it like she knows how to use it, too—while all I'm armed with are a couple rusty martial arts skills. I flash to Rachel's rifle, propped just inside the barn door, wondering if I could beat Kirtley in a dash for it. Still, reaching it in time to save myself is one thing; getting myself to actually use it quite another.

"So where is it?" Kirtley snaps, her patience beginning to wear. "Up at the house?"

"And here I just had this long conversation with Tiffany about how great you are—her words, not mine—how you're her best friend, the only person who understands her." I'm stalling, but I need to keep her talking 'til I can reach the path and make a break for the barn. She's not going to shoot me 'til she's got the log, right?

"Amazing how trusting she is after all she's been through," Kirtley says, stepping lightly as we continue our dance. "Kind of sweet, really. You know she actually swallowed the story I fed her about Allan still being alive? Consulting in New York, I think I said."

"Wasn't a total lie, I guess; the part about his being a controlling, manipulative prick was true enough. Loved having power over people, enjoyed watching them squirm—business skills he thought translated well to marriage. Tiffany seemed utterly shocked by it all."

She smirks at my look of surprise. What was it Tiffany said to me on the dock? *She's had it tough; you don't know.* "I got her to promise to keep my secret, never really thinking she would. I was hoping she'd tell people he was really still alive, confuse the issue. I mean I had to do something. It was a huge mistake, telling Clayton that Allan had fallen overboard. Man was a lot smarter than he looked."

Focus, I remind myself; keep her distracted. "Getting a little too close to the truth, was he?"

"He was a pain in the ass, frankly."

Pain in the ass or not, the guy hardly deserved to have his head stove in. And Ivan was just a kid, for Chrissake. God only knows what Clunk did to piss her off. Gail, it seems, was the only one who had her number. I picture her ruined face, a cold resolve taking shape as I gauge the distance to the shadowy trail out of the corner of my eye.

All this heinous brutality, Kirtley's twisted psychology—it's all so eerily like Hannah and the cold-blooded things she did to people. To Mary. To Weston. Atticus was the only one who knew what she was—Atticus, who loved Mary, the child he was too late to save. Mary, who loved him back and who was a Burgess like Tiffany, who herself came down from Atticus. The blending of the lines. Mary, Atticus, Tiffany.

Then, just like that, I've got it—the connection I've been trying for all along. Amazing I didn't see it before, what with the lobster shells and that letter from Hannah's father little ghostie girl kept pointing me toward. I kept thinking it was about her, but that wasn't the half of it. It wasn't even so much about Hannah as her monstrous persona—the unthinkable murder of someone who'd come to trust her, rely on her. Mary, it appears, was warning me.

Ghostie girl reaching down through the years to protect her own.

I see it now. It's Tiffany Kirtley's been circling all along, Tiffany who's the real prize here. And why? My gut tells me it's the kid's vulnerability she zeroed in on, all that need so easy to manipulate. So she uses the kid to gain access and information, all the while slowly teasing her from the pack, saving the best for last. It was brilliantly done, too—you have to give her that—and so obvious if you take Clunk out of the equation. No doubt she used him as a kind of murder litmus test to see how many official eyebrows his death would raise. But it wasn't until Clayton's autopsy was so obviously rubber-stamped that she got serious, going after Ivan and then Gail—their deaths designed to isolate Tiffany, increase her growing dependence on her special new friend. It all fits. And with the two of them out of the picture and Al consumed with grief, Kirtley was free to simply reel her in.

My God, I think, fighting panic. If only I'd listened to Al, agreed to warn her.

"So where's Tiffany now?" I manage—amazed I can manage such a conversational tone.

"Waiting for me on *Bounder*. We leave for Bermuda tonight. Seems she's as anxious to get out of here as I am." Kirtley actually chuckles at this.

I can't help myself. "Must be the ultimate rush for a monster like you, duping some vulnerable kid into loving you, needing you."

Kirtley grins in the moonlight. "See? I knew you'd understand."

Something just snaps. I haven't felt this kind of blind rage since Annika went at me with that beer bottle; it's all I can do to keep from launching myself at her. The right kick would snap her neck, I know—worth giving it a shot just to feel the satisfaction. But even in top form, the kickass speed of a Black Belt is no match for a bullet. Besides, I have to survive this or Tiffany doesn't stand a chance.

So instead I make a grab for the broken cooler and lob it at her, taking advantage of her surprise to whirl and take off—propelling myself down a path I know well enough to navigate in my sleep. Crooked, uneven, a minefield of jutting rocks and mangled tree roots I can only hope will slow her down.

I'm maybe thirty feet in when I hear the crack of a shot, the thwack of a bullet slicing into a tree to my right. So much for the theory she wouldn't shoot. I crouch, ducking and weaving the way they do in the movies, but it's tough to make much headway. I'm as scared as I am pissed off now, trying to force myself to focus on just one thing—getting my hands on that rifle. Any hang-ups about using the thing long gone.

Another shot. This one thumps dully into the pine needles at my feet and I stumble in surprise, landing hard and slamming my side on the sharp edge of a rock. Hurts to breathe, so I decide not to. I wonder vaguely if she'll kill me now; or if it even matters. All advantage gone, I consider rolling into the bushes in the hope she'll miss me in her rush to catch up. A breathy *whoof* followed by a thud somewhere behind tells me Kirtley, too, has fallen; and suddenly I'm up and scrambling again.

I can think of a hundred scenarios—none of them good. Even if I had a phone, and I don't, there's no 911 out here—just thirty rough miles of open ocean between me and a reluctant cavalry.

What would Bruce Willis do, or Schwarzenegger?

I continue ducking, jogging, weaving across the trail which suddenly seems longer than it should. I nearly panic thinking I've gotten turned around out here, veered onto some secondary path leading God only knows where. I'm trying to get my bearings when Kirtley fires two more shots—one whizzing by my head. It's the second one that's the problem, though—the nasty sting somewhere below my right knee spreading fast and slowing me down.

I trip on a root and almost go flying again, stumble around another corner to see the looming hulk of the old barn some fifty yards ahead. My shoe's full of blood, my foot making a squishing noise each time I land on my right leg; still, I put what's left of my energy into a sprint for the darkened doorway.

Another shot hits the barn as I duck inside and turn for the rifle. Only it's gone.

I try the other side of the door, but it's not there, either.

What the hell?

I whirl, desperate—peering wildly into darkened corners, my gaze grazing the walls. When I finish my three-sixty, Kirtley's standing in the doorway backlit by the moon, that gun trained on my chest.

"I mean really," she laughs. "Right inside the door? You had to know I'd search this place." Shakes her head as I hunch over my knees, sucking in air. Kirtley, I'm ashamed to say, is barely winded. "Not very good at this, are you?"

"First time—sorry," I wheeze, eyes raised just enough to keep scanning for the rifle. "Try it again?"

"Don't bother," she snaps, approaching slowly. "It's not here."

She's maybe three feet away now, just far enough to make grabbing for the gun too risky.

"I must say you've been rather a disappointment," she tells me.

"Not sexually, I hope. My reviews in that area are generally pretty good."

I stand to face her and it's then she steps in, planting herself firmly against me as she buries the barrel in my nuts—an odd smile playing on her lips. I don't so much as flinch.

"I liked you," she pouts. "Why did you have to get so nosy?"

"C'mon, now," I try, stalling for time. "Killing five people isn't enough for you?"

Her eyes widen for a split second—surprise that I've finally figured it out, maybe? Hard to tell in the gloom.

I wince as she grinds the gun in. "Easy," I breathe, the pain oddly heightening my sense of smell—damp earth, blood, something musky. Fear, I realize—my own. Death by castration, I'm thinking. How ironic. "Killing me is one thing, but why mess with the boys?"

"Can't lose what you never had, Gil. Balls, I mean." She's grown flushed, looks almost high—turned on by the power, the anticipation of watching me die. "Besides, it's not about the why. You, of all people, should understand."

"Me?" I croak.

"It's all about the hunt, for people like us. Sex is one game; I simply took it to a higher level. Killing Allan set me free in more ways than one. You said it yourself; it's the fantasy of women everywhere."

I tell myself she's full of shit, that her little analogy's a crock, but some part of me wonders if in a weird way she hasn't got me nailed. The emotional disconnect I cloak myself in; the unbridled, over-the-top way I pursue sexual conquest, then walk away—what's all that about if not some deeply aggressive urge? An odd thought, then. What if it was myself I'd really come out here to catalogue—growth, overall health, and outlook for longevity? If so, it ain't lookin' too good just now.

I feel the gun shift, inch my gaze down to find the thing aimed at my chin.

"If I pull the trigger now," Kirtley whispers, "which one of us dies?" Then, just like that, she steps away—backing up maybe a foot out of reach. "No more stalling. Tell me where Allan's log is. Otherwise I just kill you and get Tiffany to help me."

I groan inwardly, near panic at the thought of Tiffany waiting so unsuspectingly on *Bounder*. Then again, if I tell Kirtley that Al's got the log, she kills him—no question. And it's not gonna happen, not if I can help it. Still, I refuse to go out like some wimp; so with silent apologies to Tiffany—who I can only pray will somehow figure all this out before it's too late—I drop my head and make a run at Kirtley, wondering if I'll be dead before I hear the shot.

What I hear instead is a thick whoosh, a loud crack, and just like that, she drops to the dirt at my feet. My momentum being what it is, I stumble and come down hard, barely managing to miss her. Glancing up, I can only stare, my disorientation complete. Standing above us, two by four in hand, is Cash.

"Can't fuckin' leave you alone for a minute," he snarls.

Only then do I register the presence of Josh and *Hombre* in the shadows behind him.

Might not be a cavalry, but they make a hell of a good posse.

"Figured it had to be one of you," Cash says, "so we been keepin' an eye." He stoops for Kirtley's gun, tucks it in his pants. "Find some rope," he says over his shoulder. "Tie her up good."

"She killed her husband," I tell him as *Hombre* heads off. "Never reported the death. Probably killed Clayton 'cause he caught on." I pause. "I figure she killed Ivan and Gail to isolate Tiffany. The kid's waiting for her on *Bounder*, thinks they're sailing for Bermuda tonight."

He cocks his head toward the dirt, his eye beginning its telltale twitch. "She tell you that?"

I nod, glancing over his shoulder at Rachel's house squatting silent and watchful in the moonlight—hoping Mary's somehow bearing witness. I'd like to think she knows I finally figured all this out, that Atticus's great-whatever-granddaughter is safe.

I whirl at the sound of another loud thwack, the sickening crunch of shattered bone, and see Kirtley flinch—a moan escaping in her semi-conscious state.

"Fuckin' bitch," Cash snarls, raising his arm for yet another go.

"Whoa!" I shout grabbing for his arm. "Nothing I'd like better than a couple whacks at her myself, but right here in Rachel's barn? Think about it."

He stares at me, wild-eyed with fury, nodding slowly as *Hombre* returns with a pile of phone cord no doubt yanked from the house—yet something else I'll have to replace.

"You're right," Cash says finally. "No reason to bring Rachel into this."

Hombre pulls Kirtley's hands roughly behind her back and ties them. "I say we leave her with Cheryl tonight." He gives the knots an extra tug. "Won't be nothin' left by mornin'."

"Tiffany," I say. "We've got to get her off that boat."

"Row out there," Cash tells Josh. "Take her back to Al's—drag her if you have to. But don't say nothin' bout any of this, understand? And get back with the truck soon as you can."

Josh nods.

"Best you stop and fill Al in first," Cash adds. It's then he notices my leg, the blood pooling at my feet. And grins.

"I'm fine," I mumble, but I'm not—not at all. Now that all the fun's over, the steady stream of adrenaline slowing to a trickle, my head pounds, waves of pain alternating with nausea. I'm going to hurl or faint, maybe both, which should just about sew up my image here.

"And get Bill what's-his-ass back to tend to Hodge," Cash calls over his shoulder. "Gunshot wound, tell him. Lotta blood."

THIRTY-NINE

It's a couple days before I'm up and about with anything like my usual energy. Relieved, anxious, I await the forces of officialdom while limping around Rachel's drying out my soggy stuff and chowing down the series of creamy casseroles I keep finding on the back porch.

The third morning, I start to wonder just what's going on, exactly when somebody's going to show up and start grilling me about Kirtley—her confession at the dugout, the chase through the woods, all of it.

Yeah, I know, unraveling a string of murders takes time, and the cops or the Coasties or whoever handles this kind of thing out here in the hinterlands have an island's worth of hardened Matinicans to get through—most, if not all, reluctant to share anything more pithy than an ample fart with a badge or uniform.

The other problem, believe it or not, is ghostie girl. Once Tiffany was out of harm's way, you'd think she'd have vacated the place, or slipped away, or whatever spectral beings do once they've finished their business here. But no. Seems there's something more I'm supposed to have sussed out, evidence the rhythmic thumping continuing from the second floor—Her Spiritness banging her head repeatedly at my continued stupidity, no doubt. I haven't seen her this agitated, frankly, since the night I found the letter, figured out it was Hannah who killed her. Not that I'm complaining. The place would hardly be the same without her.

Bill Cutler did an admirable job with the leg, by the way. The bullet hit mid-calf, managing to miss bones and arteries and all that other important stuff as it sliced its way out the other side. Flesh wound, as they say, though the stitching hurt like hell—Bill not having much in the way of drugs to numb me out. Pretty smug when he told me this, too. Kinda made me wonder.

Cash himself stopped by last night, surprised the hell out of me. Don't think we said three words, just kicked back on the porch steps with a couple beers, passing a joint between us while a molten sun eased its way toward the horizon. Touched me; I have to say, though it's Al I really need to see. And right away. No doubt he's got his hands full trying to keep Tiffany out of all this; still I need to know just what he's told the police, whether he's given them Allan's log. No way around it, I suppose; it's the reason Kirtley used me for target practice, after all. Thing is, they'll want to know how he came by it—something bound to cause me a few legal problems of my own.

About noon I've had enough of all this waiting and decide to take my act on the road, dragging myself over to the Galley Hatch—which reopened yesterday, according to Cash—looking for answers, some buzz on the investigation. I grab a beer and take a seat, toss my cap to the counter. I can hear Al rattling around back in the kitchen, that and music wafting from upstairs—something soft and female, filled with longing. Nora Jones, maybe.

"Ah, it's you," Al nods, limping around the corner loaded down with tube steaks and rolls for the steamer.

I cock my head toward the ceiling. "How's she doing?"

"Not sure," he says, following my gaze. "Hasn't talked to me since Josh pulled her off that boat, kickin' and screamin' like you never seen. Bit him in the hand but good, too. Had to lock her in her room that night, or she'd have gone right back out there. Next morning when I ask her how she is? Tells me to go fuck myself, that tells you anything."

"Good sign."

A half-hearted shrug. It's then I notice how drawn he looks, how tired—his tee shirt gone baggy practically overnight. Christ when was the last time he ate?

"She sneaks down when she thinks I'm not around, grabs something from the kitchen; other than that she pretty much stays upstairs, plays her music."

"She'll be alright—you'll see." And I'm sure she will. Not right away, not anytime soon, but eventually.

He nods distractedly, glances toward a brown cardboard box over by the cash register, eight by eight maybe, and taped up hard. Ashes, I realize. Dad's came back in one just like it.

Hard to imagine you can shrink a person's whole existence—body, mind, a lifetime of experience—to something the size of a Kleenex box.

"Been thinking of selling out," Al says. "What with Gail gone and Tiffany heading off to school, not sure I can take it out here. Not sure I want to."

Can't blame him, really. I admit to much the same feeling. Not only that, the cataloguing project's a complete loss, though I find I'm strangely ambivalent about it—almost relieved in a way. The whole idea should have died with Ben.

"I'll be heading out myself—soon as the police are done with me," I tell him. "They gotten to you yet? 'Cause no one's been by Rachel's at all."

"I'll be sorry to see you go," Al says, loading the steamer with dogs. "And I mean that."

"You handed Allan's log over yet?" I ask. "They'll want it for sure, for all the good it'll do them. You can visit me in prison when Kirtley tells them I broke into her boat and stole it."

"Reminds me," Al says. "I went through the thing again after you left that day, found a small brass key worked into the spine. Safe deposit box or something."

Our eyes meet. "No shit." No wonder she was so desperate to get her hands on the thing.

He nods. "Could be old Allan didn't trust Kirtley as much as she'd have liked.

"Something else," he says, hefting a moldering cardboard box from the top of the Philco to the counter. "Found this when I was going through Gail's things. It's all stuff they pulled from Rachel's place during the renovation—Hannah's things, Gail figured, since they were found with the diary. All of it packed under a floorboard. Guess I'll pass it along to Rachel now; let her decide what to do with it."

I set the box on the stool next to me, stir the stuff around. A bunch of old papers, a desiccated pair of leather shoes, a moldy prayer book. Whole thing smells of decay. Then something else catches my eye.

"Mind if I keep this?" I ask.

Al glances over. "Souvenir, huh? Sure, take what you want. I don't give a shit."

I lay it gently in my pocket, glance toward the harbor expecting a wharf choked with Coast Guard zodiacs, a bunch of official types milling about the dock. But there's nothing—no cops, no inflatables—nothing.

And no sign of *Bounder*.

Confused, I turn to Al. "Police impound Kirtley's boat?"

He doesn't answer, absorbed as he's suddenly become in the scrubbing of the coffee machine. A little too much gusto for what's basically busy work.

"Al?"

Nothing.

I slide my gaze uneasily to the window, willing the glistening fifty-footer to reappear, which is when it finally hits me—the one question I should've asked Gail and never did. "What happened to Hannah, Al? She confess?"

"Eventually." He stills, considers, then turns—wiping his hands slowly on the dishtowel. "Island had its own kind of justice back then, its own way of dealin' with the likes of her. Set her adrift about ten miles out. Enough food and water for a couple days so she could contemplate her sins. Island Justice, they called it—crude but effective."

A death sentence.

"Where's *Bounder*, Al?" I ask again—more pointedly this time. "Where's Kirtley?"

"Best part is, didn't cost the taxpayer a dime. Had it right back then, you ask me."

I grow still as the realization sinks in. "Nobody called the police, did they?"

"It's been dealt with," he says. "All you need to know."

"*All I need to know*? What the fuck, Al?"

His look is a mix of triumph and defiance. "My wife's dead, Hodge—beaten to death, remember? Died slow and hard. Ask me if I give a rat's ass what happens to Kirtley Kneeland except she goes the same way. Ask Cheryl."

"Island justice," I say flatly, not bothering to hide my disgust.

"What," he snorts, "you think we'd get any if this went to court? That log of Allan's, the way we got it? That woman gets a half-decent attorney, no way it'd be admitted as evidence. And all that stuff she told you in the woods? Just your word against hers.

"Got no death penalty in Maine, either—you know that? Even by some miracle we got a conviction, you want a monster like that livin' all comfy in some country club prison for the rest of her life? And us payin' for it? Well, I've paid enough."

I open my mouth, close it again. It's just more killing, I want to plead—retribution, not justice—but what's the point? What's more—and I hate to admit this—he's right. One of the greatest ironies in all this is that Allan's money would buy Kirtley a topnotch attorney, an amenable psychiatrist. What's more, we have no physical evidence linking her to any of this. She was careful about that.

"Don't expect you to understand," Al tells me, "just go along. Another thing. Right now all Tiffany knows is I pulled her off *Bounder* 'cause I got wind she was livin' out there. She finds out we knew about their plan to sail outta here together, she's gonna start askin' questions. This way she figures Kirtley got tired of waiting and sailed off without so much as a goodbye. She needs to keep thinkin' that."

I mull this over. No question that as hard as this lie is on her, the truth would be much worse. The police start sniffing around, the whole thing comes out. All the information Tiffany unwittingly fed Kirtley, the way Kirtley then used it to target and murder her victims. Sucking up to Tiffany, pretending to be her friend and all the while planning to kill her, too. I know this kid; innocent as her part was in all this, she'd never forgive herself. Maybe it's best she thinks abandonment the worst thing that can happen to her.

I snag my cap and head for the door.

Right, then.

FORTY

Three days later, we're buckling into the Cessna for the noon flight to Rockland. Doug's his usual chatty self, talking fuel consumption and weather windows as he packs the outgoing mail and packages around our gear, inexplicably jamming in a rusty two-wheeler circa 1950, with not one but two flat tires. All the activity keeping any real conversation to a minimum, which is fine with me. Less chance for the kind of questions I'd be forced to dance around. Not that I've got much to worry about there. Tiffany's said nothing about Kirtley since the night she was yanked from the boat, not to me anyway. And why would she? She's come to expect this kind of thing—yet one more person leaving her behind, another loss to lock deep inside.

She stares dully out the window as we rumble our way through the take-off turn—Al's teary goodbye having left her subdued. As per Gail's original plan, she's heading to the sister's place in Rockland with yours truly as escort, though beyond that she's said nothing, nada—not a word about Ivan or Gail, or even if she's decided to have this baby. I figure if she wants me to know, she'll tell me.

It's my barely controlled terror that finally wins me a wan smile. Phobia, I yell over the sound of the engine, gritting my teeth against the clatter of shuddering fuselage. Only after we're safely airborne and my shaking's subsided do I risk a glance out the window where the waters beneath us seem calm enough—harmless, really, 'til the sight of a lone boat under sail calls up last night's eye-opener with Al.

Hindsight, right? Wish I didn't know now what I didn't know then—
that kind of thing. Had to ask, though; had to press him for what actually
happened out there on *Bounder*. What can I say? I was loose-lipped with
libation. Closure seemed important. Well, I'm here to tell you it's a very
overrated concept.

"Cash's scars," Al said. "Know how he got em?"

"Meth lab?" I suggested. "Freebasing heroine?"

"He was the go-to guy for propane out here, 'til a tank he was working
on exploded."

"And he survived?" I was thinking third degree burns, the kind of
immediate medical attention such things require. Not to mention the pain.

"You wanna call it that. It was his brother's tank. Guy was killed."

I opened my mouth, shut it again.

"Boats use propane, too," Al said, scrutinizing his shot glass. "Heating and cooking mostly. Accidents happen, not all that much, but often
enough. Leaks in the line, lack of maintenance—like that. Tank blows up at
sea, the whole boat becomes a fireball. Goes down pretty quick. Not much
chance of rescue, especially if the life raft's defective or maybe just ain't there
at all."

That sobered me, and fast. "Dinghy defective, too?"

"Can happen."

Sweet Jesus.

"In case you're feelin' bad about any of this, Kirtley confessed again to
killing Allan. And you were right about her never reporting the death. Reason she came out here, she needed a base, someplace under the radar. Can't
get much more under the radar than this place—Antarctica, maybe. Used
those trips to the mainland to move investments around. Remember I told
you Allan had a couple kids? Kirtley was draining the accounts a little at a
time; planned to be gone before anyone realized anything was wrong.

"And that key in the spine of Allan's log? Turns out it's some safe deposit
box where she kept her stash. No wonder she was so hot to get the thing
back."

"And you know all this how?" I asked.

"She told Cash—in the end."

I swung my gaze to him.

"Don't ask."

It was Cash who rigged the explosion, Al told me, after he and *Hombre*
slipped out of the harbor with *Bounder* the night after I was shot—Kirtley
locked in her cabin below, Josh trailing a mile or so behind on the *Mary
Kate*. Got it all set up—sliced through the propane line at the stove, lit a
candle on the table, then shut the boat up and got the hell out of there,

scuttling the life raft and dinghy on their way back in. No way Kirtley would be able to escape even if she somehow managed to free herself. Al seemed to take great satisfaction in the fact she'd be sitting there waiting for the inevitable explosion—no idea just when it would happen. He hoped she felt helpless, terrified, desperate.

I had a hard time with all this 'til he told me Josh called the Coast Guard that same night to report seeing floating wreckage. Official wheels grind slowly out here, but eventually somebody's gonna figure out who's boat it was and, ignorant of Allan's death, will no doubt assume both he and Kirtley died in some kind of catastrophic event. Which they did, of course, only not at the same time. All this so Allan's kids can collect their inheritance with a minimum of fuss. Kind of put the whole thing right for me, you know?

Tiffany yawns, announces she's hungry. A good sign, I think, and I promise her lunch when we hit land. Which reminds me.

"Got something for you," I say, reaching to my rucksack for the corn-husk doll Al let me take from Gail's box. Unwrapping it carefully, I place it in her hand—ignoring the What the hell is this? look she shoots me.

"Your great-great—whatever—grandfather, Atticus, the black sailor? He made this for a little girl on Matinicus almost two hundred years ago. If anyone should have it, it's you." High time she had a relation she can be proud of, I figure—distant as he might be. Someone who won't leave her behind. Because we never know just what'll save us, you know? A cornhusk doll, a maddening little spook, a teenager with angry eyes who wrangles her way into your sottish, self-indulgent heart. "He was a hero," I tell her. "Ask Al about him sometime."

She studies the thing resting in her palm—this offering I've made in lieu of the truth—the tiny body gone brittle with age; the dress faded color-less and fragile at the edges. Then she shoots me a crooked smile and I get a flash of that old fire. That's when I know she'll be okay, whatever the future has in store.

She leans across me, then, angling for a last glimpse of Matinicus through the window. I can only imagine what she's feeling—confusion, loss, uncertainty. Life out there will never be the same, of course. Still, it *is* home.

"You'll be back soon," I assure her, feeling oddly paternal. "Thanksgiv-ing's what—couple months away?"

She shakes her head like I've said something funny, turns a smug, almost triumphant look on me.

"I know it was Kirtley told Josh I was on the boat." She looks to me for confirmation and it's all I can do to keep my face neutral. Talk about guilty knowledge. "I mean who else knew, right? We were supposed to leave the island that night. She told me to hide below, said she'd be back after she took care of some stuff."

Yeah, I think—like trashing the dugout, lying in wait for me.

"Only she never came. Well, she's just a liar, that's what. Pretending to be girlfriends, sharing secrets and stuff when all along she planned to ditch me. Well fuck her, and fuck Josh, too, the prick. Fuck all of 'em, 'cause I got away anyway. No one left to stop me now. And no way I'm going back—not ever. You can forget about Rockland, too."

Huh? "Whoa, kiddo. I know you're upset, but…"

"Whole thing's Uncle Clayton's fault, really—I mean when you think about it. None of this would have happened if he left me the money he promised. He knew I needed it to go find her. But then Clunk had to go and die, and Aunt Sylvie was gonna move in with Clayton since she was his sister and all, which meant he'd probably leave *her* all his money and I'd be good and fucked, you know? Turns out he didn't leave me anything, anyway, which is just about the way things always go for me."

I struggle to connect the dots. Find who—her mother? What money? And who the fuck's Aunt Silvie? "Tiffany…"

"People are so lame, you know? Like Uncle Clayton, leaving that crowbar in plain sight like that, where anyone could come along and grab it. How dumb is that? And the Coasties? I bet even if they knew it wasn't an accident killed him, they'd never think to go looking in his own barn for a bloody old crowbar, they're that stupid."

I search my memory for talk of a crowbar, any crowbar, and come up empty. Have I perhaps had a stroke? Some weird, instant-onset dementia?

"And Ivan? He's another one dumber than shit. Boy never was careful with one thing his whole life. No way he shoulda been under that truck with the jack all wobbly like that. Too easy for someone to reach out, maybe give the truck a little push—just to see what would happen, you know? He should've been more careful. Joke's on him, right?"

More word salad. I mean they all fit together well enough; it's their meaning I can't quite get—what with the sludge of visceral alarm choking off my thought process.

I flash to something she muttered that morning at Rachel's, just after she found out for sure she was pregnant. *Don't need him makin' claims—'specially not now.* Hours later he turned up dead.

Pesky thing, the truth. Getting a whiff can ruin your whole day.

Something else she said slides into place, this time down on the dock just after Gail died. How she panicked when Gail told her she was planning to have Kirtley kicked off the island—words that only now take on a clearly sinister meaning. So just how panicked was she?

"Gail?" I breathe—every sweat gland on my body seeming to let go as I fight the image of her bloodied body at the bottom of that well.

Tiffany swings her gaze, considers me. "I tell you we had a big fight the day she died?"

Somehow I manage a nod.

"I was so pissed I spit it all out—told her I was pregnant, that I was gonna leave the island with Kirtley and fuck what she thought. Well, the shit hit the fan but good. God, was she mad—huffing off to send Kirtley packing right then and there. Never even turned around once, see if anyone was following."

No one left to stop me now.

I glance casually toward Doug to see if he's getting any of this, but he's oblivious—ears pillowed by those enormous noise-canceling headphones.

"Way I figure it? This baby was meant to be, like that crowbar in Clayton's barn, and that old well being right where it was in the woods. All of them signs, showing me the way. Like it was God saying *Here's what you need, now go do what you gotta do.*" Smiling at the thought. "Baby'll be a girl, too; I just know it. And I'll name it Deb after my mother to show I've forgiven her. It'll be like a do-over, you know? The two of us raising little Deb together.

"Because one thing I know for sure. When everyone else turns their back and there's nobody left who loves you—nobody at all—your little girl always will. Because that's what kids do. They love their mothers." Face serene as she turns again to the window. "For always."

I'm sure I must look stunned; how could I not? I mean, all this just because she wanted her mommy?

"Relax, Hodge," she laughs—settling back and closing her eyes. "Everything's worked out perfect."

This can't be happening, I think, only it clearly is. My God, didn't anyone think to ask where this kid was when these people died? I know I didn't. Out of the blue I remember the rest of what Al told me about that interrogation on *Bounder*, the part I'd so conveniently tossed off in my rush to make everything fit my Kirtley-as-killer scenario.

"Funny thing," he said. "She swore up and down it wasn't her killed the others. Even at the end, when she knew she'd never get off that boat alive."

"'Course she did," I told him, feeling the smallest twinge of—what exactly? Disappointment? Uncertainty? "Why make things any worse than they have to be?" She'd been determined to kill me, too, I reminded myself—and would have if Cash hadn't turned up at the barn when he did.

I zero in on that night, trying for Kirtley's exact words during the five excruciating minutes she held that gun on me—exactly what she said about Allan's murder and, more importantly, what she didn't say about the others. What stands out most for me, I realize, was that flash of surprise when I accused her of the killings. Surprise, I wonder now, or confusion?

What really clinches all this for me, though, is ghostie girl—all that continued bumping and thumping once Kirtley'd been carted off finally making sense. I mean her work was done; Tiffany was safe. She should have been happy, only she clearly wasn't. I knew I was right about the connection between Mary and Atticus and Tiffany—no question—it's just I'd gotten the permutations wrong. It wasn't that Tiffany was in danger; it's that she *was* the danger.

All this puts me in a hell of a spot, as I'm sure you can imagine. Feigning nonchalance, I tug Dad's cap down and inch back in my seat to ponder the options. My immediate reaction is to suck it up, come clean with Al and Cash about my humiliating miscalculations and let the chips fall where they may—only this means Tiffany might well suffer the same fate as Kirtley. Something I can't let happen, despite everything this kid's done. I simply can't. There's been far too much carnage already.

The saner, safer option would be to turn her over to the cops once we hit land—safe being a relative term, of course. Problem is proof. I mean forget bringing up the whole Kirtley debacle; half the island would be arrested for colluding in her murder. Besides, I'd say I've done enough damage there already, wouldn't you? It's also clear that Tiffany's comments, while convincing enough to me, prove absolutely nothing. She never came out and actually confessed to anything; she was careful about that. And even if she had—well, it's my word against hers, right? And then there's ghostie girl—my psychic ace-in-the-hole—and wouldn't that go over big. Which leaves squat.

I cock an eye to find Tiffany's dropped off to sleep clutching the cornhusk doll—her neck drooping sideways at an impossible angle, fingernails bitten to the quick. She doesn't look ten.

You see my problem. The proverbial rock and hard place. It's not that I'm not outraged or disgusted, because I am—no question. What she did was horrific, inconceivably monstrous, but she's hardly the only one to blame here. I mean, when's this kid ever caught a break? No father, mother does a flyer—dumping her on a woman who, for all her good intentions, simply didn't have the kind of warmth that might have saved her. Not to mention an island full of relatives too self-absorbed to reach out in any meaningful way. Even I own a piece of this mess, not having once picked up on anything odd—of which, with the stunning twenty-twenty of hindsight, I realize there was much. Crimes of omission, you might say.

So say she gets her chance. I know; I know, but hear me out. I mean the killing's over, right? She got what she wanted, she's off the island and about to do the one thing she's dreamed of most of her life. No way she'll ever find the woman, of course—chick's been gone now, what, ten years?—but at least she'll get a shot. Which in some twisted way makes me feel a little better about all this. Bizarre, I know, but there you are.

Still, just setting this skitzy, delusional kid loose on an unsuspecting population would be beyond irresponsible. Unless, of course, there was a kind of contingency plan in place.

I sit with this as Doug begins his descent—the subtle changes in cabin pressure enough to wake Tiffany, who rises from the sleep of the not-so-innocent in a long, luxuriant stretch.

Sighing, I reach for my wallet, snag a business card—fully aware of the innumerable felonies I'm about to commit. Praying that some part of Gail, the part that once cared enough about a lost little girl to take her in, would be okay with what I'm about to do.

"You'll need help," I say, scribbling my various numbers on the back. "Certainly money." Not to mention a world-class shrink to try and unlock the twisted reasoning behind all this, but one thing at a time. Folding my last few Matinicus Ones over the card, I hold it toward her—hanging on when she goes to palm it 'til she raises her eyes to mine.

"I expect to hear from you at least once a month," I tell her. "I'm serious. If I don't, the police will get a call from me, and we both know where that will lead."

"No prob," she says brightly, tucking the card and money in her jeans pocket. "I get a ride to the bus after we eat? I figure she went to Portland first; that's where I'll start."

I nod—wondering what the hell I'm gonna tell Al, who's panicked call I can no doubt expect in a matter of hours. Followed by a visit from one of the island hotshots, most likely Cash, determined on answers. But by then she'll be long gone.

Tiffany reaches for my hand, squeezes it against the bounce and shutter of the Cessna hitting the tarmac—or maybe she's simply sealing our deal, who's to know?

Thus, having allied myself irrevocably with a mass-murdering teen—a move certain to return one day and bite me in the ass—I settle back, prepared for some flicker of remorse, that inevitable *Oh Shit* moment. Only it doesn't come, trumped as it's been by my sudden, crazy-ass desire to right a few egregious old wrongs. Were I a better man, this would probably bother me. But I'm not, so it doesn't. Not yet anyway.

No, this one's gonna lie in wait, sneak up on me some night in the wee hours—which is when all my ghosts come to call—in a heart-racing, what-the-fuck-was-I-thinking wake-up call.

Count on it.

Coming Soon:

Reese's Leap

Book Two in Darcy Scott's Island Mystery Series

S till licking his wounds after the debacle on Matinicus some three summers before, a chastened Gil Hodges takes a Sunday afternoon joy-ride that lands him right back in the thick of things.

Six longtime friends have arrived for their annual, all-female retreat on Adria Jackman's rugged, 200-acre enclave of Mistake Island. Freed from their complicated lives for a blissful week of hiking, sunning, and partying in a rustic, hundred-year-old lodge, the women find themselves forced to host Gil and his buddy, David Duggan, when an unrelenting fog strands them on the island for what could be days.

While initially delighted at the layover, Gil soon finds the verdant, primordial glens and moss-covered trails deceptively bucolic, the women a little too intriguing for comfort—stirring both glorious memory and profound regret. When a manipulative stranger slips among them bent on a twisted and brutal revenge, Gil's forced into the ultimate face-off between blind self-interest and emotional honesty if anyone's to make it off the island alive.

Read on for an Excerpt

PROLOGUE

Subject: Island Women Week
From: a.jackman@cambridgebooks.com
To: Nora2736@yahoo.com, paddlechick@hellerfamily.net,
Lily@kilabukdesign.com, shelleybelly@aol.com, wildyogathing@yahoo.com

Greetings, Island Women!

Okay, this is my final email before I see you on Saturday—promise. And Shelley, what's this shit I hear about you bailing on us to "work on the relationship?" Damn, girl, how can this new man, whom none of us have met by the way, be worth giving up an entire week on the island? Seriously, put the boy-toy on hold and get your ass up here.

Reminders. Still no electricity on Mistake, so don't bother bringing anything that plugs in. That goes for cell phones, too, though I know you'll bring them anyway. And, no, the signal hasn't improved any. (Sorry, Margot, the biz will just have to do without you for the week.) On the plus side, brother Drew has rebuilt the solar shower and filled the propane tanks; the gas lights that were on the fritz last year have been replaced, and while the broiler on the stove still goes out any old time it wants, Frosty Frieda and that temperamental pilot light of hers are finally gone, replaced by a brand new gas fridge! A couple new carts this year, too—the larger ones able to carry two of the big water jugs instead of just one, which means lugging the stuff from the well will go faster. I can hear you all grumbling now; just think of it as your aerobic exercise for the week (except for Margot, who will probably hike ten miles and kayak around the island twice each morning before the rest of us are even up).

Accommodations in the Birches will be first-come, first-serve this year; seems only fair considering three of you have asked for the same bedroom. New futons in two of the rooms, though, so the sleeping should be better. And there are always the porches with their hammocks. Plus, we finally tossed the fuggy mattress that was in the Twig and brought in two singles. Still a squirrel problem down there (who wouldn't want to make their nest in that sweet little cottage, right?), so I'm thinking Brit and Lily for that since Lily's bringing Faye. The scent of a dog always keeps them away.

Please be on time at the boat ramp. Seriously. The tide won't wait for you, so neither can I. My current plan is to pick Margot and Nora up at the high tide just before noon. Last I heard, Lily and Brit were riding together, but I'm fuzzy on the timing, so try for as close to that as you can. Might want to call and confirm when you're getting close, but remember that cell service drops out just past that little gourmet market on Bourne Road.

Okay, clothes. Lots of layers. It can go from hot to chilly and damp in a matter of minutes out here. Remember last year? Comfortable shoes—sneakers, Tevas, etc. Something for hiking. A bathing suit, if you absolutely must. We're very much alone out here, so think lots of skinny dipping. I, for one, plan to give those lobstermen something to remember!

What else? Books, books, books, of course. Flashlights, bug dope, water bottle, back pack for day hikes. Candles are nice, too. We're about out of lamp oil, so bring some if you can find it anywhere.

As far as dinners go, I'm going to make it easy on everyone and do Saturday night, just to get things rolling. I'm thinking that Thai Chicken Salad you all liked so much last year. Stick with a winner, my mama always says. Margot's taking Sunday night. That leaves the rest of you to choose a night to cook for the group. Remember, you're responsible not just for the meal, but the wine and munchies for cocktail hour (see my last email). There's that supermarket just off the highway and the little gourmet place for provisioning, or you can wait and make a trip in later on in the week. Pick up your own stuff for breakfasts and lunches, beverages of choice. Wine, wine, and more wine. Is there ever enough? And Brit, maybe you could bring that big cooler of yours again? Really helped with fridge overflow last time.

I'm sure Margot will let me know if I've forgotten anything; she usually does. Remember, this week is yours to do whatever. Read, relax, play, and just be with other amazing women without the distraction of men and other assorted children—hah! Oh, and a caveat to that long list of things I just suggested you bring? Don't forget it's a good half-mile slog from dock to house, and the only person schlepping your stuff will be you. Guaranteed.

Have to run; got a new author coming in for a reading.

Island Women rule!

Adria

SUNDAY

GIL

"The friendship was pretty much over before this whole thing happened, and now—well."

No idea where Duggan's going with this, so I say nothing. Something about yet another falling-out between Lily and what's-her-name, the ex-roommate. Gotta admit my mind's been wandering, the bulk of the drive down I-95 from Bangor from whence I was fetched for this little joyride little more than a stream-of-consciousness venting on life without son Matt, whose bizarre death a month ago has left everyone reeling.

A cream-colored Lexus whizzes by in the left lane; this time even I crane for a look at the plate.

GD2BLV

David breaks from his spiel to interpret, a game he's recently taken up as part of his obsession with all things literary. "Good to believe," he announces, and I place a mental tic on the plus side of the Duggan mood-o-meter—having weeks ago charged myself with keeping my finger on his wildly fluctuating emotional pulse.

Not that I'm complaining. David Duggan's more than simply a col-league—Writer in Residence at Dartmouth to my currently rather sketchy position at UMaine—he's a friend of considerably long standing, which in my book means he can bend my ear anytime and for as long as needed. Losing a kid sucks, as I well know. Not my own—parenthood having so far eluded me, thank God—but Rachel Leland's son, Ben. By far the best student I ever had, possibly the finest the Urban Forestry Program at UMaine ever attracted. Not to mention an all-'round terrific kid, thanks in large part to his mother, on whom I've nurtured a spectacularly unrequited crush for years. Sadly, any chance I had with her, while admittedly slim from the start, quickly vaporized—just one of the many things I've so gloriously fucked up over the years.

EZ2LUV, I spontaneously decide. Much 2.

But back to Ben. While his death was truly tragic—carried off as he was by a particularly aggressive form of Non-Hodgkins lymphoma—Matt Duggan's demise was one of pure, unmitigated stupidity. Complicated history here; suffice it to say he's been addicted to virtually every illegal substance at one time or another, in and out of rehab since his early teens. Various therapies and psychotherapists, all of it crushingly expensive and in the end utterly useless. Last few years the kid seemed to be slipping even further away, spending a year in jail on a drug charge—a time David still can't bring himself to talk about—and eventually dying alone in a dingy studio apartment up in Claremont when the frozen pizza box he'd stupidly parked atop the stove's pilot light caught fire, the innocuous-looking plastic tray inside releasing a toxic stew that overwhelmed his miserable little ass while the rest of the closet-sized kitchen burned around him. I kid you not. To put it bluntly, Matt Duggan burned to death. That he was blotto on booze, weed, and God only knows what else, and thus had the reaction time of a concrete block, no doubt contributed to the tragedy. Twenty-two fucking years old.

David nudges me as a boxy green thing screams by. "Now *that* one's good."

I pull my mind from Matt, just managing to make out the plate.

IMINMY

Huh.

"It's that Honda thing—you know, the Element?" He waits for me to get it, then sighs. "As in *I'm in my*? Christ, Hodge. Okay, hold on."

I make a wild grab at the doorframe as he downshifts, shooting me a maniacal grin as the engine screams and we barely make the tight wind of the highway off-ramp onto 1-A south. "Cornering on this thing's the balls," he purrs.

I grunt, tugging Dad's old '55 Dodgers cap down where it joins the cheap Maui Jim knockoffs I was forced to shell out for in order to do battle against the scorching yellow ball burning its way through the windshield of David's brand new cherry-red Miata—a purchase I remember arguing strongly against. Forty-five-year-old men, I cautioned—a demographic into which we've both recently slid—should avoid fixating on little red sports cars, lest it be interpreted as some attempt at anatomical compensation.

Still, I suppose it's relatively harmless as outlets for grief go. Expensive yes, and no doubt dangerous as shit with the top down like this, but—and here's the thing—it gives him the lift he so desperately needs while requiring absolutely no emotional investment in return.

Thus it is I crammed my six-foot-two frame into the absurdly cheery thing, put up with the sun and Duggan's venting, not to mention his maniacal driving, for what is essentially a spontaneous drop-in on the aforementioned Lily—his current lady-love and a cute-as-a-button landscape designer who, only yesterday, began an annual week-long retreat with other high-octane women. Chicks only. On a private, two-hundred acre island, no less. Why he thinks we'll actually be welcome out there, regardless of the half-hearted invitation flung his way as Lily was heading out the door, is beyond me. Then there's the fact we have no boat.

I admit he got my interest with the bit about the women, though. A recent departure for me, I have to say—an apparent reawakening of the old Gil, gone and I'd hoped forgotten, my libido having been beaten into submission by a series of leather and lace types. Suffice it to say I've been a good boy in that regard for the better part of three years now, since the debacle out on Matinicus. Almost getting my nuts shot off has that effect on me.

I veer from the thought, distracting myself with the promise of Mistake Island's old-growth interior, which is legendary. High time I made it out here, anyway, I tell myself—no matter the reason. I'm a botanist, dendrology specifically, which means I study trees. I teach as well, or did until relatively recently, and the change still has me reeling. Whole other story.

We're doing at least twenty over the limit, screaming down a country road blessedly shaded by glorious red maples, when we veer wildly into the parking lot of a small, cedar-shingled market—Duggan being determined on an offering to the island babes—and thump to a stop inches before taking out an ice machine. Red and white-striped awning, big urns erupting in profusions of wildflowers. An old Mom-and-Pop convenience store in its former life, I figure, before it went gourmet.

"Want anything?" Duggan asks, unfolding his doughy, urbanized frame from behind the wheel.

Short of an I.V. of ice water? "Cold Heineken or Moosehead would be nice." A bit optimistic, to be sure, considering the swinging corrugated sign promises sixteen-ounce cans of Narragansett, no doubt a staple of the local bass-fishing crowd.

Duggan being Duggan, he does me one better—pushing through the screen door five minutes later cradling an entire six-pack of Moosehead and a cutesy little paper sack nipped at the top with an embossed gold seal, tossing the thing to me as he climbs in. I peer around the seal at a chocolate bar whose name I can't begin to pronounce, a cry-o-vac of organic dried fruits, a jar of fat-infused avocado dip—the kind of stuff I can't imagine Lily will actually consume, being not only a chick of the holistic, veggie-leaning variety but hands-down the smallest female I've ever set eyes on—that Inuit extraction, no doubt. Petite—five feet tops would be my guess. Might weigh a hundred pounds if she were dipped in molasses.

We reach the parking lot at the boat ramp just after two—Duggan fussing with the car's top while I'm left to fork over five bucks for an afternoon's parking to an old guy who appears out of nowhere determined to lighten my wallet. Then, grabbing my rucksack—a traveling office of notes, trail mix and bug repellent—I join Duggan at the top of the boat ramp, a truly hoppin' place. The great weather's brought out every fisherman in probably twenty miles, a long line of pickups towing various craft waiting their turn to back to the water and drop their load. The guy at the market told Duggan the bluefish were running, which explains it, I suppose—if you don't mind beating your food to death. Bluefish make great eating, but you gotta come prepared to do battle. They're a vicious, hard-fighting species; catch one and you gotta kill it soon as it's in the boat or it's likely to chew your leg off.

The two men currently working a boat down the ramp—a forty-ish guy in waders and a man of about sixty back in the cab—look to be a father and son out for a day of it. A lifetime of easy together, looks like; their hand signals relaxed as the younger guy gestures the boat back—no easy task considering the wall of boulders on either side.

I turn to see Duggan heading down the side of the ramp to where an admirably toned woman is maneuvering a wide skiff into the water, a handful of plastic grocery bags in the stern. Nordic features, ash-blond ringlets fisted into a ponytail, dressed in the kind of techie gear so popular with wanna-be athletes these days—lime-green racerback tank and tight black kayaking shorts. Only on this chick it works. Not an ounce of fat on her; the muscles tensing along her arms signaling serious upper body strength. Competitive swimmer, maybe—that or a rock climber. She turns as we approach, and Duggan jumps right in.

"You heading out to Mistake, by any chance?"

Now I'd have hung back and flirted with her a little first—old habits being what they are—maybe helped with the boat to win some points; but therein lies the single biggest difference between Duggan and myself. Love him to death, I do, but the guy's got no subtlety. An old flame of his once told me he wasn't much for foreplay. Not sure who I felt sorrier for.

Nordic chick says nothing—eyes traveling Duggan as she works the boat, her gaze sliding my way where it settles briefly on my Heineken. No fool, this one. Hell if she's gonna reveal her plans to a couple middle-aged, beer-swigging perverts accosting her on a boat ramp, at least not without first being introduced.

"Gil Hodges," I say, offering up my goofiest grin as I extend a hand.

6

"Want some help with that?"

She ignores me, chin-nods at Duggan. "You looking for someone on the island?"

"Hoping for a ride out, actually."

More ocular appraisal. I glance down, wondering exactly what it is she finds so fascinating. My usual ensemble—faded jeans and worn hikers, my favorite Frank Zappa tee—looks okay, if you ignore the small ketchup stain from lunch. Even David, in today's natty semi-nautical attire, is nothing out of the ordinary. Chinos, polo, Docksiders sans socks.

"Problem is we've booked the island for the week," she explains. "All-female retreat—no men. No offense, it's just this thing we have."

Duggan's wearing the look of mild befuddlement I've seen him use on students, though the woman's clearly in her thirties and obviously too intelligent to be so easily thrown. Over her shoulder I spy a large island a mile or so off, the tops of its towering pines just visible through the steaming haze. Mistake, I'm assuming, which is frankly how all this is starting to feel.

"I'm a friend of Lily Kilabuk's," Duggan tells her. "She invited me out for the day." As proof of his veracity he holds up the twee little bag wherein that twenty dollar bar of chocolate is doubtless fast turning to goo.

She snorts a laugh. "Well, then, by all means." Shaking her head as we climb aboard, she gives the skiff a final shove and hops on. "This oughta be interesting."

Some ten minutes later—after picking her way through a tricky, rock-strewn approach—our guide, who's somewhat belatedly introduced herself as Margot, ties off to a small float. A long aluminum ramp leads us beneath a canopy of shaggy, tightly-packed conifers, disgorging us onto a blessedly cool trail—narrow, rocky, and cumbersome to navigate what with the heavy crosshatch of tree roots so common to islands where granite underlies the forest floor and the ground is mostly duff, or decaying spruce needles, rather than actual soil.

A few minutes of this and we're dumped into a broad, open meadow filled with the busy grind of cicadas—the scientist in me taking note as we go. Ground cover of bunchberry, or Cornis canadensis, a green-leafed shrub sporting the cheery red berries of childhood nursery rhymes. Lots of wild low-bush blueberry and creeping raspberry here, too. The trees are red oak and birch for the most part, set off from which are two of the most enormous arborvitae I've ever seen, each spanning some thirty feet.

Nordic chick moves quickly—the bugs are ferocious out here—passing a well of the old hand-pump variety, a few outbuildings. I glance back at Duggan, gamely trying to keep up. Have to say, for a guy who regularly beats me at squash he seems oddly clumsy in the out-of-doors. The extra weight doesn't help, of course. When we met years ago, he could have leapt from the pages of an L.L Bean catalogue—muscled and fit, wide shoulders, serious brow. Hair the color of wet sand. The ten extra pounds he's picked up since having ballooned to twenty or twenty-five since Matt's death.

We tuck back beneath the pines at the far end of the meadow, and another hundred yards along I catch snatches of a house through the trees. An early twentieth-century hunting lodge, by the look of it—long and low, cedar-shingled, slung atop an outcropping of rock and birch trees.

Shafts of sunlight strike through the boughs, revealing movement in the dooryard. Glimpses of flesh. A woman, I realize, as the trees part before me—svelte, long of leg, and gloriously naked—bent at the waist as she rinses her dark, cropped hair, water sluicing over her head, her neck. Her movements slow and languid, unselfconscious as women can only be when they believe themselves to be unobserved.

For the briefest of moments my heart all but stops—certain as I am that the woman before me is Rachel, the astronomical odds against such a thing be damned. Hair's all wrong, of course; she of my fantasies wore hers in long, curling ropes of auburn. Still, I drink her in, the physical similarities enough to kick-start the old longing again.

"Cover up, girls," our reluctant guide calls as she sets the groceries at her feet. "Men doth approach." Amusement in the glance she flicks our way. Let the butter melt, that look says, the milk curdle. No way I'm gonna miss this.

The vision before us whirls, grabbing up her towel and covering herself best she can as she scrambles for the screen door—through which, once opened, a furry black projectile launches itself toward us amid bursts of staccato yapping. Lily's cocker spaniel, I realize. Faith, Fran—something like that.

A full minute goes by, time I spend trying to spit-clean my miserable knockoff shades—replacements for the Ray-Bans that rather inexplicably disappeared from my campus office sometime over the last few days. Or maybe not so inexplicably. But more on that later.

Still nothing from the house. I shift my rucksack, slapping at mosquitoes while Duggan appears unperturbed by the continuing delay—patiently kneeing the pooch away from the foolish little bag still dangling from his hand.

A cackling laugh from somewhere within, and Lily finally pushes through the door, looking about as irritated as I'm starting to feel—a freckled, gum-popping redhead fast on her heels. She of the laugh, no doubt, the irreverent sound of it somehow in keeping with the tatts wrapping an otherwise bare upper arm.

"Hey, Lil," Duggan grins, extending the bag. "Brought you a little something. Hello, Brit."

Brit. The name is familiar, as is the lopsided, challenging grin. Do I know this chick? I nearly panic at the thought she might be some ex-student-cum-lover—one of many I've left in my wake. An unfortunate specialty of mine. They've been popping up with alarming regularity lately; I ran into one in a bar in Portland a few months back, nowhere near my home territory, and she actually tried to deck me. But Brit shows none of the usual signs of recognition—disbelief tinged with the almost pathological level of rage I've grown so used to—so I relax.

Lily, on the other hand, is visibly shocked to see us. She may have invited Duggan out here vis-à-vis some halfhearted invitation, but she clearly didn't think he'd show. And my presence isn't helping things any.

"What's he doing here?" she demands. Meaning me, of course.

I should tell you that Lily doesn't like me much, having quite mistakenly pegged me as the reason Duggan has not yet slid into marital mode. True, the two of us have been spending a lot of time together since Matt's death—okay, we've been pretty much inseparable—but I refuse to apologize for that. The guy needs me right now. Love, like sex, runs hot and cold, and I expect the emotional ups and downs he and Lily are going through—her relationship with Matt was never easy—are a bit much for him just now. Friendship is simpler, cleaner. Road trips, ballgames, bar-hopping—I'm there.

Strangely enough, though, I like Lily. Her funky, spiritual bent's a bit of an eye-roller, but she's sweet and for the most part sincere—two attributes I've come at long last to appreciate in a woman. And I actually have hopes for the two of them. Perhaps David can accomplish the thing I seem so singularly incapable of, that being sustained monogamy. He came close with Matt's mother, as I remember, and I've often wondered if things might have turned out differently for Matt had the two of them stayed together, or if the kid had seen more of Duggan than he did in those early years.

The screen door snaps open yet again, this time disgorging a stunning black woman come to check out the commotion. Petite and lean, hair cropped close and tight highlighting a serene countenance lit by a sunny smile. A cropped top and beige cargo pants rolled to just below the knee reveal long, graceful limbs. My God. How many more such lovelies can there be?

"Sorry, Adria." Lily says, clearly embarrassed. "Forgot to mention I invited David out for the day."

Ah, I think. Head chick at chick week.

"Dr. David Duggan," he announces in the stentorian tones normally reserved for book tours and ladies' club appearances. Extending a hand as she trips lightly down the short run of stone steps from house to path. "A pleasure."

"The novelist. I know your work," she says, grinning broadly as they shake. "Adria Jackman. It's great to finally meet you. I carry your books in my store—Cambridge Books in Boston. Love to have you in for a reading."

"I'd be honored."

David's very old school, if a bit fusty at times; not to mention he's an absolute sucker for this kind of thing—probably 'cause it happens all too infrequently these days—and I feel a warm flush of gratitude toward this woman. Who cares if she really means it? David's books, mysteries mostly, are considered a little, well, light. The night I met him, his breakout novel, *Murder on Monhegan*, had just won some prize from the Mystery Writers of America, so he was flying pretty high. He was in Portland for a series of lectures and signings, and I remember spending a good chunk of the night with him taste-testing our way through top-shelf single malts at the Olde Port Tavern. A couple more books followed, including a better-than-average swashbuckler series pitting colonists against Native Americans, which proved surprisingly popular. All of this back in the mid-nineties, his artistic muse having for the most part eluded him since.

"This is Gil Hodges," he says, turning to me. "A botanist friend of mine specializing in trees. He's doing a book about the Maine islands."

"Biodiversity of Maine's outer islands," I correct as we shake. I, too, could trot out my credentials, but it's been my experience that women of this quality really don't give a shit. "Hope you don't mind my poking around while these two are visiting." Visiting being a euphemism, of course. Based on the tension-charged looks Lily's still shooting our way, it's a safe bet they'll spend the time either fighting or screwing. Probably both.

"Absolutely," Adria says. "Day visitors are always welcome. One of us will ferry you back to the mainland about five, if that works." Something about the way she says this reminds me of a bumper sticker I once saw on a rusted-out pickup rambling down I-95: *Welcome to Maine—now please go home.*

I nod. "My folks had a Carolina Skiff much like yours—fourteen-footer. Brings back memories. A lot like trying to steer a bathtub, as I remember."

Margot snorts a laugh. "Dumpster's more like it."

I shoot her a glance. A couple years back I'd have put some serious effort into flirting with this chick, wedding band or no, but I've sampled others of this hyper, controlling type whose names momentarily escape, thank God—women bent on correcting and psychoanalyzing me—with alarming results.

Adria points to where the trail we took in continues beyond the house.

"Follow this path past the Twig—that little cottage maybe a hundred yards down the hill—then bear right. It'll take you around the south side of the island and back to the dock. About a two-hour hike. The interior's a lot tougher to explore, I'm afraid, unless you're into slogging your way up mountain trails."

Thanking her, and tossing a final fruitless glance toward the screen door for a glimpse of she-who-stands-naked-in-dooryards, I heft my pack and head off.

Islands have their own distinct personalities, I've found—subtle patterns of creation resulting from the intimate interaction of flora, fauna and climate—the most fascinating having suffered only minimal human interference. And so it appears here. Maybe thirty minutes after leaving Duggan to navigate the tricky emotional minefield of our visit, I'm starting to get a feel for the place. It seems the owners are good stewards indeed, for the most part allowing nature its head. No clearing of brush or blow-down, other than to keep the trails open; where streams need to be crossed, simple plank bridges have been crafted of native materials.

Working my way around toward the southeast, where the sharply-scarped granite shelf drops some forty feet to a series of rocky inlets, I find a mixed forest of hardwoods and spruce—white, the Picea glauca variety. Far more interesting, though, is the heady, resinous scent of the interior wafting toward me from an intersecting uphill trail, the quick glimpse of a small stand of red spruce through the dappled light of a deeply still woods. I decide to strike inland despite Adria's warning, or maybe because of it. I'm funny like that.

Amazing the amount of deadfall in here. Last time I encountered this much of the stuff was on Matinicus—a period in my life I try not to dwell on. Oddly enough, it was Rachel's son Ben who first lured me out there, promising not only his mom's stellar home cooking, but a phenomenal seven hundred species of flora on an island less than three miles long— including some forty-four different kinds of trees and a purported twenty-two species of wild orchid, many of which Ben claimed to have catalogued himself. A botanical treasure-trove, assuming it was true. Skeptical as I was, I was nonetheless up for adventure—figured we'd drink a lot of beer, do a bit of camping and, if lucky, I might somehow manage to get laid. Sad, I know, but that's who I was back then. Meeting Rachel for the first time knocked me on my ass—my gleefully sophomoric and ultimately failed attempts at seduction something I can never possibly live down. I should mention that Rachel's not simply beautiful; she's poised and graceful and an artist, it happens, of considerable talent. The proverbial one that got away.

Fast-forward a couple years. Ben had died by then, and I was on what you might call a strongly encouraged sabbatical when I flew back to the island for a much needed break from academia—not to mention my own self-destructive tendencies, or so I was told at the time. I'd recently ended a wildly inappropriate fling with a psychotic, possibly homicidal grad student whose desire for me had morphed into a determined attempt to ruin my life. Best way to avoid her, I figured, was to leave town. Indefinitely. Matinicus was perfect—a place so remote, so rugged, so utterly unwelcoming to strangers it would deter even this chick.

Of course I convinced myself I was heading back out there to complete the cataloguing Ben had begun before he got sick. I had some vague idea of producing a botanical write-up of the island in all its mind-boggling biodiversity, the kind of obscure scholarly drivel so valued in academia and with which I could redeem myself in the eyes of my peers. Sneaky thing, the libido, 'cause all the while I was angling for another chance at Rachel. You see the problem. I never finished the cataloguing work, which surprised no one—especially not me. Instead, I got dragged into a couple particularly grisly murders and was stupid enough to get shot by someone I knew all along I couldn't trust—all the while living cheek-by-jowl with a little island girl two hundred years dead. Yeah, yeah—laugh all you want. You weren't there.

Kicker was, I never did meet up with Rachel, which would've made everything else bearable. She was off-island the entire time, and no sign of her since, which has only increased my longing. Thus my reaction an hour ago when I thought for just an instant I'd seen her at the house. Hope springs eternal; never more so, I've found, than when there's no hope at all.

All of this is particularly ironic, because the paper I eventually did write—a kind of eco-socio treatise on the interdependence of all that bio-diversity and its various metaphors to the decline of island life, blah, blah, blah—attracted a lot of attention in the field and resulted in my being offered the contract to do the book on Maine Islands. On top of that, after news of the book deal made its way up the ancient, creaking ladder of academia, the university bigwigs started getting nervous about the possibility I might leave their fold—a prospect that would have delighted them less than a year before. So instead of being shit-canned for years of admittedly inappropriate behavior, I found myself Chair of my Department which, in our particular institution, is rather vaguely defined and involves very little actual teaching. Which, strangely enough, I find I miss. Still, I'll probably live longer this way.

Nothing like slogging through the thick brush of a mountain trail for begging unwelcome introspection, so I'm more than relieved to reach the top of this one. Stepping into the small clearing, I envision miles of glistening, dappled water dotted with islands, a sailboat or two straining into the wind—anything to take my mind off my past misdeeds and the longing that's kick-started in my loins. But, like so much of what I take for granted these days, expectation is once again turned on its ear.

Two thoughts occur as I glance toward the sea. Shit. And shit again. Because despite the day's heretofore stellar conditions, a solid wall of fog is slowly and inexorably heading this way—reminding me of that amorphous mass of extraterrestrial protoplasm for which the old sci-fi classic *The Blob* was named. Steve McQueen in one of his dumber roles, as I remember. And that's saying a lot.

No time to backtrack along the perimeter trail; if Duggan and I are gonna get out of here, I quickly realize, it's got to be now. Sighing, I set off down the back side of the mountain, double-timing it along a trail that instinct says will dump me somewhere near the stone wall I noticed bordering the meadow.

Man, I think. Lily's just gonna love this.

ABOUT THE AUTHOR

DARCY SCOTT is a former symphony orchestra marketing director who works as a freelance writer and marine industry publicist when she's not off adventuring. An experienced ocean cruiser, she's sailed to Grenada and back on a whim, island-hopped through the Caribbean, and been struck by lightning in the middle of the Gulf Stream. Her favorite cruising ground remains the coast of Maine, however, and her appreciation of the history and rugged beauty of its sparsely populated out-islands serves as the inspiration for *Matinicus* and the other novels in her Island Mystery Series. She recently completed book two, *Reese's Leap*, and is drafting the final book in the trilogy. Her debut novel, *Hunter Huntress*, was published in June, 2010 by Snowbooks, Ltd., UK. Learn more at www.Darcyscott.net.